CHILD OF
THE ANCIENTS

SHIRLEY BIGELOW
DEKELVER

Solstice Publishing - www.solsticepublishing.com

Child of the Ancients

by

Shirley Bigelow DeKelver

Dedicated to everyone who believes in magic!

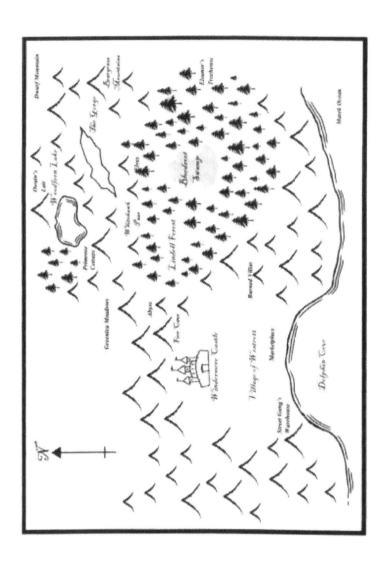

Prologue

The flames crackled and furled, devouring everything in its path. She backed down the stairs, shielding her face from the intense heat. Flinging open the front door, she ran outside. Two mounted soldiers were watching the house, the nearest rider pointed in her direction, and then he spurred his horse and galloped straight towards the porch where she was standing. She jumped off the steps, tore across the yard towards the heavy trees, her heart pounding. Her throat was raw from inhaling the caustic smoke. A sharp pain in her side doubled her over.

A muscled arm grabbed her around the waist, throwing her face down across the pommel of his saddle. Kicking and screaming, she tried to break free, but the soldier only tightened his hold, warning her to settle down, or he would thrash her soundly. He galloped back to his companion, who had dismounted and was standing next to a crude cage hidden in the shadows. Her captor handed her down to his companion, who unlatched the door, and shoved her roughly inside. She lay motionless trying to catch her breath. A stirring in the corner caught her attention. A boy, covered in bruises and dirt, was holding a sniveling child in his arms.

She grabbed the wooden bars tightly as the wagon pulled away. The farmhouse walls collapsed inward, and she heard a piercing scream over the roar of the flames. An unbearable anguish overwhelmed her as she collapsed, moaning and keening in agony. Then everything went dark.

Part I

Coming of Age

Chapter One

The entire day was one disaster after another, Aurie had a pounding headache, and she could not throw the anxiety that cloaked her like a mist. The kitchen staff had been cooking since sunrise, preparing a feast for visiting dignitaries from a neighboring borough. The head cook, Mrs. Black, had turned into a raging tyrant, relentlessly pushing, until everyone was exhausted and short-tempered.

When the demanding woman snapped at her to bring a pitcher of buttermilk to the sideboard, Aurie was so flustered her boot tangled in the hem of her skirt. Before she realized what was happening, she was sprawled on the stone floor. The pitcher shattered, and the buttermilk splattered on her dress and down the side of Mrs. Black's apron.

"Stupid girl," Mrs. Black screeched, grabbing Aurie's arm and yanking her roughly to her feet. "Can't you do anything right?" she raged, slapping her hard across her cheek. Aurie twisted sharply, breaking free, and fled to the far side of the room. Tasting blood in her mouth, she sullenly wiped her hand across her mouth.

Mrs. Black angrily brushed her dress where the buttermilk had left a stain. "Clean up this mess," she ordered pointing at the floor. "When you're finished you can change into those leggings and shirt going to the poor house, they'll have to do for now, your dress is filthy." Fuming, she headed towards the back door, stopped and looked over her shoulder. "And there'll be no supper for you tonight. Maybe next time you'll be more careful."

Then she left the kitchen and disappeared down the corridor.

Aurie touched her swollen lip and flinched. The room was quiet. The staff had stopped to watch the altercation. A few of them had smirks on their faces, but not one of them offered her a hand to pick up the shattered pieces of glass.

Dora, the assistant cook, was standing next to the open hearth turning a huge roast on a spit. The heat of the flames had flushed her face, and she wiped the perspiration from her forehead. "Everyone back to your chores," she said sharply. "Mrs. Black come back and see you all gawking like a herd of sheep, we'll all be going to bed hungry."

Aurie walked over to the broom closet and grabbed a wooden bucket and a scrub brush. She gathered the glass and cleaned up the buttermilk, all the while keeping a watchful eye out for Mrs. Black.

"See what you can do about your dress," Cora said, turning to face Aurie. "You'll need it tomorrow, those clothes going to the poor house are over at the keep, but I ain't got time to fetch 'em for you. You got to make do 'til I'm done here."

Aurie nodded, and then fled down the hallway to the sleeping quarters. She walked over to her pallet and stood rigidly, her hands fisted so tightly her knuckles turned white. Looking down she groaned angrily, the buttermilk, along with the soot and the grease that covered the kitchen floor, had left an ugly stain. She sat down on her straw pallet, refusing to cry. Suddenly her arms started tingling. She began to tremble, then felt nauseous and light-headed. Bright sparks streaked from her fingertips, hitting a glass mug sitting on a shelf on the far side of the room. It shattered and tiny shards flew across the room, landing on the dirt floor. In horror, she grabbed her blanket and flung it over her head. She took a deep breath, trying to calm her pounding heart. What had just happened? Had she just performed magic! How was that possible?

A shuffling noise from the outside corridor startled her. She stiffened and slowly lowered her blanket. She was alone in the room. She wrapped her coverlet tightly around her shoulders. An icy dread spread through her body; sorcery was forbidden and meant immediate arrest and imprisonment. Prince Kalian, the merciless ruler of Westcott, had imposed a royal edict banning the use of magic anywhere in the kingdom. She lay for hours staring at the ceiling, her mind numbs with shock, recalling over and over what had happened. Perhaps the mug had been sitting too close to the edge of the shelf and had fallen off. She knew this was not the case, she had just performed magic, and she was in danger. No one must ever find out what had happened.

Aurie lost all sense of time. It might have been minutes or it might have been hours when Dora slipped into the room. Bess and Kate, two kitchen maids, who also shared their sleeping quarters, followed her into the chamber. Dora was carrying a lit candle, which she placed on the shelf above her sleeping pallet. "What's that girl done now?" she said tiredly spotting the glass on the floor. "I'm too worn out to pick up after her; she can clean this up in the morning."

Keeping her eyes tightly shut, Aurie pretended to be asleep. The women quickly undressed in the cooling room, Dora blew out the candle, heaving a sigh of relief as she settled on her pallet. The three exhausted women were soon fast asleep. Tossing and turning for hours, Aurie finally fell into a restless sleep.

She woke with a start. Dora's snores filled the room. She shuddered under her covers, brought on more by her deep-rooted fear of what had happened than the clinging dampness of her dress. There was something lying across her feet, and she reached down and touched clothing. Cora must have retrieved the pants and the shirt from the bundle going to the poor house, and had left them at the foot of her pallet. She grabbed the clothes and then groped around in the dark until she found her boots. She shuffled across the pitch-dark room. Arriving at the closed door, she carefully opened and then closed it. She crept down the long corridor feeling along the walls until she arrived at the kitchen.

A few embers buried in the ashes glowed in the huge hearth, providing enough light to allow her to move around without bumping into anything. She removed her damp dress, shivered in the chilly air, wrinkling her nose at the smell of the sour buttermilk. Folding it neatly, she placed it in a pail in the broom closet, intending to wash it after she had finished her morning chores.

The pants and shirt were threadbare, the legs and arms too short. They would have to do for the time being. Sitting on a wooden bench, she struggled with her worn boots, her toes poked out of the top, and there was a hole in the right sole. Although they cramped her feet, it was better than having no shoes at all, especially during the bitter winter months.

She walked over to the window, it was dark and the courtyard was deserted. Retrieving her coat and cap, she quickly put them on then went to the vegetable bin, grabbed two carrots, and stuffed them in her pocket. Opening the huge oak door, she crept outside, quietly shutting it behind her.

Although it was early spring, the weather was cold and brittle. During the night, it had snowed leaving a light skiff covering the buildings and ground. Aurie shivered in her jacket, it did little to protect her from the bone-chilling dampness. She blew into her chapped hands, wishing she had woolen mittens and a scarf.

Turning left, she walked towards the stone barrier surrounding Windermere Castle. Keeping low and out of view of the guards patrolling the parapets, she followed the wall until she arrived at the horse stables. Her night vision had always been good and she had no problem finding her way in the shadows. The horses were off-limits to everyone except the soldiers and the grooms, who were careless at times and left the side door unlatched. Today she was lucky, the latch opened quietly.

She went directly to Cesar's stall. The huge white warhorse greeted her by rubbing his muzzle against her jacket. Smelling the carrots, he nudged her lightly. "Always thinking about your stomach," she said, patting his muscular neck. The formidable horse had a reputation for being dangerous and unpredictable, yet he was always gentle with her. She had planned to stay for just a few minutes, but the straw in Cesar's stall looked so inviting she crawled under it, and immediately fell asleep. She awakened with a jolt when Cesar kicked over his water bucket. A weak light forced its way through the windows, and she realized it was dawn. It would not be long before the grooms arrived to tend to the horses.

Creeping quietly out of the stall, she left the barn by the back entrance. Sometime during the night, the snow had changed into a light rain, and a fog crept into the castle grounds. Staying close to the walls, she followed the path until she arrived at the livestock barn, which was located adjacent to the stables. Just as she stepped around the corner, she spied Cora striding across the courtyard, mumbling angrily under her breath. Aurie retraced her steps, raced to the back of the livestock barn, and entered through the side entrance. She quickly found refuge behind a wooden barrel.

The front door flew open with a bang, and chickens scattered in all directions. Cora stormed in, grabbed a pitchfork leaning against a weathered saddle and entered the nearest stall, jabbing the tines into a pile of hay. Still mumbling, she left the stall and walked towards a mound of burlap sacks stacked in the corner against the far wall. "Aurie, I just seen you running away, so I know you're hiding in here somewhere," she said as she kicked the sacks, scattering them across the floor. "Mrs. Black's having one o' her fits; the kitchen's as cold as the outdoors. Where's your mind, girl?"

Aurie shook her head in dismay. Mrs. Black would be livid with anger, especially after the mishap with the buttermilk and now neglecting the fire and failing to feed the hungry livestock. It seemed she was always in trouble with the unforgiving cook.

A scuffling noise from above caught Cora's attention, and a piece of straw floated to the floor. "Don't mean nothing to me if you want to be stubborn, girl," she said, as she looked up into the hayloft. "Just so you know, she's threatening to lock you in the tool shed again, and we know how much you like it in there."

Not getting a reply, the disgruntled woman returned to the front of the barn. "This is your last chance girl, don't do you no good hiding, it'll only make things worse." Shrugging, she returned the pitchfork to where she had found it, pulled open the cumbersome door and left. A few seconds later, the sound of the kitchen door slamming shut echoed across the courtyard.

Aurie stepped out from behind the barrel. She did not fault Cora in seeking her out, as she knew the busy woman was only obeying Mrs. Black's orders. She hoped the cook would not be too harsh with Cora when she returned to the kitchen empty-handed.

Aurie walked over to the door and cautiously peeked outside. The courtyard was deserted. On the far side of the bailey, the stone cookhouse was barely visible in the mist that had wrapped itself hungrily around its walls. The thick fog drifting into the compounds of the castle had swallowed the keep and main building, as well as the surrounding curtain wall.

Aurie realized she had to face Mrs. Black sooner than later. The longer she waited to return to the kitchen, the angrier the head cook would be, and the harsher the punishment. She left the shelter of the barn and scurried over to the woodpile next to the corral, loaded her arms with firewood and raced across the courtyard. Arriving at the kitchen door, she shifted the wood higher in her arms. Reaching forward, she lifted the heavy latch, then pushed the door with her foot, causing it to slam against the inside wall with a loud bang. She froze, expecting Mrs. Black to swoop down on her, but the kitchen was empty.

She stacked the logs neatly in the woodbin. Then she swept up the cold ashes in the hearth, grabbed a handful of kindling and several chunks of firewood and tossed them onto the embers she managed to salvage from yesterday's fire, and soon the wood was burning hungrily. An iron kettle filled with water was sitting on the floor, and she hung it on the trammel hanging from the lug pole. She grabbed a milk pail from a hook above the table, and closed the door quickly when she left, keeping as much of the heat inside as possible.

When she arrived at the corral, she lifted the wooden bar, pulled open the heavy gate, and bolted it quickly. Remembering Cora's words about the garden shed, Aurie's thoughts returned to the middle of winter. She had forgotten to close the gate, and the cows had escaped and stampeded through the bailey, creating havoc and trampling the ground into a sea of mud. It had taken over an hour to herd them back into the paddock, and Mrs. Black had been so furious, she had beaten Aurie and locked her in the unheated garden shed for two days. There was a small window located high on the back wall, and Aurie had watched the swirling snowflakes as they drifted to the ground. The only protection she had from the cold was a tattered burlap sack she had found stuffed in the corner behind some garden tools. The scurrying sounds of rats as they scrounged among the seed bags had terrified her. Ever since then, she had a deathly fear of dark confined spaces and the disgusting rodents.

Aurie's mind returned to the present. She stared at the churned mud in the corral, the muddy puddles dotting the courtyard, and the overcast sky. Windermere Castle was a dismal place this time of year, and she wished for the warmth of the sun and the scent of new spring flowers. She spotted an oak leaf lying in the frozen mud, picked it up, and marveled at its intricate design and texture. Sighing, she opened her hand and watched as it drifted slowly to the ground.

Castle rules dictated slaves and free servants were not to mingle and as Aurie was the only slave working in the kitchen, she spent most of her time alone. Her quiet disposition and unique appearance set her apart from the others, and as is often the case when a person is different, people have a tendency of being cruel and hateful. If Aurie had not discovered she preferred the company of animals to people, her life would have been intolerable.

Clucking and whistling softly, she approached the dairy cows, steering the docile animals into the barn. She led Blossom, her favorite Guernsey, into the first stall. She took off her cap and stuffed it inside her coat, tucking her hair behind her ears. She hummed softly, enjoying the early morning sounds of the cows' quietly munching hay, and the chickens clucking and scratching in the straw, searching for seeds. She smiled when a barn owl hooted in the rafters.

The grating of the back-door opening disturbed the quietness. She froze, wondering who else was in the barn this early in the morning.

"Quiet, did you hear something?"

Aurie gasped; it was Mrs. Black

"I told you to stop worrying," a man's raspy voice replied. "There's nobody here but us."

"That's easy 'nuff for you to say," Mrs. Black replied sharply. "But we can't take a chance of anyone overhearing us."

"Quit fretting. You're absolutely sure what you saw?" the man's voice asked.

"If you don't believe me," Mrs. Black replied, "I can always do this without you."

"I'm sure you'd like nothing better than to keep the reward for yourself, dear sister," the surly voice snarled. "But as long as you can vouch you saw the girl using magic it shouldn't be too hard to persuade her to confess."

In shock, Aurie clamped her hand across her mouth. They were talking about her. There had been someone watching outside the sleeping quarter's door last night, it was Mrs. Black and she had seen Aurie using magic.

"Just make sure you don't injure her," ordered Mrs. Black. "If you do, not only will there be no reward, but Prince Kalian will make sure we spend the rest of our lives rotting in his dungeon."

"You take care of your part of the bargain," said the gravelly voice, "and I'll take care of mine."

"Come get her tonight. I'll lock the girl in the garden shed, nobody will be suspicious. She's spent enough time in there."

"I doubt if any of your staff would have the courage to speak up," the man replied sarcastically. "You're not exactly known for your tolerant nature?"

Mrs. Black grunted at the derisive remark. "I always thought there was something funny about that girl what with her strange looks and manners."

"You ain't got no call to complain. Not many peasants can brag 'bout owning their own slave."

"I ain't no peasant. I got that girl fair and square."

The man snorted at Mrs. Black's comment. "I'm surprised you're turning her in," he said. "All you got to do is keep quiet and nobody would ever know and you get to keep your slave."

"Nobody 'cepting Prince Kalian, can't hide nothing from him, and you know the penalty for keeping quiet 'bout something like this."

"Don't forget I'm one of his troopers, I know more than you ever will."

"I'll give you a few minutes to leave," Mrs. Black said sharply, "and then I'll head back to the kitchen, Cora should have found that stupid girl by now. She'll have no idea what's happening until it's too late."

Realizing she did not have time to leave the stall, Aurie ran to the far corner and quickly crawled under the hay, covering herself and the pail seconds before Mrs. Black strolled into view. Mrs. Black was an obese, slovenly woman, with unkempt red hair streaked with grey and deep piercing brown eyes. She stopped and stared at the Guernsey standing complacently in the stall. Scratching her head, she shrugged her shoulders, and left the barn.

Aurie remained in her hiding place for a few minutes, absorbing what she had just heard. It would not take Cora long to report she was unable to find her, and Mrs. Black would certainly send one of the unruly kitchen boys out to continue the search. They were a lot nastier than Cora and would not give up as easily.

Aurie brushed the straw from her hair and clothes. Reaching inside her coat, she grabbed the gold medallion that was hanging around her neck, creating a warm glow that radiated through her body. Gradually the panic subsided. For as long as she could remember, she had owned the pendant, and had kept it hidden under her shift realizing if Mrs. Black ever found out about it, she would have confiscated it for herself. Aurie knew the valuable medallion connected to her past, yet she had no memory of who gave it to her.

She must think of something fast; time was running out!

Chapter Two

Aurie left the stall and ran to the back of the barn, grabbed one of the burlap sacks, and wrapped it around her shoulders for warmth, tying it in a knot. The castle was constantly under guard and if Mrs. Black had put out the word she was a runaway, she knew she would not make it halfway across the compound before detection. It was then she remembered a different exit, one she had not used in a long while.

She opened the barn door and peeked outside. She was facing a field, not fifty yards away the curtain wall rose sharply. The fog provided a small measure of cover, but it was just starting to lift. She raced across the field, crouching low in the brittle grass. When she reached the wall, she hid in the tall thistles, it was quiet and the only sound was the chirping of swallows nesting beneath the eaves of the barn. Following the wall closely, it was not long before she came to a wooden door, standing no higher than four feet in height. She gripped the rusted handle, and tried to lift it, but it would not budge. Bracing her legs, she grabbed it with both hands and frantically pulled as hard as she could. The door refused to open, she looked around in panic, expecting at any moment for the guards to notice her. Suddenly she felt the same tingling feeling she had earlier, sparks flew from her fingertips, and the latch lifted without a sound. She pushed the door open, slipped through, closing it quietly. She heard the latch drop back into place on the other side.

She was standing on an overgrown path, if she turned right, she would come out near the gatehouse. The left path veered away from the castle towards a clearing, which bordered a stream following Lindell Forest. The only time she had ever entered the woods was when she and Cora had gathered mushrooms for Mrs. Black a few years back. They had not ventured far, staying close to the castle, as the gigantic trees were dense and intimidating. Aurie remembered sensing a menacing presence, but she said nothing of her fears to Cora, as the practical woman would have scoffed at her jumpiness.

Not finding the courage to take the path leading into the forest, she turned right, took a few steps, and then stopped abruptly. She must disguise herself, as she would be identified immediately. Twisting her silver-blonde hair into a knot, she removed her cap from her pocket and put it on her head, pulling it down as tightly as she could, covering her pointed ears and part of her face. Grabbing a handful of dirt, she rubbed it across her forehead and her hands. She thanked her luck she was wearing the pants and shirt instead of her dress as anyone seeing her would think she was one of the castle boys, the bruise on her lip making her disguise even more believable.

She walked quickly, keeping close to the wall. The guards patrolling on the parapet would not see her unless they looked directly down. Soon the trail tapered off and the wall ended. Breathing heavily, she strolled purposely around the corner and almost barged into Rufus, one of Prince Kalian's guards. He was leaning against the castle gate, chatting companionably with Bess. Aurie did not like Rufus, as he was cruel, always-making snide remarks about the shape of her ears and the unusual color of her hair and eyes. If either of them should suddenly turn around, they would be looking directly at her and would immediately recognize her. Rufus was naturally suspicious by nature, and he would not believe anything she told him, he knew Mrs. Black never allowed her to leave the castle grounds.

Bess giggled, and Rufus leaned over and whispered in her ear. Aurie walked rigidly past them, expecting recognition, but neither of them took any notice as she strode quickly down the drawbridge and turned left on the cobblestone road. Although it took all her willpower, she continued to walk slowly away from the castle, keeping her pace steady. She caught up to a crowd of villagers, and blended in with them. As soon as the castle was out of sight, she dodged down an alley, hoping to find a less travelled route. She passed by piles of fly-infested garbage stacked against the walls of the rundown tenements. Walking cautiously towards a dilapidated fence, she searched for a gate or an opening. She stepped on the tail of a huge rat, and the disgusting creature squeaked noisily. Shuddering, she fled from the alley and returned to the main road.

She walked steadily, infiltrating deeper and deeper into the bustling village. Most of the mist had dissipated, the sun was feebly attempting to break through the low lying clouds and the snow had long since melted. She was cold, exhausted, and hungry, but she dared not stop, she must find a place to hide. For their personal protection and survival, most of the street kids belonged to gangs, a young girl, or for that matter, a young boy, would not survive long on their own. The soldiers patrolled the streets and alleys continuously, if you were unfortunate enough to be captured you either ended up working in the castle, or in the case of the older boys, as a laborer in Prince Kalian's quarry.

She wandered through the side streets and down abandoned alleys. It was turning colder and it would not be long before nightfall. Finding herself in a bustling marketplace, she strolled towards the orderly booths, hoping she would find a compassionate soul who might offer her food. The merchants were more interested in selling their wares before closing their booths for the night, and took no notice of a dirty street urchin dressed in tattered clothing.

A piercing scream on the far side of the bazaar startled Aurie. A second shout followed closely, and merchants and vendors ran frantically in all directions. More than half a dozen-armed soldiers galloped into view, the head guard signaled the riders to stop. "Check under those stalls," he barked. She recognized Rufus' deep booming voice, and she quickly ducked behind a pile of empty baskets. The soldiers dismounted and began their search, adding to the chaos of the scurrying villagers, rummaging through the goods and produce, tossing them on the muddy ground and trampling them under their feet, smashing pottery and upsetting barrels of food. Aurie looked anxiously around, it would not take them long to reach her. Off to the right was a dark alley, leaving her hiding place and staying as low as she could, she crept towards it.

"Quick, take cover under here," a scratchy voice said. "They'll find you if you try to hide in there, it's a dead end."

The voice came from under a wooden cart that was backed-up against the wall of a tenement. There was no time to reflect on whether she was making the right decision or not, she darted under the cart, sliding as far back as she could. She glanced at her companion. He had a wild mass of curly black hair, dark blue eyes, and looked to be around sixteen years old.

She edged slightly forward and peered from under the wagon. Two muscular guards walked down the alley, poking under the piles of garbage and litter with their spear tips, while two others made their way over to the wagon.

The boy touched her arm and pointed behind him, he rolled out from under the cart, pressing his body tightly against the wall of the building. Directly in front of him was a door that was slightly ajar. Before Aurie realized what was happening, he disappeared. Without hesitation, she followed.

The musty smell of mildew and dampness permeated from the decaying walls and floors, a window on the far side, covered in filth, permitted tiny light to filter into the room. She could barely make out her companion's outline a short distance away.

"Come on," he whispered. "And be quiet."

She followed him to the back of the room. He bent over and lifted the corners of a frayed carpet. Underneath was a hidden trapdoor, he reached down and lifted a metal latch, and the heavy door opened without a sound.

"There's a wooden ladder inside," he whispered. "Climb down until you get to the dirt floor at the bottom, then wait for me. Hurry."

Aurie lowered herself over the ledge, cautiously placed her foot on the first rung and then she froze, her old fear of dark cramped places engulfing her. A heavy boot smacked the top of her head.

"Ow," she yelped.

"Why are you stopping?" the boy said gruffly. "Keep moving and be quiet."

Fighting back her fear, she closed her eyes and descended into the black hole until she reached solid ground. She moved over to the side and sensed the boy standing next to her. There was a scraping sound and a weak light filled the darkness. A dented lantern was hanging from a nail on the ladder. They were standing in a bowl-shaped dugout with dirt walls.

Aurie took a closer look at her companion, he was at least two heads taller than she, and would probably be well over six feet when he finished growing, his shoulders and arms were muscular, suggesting he was no stranger to arduous work.

"Stay close to me," he said, taking the lantern off the hook. "There's a tunnel straight ahead."

She followed him through the dark passageway. The walls were dirt with weathered posts held up by wooden beams. She wondered if they were in an old mining shaft as the entire structure did not look too stable. The tunnel continued to twist and turn, numerous passages branched off in all directions, and in no time, she was confused and disoriented. It would not have taken her long to get lost in this underground labyrinth, the thought made her tremble, as she realized her life was in the hands of a stranger.

The dull light from the lantern cast eerie shadows on the walls. They walked steadily, never breaking their stride. Turning a sharp corner, she spotted an oak door. The boy rapped three times, waited a few seconds, and then rapped twice. The door creaked opened and a thin, hollow-eyed boy, his clothes hanging untidily on his frame, stood before them. He gaped in surprise as Aurie's rescuer gestured her to follow him into the room.

They were in a large space, which looked like it might have been part of a warehouse at one time, the walls were crumbling and portions of the roof were caving in, exposing huge gaps of sky. Wooden crates and bulky barrels were stacked haphazardly on the far side of the room, while piles of filthy clothing and debris lay strewn across the floor. A window on the far wall had no panes, and there was a tattered piece of cloth nailed across the opening to keep out the rain and wind. There was a wooden door, barred from the inside, and presumably leading outside.

In the middle of the room was a small flickering fire, curls of smoke drifted lazily upward making its way out of the holes in the roof. A heavyset boy was sitting on a bench warming his hands over the open flames. When he saw them, he jumped up, an annoyed look on his face.

"You stay here," Aurie's rescuer said, and then he and the thin boy strolled over to the fire pit. Soon all three of them were talking in hushed tones. The conversation became animated, and the husky boy raised his voice, he looked over at Aurie and scowled. The boy who had led her through the tunnels motioned to her, and she walked nervously across the floor, stopping just short of the small group.

"I'm Tony Drummond," her rescuer said. "He's Sam Murdoch," he said pointing at the thin boy, "and this guy with the pouty face is Fred Smith."

Sam appeared to be younger than Tony by a few years. He had brownish-red hair, light blue eyes, and a pale complexion. She nodded and he smiled shyly. Immediately she liked the quiet boy, sensing he had a gentle soul.

Fred, however, was quite the opposite, he was short and squat, had dark greedy eyes, and a shaved head. "So, what's your name?" he asked her brusquely.

"Aurie," she answered, as she slowly turned and faced Tony. "Thanks for helping me back there at the market place."

"Want to tell me what that was all about?" Tony asked.

Aurie's mind was racing frantically, trying to think of a plausible story. "Me and my pals usually hole up by the wharf," she said, slipping into street jargon. "Them soldiers have been making our lives miserable for days. There's been lots of kids disappearing lately, so when the troopers suddenly took after us, we thought it safer to separate."

"Smart move, it's not safe on the streets anymore," Tony said nodding his head.

"They got my friends, and I thought I could lose them in the crowds at the marketplace. If you hadn't helped me, they would have caught me."

"You're lucky I finished work early today, otherwise things might have turned out differently," Tony responded. "You better lay low for a while. You can stay here with us for the time being, at least until I decide what to do with you."

"Are you serious?" Fred blurted angrily. "There's barely enough food for the three of us, let alone someone else."

"You know my code, we don't turn anyone away if they need help," Tony commented, looking darkly at Fred. "Besides, he doesn't have anywhere to go what with his pals getting picked up by the troopers."

"I've told you before, Tony, you're gonna get us into big trouble one of these days, we can't help every hard-luck case that comes our way."

"You let me worry about that okay. You got anything else to say?"

Fred's face turned a deep red and Aurie sensed the anger and tension between the two boys.

"Naw," Fred shrugged, backing down. "Your decision makes no difference to me, long as I get my fair share."

"Then it's settled," said Tony as he turned and faced Aurie. "You hungry?"

Aurie nodded, having gone all day without food and being denied supper the night before, she was famished.

"You can help yourself to whatever's simmering in that pot," Tony said. "May not taste too good, but it'll stick to your ribs?"

"Thanks."

Aurie picked up a tin plate and an old battered spoon lying on top of one of the boxes. She walked over to the fire and looked inside the pot, there were potatoes, turnips and something brown and lumpy that passed as meat.

She scooped the food onto the plate, and then sat down on the wooden seat recently vacated by Fred. The heat was welcoming and she could feel the numbness leaving her toes and fingers. Tony strolled over to the far side of the fire and sat down on a large flat rock. "I'm not giving you a free ticket okay. You gotta pull your weight around here. You contribute to the pot and you can stay, otherwise, you go. Understand?"

Aurie nodded.

"You're pretty scrawny looking," Fred said.

"Whatcha want me to do?" Aurie said to Tony, once again ignoring Fred.

"We try and pick up jobs wherever we can, sometimes we find work at the docks helping the fishermen unload their catch," Tony replied. "But that's real strenuous and there's a lot of lifting."

"Yeah," Fred smirked. "Don't look like you're used to heavy work of any kind."

"I'm stronger than I look, and I knows my way 'round a barn," Aurie answered defiantly, trying hard to disguise her dislike of the judgmental boy.

"That's good to know," said Tony. "I work at the castle, at times I get really busy, and a second hand wouldn't hurt."

Aurie felt the color draining from her face. "You work at the castle?"

"Yeah, I'm a groom at the stables," Tony replied. "I'm always looking for someone to muck out the stalls and clean tack, the pay is sad, but it all helps. Sam and Fred are going to the docks tomorrow, so you can come with me."

Aurie lowered her head and stared at her plate, a lump of potato lodged in her throat, she said nothing.

"We better call it a day," Tony continued, mistaking Aurie's silence for acceptance. "We have to be at the castle gates before sunrise. They're only open for a few minutes, and if we're late, we don't get in."

"Why do they lock the gates?" Aurie asked lifting her head, a confused look on her face.

"It's a new law that's just been passed," Sam said. "Anyone living in the village and wanting to get in has to arrive at sunup, after that, the gates are closed, and if you're inside, you don't get out until sunset."

"Oh, I've never actually been inside the castle grounds," Aurie replied. She had always despised lying, and hoped the tone of her voice would not give her away.

Aurie was not surprised to hear about the tight security at the castle, but she had not been aware of the closed gate policy recently passed. If she had not left by the back gate this morning, she would not have made it out of the castle at all. With Prince Kalian increasing his efforts in finding anyone with magical abilities, he must have implemented this new law to tighten security. Her disappearance would only add to his frustration and his soldiers would be everywhere, merciless in their pursuit.

"There's a lot of instability in Westcott right now," Tony said, as if reading her thoughts. "With Prince Kalian arresting anyone using sorcery, this is just another way for him to tighten his control over the villagers."

"Things are kinda bad then?" Aurie said, keeping her face down and hoping none of the boys would notice her nervousness. She poked a piece of turnip, moving it slowly around her plate.

"There's no work, and Prince Kalian keeps raising taxes and confiscating crops to feed his growing army. The villagers are starving and it does them no good to complain, if they make too much noise they end up in the dungeons or working at the quarries."

"Never thought much about stuff like that," Aurie replied quietly.

Tony shook his head in frustration. "Unfortunately, that's the way too many people think, it's safer for them to hide their heads in the sand than to stand up for their rights."

"Maybe they're afraid?"

Tony looked at Aurie, a frown creasing his forehead. "And that's why Prince Kalian is becoming more powerful all the time, he feeds off their fear."

"Better not get him started," Fred grumbled. "Tony doesn't have much love for Prince Kalian."

"It's hard to respect or like a tyrant, Fred," Tony said through clenched teeth.

"Yeah, but you better remember that you're working for him, and you do anything to get on his bad side, he'll throw you out in the streets."

"The only reason we're surviving," Sam interrupted, sensing the tension between Tony and Fred, "is because Prince Kalian needs Tony, not because he wants to help the needy."

"Whatcha mean?" Aurie asked anxiously, suddenly wondering if Tony was one of Prince Kalian's soldiers.

"He's the only person in Westcott who can handle Prince Kalian's horse which is lucky for us, because Tony has steady work, while Fred and I have to take whatever we can find. We haven't had a job in a while, but we finally managed to find something for the rest of the week."

"Look, let's forget we even talked about it, okay?" Tony said stiffly.

Aurie nodded, sensing his anger. She gladly let the matter drop, because talking about Prince Kalian frightened her so badly she found it hard to breathe.

Sam went to the fire and tossed some weathered boards onto the smoldering coals, humming quietly to himself. Fred disappeared into a dark corner of the room, Tony visibly relaxed, and Aurie got the impression that Sam's quiet demeanor often kept peace between the boys.

"Grab that old rug over there by the wall," Tony said. "If you dig through those piles of clothes, you might find something to use as a cover to keep you warm."

"Thanks for everything, Tony," Aurie said.

"Sure," Tony said as he walked away. Aurie sensed he was embarrassed from his recent outburst, and probably not used to receiving thanks.

Finishing her meal, she scrounged through the clothing, digging out a blanket that was full of moth holes. She also found an old worn jacket, which should work well as a pillow.

Each of the boys had their own sleeping area, so Aurie set the rug up next to the wall on the far side of the fire. She covered herself with the threadbare blanket, and stuffed the jacket under her head. It had a lingering odor of onions and dried sweat, and she wondered who the previous owner might have been.

She listened to the boys settling down, realizing how lucky she was in getting off the streets for the night. If she helped to contribute by getting a job, maybe Tony would let her stay. She reached inside her shirt and grasped the medallion, it started to glow, and soon her uncertainty dissipated, leaving her warm and relaxed. It was not long before her eyelids closed and she fell into an exhausted sleep.

Chapter Three

It took Aurie a few moments to realize the sound that had awakened her was the crackling of burning wood. The three boys sat around the fire, holding tin cups in their hands and chewing bread. Fred dunked a huge chunk into his cup, scooped it out, and wolfed it down greedily.

"You know, I've been thinking," Aurie said as she walked over to the warm fire. "It's only been a few hours since them soldiers were after me, and I thought it might not be safe to go to the castle right now, just in case they recognize me."

"So, what you gonna do then?" Fred asked snidely. "Take a holiday?"

"I'm thinking I could stay here and clean up a bit, and I'm a really good cook."

"You can cook?" Sam asked, smiling happily.

Aurie nodded. "Iff'n you tell me whatcha do for food, and where you got your wood, I'll have a hot meal ready when you get back."

"I'm okay with that," Tony shrugged. "Besides, this place can use a good cleaning, and you might as well find out how to get to the market place. It'll save me having to go there today, and I can get in a few more hours of work at the stables."

Sam nodded without hesitation. Fred scowled angrily, shaking his head in denial. When he saw the look on Tony's face, he grabbed the last piece of bread and stuffed it into his mouth.

"Here's some coin," said Tony, as he reached inside his pocket and handed Aurie two pennies. "You should be able to get some bottom-of-the barrel vegetables, and maybe some stale bread at the market. Go out the front door, and head straight down the hill, there is a junk yard at the bottom, just cut through and turn left when you get to the gate. Watch out for the old codger who lives in the shack next to the fence. We've known him for years and he keeps spouting off about getting a guard dog, he's too lazy to chase us, and so far, his threats are mostly hot air."

"There's a pile of wood over there," Sam advised. "It's pretty rotten, so you shouldn't have any trouble breaking up the pieces and burning them."

"Thanks," Aurie answered.

"Let's get a move on," said Tony. "The sun will be up soon and we all have a long walk ahead of us. I have to get to the castle before they close the gates."

Sam opened the lid of the wooden barrel located next to the fire pit. He reached inside and took out the rest of the bread they had been eating. He tore it into three pieces and handed one chunk to Tony and one to Fred, who quickly stuffed them inside their jackets. Aurie was aware it was their only food for the day. When they got to the door, Fred turned sharply and said. "If we come back tonight and you're gone and anything's missing, you'll wish you'd never been born, hear?"

Aurie glanced fleetingly at the surly boy, disdainfully, she turned and concentrated on the far side of the wall, she was terrified she would lose control of her powers, her growing dislike for Fred could prove to be her undoing, and she knew she had to be careful.

"Let up, will you Fred," Sam said abruptly. Fred growled under his breath, lifted the wooden bar and yanked the door open. He stepped outside and disappeared into the darkness.

"Don't mind him," Tony said as he followed Sam out of the door. "He's always suspicious at first. Just give him time to get to know you."

Aurie nodded, although she felt she would never like Fred, she had spent too many years avoiding people like him at the castle.

She understood Tony was giving her a chance to prove she could be trusted, she had only known him a few hours, but instinctively felt he was a decent sort. However, she also knew if she did not earn her keep, he would turn her out without hesitation, you did not survive on the streets without being tough.

She closed the door and returned to the fire pit. A dented coffee pot was sitting on a rock next to the coals. She picked it up and shook it. There was not much left, but she managed to get half a cupful, it tasted like mud, but at least it was warm. Aurie had a quick look around to see if there was anything else to eat. She checked inside the barrel where Sam had retrieved the bread, but it was empty. She lifted the lid off the stew pot holding yesterday's food and cringed, there was a greasy film floating on top of a few pieces of shriveled meat and colorless vegetables. Gingerly, she scraped out as much of the food as she could and swallowed it quickly. It was disgusting, but it helped to slake her hunger. She had to make sure she got up in the morning the same time as the boys, or Fred would eat her share as well as his own. If she did not stand up for herself from the start, she would be going hungry.

She spotted a metal pot on one of the boxes, it was black with soot and the handle was missing, replaced by a piece of twisted wire. It was full of water, so she poured half of it into the empty stew pot, and then she placed both pots on the coals.

While she was waiting for the water to boil, Aurie decided to do some exploring. The oil lantern Tony had used yesterday was sitting on the ground next to the huge boulder. She knew how difficult it was to get fuel. She spotted a half-burned candle sitting on top of one of the barrels. She held the wick under the flames until it caught. It did not provide much light but at least she would be able to move around the warehouse without tripping. Having good eyesight had its advantages.

She pried open wooden crates and lifted lids off the barrels, peering inside to see if they contained anything that might be useful. There was old, mildewed clothing, rusted wire, broken lanterns, and books with the pages torn or missing. She reached down and took an old book bound in leather from one of the barrels, it was about weaponry, and she slowly browsed through the pages, holding the candle above her head to make it easier to read. She wondered who had owned the books before they ended up in the warehouse. She had always been able to read, although she could not remember who had taught her. It was something she had never told anyone. Intuitively, she knew how dangerous it would be to let anyone know her secret. Slaves did not know how to read. She returned the book to the barrel and replaced the lid.

Gradually the darkness dissipated, and the sun shone weakly through the hole in the roof. The candle had burned down to a stub. She returned it to the top of the barrel, and made a note to tell Tony she had used it so Fred could not accuse her of stealing.

She strolled towards the door, and opened it cautiously. The warehouse was located on a hill overlooking the rooftops of a row of run-down tenements. She stepped outside and walked cautiously across a field covered in white clover and nettles until she arrived at the edge of an embankment. In the far distance, the dark expanse of Lindell Forest disappeared into the horizon. She recalled hearing stories of people who were venturesome enough to travel through the forest, although they journeyed in large numbers or with hired protection.

Frightening myths telling of beasts and fearsome magical creatures were enough to deter even the bravest of men.

Through the rising mist, she noticed the outlines of burned houses, the vegetation and undergrowth reclaiming those that remained standing. She wondered who had lived in them as it was evident they were once magnificent villas.

Looking south, she saw Dolphin Cove with fishing trawlers floating calmly on its surface, and any ships approaching the harbor were visible for miles, thus eliminating the threat of a surprise attack. Although the route was longer, most travelers opted to sail by ship to their destination rather than travelling through Lindell Forest.

On the north and the west side of Westcott, craggy mountains formed a natural barricade. The mountain passes heading west were treacherous and almost impassable due to unpredictable weather and avalanches in the winter months and rockslides in the summer. The merchant ships brought in the commodities not available in Westcott in exchange for the pottery and leather goods for which the villagers were famous.

Windermere Castle built on the highest point, looked down on the village. There was a dry moat surrounding the stronghold. With the protection of the royal army and its location, Westcott was almost impenetrable. Tony's remarks about Prince Kalian made her realize how powerful the man had become, and the formidable hold he had over the village and its inhabitants.

A path wandered off to the left and Aurie followed it around to the back, it did not take long for her to discover where it led. The reek emanating from an outhouse concealed in the bushes made her gag. The door was hanging by a rusted hinge. Peeking inside, she noticed an old wooden bucket propped against the wall, a hornets' nest hanging in the corner, and spider webs covering the walls and ceiling. She cringed in disgust, deciding her last chore for the day would be to tackle the privy. Much as she hated to do it, she quickly dodged inside and used the bucket.

Adjacent to the outhouse was a huge pile of rotting logs and boards. At least she knew now where they kept their wood supply. A stream trickled off to the left, and she assumed this was the water source, it was brown and murky and she made a mental note to boil all water before drinking.

Aurie retraced her steps and went back inside the warehouse. She took the metal pot off the coals and poured some of the heated water into a basin she found on a crate. She pulled off her cap and her hair cascaded down her back. There was a cracked mirror hanging on the far wall and she stared candidly at her reflection. The cut on her swollen lip was healing well. She had always healed quickly and was not surprised to see the bruise had almost disappeared.

She remembered the first time she had seen her image, shortly after she had come to the castle. Startled by her appearance, she had realized how different she looked from anyone else. She lifted a lock of her thick hair, twisting it around her finger. It was silver in color with golden highlights. She traced her finger along her pointed ear, her skin was pale, her face heart-shaped, and her eyes, her most prominent feature, were deep violet. She could not recall having seen anyone at the castle who had her coloring, or for that matter, who looked even remotely like her.

She returned to the basin and scrubbed off the dirt covering her arms and face. She had always had an aversion to filth and tried to keep herself as clean as possible. Mrs. Black used to nag her constantly about her cleanliness, telling her she was putting on airs, and warned her that if she washed too often she would come down with the lung sickness. Aurie was aware the selfish woman was not concerned about her welfare but did not want to chance losing the status of having her own slave. The only people wealthy enough to possess one were the nobility and the upper classes, and Aurie often wondered how she had become Mrs. Black's property. It was another unsolved mystery from her past.

When she had finished washing, she knotted her hair and piled it on top of her head. The most sensible thing to do would be to cut it short, but she did not have a knife that was sharp enough to do the job. She placed the cap back on her head and pulled it down snugly to cover her ears. She turned from the mirror and looked around the room, not sure where to begin. She picked up soiled clothing and worn boots and tossed them into the empty boxes, she found an old broom leaning on the back wall and swept the floor, which did not help at all. There was so much dust floating in the air, she found it difficult to breathe and decided it was best to leave the floor in its present condition.

After tidying up as best she could, she returned to the fire, lifted the filthy stew pot off the coals, and started scraping the sides with a spoon. It took her well over an hour before she was satisfied it was sanitary enough to cook in again.

Realizing it was time to go to the market place she grabbed her burlap sack, and left the warehouse. Following Tony's directions, she walked across the field, found a worn path leading down the embankment, and soon arrived at a tall wooden fence. She peeked between the slats, inside was a junkyard buried under towering stacks of metal, wood, and rocks. She spotted an old shack off to the right. It must be where the junkman lived, she could not see him anywhere, and she hoped he would not notice her cutting through the yard.

The fence ran in both directions, and she turned left. She walked for a few minutes until she found a loose board, this was probably how the boys got inside the yard. She lifted the plank and squeezed through, letting it drop behind her.

On the far side, she spotted the top of a gate and walked quickly down the path, skirting piles of rusted metal. She was half-way across the yard when she heard frenzied barking, she spun around and saw a huge mastiff running directly towards her. The junkman had obviously acted on his threat and had obtained a guard dog.

In panic, she realized she would not be able to make it back to the fence or to the main gate in time. Again, she felt the energy flowing into her body. When the ferocious dog was almost on top of her, she lifted her hand and sparks flew from her fingers, hitting it squarely in its chest. The dog stopped in its tracks, as if slamming into a brick wall, yelped in pain, and lowered itself to the ground.

"Go," she shouted angrily, hoping she had not caused him a lot of distress. The frightened dog whined, turned and raced down the path, heading back in the direction from where it had come.

Shaking violently, she checked around to make sure she had not been seen using magic. She did not understand where her powers were coming from, and although this time it was to her advantage, she realized she had to learn to control her emotions, because it seemed that every time she got frightened or angry it happened. If someone should see her using her powers, she would soon find herself in Prince Kalian's dungeon.

It did not take her long to get to the gate. Although bolted, it was slightly ajar, and she managed to squeeze her slim body through the opening. She turned left onto the cobblestone road, and after walking for a short while, arrived at a market place. She was dismayed to see it was the same one where Tony had rescued her. Everything appeared to be peaceful, and the merchants had cleaned up the damage caused by the soldiers and were once again selling their merchandise. She approached one of the stalls. The merchant noticed her tattered clothing and frowned.

"Get along now, you thieving brat. There's nothing here to interest you."

She shrugged and left, not wanting to attract undue attention. She wandered over to a second booth, piled high with baskets crammed full of vegetables.

"Can I help you, young sir?" a voice boomed.

She lifted her head and inhaled sharply, the merchant standing behind the counter was enormous, with a thick neck, broad shoulders, and muscular arms. He had a long, dark beard, thick bushy eyebrows, and black penetrating eyes.

"How much?" Aurie gulped, pointing at a bin full of potatoes.

"How much you got?"

"Not 'nuff to pay your price, but 'nuff to pay what they're worth."

The beefy merchant looked at her in surprise. Suddenly he threw his head back and laughed boisterously. "Pretty brave for such a small mouse, aren't you?"

"Just don't likes being gypped, that's all."

"Two pennies and you can have two spuds, four carrots, and a turnip and an onion."

"Are you kidding? Them's last fall's crop, they're all bruised, I'll give you one penny for half a dozen spuds and a bunch of those wilted carrots."

Shrugging his massive shoulders, the merchant let out an exaggerated sigh. "You drive a hard bargain, young man. Give me your sack."

"Thanks mister," Aurie said as she handed him her bag and one of her pennies. "It's been a real pleasure doing business with ya."

The merchant picked through the bin and tossed a handful of potatoes into her sack. Then he started digging through the carrots.

"Leave the tops on," she said. Some merchants would remove them and try to sell them separately, but she liked the flavor they added to a stew.

"Maybe tomorrow you can pick on someone else," said the merchant good naturedly, as he handed her the vegetables.

"And miss all this fun!"

The merchant grinned. "What's your name lad?"

"Aurie," she replied, belatedly wishing she had used a different name.

"I haven't seen you around here before, are you new to Westcott?"

Aurie stiffened, realizing she had to be careful in answering. There were spies everywhere, and she did not know who might be reporting to Prince Kalian.

"Naw," said Aurie. "I just live a few blocks away. Ma thought I was old 'nuff now to start buying at the market, says she's got her hands full taking care of all us kids, what with me da never being home half the time."

The merchant nodded, as if it was a story he had heard far too often.

"I'll tell you what. You come back tomorrow when the market closes and if there are any vegetables I have not sold, you can take them off my hands, all for a penny. What do you say?"

"That's great," she said gratefully, tossing the sack over her shoulder. "Thanks mister."

Aurie strolled around the market place, overwhelmed by the sounds and smells, the ripple of voices haggling, laughing, and shouting adding to the atmosphere.

A short distance away, an elderly beggar sat on the curb clutching a tin cup in his gnarled hand, he had no coat, and around his neck was a tattered scarf. Occasionally, he grabbed the back of a passerby's jacket, begging for a coin.

Young girls, more than likely servants working for the more affluent families in Westcott, moved from booth to booth, searching for the freshest fruits and vegetables. A stout woman holding a basket in her arms stopped at one of the stalls and pointed into a large wooden bin. The vendor must have quoted her an exorbitant price, because she shook her head vehemently, her face red with anger. They haggled for a few minutes, then the woman nodded curtly and the vendor leaned over and plunked a large fish in her basket. Aurie relished the liveliness of the interchange, chuckling quietly to herself as she watched the merchant bite the coin the woman handed him before he pocketed it.

Loud laughter erupted from behind the booths, and Aurie strolled over to see what was happening. A juggler was throwing apples into the air and catching them with one hand, and then he jumped high into the air, did a backwards flip, and landed nimbly on his feet. Aurie laughed, laid the burlap sack on the ground, and clapped her hands, greatly enjoying his performance. An elderly man and a garishly garbed woman were standing close by. The woman was singing off-key and the man was talking loudly, wildly waving his arms. It took Aurie a few seconds to realize he was a storyteller, and soon she was engrossed in his tale. With a start, she realized how much time had passed. She must not allow herself to get distracted.

A well-groomed man dressed in a velvet jacket, and riding a dappled horse, stopped to chat with an acquaintance. He was wearing a sword and his shield bore

Prince Kalian's crest. Aurie grabbed the burlap sack, lowered her face and quickly stepped behind one of the stalls. The young man laughed, spurred his nervous mount, and galloped through the throngs, scattering merchants and villagers in all directions. The air was thick with the sounds of cursing and angry voices. A young strapping lad picked up a rock and threw it at the back of the disappearing equestrian. His companion grabbed him by his arm, and pulled him quickly away. Aurie watched the foolhardy boy as he disappeared into the crowds, and recalled Tony's words that the townspeople had no love for the soldiers. They were cautious enough to realize any show of open rebellion could prove to be not only dangerous, but also deadly.

Aurie wandered casually around the stalls, admiring the diverse displays of wares for sale. The pottery and the quality of the leather boots and saddles offered were unmatched, and she remembered overhearing the kitchen maids commenting on overhearing visiting dignitaries praising the workmanship of the Westcott artisans.

She stopped before a booth with a display of freshly baked bread, cream filled pastries, and plump raisin buns, the aroma made her stomach grumble. A young girl, a few years older than Aurie, waited on an elderly woman. When she had completed the sale, she turned towards Aurie, and asked pleasantly, "What can I do for you today?"

"Any day-old bread, miss?" Aurie asked.

"I'm sorry, but all our bread is fresh. How about a delicious raisin bun? It's only one penny?"

Shaking her head, Aurie turned and walked away.

"Wait just a minute, young man. I have this loaf of herb bread. It's burned on the bottom so it probably won't sell, you can have it for a penny."

Grinning, Aurie raced back to the booth and paid for the loaf of bread. She placed it in her bag, staring openly at the young merchant. She was very attractive, with long auburn hair, and green sparkling eyes.

"You're new around here, aren't you?" the young girl laughed, noticing the admiring looks from Aurie.

Aurie nodded suddenly aware she had been openly staring. Her face turned red in embarrassment and she hoped the young woman would not think she was being rude.

"I've noticed you wandering around the marketplace."

"Yes, miss."

"My name's Jasmine Bates, but you can call me Jasmine."

"I'm Aurie."

"Pleased to meet you Aurie. You wouldn't by chance be looking for work, would you?"

Aurie nodded eagerly.

"You know, you might be just what I'm looking for. I need someone to help load the cart in the mornings, and to keep the booth tidy while I wait on customers. Come by the Blue Dove Bakery on Tupper Road tomorrow at dawn, and I will give you some chores to do? I'm sorry, I can't pay you any coin, but if you agree, I can let you have any baked goods left at the end of the day, there's usually a loaf of bread or some buns."

"That would be great miss. I'll be by first thing in the morning."

Aurie could not believe her good luck. If Tony agreed to let her work at the bakery, then she would not have to go to the castle with him the next day. Along with the vegetables, she would bring home enough food each day to feed the four of them.

She raced back to the warehouse, stirred up the coals in the fire pit, and threw in a few pieces of dried boards, stoking up the flames. She poured half of the remaining water from the metal pot into the stew pot.

She cleaned the potatoes and the carrots, scraping away as much of the dirt as she could. Then she dug out an old rusted knife she remembered seeing in one of the barrels and hacked the vegetables into small pieces. To her surprise, she found a large onion lying at the bottom of the sack. She smiled and reminded herself to thank the kind hearted merchant tomorrow when she picked up the promised vegetables.

While scrounging earlier around the room, she had discovered an old jar half full of dried chicory. She used the rest of the water to brew a pot of the unsavory liquid. The first thing she would do in the morning before she left to go to the bakery would be to give the coffee pot a good cleansing, now that she knew where their water supply was located.

It was not long before Tony arrived. He looked around at the much-improved warehouse and smiled. "That smells pretty good," he said, inhaling deeply. He handed her a package tied in brown paper, Aurie opened it and found a chunk of meat.

"It's a bit off, but if you cook it long enough, it should be okay," Tony said.

Aurie chopped it up and threw it in the pot along with the simmering vegetables. She had just started to tell Tony about her good luck in finding work when they heard voices outside the door. Sam and Fred entered the room. Sam walked over to the fire and lifted the lid off the stew pot.

"Looks like you did pretty well for your first day Aurie," he said, inhaling deeply.

Fred did not say anything. He took his jacket off and tossed it in the corner next to his pallet, grabbed a tin cup and poured a cup of the brewing chicory.

"Aurie was just telling me he managed to pick up some work today," Tony said.

"It's at the bakery on Tupper Road. I ain't getting no money, but the girl who works there says if there's any bread or buns left at the end of the day, I can have those," Aurie said. "And one of the vendors is letting me have his left-over vegetables for only a penny."

"Great job Aurie, food's as good as coin," Tony remarked. "I'm surprised anyone would hire a street kid, though."

"I guess since they weren't paying me nothing, no one else would want the job."

"Whatever works," Tony grinned.

"Guess it doesn't hurt when you look half-starved," Sam chuckled. "I bet all you had to do was bat those big violet eyes and you had that lady eating right out of your hands."

Aurie could feel her cheeks turning red. She laughed along with Tony and Sam, although she felt uncomfortable. The boys who worked in the kitchen and in the barns teased and joked among themselves in the same way, and she had to remind herself to not act surprised when Tony, Sam or Fred did the same.

"More than likely felt sorry for him," Fred grumbled irritably. He did not congratulate Aurie on her luck.

"Speaking of money," asked Tony. "How did you two do today?"

Sam dug into his pocket and dropped a couple of coins into Tony's hand. Fred hesitated for a few seconds, and then he begrudgingly did the same.

Tony walked over to his sleeping area. He pulled back a loose board, reached inside, removed a small sack, deposited the money, and returned the bag to its hiding place.

Aurie felt uneasy. She turned and looked at Fred. He was staring openly at her, a sneer on his face. She could not understand why he disliked her so intensely.

The next morning Tony gave Aurie the directions to the Blue Dover Bakery. "Cut through the market place and you'll save yourself ten minutes, when you get to the main street, walk a few blocks, and then turn right on Tupper Road, the shop is half-way down the block, on the left-hand side."

When Aurie arrived at the bakery, she tried to open the door, but it would not budge. She leaned against the outside wall, waiting for the shop to open. Just when she wondered if anyone was going to show up, the door opened and an elderly man carrying a broom and dustpan stepped out. He was thin as a post, and his face was wrinkled and dark as leather, he started sweeping the sidewalk, ignoring Aurie. When she did not move away, he turned and faced her, "You waiting for someone lad?"

"Yes sir, a young lady, with auburn hair and green eyes. I met her yesterday at the market. She said her name was Jasmine."

"She's inside getting things ready for the market. You must be the young lad Jasmine mentioned, go on in."

"Yes, sir."

"And don't leave the door open any longer than you must, I don't want to spend the day swatting flies."

Aurie nodded and entered the shop. Jasmine was standing behind a wooden counter. She lifted her head when the doorbell rang, smiled, and pointed down a hallway to rows of baskets filled with baked goods. "You're here bright and early. Why don't you stack those in the wooden cart in the back alley?"

Aurie quickly went to work. The old man Aurie had talked to earlier came back into the shop and took several loaves of bread and a batch of raisin buns out of a huge oven.

"Aurie, this is Jack Mudd."

Jack nodded, and then returned to his chores. Aurie could sense the comradery between the old man and the young girl.

As Aurie and Jasmine were walking out the back door, Jasmine called to Jack. "Uncle Nathan should get here any time. He spent half the night at the pub, so keep out of his way if you can."

Jack nodded solemnly and waved as they left.

"Poor Jack," said Jasmine. "He's in for a long day, I'm afraid when Uncle Nat gets into the suds, he can be pretty nasty." Aurie did not say anything, as she assumed that Uncle Nat was the owner of the bakeshop, and she knew it was best to keep her thoughts to herself.

Soon they arrived at the market place. On their way to Jasmine's stall, they passed the vegetable booth, Aurie stopped and thanked the friendly merchant for the onion, and then she joined Jasmine.

"I didn't know you were friends with Seamus Stark," Jasmine commented.

"I ain't, didn't even know that was his name. I just met him yesterday, he's real nice."

"He doesn't usually make friends with anyone. Most of the merchants keep clear of him. He's someone you don't want to cross."

"He's been kind to me."

"Not to most people, you must have a magic touch," Jasmine said, shrugging indifferently.

Aurie quickly lowered her head, thankful that Jasmine did not notice the look on her face at how close to the truth her comment had been.

Aurie kept busy restocking the table with the baked goods from the cart, keeping the booth tidy, and running on small errands for Jasmine. In the early afternoon, Jasmine untied a piece of cheesecloth, removed a slice of bread spread with lard, and took a bite. Aurie kept on working, ignoring the hunger pangs in her stomach.

"Why don't you help me with this," Jasmine said as she tore the bread in half. "It's way more than I can eat."

'Oh no miss," Aurie said quickly. "I'm fine."

"Nonsense," Jasmine said. "Tomorrow I'll bring two slices. Since you're working for no coin, the least I can do is provide you with a piece of bread during the day, it won't break Uncle Nat."

Aurie thanked the generous girl, and happily returned to her chores. Before she knew it, the day was over and Jasmine asked her to load the empty baskets back into the cart.

"Seamus is coming over," Jasmine commented. "I wonder what he wants."

The huge man plodded over to the cart, nodded to Jasmine, and waited until Aurie had finished her chore. "Don't forget to pick up the vegetables I promised before you go home. Hope your Ma had enough to feed all those kids at your place."

"Yes sir, she did. I'll be right over to get them," Aurie replied, keeping her head down. Seamus returned to his stall.

"I didn't know you lived near here," Jasmine asked. "You never mentioned anything about having a family."

"Didn't think you'd be interested that's all."

Jasmine did not say anything. She lifted the poles of the pull cart and started to walk away. Stopping, she grabbed a package from inside the cart, and tossed it at Aurie.

"Here's your bread. See you tomorrow bright and early."

Aurie stopped at Seamus' stall to get the promised produce and handed him her coin. She knew he was giving her considerably more than a penny's worth, and was thankful for his charity.

On her way back to the warehouse, Aurie recalled the look on Jasmine's face when Seamus had asked about her family. She had to be more careful in the future and ensure her story was the same with everyone she talked with. Much as she was getting to like Jasmine, she did not want her to start asking questions, she needed to be diligent and on alert. One mistake could be disastrous.

Chapter Four

Time went by quickly, and before Aurie knew it, a month had passed. She got along well with Tony and Sam, and Fred reluctantly accepted her presence long as she provided the food. She had to remind herself to talk like the street kids, sometimes forgetting, and when she did, she noticed Tony watching her closely.

Prince Kalian's troops seemed to be everywhere, and it did not look as if he was going to give up his search. Aurie could not understand why he was so intent on capturing her and why he had such a hatred for anyone who possessed magic. She kept herself hidden from view when the soldiers came anywhere near the marketplace. Posters nailed on the sides of houses and on posts gave a description of a runaway slave girl with long silver-blond hair, and pointed ears. A crude drawing of her likeness nailed on trees and the sides of the stalls, was prepared for the benefit of the villagers who did not know how to read. Thankfully, the drawing was so inaccurate. Aurie did not feel threatened by the image. The posters said she used sorcery, and anyone knowing of her whereabouts was to inform the troops immediately. At the bottom in bold letters was a warning that anyone helping runaways would "be arrested and punished severely."

The merchants at the marketplace came to know her by sight, and she managed to pick up extra jobs when Jasmine could not keep her busy throughout the day. Seamus always found something for her to do, which added an extra onion or turnip in her sack, and it was not long before a friendship grew between her and the kindly giant.

She woke one morning shivering under her blanket. Sam, whose job it was to start the fire in the mornings was already up and stoking the coals. The room was damp and chilly, and rain was falling through the holes in the roof, leaving puddles on the dirt floor. "It's going be a wet one today," he said quietly when he heard her stirring.

Aurie groaned and slowly stood up, and then she raced outside to the outhouse before the other boys awoke. She did not relish the idea of standing in the pouring rain at the marketplace. On such a bitterly frigid day, sales would be slow and it would be difficult to pick up work from the other vendors.

After everyone had eaten a hasty meal, the three boys left for the day. She followed them down the hill and through the junkyard. The mastiff kept his distance and Fred's scornful remarks about the dog's cowardliness irritated her. She wanted to defend the animal, as she felt it was an intelligent and faithful guard dog, but she realized it was prudent to remain quiet.

Sam and Fred took a different route as they had both managed to find work at the rock quarry located a few miles outside of Westcott. It was only for a week, but the pay was better than what they made at the docks.

"Why don't I go with you to the bakery to see if your friend Jasmine is going to set up today?" Tony asked. "If she doesn't need you, come with me to the castle, I could use an extra pair of hands, and at least you'll not have to stand outside in the pouring rain. The market's going to be quiet today, and it's dry in the barn."

Aurie sloshed sullenly through the puddles, following closely behind Tony, when they arrived at the marketplace, she noticed that a few of the regular merchants had already arrived and were setting up their booths. Many had raised tarps over the tables and stalls to provide some protection from the relentless downpour. She waved at Seamus and he waved back.

They finally arrived at the Blue Dove Bakery. Aurie stopped Tony at the door. "I'll run around to the back door. They're not open yet, and I'll let you know in a second," she said.

Tony nodded and took protection under the eaves as Aurie raced around the side of the shop and opened the back door. Jasmine was helping Jack take loaves of bread out of the oven. When she saw Aurie standing in the doorway, dripping water all over the floor, she grabbed a towel and walked over to her. "Here, let me dry you off. You're soaking wet."

Aurie jumped back just as Jasmine reached for her hat. "I'm fine Jasmine. I just wanted to know iff'n you'd need me today at the marketplace."

"Not today. It's too wet."

"Should I come around tomorrow?"

"Not unless it stops raining, the customers generally come to the shop to buy their baked goods when it's this wet."

Aurie thanked Jasmine, and turned and left, joining Tony at the front.

"Well?" he asked.

"She says she won't need me again 'til the rain lets up."

"Great, that works out just fine," Tony said, as he companionably slapped Aurie's back. "I have more than enough work to keep both of us busy, come on, we're running late, and Prince Kalian doesn't take kindly to slackers."

Hearing Prince Kalian's name visibly shook Aurie and as was always the case, she found it difficult to breathe. Her terror of the man left her rigid with fear, and she often wondered what her reaction would be should she ever meet him face to face.

If she continuously refused to go to the castle with Tony, he might get suspicious and start asking her dangerous questions. She realized the only way she was going to survive away from the castle was to stay with Tony's group. Without their protection, she would not last more than a day on the streets.

Before long, they arrived at the castle. The guard, who was standing under a protected walkway to keep dry, waved at Tony and hastily opened the gate, ushering them into the lower bailey. "You got here just in time, almost time to lock the gates," he remarked. Tony grinned and saluted good-naturedly.

Aurie looked around at the familiar surroundings, wishing she were anywhere but here.

"Over this way," Tony said to Aurie, pointing in the direction of the stables. She followed closely, praying no one would recognize her.

Tony walked around to the back and they entered by the side door. A tall reed-thin boy was mucking out one of the stalls, while a second boy, shorter and stockier was pitching hay into a nearby stall.

"I thought you said you were bringing someone to give you a hand," the tall lad commented to Tony. "But it looks like you found yourself a little Pixie instead."

"Don't worry, James," Tony replied. "He's small, but he's a good worker, he can do twice the job you two lazybones can with one hand tied behind his back."

James and his companion laughed at Tony's ribbing, and Aurie saw the three of them were good friends. It seemed that most people who knew Tony respected and liked him.

"Aurie, I'd like you to meet James and Randy. Don't let them give you any trouble, okay?"

"Good thing you got here when you did," James said, his face dark with worry. "Prince Kalian's taking the troops out today and he wants that nasty piece of horseflesh saddled right away."

"Tsk, tsk, shame on you James. A big strapping boy like yourself, and you don't even know how to saddle a horse," Tony joked.

"I can saddle and ride any horse in this barn, but you know full well that horse is the devil himself. Beats me why he lets you near him, when even Prince Kalian has trouble controlling him."

"You just need to earn his trust, he's a magnificent creature."

James snorted, and then returned to mucking out the stall. Tony gestured for Aurie to follow him. They walked to the back of the barn and entered the tack room. There were saddles everywhere, with bridles, bits, and reins hanging from pegs on the far wall. Aurie was amazed at the amount of riding equipment available and saw that Prince Kalian spared no expense for his troops.

Tony went over to a mahogany brown saddle covered with silver studs and intricate designs imprinted into the soft leather.

He noticed Aurie staring. "It's a masterpiece, isn't it? Fit for royalty?"

For a moment, Tony's face darkened into a scowl, and then just as quickly, it disappeared. He grabbed the saddle and left the room, heading towards the front of the barn. He walked over to a stall, opened the gate, and walked in. Aurie smiled, as she immediately knew where she was. Without pausing, she followed Tony, he stopped abruptly, and she walked into him, smacking her nose on the side of his arm.

"Whoa, not so fast," he grunted. "This stall is off limits to everyone but me, okay?"

"Why?" Aurie asked, rubbing her nose.

Tony moved over to the right, stepping out of her way, and it was then Aurie spotted Cesar. He was tossing his head and flaring his nostrils. She was so happy to see her friend she almost raced over to him, but at the last second, stopped. It would have been difficult to try to explain to Tony how she and Cesar knew each other, especially when she had told the boys she had never been inside the castle.

"This is Cesar, Prince Kalian's warhorse."

She stared in astonishment, realizing only someone as rich and powerful as Prince Kalian would own a horse as regal as Cesar.

Tony steered Aurie out of the stall, and firmly closed the gate. He turned and approached Cesar, talking softly to the nervous horse. Cesar accepted a piece of apple from Tony, then walked over to the gate, lifted his massive head over the sides, and as was his way in greeting her, placed his muzzle against her jacket. Aurie stroked his neck, and scratched behind his ear, happy to see her old friend.

"Wow, I have never seen him do that before," Tony said. "Maybe you are a Pixie, or for that matter, a powerful wizard."

"Don't be silly." She murmured, laughing softly as she stared openly at Tony. "If that was the case, you'd have to have me arrested. After all, using magic is against the law."

Tony returned Aurie's stare, and for the longest time he said nothing. "I better get Cesar saddled. Prince Kalian doesn't like to be kept waiting."

Aurie gulped, expecting to see Prince Kalian emerge at any moment.

"Why don't you start cleaning out those stalls over there?" Tony suggested,

Heading in the direction where Tony pointed, Aurie grabbed a shovel leaning on the wall, and began mucking the floor. She was shaking from head to toe. Tony's reaction to her teasing was completely unexpected, she was positive she had seen something in his eyes when he had stared at her. Maybe being back at Windermere Castle and so close to Prince Kalian was making her jittery.

If she was lucky the rain would stop by tomorrow and she could return to the bakery. Unfortunately, as luck would have it, the rain continued to fall. Aurie dreaded the mornings when they walked across the castle grounds. Every time she passed through the castle gates, there was a chance of discovery.

At first, she made a point of staying as far away from Cesar's stall as she could in case Prince Kalian showed up unexpectedly. She spent long hours in the tack room, polishing stirrups, spurs and tack, and oiling and buffing the saddles until they shone with a bright luster. Eventually Tony allowed her to take over the care of Prince Kalian's saddle. Aurie marveled at its beauty and artisanship. She recalled the look on Tony's face when he had looked at it, and wondered why he had reacted so passionately. Maybe the thought of Prince Kalian owning a saddle that was worth more than it would take to feed a whole family for a year weighed heavily on his mind.

If it had not been so dangerous, Aurie would have preferred working alongside Tony. He joked with her, was patient when she made mistakes, and provided invaluable information about horsemanship. Perhaps one day these skills would prove to be worthwhile, so she listened intently. She had never had the opportunity to learn anything but kitchen work while she was under Mrs. Black's thumb. She came to realize how little she knew about the world around her, and she hung onto Tony's every word.

She soon discovered Prince Kalian seldom came to the barn. If he wanted Cesar he would send a messenger to Tony, and Aurie began to feel safer and more relaxed.

After it was apparent Cesar meant her no harm, Tony allowed Aurie to go into his stall. James and Randy just shook their heads, and laughingly joked that Cesar had no sense when it came to choosing friends.

On the fourth day, Tony asked Aurie if she would like to accompany him while he exercised Cesar. "You're probably going stir-crazy being cooped up inside this musty barn all day, the rain has let up a bit, and so we won't get too wet."

Aurie happily followed him to Cesar's stall. Cesar knew he was going for a run, and he tossed his head impatiently. As Tony was leaving the stall, the big horse reared and then bolted towards the back exit. Tony pulled back on the reins, quietly reprimanding the excited animal. James and Randy high-tailed it to the back of the barn putting as much space as possible between themselves and the spirited warhorse.

When they arrived at the corral, Aurie climbed the fence and balanced herself on the top rung. Tony climbed onto Cesar's back and trotted him around the enclosure. The horse's weight soon turned the ground into a mire of mud. Tony shook his head and steered Cesar over to where Aurie was sitting "It's getting too slick in here. I cannot chance he will fall. Jump on behind me and we'll take him to the grass field outside the castle."

"Are you sure it's okay? I thought Cesar didn't like anyone riding him but you."

"Of course, it's okay, he's gentle with little kids. It's Prince Kalian he particularly dislikes, shows how much horse-sense he has."

Aurie lowered herself into the saddle. For some reason Tony's remark about her being a little kid annoyed her.

Tony spurred Cesar out of the corral and Aurie hastily wrapped her arms around Tony's waist. She had never ridden on a horse before, and the sensation was exhilarating.

They trotted across the bailey, and Aurie spotted the kitchen on her right. She slouched down in the saddle, turning her face away, praying no one would come out and see them. When they arrived at the castle gate, she relaxed, not realizing she had been holding her breath.

The guard grinned when he saw Tony. "Taking that bundle of energy for a run, I see?"

"The corral's too dangerous, I can't chance he'll fall," Tony commented.

"Can't say I blame you. If anything should happen to that horse you'd be locked in irons for the rest of your life."

Tony chuckled and the jovial sentry opened the gate and waved them through. Exercising Cesar gave Tony the freedom of leaving the confines of the locked-down castle during the day.

They rode down the drawbridge, and without hesitating, Tony steered the horse onto the road. The streets were almost empty, and the only sound was the clip clop of Cesar's massive hooves striking the cobblestones.

Then Tony guided Cesar away from the road and towards the moat. Usually the moat was dry, but with the persistent rainfall, it was half-full of brown, churning water.

Cesar slithered down the steep bank, moving cautiously through the slippery mud. Without hesitating, he strode into the moat. As the water rose, Aurie raised her legs to keep from getting wet. Cesar climbed the embankment on the far side without breaking his stride.

Before them was an open field and Aurie realized where they were. Not more than ten feet away was the trail she had taken when she had run away. She looked nervously around, although she knew it was highly unlikely anyone would use the secluded side gate or the trail, especially in such foul weather.

Tony steered Cesar into the tall grass, which brushed against their legs, leaving their leggings damp. They soon arrived at a path leading away from the castle, and Tony urged Cesar to pick up his speed. The horse trotted for a short distance, and eventually they arrived at the creek. Cesar lowered his head and took a drink, but Tony pulled back on the reins. "Whoa boy, not too much water. Wait until after you've had your run."

Cesar stepped back and tossed his head. "Why don't you jump down?" Tony said to Aurie, chuckling at the horse's impatience. "You should be able to keep yourself busy while I'm gone."

She slid off the saddle, landing on the soggy ground. Tony clucked quietly and Cesar kicked his heels then raced across the field, creating a path through the overgrown weeds. It was not long before the huge horse and rider disappeared over a knoll. Aurie stood quietly, looking around at her surroundings. She did not feel comfortable standing in the open.

Along the banks of the stream, delicate windflowers and violets peeked through the moss. Although it was late spring, the rain was cold and the buds on the trees were slow in opening. There were large rocks forming a natural bridge to the far side. Usually Tony liked to exercise Cesar for over an hour, so Aurie decided she would have time to do some exploring. If she was careful, she should make it across without getting too wet. She slid down the embankment, the water flowed strongly, but not enough for her to lose her footing and she jumped from one slick rock to the next until she arrived safely on the other side.

The bank was higher on this side, and she grabbed the branches of a small bush to pull herself up. She stood in the lush foliage, wondering which direction to take. Pushing the closely packed ferns aside, she was surprised to see an overgrown trail, having her decision made for her. She headed down the path, wondering where it led.

The footpath wound its way around rocks, trees, and lustrous ferns. The heavy branches of the cedars and pines formed a natural canopy overhead, while a light drizzle of rain fell gently to the forest floor. She remembered the anxiety she had experienced the last time she had entered these woods and hoped her fears were unfounded.

She walked for a short while, keeping a vigilant lookout, just when she thought it would be prudent to turn back, she spotted a hollow tree trunk at least six feet high. She would not have paid any attention to it, except there was a rope hanging over the side. It was probably a fort built by some village kids, but her curiosity got the better of her. She grabbed the cord and gave it a yank, and it held firm. Wrapping her legs around the line, she quickly climbed up. When she reached the top, she looked inside, and was surprised to find a ladder hooked over the edge. She took a quick look around, the woods appeared to be deserted, and there were no signs posted warning people to keep out. She flung her leg over the top, placing her foot on the top rung.

Suddenly her body felt tingly, and there was a pressure at the back of her head. Instinctively she knew she was sensing magic. She climbed down the ladder, there was sufficient light penetrating from above that she could make out the shadowy outlines of the walls. She noticed several oil lanterns and a flint lying on a shelf, she grabbed the nearest lantern and lit it. Raising it above her head, she turned slowly around in a circle.

Stairs carved out of stone disappeared into the bowels of the earth. The sensation she felt intensified, the magic was stronger.

She took one of the flints and placed it in her jacket as the thought of being underground and having the lantern go out was terrifying. She stepped down onto the first step, took a deep breath, and gritting her teeth took another step and then another, the faint light glowing from the lantern created sinister shapes on the ceiling. The walls were clammy and slippery with slime, the air became hotter and more humid the deeper she descended and beads of perspiration dotted her forehead. Her hair clung to the back of her neck and her body felt sluggish.

The steps suddenly ended, and Aurie found herself in a large circular subterranean cave. A dark pool covered most of the area, and in the middle, a stone pillar rose sharply. Sitting on top was a glass container and inside was a brilliant crystal. The air pulsed with magic and her head pounded in agony, she massaged her temple, trying to appease the pain.

She placed the lantern on the ground, walked over to the pool and reached down to get a drink. She touched the water, and at once the crystal became brighter and a hum resonated through the cave. Aurie flew backwards, landing heavily on the ground. She stood up, rubbing her scraped hands against her leggings. The sensation she felt was very different from what she had experienced before, and for some reason it felt wrong, almost sinister. She had not used her powers, of that she was positive.

Aurie walked cautiously back to the water and almost immediately the humming started, she felt nauseous and her head pounded even harder. It was then she realized the sound was coming from the crystal!

She picked up the lantern and walked carefully away from the pool, wandering deeper into the cave. The farther away she got from the pool, the better she felt.

A piercing scream reverberated off the rocks, sending chills down her back. She spun around in panic, trying to pinpoint the source. Before her was a dark tunnel, and she approached the entrance. She heard footsteps and muffled voices coming towards her. Looking anxiously around, she spotted a large boulder. Quickly she blew out the lantern, squatted down behind the huge rock, and flattened herself against the wall.

Two men wearing tunics with Prince Kalian's crest stepped out of the tunnel and entered the cavern. One of them was holding a lantern, he was tall and reedy, with deep-set eyes and a gaunt appearance, and he was looking nervously around, his eyes darting in all directions. Aurie crouched closer to the ground, hoping he would not see her in the shadows.

The second man was muscular with a grim look on his face. The soldier carrying the lantern stopped abruptly, grabbing his companion's arm.

"Did you hear that?"

"Hear what?" grumbled his short-tempered companion.

"I don't know, I thought I heard something moving around."

"Probably rats, come on, we have to report back to Prince Kalian."

"Just remember, I'm not taking the blame this time. You can tell him what happened."

The second soldier shrugged. "I don't know why he even bothered with this one. Her powers were so weak she evaporated before we even started."

"He must be getting desperate if he'll take anyone with even the slightest trace of magic, soon there won't be anyone left in the entire kingdom, let alone Westcott, that will satisfy his needs."

The muscular soldier snorted, and walked towards the pool. "You better keep your opinions to yourself. If Prince Kalian heard you talking like that, you will be working in the quarry for the rest of your life. Just keep your mouth shut and do as you're told."

After five minutes had passed, Aurie cautiously crept from behind the boulder. The conversation between the two soldiers left her visibly shaken.

Returning to the surface would have been the sensible thing for her to do, but she could not get the sound of the screaming out of her head. She had to find out where it came from.

The glow from the crystal provided enough light for her to retrieve the flint from her pocket to re-light the lantern. She hoped when the two soldiers got to the ladder they would not notice it was missing. She headed apprehensively down the tunnel, eventually it ended, and she found herself in a small antechamber. There were several wooden cages located around the room. She approached the one nearest to the entrance. Except for a pile of filthy blankets and a tin plate lying on the dirt floor, the cage was empty. The odor was so overpowering she covered her nose, breathing raggedly through her mouth. She could still sense a slight trace of magic, and a lingering odor of Sulphur permeated the air. She walked slowly around the room, examining every corner, people just did not mysteriously vanish, and the only way in and out of the small chamber was through the tunnel.

If she was discovered her fate would be no different from the poor souls who had ended in these cages. She must never say anything about what she had seen today to anyone, not only for her own protection but for Tony, Sam, and Fred's as well. She did not understand everything the two troopers were talking about but she knew it was something she should never have overheard.

Quickly she retraced her steps, skirted the pool carefully, raced up the stairs, blew out the lantern and returned it and the flint to their original places. She scampered up the ladder, hesitating when she got to the top. Raising her head over the edge of the trunk, she looked around, there was no one in sight and the only sound was the soft patter of rain.

She raced back to the stream. Tony was lounging comfortably on Cesar, his back turned away. She climbed down the embankment, dislodging rocks. He heard and twisted in the saddle. Waving, he trotted Cesar over to the edge of the creek.

She concentrated on not slipping on the stones, when she was standing next to Cesar Tony grabbed her hand and helped her climb into the saddle.

"Did you find anything interesting in the woods?" he asked.

She shook her head.

"After I left, I suddenly realized I should have warned you to not wander too far. There are tales about people disappearing in Lindell Forest, disappearing forever. I imagine it's easy to get lost if you don't know where you're going."

She swallowed nervously, her eyes widening.

"Don't worry," Tony chuckled when he saw the frightened look on her face. "I'm sure it's just stories the villagers make up to keep their children from wandering off. I wouldn't make any mind of it."

She did not answer. She wished she could tell Tony just how true the stories really were.

Chapter Five

The remainder of the week passed quickly and eventually the rain subsided. The weather turned warmer. Aurie reminded Tony it was time for her to return to the bakery. Although she was anxious to get away from the castle, she was going to miss Cesar and the camaraderie of James and Randy. Tony seemed to enjoy her company but he was aware that the bread she earned from Jasmine and the vegetables she bought from Seamus provided enough food to feed all four of them. The food was more important than the few coins she earned at the stables.

The next morning, Aurie ran to the market, stopping for a few seconds to greet Seamus and to let him know she was back. Arriving at the bakeshop, she flung open the door, expecting to see Jasmine standing behind the counter. A muscular dark-haired man was facing away from the door; he spun around, glaring crossly at Aurie. "Who are you?" he asked in a menacing voice.

"Please master," said Jack, who was standing next to the oven. "He's the young lad helping Jasmine out at the market."

"What young lad?" the man said angrily. "Jasmine, get yourself out here this minute."

Jasmine raced into the room, a worried look on her face. "Yes, Uncle Nat."

"Jack told me you hired this street kid to work for you."

"Yes, sir. He helps me load the cart in the morning and set up the booth, it was too much work for me to do alone."

"I don't make enough to pay another worker."

"He's not getting paid. I give him a loaf of bread or any buns left over at the end of the day. He's a hard worker," Jasmine replied as she nervously twisted her apron into a tight ball.

During the entire exchange between Jasmine and her Uncle Nat, Aurie had stood in horrified silence. The moment Nat had spoken she immediately realized who he was. He was the man she had overheard talking to Mrs. Black in the barn, the same man who had planned to turn her over to Prince Kalian. Aurie would never forget the raspy sound of his voice as long as she lived. Her heart was hammering in her chest, and she felt lightheaded from the shock of meeting him face to face.

"You from around here?" he said, as he turned and faced Aurie.

"His family lives a few blocks from here," Jasmine answered. "He came to the market place about a month and a half ago."

"Let the boy speak for himself," Uncle Nat interrupted. "What's your family name?"

"It's Mundy, sir." Aurie replied. She had seen the name painted on the side of a wagon hauling pigs to the marketplace a few days back.

"I don't know anyone in the neighborhood with that name. What does your old man do?"

"We've only been here a little while, Sir. Da sometimes picks up work at the docks, or at the rock quarry."

Uncle Nat stared at Aurie for the longest time. Slowly she backed towards the door, intent on fleeing in case he decided to ask questions she would not be able to answer. He shrugged, dismissing her as if she was no more than a fly on the wall.

"Well, you best get that cart filled and get to the market," he said turning to face Jasmine. "Take the lad with you for the day. We'll discuss this tonight when you get back."

Aurie grabbed an armful of bakery goods and left hastily through the back door, Jasmine following closely behind. Aurie noticed the young girl was close to tears, and recalled the fear in her eyes when Uncle Nat had reproached her.

While they were setting up the booth, Aurie started trembling. She realized it was the shock of discovering who Uncle Nat was. If he should start asking around about her make-believe family, he would soon realize she was not who she said she was. It would not take him long to realize who she was, a fugitive being hunted by Prince Kalian's soldiers.

The day seemed to drag on forever, but finally it was time to close. Jasmine handed her a loaf of bread and at the last second, a sticky bun. She told Aurie it was a treat as she had missed her during the week, and was happy she had returned.

Jasmine reached over and put her arm around Aurie's shoulder. "Now don't you worry about Uncle Nat? I will talk to him tonight about how hard you work, and convince him that he is getting the better part of the deal. It won't take him long to realize how lucky he is to have someone working for him for only a loaf of bread or a few buns."

"Jasmine, are ya gonna get into trouble for hiring me? Your Uncle Nat was really angry."

"Don't you worry. I can take care of myself. I'll just remind him that he's not paying me a wage either."

Aurie's mouth flew open in shock. "But how can he get away with that?"

"He's not really my uncle. His name is Nathan Trent, and I am his indentured servant. In four more years,

I'll be eighteen, and my debt will be paid off, then I'll be free of him forever."

Knowing what Nathan Trent was capable of, she still worried he might do something terrible to Jasmine. As she watched the young girl leaving the marketplace, she wished she could have told Jasmine everything she knew about the cruel man.

Trying hard not to show any emotion, she walked slowly over to Seamus' stall to pick up the vegetables. He grinned as she approached his booth, but when he saw the look on her face, his smile disappeared, "You're a bit down in the dumps. What's ailing you lad?"

"Nothing, just tired, I guess."

She took the sack from Seamus and quickly left the market place. When she got to the street, she turned and waved, Seamus was watching her closely, a look of concern on his face. She would miss him terribly.

Aurie did not get much sleep that night, she tossed and turned, wishing she did not have to leave, but realizing it would be safer for everyone if she did. After a quick breakfast of bread and raw onions, they left just as the sun rose over the crest of the mountains. She walked with the boys as far as the market place, and waited until they were out of sight, then she turned and raced back to the warehouse. She rolled up her tattered blanket and put it in the burlap sack, wandered around the room lifting the lids off the barrels and opening some of the boxes. She remembered an old dented pot that was in one of the containers. After locating it, she went to the barrel where she had found the books. She dug out the one on weaponry and a second about herbs and wild flowers, something that had always interested her.

When she was finished packing, Aurie looked around the warehouse one last time. It may be old and crumbling, but over the past six weeks, she had come to look at it as home, she was going to miss Tony and Sam. She opened the door, and raised her hand to her mouth, stifling a scream. Fred was standing in the doorway, his face red with anger. "Told you he was up to no good," he sneered. "He's probably robbing us blind."

Sam and Tony stood immediately behind Fred, blocking the doorway.

"I don't know what you're talking about," Aurie said.

"Then you won't mind if we look at your sack," Fred said, as he grabbed it roughly out of her hand. Stepping back from the door, he turned it upside down, and gave it a shake. The contents spilled onto the ground.

"It's just my stuff, and an old pot and some books," she replied quietly.

"Were you leaving without saying goodbye?" asked Tony, raising an eyebrow.

Aurie looked at him, unable to find the words to answer. No matter what explanation she gave she knew he would not understand.

"Look, that's not all he's got," Fred, said in a voice that was a little too loud. He was kneeling on the ground with his back to everyone, and was shuffling through the scattered articles. He held up a bag, and gave it a shake, the sound of jingling filled the air, and everyone realized what it was. It was Tony's bag of coins.

Aurie's mouth flew open in shock, she spun around and stared at Tony who had a look of disbelief on his face.

"Tony, please, I didn't do this, I just saw Fred put it on the ground. He's trying to frame me."

"I told you right from the beginning he was bad news," Fred interrupted. "I never trusted him."

Aurie stared in disgust at Fred, trying hard to control her feelings. The anger forced its way to the surface, and without warning a streak of light exploded from her fingertips. In horror, she twisted her body at the last second, there was a loud crack and the wall of the warehouse exploded.

At first, there was deathly silence, and the three boys stared at her in astonishment.

"You can do magic," Sam whispered in awe.

Fred's face had gone a pasty white, and when he had composed himself, he jumped up waving the bag of coins in Aurie's face. "Did you see that? He tried to kill me."

"No, I didn't, you know that's not true," Aurie said as she looked beseechingly at Tony and Sam. "It was an accident."

Tony stared at Aurie for the longest time. "That's why the soldiers were chasing you, wasn't it?" he whispered. He reached over and grabbed her cap, yanking it roughly from her head. Her hair cascaded down her back.

"I guess I've always had my suspicions," he said coldly. "Why did you pretend to be a boy?"

"The soldiers were looking for a girl. That's why I disguised myself."

"But why did you keep up the ruse with us?"

"If I didn't, would you have let me stay? You know I contributed most of the food and kept the warehouse clean. I wouldn't have gotten work at the bakery or the stables, it shouldn't make any difference if I'm a girl or a boy, but you know as well as I do that it does."

"Stealing is bad enough," Fred said scornfully. "But we all saw her using sorcery and that's illegal."

Tony shook his head angrily. He turned and stared into the distance. Aurie sensed how upset he was, and knew he was waiting for her to say something to defend herself, yet no matter what explanation she gave him, there was no way she could deny what he had just seen.

Tony turned and faced the small group. She saw the hurt in his eyes, and it cut her like a knife. Sam was staring intently at the ground, shuffling his foot in the dirt. Fred was standing next to Tony, keeping well away from her, and Aurie realized he was afraid of her, and for some reason, she felt a small sense of pleasure in knowing that.

"Please Tony," Aurie pleaded. "You know I'm innocent, I'd never steal from you. Just let me go."

"I know you didn't steal anything," Tony responded. "I'll deal with that matter later. We all saw you use magic and I have no choice. I must turn you in. There are others than just us I have to think about."

She realized Tony was telling the truth, she nodded in silent resignation.

"Come on, let's get this over with," he said gruffly. He gently took her elbow, steering her towards the path leading down the hill. She took a few steps, and then stopped abruptly. Without turning she said loudly, so all three of the boys could hear. "You might want to get the coins back from Fred. I believe they're in his pocket."

Holding her head high, she continued walking down the path. She would not give any of them the satisfaction of knowing how terrified she was.

Chapter Six

It was not long before they arrived at the marketplace, Fred grabbed Aurie's arm tightly and hissed in her ear. "Don't make a scene, or we'll let everyone know who you are. I'm sure there are a few merchants and villagers who won't appreciate they've been fooled all this time by a runaway slave."

Aurie angrily pulled her arm away. She stared defiantly at Fred, and again felt a sense of empowerment when he looked away first. She walked across the cobblestone yard, looking straight ahead. Peering out of the corner of her eye, she saw Seamus standing a few yards away, when he started to walk in her direction, she caught his eye, shaking her head. He slowly backed away and disappeared into the crowd, understanding immediately that she did not want him to intervene. She would never forgive herself if he tried to help her and the soldiers arrested him.

After what seemed like an eternity, the small group finally arrived at Windermere Castle. Tony had not said a word since leaving the warehouse. They walked up the drawbridge towards the gatehouse, cautiously approaching two guards on duty. The friendly young soldier who had joked with them earlier in the week was missing. She groaned quietly, suddenly realizing one of the sentries was Rufus. He watched closely as they strode towards him.

"We'd like to see Prince Kalian," Fred said.

"Now why would Prince Kalian want to have anything to do with the likes of you?" Rufus asked, his voice dripping with sarcasm.

"We have a present for him," Fred answered, pushing Aurie forward.

"Well, well, well, looks who's returned," Rufus growled, immediately recognizing Aurie. He stepped forward and pulled her roughly away from Fred.

"Leave her with me boys, and I'll see she's taken care of."

"I'm sure you'd like that," said Fred scornfully. "But the reward belongs to me, I mean us. We'd prefer to talk to Prince Kalian personally."

"Suit yourself, it's your funeral," Rufus answered, his eyebrows raised disdainfully. He motioned to one of the guards standing a few feet away. "Run and get Prince Kalian."

The young sentry's face turned pale. "But Sarge, you know he don't like being disturbed this early in the morning."

"He'll come, just tell him his prize runaway has been found."

The guard nodded then turned and headed towards the keep.

Aurie's inherent dread for Prince Kalian surfaced and she stared at the ground, her mind racing, there was no way she could escape, not with Rufus's iron grip on her arm. Instinctively, she understood using magic to escape would be madness, as she had no idea how the soldiers might react.

A young boy strolled past, carrying a wooden bucket. He headed towards the well located in the center of the bailey.

"Scram," Rufus shouted angrily. "Get out of here, or I'll box your ears."

The terrified boy yelped, turned quickly, and then raced towards the huts located on the far side of the compound. Aurie turned away in disgust, remembering the times when Rufus used to torment her when he came to the kitchen. She found herself staring directly into Tony's eyes, for a moment, she thought she saw remorse written on his face, but just as quickly, it faded. He scowled, turned, and walked over to where Sam was standing.

Soon the nervous guard returned, followed closely by a tall, gaunt man with long black hair, a pale complexion, and sharp piercing eyes. He was dressed in a flowing black robe and was carrying a crop he slapped sharply against his boot.

"You better have a sound reason for disturbing me this early in the morning Sergeant," Prince Kalian said as he approached Rufus.

"Yes, my lord," Rufus replied. "These boys ... "

Prince Kalian raised his hand, commanding Rufus to stop talking. Looking directly at Tony, he asked abruptly, "What's this about, Drummond?"

Tony noticed the scowl on Rufus's face, but the well-trained soldier said nothing, he obviously knew better than to display disapproval towards any of Prince Kalian's actions or orders.

Before he could answer, Fred, who was standing behind Aurie, pushed his way in front. Tony clenched his fists, hoping Fred would not say anything that would get them all in trouble.

"We saw this girl using magic, your Highness, so we brought her in."

Prince Kalian glared at Fred, a look of repugnance on his face. He grabbed Aurie's hair and pulled her head back.

"Blond hair, pointed ears, slim build. You definitely match the description given by Mrs. Black."

"See, I told you she was the fugitive in the posters," Fred said to Tony and Sam. "She may have had you guys fooled, but I knew all along something was fishy, never did trust her."

"I'll take her," Prince Kalian said to Rufus, who nodded and released his hold of Aurie's arm.

"If you still want a job Drummond, you better get to work," Prince Kalian said to Tony.

"Yes, My Lord," Tony replied.

"Excuse me My Lord," Fred said, stepping boldly forward. "Where do we go to get our reward?"

Prince Kalian, who was walking away from the small group, stopped abruptly. "I would suggest you boys leave immediately," he said in a steely voice without turning to face them, "Let's just say your reward is walking out of here alive."

Fred's face turned an angry red. Before he could respond, Tony grabbed his arm, giving him a warning glance as he did. Fred struggled but Tony only tightened his hold, leaned over and said something in the agitated boy's ear. Fred immediately settled down. Tony glanced at Sam and nodded, and Sam turned and walked down the ramp, with Fred following closely behind.

Prince Kalian grabbed Aurie's arm and dragged her across the bailey. She was surprised when he led her to the stables, where they entered by the side door.

Tony had arrived before them, and was talking to James and Randy, who were working in the stalls. When they saw Prince Kalian and Aurie, the two boys immediately laid down their pitchforks and disappeared. Tony walked over to Cesar's stall and began currying the horse.

When they passed Cesar's stall, the warhorse butted his head on Aurie's arm, she automatically reached up and patted his neck.

"Keep your hands off my horse," Prince Kalian threatened, as he pushed her towards the tack room. Once they were inside, he slammed the door. Walking over to the wall, he reached up and tugged sharply on a rope hanging from the ceiling, the wall parted, and before them was a large wooden door. Raising his hand, he touched the handle and it opened without a sound.

There was a steep stairway heading downwards. It was dark and Aurie placed her hand on the dirt wall for support as she walked carefully down the steps. She remembered all the happy hours she had spent in this room, not realizing all the time she had been only a few feet away from a hidden doorway leading beneath the castle grounds.

When they arrived at the bottom, there was a second wooden door barricading their way. Prince Kalian knocked twice, and it slowly creaked open. A slovenly guard with a toothless grin peeked around the corner. He stepped aside and let them enter, and then firmly closed the door. He reached over and grabbed Aurie's arm when a flash of light hit him square in his chest. He howled and keeled over.

"Touch her again, and I won't be so nice," Prince Kalian sneered. "This one's off limits. Nobody goes near her but me, understand?"

"Yes, My Lord," groaned the guard, rubbing his chest.

Aurie was astounded. Prince Kalian had just used magic. When he noticed her staring at him, he reached over and touched her lightly on her cheek. "You see, my dear, you're not the only one who has powers." Aurie shivered inwardly, her fear and loathing for the man written clearly on her face.

Prince Kalian led her down a narrow, ill-lit corridor, off to the left was a passageway, and he steered her in that direction. There were cells on both sides and Aurie realized they were in the dungeons.

The only light was an oil lamp sitting in a smoke blackened sconce half way down the corridor. The cells were empty, except for the second one from the end. A man wearing a soiled robe was lying on a pallet on the straw covered floor, the emaciated figure did not stir, and Aurie wondered if he was alive.

Prince Kalian shoved her into the last cell and slammed the door, "Make yourself comfortable. This is going to be your home for a while." Then he turned and walked away from the cells, disappearing down the dark corridor.

The floor was filthy and reeked of urine and excrement, it made Aurie's eyes water and her stomach heaved. A scuffling noise came from the corner and she started. Staggering over to the back wall, she slowly lowered herself to the floor, trembling violently. She placed her head on her knees, clasping her medallion tightly against her chest. She drew from its warmth and could sense the strength coursing through her body.

She did not know how long it would take, but one day again she would confront Fred, and when she did, she would seek her revenge. As for Tony, she thought they had become friends, someone she could trust, but she had been terribly wrong. He could have released her, but he too easily agreed with Fred in turning her over to Prince Kalian. She could understand Fred's vindictiveness, but as for Tony, she would never forgive him for betraying her.

Chapter Seven

Something heavy was lying on her chest. She heard a squeak, and then the scuffling sound of an animal scurrying away. Aurie jumped up in panic, the torch had gone out, and it was dark as night in the cell. Reaching inside her shirt, she pulled out her medallion, clasping it tightly in her hands.

"It's only a rat. It won't hurt you."

Startled, Aurie looked at the adjacent cell. The glow radiating from her medallion allowed her to make out the outline of the man she had noticed earlier, he was sitting propped against the back wall of his cell, a tattered blanket draped over his shoulders.

"I hate rats," she said in disgust.

The man chuckled quietly. "Well, I can't say they're my favorite animal either, but it's just curious and was merely seeking some warmth. Are you alright?"

"Yes sir," Aurie replied, nodding slightly.

"What is your name, child?"

"Aurie."

"What is your family name?"

"I don't know. All I've ever been called is Aurie."

The man stood up, walked over to the bars and looked down at her. He was very tall, with long dark hair and a flowing beard, both lightly peppered with grey. Aurie stared into his eyes, and was astonished to see they were silver. She sensed an aura of energy emanating from him, and knew him to be a man of great wisdom and power.

"Well Aurie with no name, I'm called Armitage Ravenswood. Where do you live?"

Aurie hesitated to answer, but intuitively sensed that the man would not harm her.

"For as long as I can remember, I lived here in the castle, working in the kitchens, but in the past six weeks I have been living with some street kids."

"And before that, when you were too young to work in the kitchens, where might you have lived?"

She shrugged. "I don't know. I don't have any memories of my past."

"What about your parents or family?"

Aurie shrugged.

The man crossed his arms and smiled. "How did you come to live at the castle?"

"Mrs. Black, she's the head cook, says she found me at the foundling home, my clothes were covered in soot and smelling of smoke. I think I was around five or six years old, otherwise she wouldn't have picked me as she needed someone to help with the kitchen chores. I don't remember anything before that time."

Armitage massaged his chin, frowning deeply. "I noticed a light glowing in your cell. Did you cause it?" he asked quietly.

"No sir, it wasn't me, it was my medallion."

Armitage gestured for Aurie to approach him. "May I see it?"

Aurie rose, and walked towards Armitage, she took the amulet off and handed it to him through the bars, and he examined it closely.

He did not say anything for the longest time. "How old are you?"

"I don't know, sir, I've never been told my age, or when my birthday is."

"How long have you been using magic?"

Aurie paused before answering. She wondered how he knew she had powers, would it be wise to admit it to a stranger. For some reason, even though she had just met him, she trusted him. "About six weeks, I guess. How did you know?"

"Prince Kalian would not have been interested in you unless you did possess magical ability. If you've just started using your powers, then you must have just turned twelve."

"How do you know that?"

"I'm a very wise old man," Armitage said, smiling at Aurie.

"They just started suddenly, but I don't know how to control them."

"Of course, you don't, there was no one to warn you that it would happen. I'm sure you're doing marvellously, and handling it as best as you can."

"Excuse me sir, can you..."

"Child, I'm sorry to interrupt, but I can't tell you anything more right now, we might be overheard. You must promise me something, do not tell Prince Kalian that we have talked, and do not let him get hold of your medallion. Don't mention it, even if he asks, as he will know immediately that it has magical powers and could use it against you."

"Yes sir."

"Another thing you must remember, under no circumstances are you to admit to him that you have magical powers, there is nothing he can do to you unless you admit to him that you do."

Armitage returned the medallion to Aurie and placed his hand on top of her head. "Now, try and get some rest, in the next few hours, you must be very brave."

"Yes, Sir."

Aurie returned to the corner of the cell and lowered herself to the floor. For the longest time, she lay awake, clasping her pendant tightly in her hands. She wondered why Armitage had been so interested in it. She looked at its familiar shape, it had a cross in the middle, with a gemstone in the center, and there was writing around the outside. Aurie had never been able to understand what the words meant.

Suddenly she remembered the old man's warning. It would be safer to hide the medallion now, as she had no idea when Prince Kalian would send the guard to retrieve her. She groped around until she found a loose stone in the corner of the cell, prying it away from the wall. She stuffed the medallion tightly inside and replaced the stone.

Although she was exhausted, she had a tough time falling asleep. She missed the comfort and security of the medallion. When she finally dozed off, she tossed and turned, dreaming of dark shadows and huge, vicious rats.

A sharp kick woke her. The surly guard was standing over her, holding a lit torch in his beefy hand. "Get up. Prince Kalian wants to see you right away," he ordered. "And make it quick, he don't like to be kept waiting."

Aurie got unsteadily to her feet. The guard grabbed her arm and dragged her to the cell door, he pointed towards the exit at the end of the corridor. Armitage opened his eyes and looked fleetingly at her as she walked past. He smiled and nodded. Aurie felt the panic subside and her courage slowly return.

The guard led her through the entrance, turning left instead of heading up the stairs that led to the tack room. They had not gone far when they arrived at a door, it was slightly ajar, and the guard pushed her through, slamming it loudly behind her.

There was a lit lantern sitting on a rough wooden table, but the light did not penetrate the corners of the room. The walls were made of solid rock, and Aurie assumed the dungeon abutted the mountain, as was the case for most structures in Westcott.

Prince Kalian was sitting in a high-backed chair, and a second chair was facing him. He gestured for Aurie to approach, and then he indicated for her to sit. He did not say anything for the longest time. Aurie closed her eyes, and forced herself to stay calm.

"What's your name?"

"Aurie," she whispered.

"Open your eyes and look at me," he said curtly.

"Yes, your Highness."

"What is your full name?"

"I don't know I've always been called Aurie, nothing else."

"How old are you?"

"I don't know. No-one's ever told me."

"How long have you lived here in the castle?"

"I live in the village."

"Do not toy with me, girl. Now, how long have you lived here at the castle, and I would suggest you answer truthfully."

Aurie discerned the threat in his voice. "About five or six years."

"Do you remember anything before that time?"

She lowered her head and stared at the tabletop. "No sir."

"You're lying."

"I'm not lying, I can't remember anything."

"I can sense you're lying. Now tell me the truth."

Aurie did not answer. Suddenly a bolt of light hit her chest. She screamed and fell out of the chair, landing heavily on the stone floor.

"Now," said Prince Kalian. "Are you ready to answer my questions truthfully?"

Aurie wiped her arm across her eyes, forcing back tears. She grabbed the edge of the chair and pulled herself up. "I told you already. I do not remember anything. Please, I'm telling you the truth."

The second bolt came so quickly, she was not prepared. The pain was excruciating, she gritted her teeth and gripped the edge of the table, willing herself to stay conscious.

"I can see this isn't getting me anywhere," said Prince Kalian with a scowl, as he rose angrily and began pacing around the room "When you first came to the castle, did you own anything at all, something to show where you came from, a talisman?"

Aurie lowered herself slowly into the chair, afraid to look at him.

"If I did, it was probably taken from me a long time ago," she answered, remembering Armitage's warning. "Mrs. Black would never have allowed me to possess anything, especially if it was valuable."

Prince Kalian did not pursue the matter and Aurie hoped he was satisfied with her answer. He continued pacing, and then suddenly he walked over to the table and slammed his fist down hard on the surface. "How long have you been using your powers?"

"I don't know what you mean. I don't have any powers."

"I can feel the magic in you girl, don't lie to me."

"I'm not lying."

"That's not what Mrs. Black tells me."

Prince Kalian grabbed her chin roughly, forcing her to raise her head. "She swears she saw sparks shooting from your fingers and shatter a cup on the far side of a room."

"Mrs. Black made up that story because she hates me, she always has. She just wanted to get rid of me."

"I hardly doubt that's true. Someone in her position does not usually have the luxury of owning a slave. She has proven helpful to me over the years, so I indulged her by allowing her to have you. I am amused she chose you. Your looks and mannerism are quite extraordinary. However, she will be particularly happy to know you've been returned. I was quite perturbed when she "misplaced" you."

Aurie lowered her gaze and stared at the top of the table. Although she had no love for Mrs. Black, she knew the woman must have suffered greatly at Prince Kalian's hand over the past few weeks.

Prince Kalian returned to his chair and sat down. "How is it that you know Tony Drummond?"

Aurie took a quick breath. "Who?"

"The dark-haired boy who turned you in. How long have you known him?"

"Not long. He was not the one who turned me in. It was Fred, the fat ugly one."

"Ah, the one who claims he saw you using magic."

"Fred's always been resentful of me, ever since I joined their gang. I knew a girl could not survive on the streets, so I disguised myself as a boy. He concocted up this wild story that I was a runaway with magical powers, I think he saw a poster somewhere at the marketplace. The other two boys had nothing to do with it."

Aurie prayed that Prince Kalian would believe her story. Much as she was still angry and disappointed in Tony, if anything happened to him or Sam, she would never forgive herself.

"Well I'm glad to hear that Drummond is innocent, because for some unforeseen reason, he's the only one who can handle my horse, and I'd hate to lose him."

Aurie relaxed, realizing she had been holding her breath.

"But you still haven't answered my question about your powers, and I'm losing my patience," Prince Kalian said harshly. He stood up, walked over to the door, and flung it open. "Maybe more time without water and food will get you to talk. Guard, take the prisoner back to her cell."

Aurie trudged wearily down the corridor, waited until the guard slammed the cell door shut behind her, and then walked over to the far corner and lowered herself to the floor. She lay on the musty straw and curled up into a tight ball. The guard must have left the torch burning in the bracket in the hallway, as there was sufficient light in her cell to see vague outlines and shadows.

"Aurie," whispered Armitage. "Are you okay?'

"I didn't tell him anything, My Lord. I didn't tell him a thing."

"You've been very brave child. Now listen very carefully to what I say, later tonight we are going to have a visitor. He's going to get both of us out of here."

Aurie stood up and rushed over to Armitage's cell, grabbing the bars in her hands. "Who?"

"A good friend, he lives in the village and has been posing as a merchant. He's been waiting for my signal, which I sent while you were being questioned."

"How could you send a signal from here? How will he break in when there's guards everywhere?"

"Hush, I'll answer your questions later. We can't take a chance we'll be overheard." Aurie nodded happily.

"And don't worry about my friend. He can take care of himself. Now, lie down and rest, you're going to need your strength, I'll wake you when he gets here."

Aurie returned to the corner of her cell, closed her eyes, her mind racing, going over and over everything that had happened since she woke up this morning. Was it only just a few hours ago this nightmare had begun?

She fell into a fitful sleep.

Chapter Eight

Aurie jerked awake, and looked groggily around her cell. She heard a crash, followed by a grunt. Armitage was standing in his cell, he bent down and reached under the straw where he had been sleeping, retrieving a long metal staff. He pointed it at his cell door and it unlocked, swinging quietly open. He strode over to Aurie's cell and opened her lock in the same manner.

He gestured for her to follow, raising his finger to his lips to warn her to be quiet. Aurie was half way out when she turned, went to the far corner and dug under the loose rock, retrieving her medallion. In her haste, she had almost forgotten it.

Aurie ran to catch up with Armitage. Suddenly a large figure stepped out of the shadows, and Aurie shoved her fist in her mouth to keep from screaming. It took her a few seconds to realize it was Seamus. Her burly friend opened his arms and she flew into them, hugging him tightly. He smiled when he noticed her long hair and eyes, realizing immediately she was a girl.

"Ah," said Armitage. "I see you two have met. Come, we don't have much time before the guards change their shifts and discover we're missing."

Aurie and Seamus followed Armitage down the corridor. The guard was lying unconscious on the floor. Instead of heading towards the exit, Armitage turned left. Aurie stepped cautiously over the prone body, while Seamus followed. Armitage led them to the room where Prince Kalian had questioned Aurie. He raised his staff and the door swung open, closing silently behind them after they had entered. Armitage walked over to the back wall and began to chant quietly, the tip of his staff began to glow, and suddenly a jagged crack opened in the rock. He stepped through and disappeared, Aurie and Seamus quickly followed, and the gap closed behind them.

They were standing in a large cave, the light on the staff reflected off a thousand stalagmites hanging from the ceiling like fossilized icicles. Aurie stared in fascination at the brilliant colors. They walked down a winding path, in single file, Armitage leading, Aurie in the middle, and Seamus bringing up the rear. They passed deep chalky pools of water and astonishing formations in the rocks. A shimmering waterfall cascaded from the columns and fell into a small pond that glimmered like a mirror. Armitage left the path and walked over to the edge of the pond. He knelt and took a deep drink. "Come," he said to Aurie. "This water will revive you. But do not take too much and drink slowly."

Aurie had never tasted anything as delicious in her life, the hollowness in her stomach dissipated and warmth spread through her body. Suddenly her medallion started to glow, and a deep resonant melody filled the cave. Aurie spun around in a circle, her hands extended high above her head, 'Where's the music coming from?" she laughed.

"From your medallion, I believe," Armitage replied, as he smiled at Aurie's antics. "Come child, we must keep going. We have a long way to go."

The cave was very quiet, except for the occasional sound of rocks being scattered beneath their feet. They walked for many hours, descending deeper and deeper into the bowels of the earth. The water had rejuvenated Aurie, but she had not eaten in a long time, and the few hours of sleep she got when imprisoned left her exhausted. When she felt she could go no farther, Armitage left the trail and entered a small alcove. Stone shelves, located on the far wall, were sculpted out of the rock and covered with fur rugs. A small fire pit was in the middle of the room.

Armitage rested his hand on Aurie's shoulder. "We'll eat something and get a few hours of rest."

Then he raised his staff and started a fire, there was no smoke, and Aurie looked up to see if there was a hole in the ceiling to draw it out. She saw nothing. Seamus poked around in one of the boxes scattered around the cavern and found some provisions. Soon the smell of a delicious stew permeated through the cave. When it was ready, he filled a metal plate and handed it to Aurie. He grinned when she asked for a second helping.

By the time Aurie had finished eating, she was having difficulty keeping her eyes open. Armitage noticed her yawning and pointed to one of the shelves. "Why don't you rest for a short while?"

She quickly slipped under a fur rug, closed her eyes, the last thing she remembered was the fire flickering on the walls of the cave, and the murmur of Armitage and Seamus' voices.

All too soon, someone was shaking her arm, and Aurie opened her eyes and stared into Armitage's silver eyes.

"Come along child, we must continue our journey," he said.

She rubbed her eyes and stood up unsteadily, not feeling as if she had slept at all. She realized they had to keep going. Once Prince Kalian discovered they had escaped, he would be relentless trying to recapture them. In addition, he would have deduced by then that his other prisoner was much more than a poor peasant.

The fire had gone out and the cavern was damp and cold. Seamus crammed supplies into three backpacks, handed one to her and the other to Armitage. They resumed their trek, their footsteps echoing off the walls of the cave, periodically disturbing bats hiding in the high deep crevices. Soft scuffling sounds heard in the rocks and furtive movements in the shadowed recesses alarmed Aurie, and she peered back nervously at the path.

They stopped hours later at one of the numerous underground pools. "How much longer are we going to be in this cave?" Aurie asked Armitage, as she chewed on a piece of dried meat.

"If we make appropriate time we should arrive at the exit sometime tomorrow afternoon."

"Tomorrow afternoon? Wow, it must be gigantic, how did you find it?"

"I did not find it. It has always been here, since the beginning of time. This is the Fire Cave. Come, the path broadens just around the corner, and you can walk next to me. Before you can truly understand how things have come to be, you need to know the history of Westcott and its inhabitants."

As he had stated, the path soon widened enough for the two of them to walk abreast, while Seamus followed closely behind.

"For hundreds of years, the Ancients and the Alden have co-existed in Westcott," Armitage began. "The Ancients were fair, tall of stature and possessed magical abilities, while the majority of the Alden's were darker and stockier in build, having no powers, but well-known throughout the kingdom for their unsurpassed craftsmanship in leather tooling and pottery.

"For many years, both races prospered. Sometimes, an Ancient and an Alden would marry and have offspring, and a few of them were born possessing magical abilities.

"King Thomas, of the House of Whitmore, ruled Westcott. His father was Alden and his mother was Ancient. He was a caring and generous ruler to his subjects, and he deeply loved his wife Queen Wilona, who died giving birth to their son, Prince Donahue. King Thomas was so disheartened in losing his beloved queen, he lost his desire to rule, and he slowly handed over the reins of power to his younger brother, Prince Kalian. Unfortunately, they were as different as night and day.

"The Ancients did not interfere with the governing of Westcott. King Sebastian of the House of Hawthorn, and his wife, Elyse Elderberry, an Eldoran princess, were the reigning royals of the Ancients."

"What's an Eldoran?" Aurie asked.

"The Eldorans, or High Elves," Armitage said, smiling at Aurie, "are a magical tribe living in the realm of Fey Wild, and have very little contact with the natural world. When an Eldoran marries a mortal, in accordance with their laws, they lose their powers as well as their longevity. Elyse's family were very much opposed to her marriage to King Sebastian, but in time, their union was accepted.

"Over time, Prince Kalian replaced Westcott's army with men he had handpicked personally. He was aware the Ancients were skilled warriors and powerful magicians. He waited, and when the opportunity presented itself, he made his move. He ordered his army to wipe out the Ancients pillaging and burning their villas to the ground. Entire families died in their sleep. A few managed to escape, and fled into the mountains."

Armitage stopped and hitched his backpack higher on his back. "King Sebastian and Queen Elyse were among them."

"The army pursued them for months, and they finally gave up when the winter snows forced them to return to Westcott," Seamus said.

"Are you and Seamus both Ancients?" Aurie asked

"I am Alden, and Lord Armitage is an Ancient," Seamus replied.

"And what am I?" Aurie asked a puzzled look on her face.

Armitage placed his hand on Aurie's shoulder and gave it a squeeze. "Because you have magical abilities, and with your hair and eye coloring, and the shape of your ears, you probably have Elf in your bloodline, unfortunately we have no way of knowing if that is the case."

"I don't really believe in Elves and Faeries, "Aurie shrugged. "I know there's magic, all that other stuff is make-believe."

Seamus and Armitage exchanged looks, but neither spoke. Armitage stopped in the middle of the path, removed his backpack, and then he pulled out his water flask. He took a deep drink, then replaced it and continued walking.

"A few days before the massacre, I had been summoned by Prince Kalian, who advised me that my close friend, Viscount Baguley, had gone on a diplomatic visit to a neighboring borough but had not returned. He had travelled through Lindell Forest rather than by sail, and we feared for his safety. Prince Kalian was aware I would go and search for him."

"Of course, the whole tale was fabricated," Seamus continued. "Lord Armitage is High Wizard of the Ancients, and if he had been in Westcott at the time of the attack, he would have intervened and things would have turned out quite differently. Prince Kalian's plan was to have Lord Armitage secretly followed and then slain."

Seamus cleared his throat. "It was I who was sent out to slay Lord Armitage. I followed him for hours, and eventually he made camp in a small clearing. I settled back, waiting for him to fall asleep before I made my move. He was sitting with his back against a large rock. Raising his head, he stared directly at me, waving me over. At first, I hesitated, but realizing he knew I had been following him for hours, I decided to join him. He was holding a water skin, and he filled two mugs, giving one to me, and keeping the other for himself. He took a deep drink, and I waited a few minutes. When nothing happened, I took a sip. I was pleasantly surprised to discover the liquid was mead, the Ancients brew the best honey mead in the kingdom."

"I remembered that Seamus had a fondness for that particular libation," Armitage said, chuckling quietly.

Seamus grunted. "I had only taken a few swallows, when suddenly I got dizzy, and then everything went dark, when I awoke, I was alone. It was morning and I was lying in the dirt with a terrible headache. I didn't find out until later that Lord Armitage had slipped a magical sleeping potion into my ale."

"Then what did you do?" Aurie asked, enthralled by the tale. "Did you return to Westcott?"

"Prince Kalian is not a forgiving man, and if I had returned to tell him I had failed in my orders, I would not have lived to see another day. I had to finish what I started and trying to find an obscure wizard is a daunting task.

"I walked for miles, and eventually arrived at a lake, where I spotted a small, white cottage on the far side of a meadow. I crept through the underbrush until I was close enough to peer through the window. Lord Armitage was resting in a chair in front of the fireplace and appeared to be dozing."

Aurie was so engrossed in the story she turned and faced Seamus. She tripped on a rock, and almost landed on top of Armitage.

"Sorry My Lord," she murmured sheepishly. Armitage chuckled, not slowing his pace.

"The door was slightly ajar, so I quietly entered, I unsheathed my sword, and suddenly I couldn't move. I was frozen."

"Really?" Aurie said.

"Lord Armitage was looking right at me. I suddenly remembered I was facing the most powerful wizard in the kingdom and I wasn't sure if he would disintegrate me or turn me into a turnip."

"That's the best story I've ever heard," she exclaimed, giggling at Seamus' silliness. "Then what happened?"

"Realizing I was outmatched, I laid down my sword, and surrendered. After he unfroze me, of course."

"You became his prisoner?" Aurie asked in disbelief.

"I made a pot of tea, and then we spent the rest of the night talking," Seamus continued. "Lord Armitage had sensed that something terrible had happened in Westcott, and was aware of my orders. He also knew many Ancients had perished, and that King Sebastian and Queen Elyse had escaped."

"Realizing Prince Kalian wanted both of us dead," Armitage reflected. "We thought it best to disappear for a while, should Seamus have returned to Westcott, he would have been disposed of immediately, as the last thing Prince Kalian wanted was a witness."

"I pledged my allegiance to Lord Armitage that very night," Seamus said.

"For the last twelve years, we have been searching for the survivors, but it was as if they had fallen off the face of the Earth," Armitage said solemnly "We had also learned that shortly after the massacre, King Thomas had been slain and those who had remained loyal to him were also put to death. We could only assume Prince Donahue died along with his father, he was only four years old. As the years went by, more and more villagers disappeared. I tried talking to the people in Westcott, but they were terrified, and refused to communicate. I posed as a beggar, stole from the marketplace, and soon found myself in the dungeons."

"That's why you were in the cell next to mine?" Aurie mentioned.

Armitage nodded. "I would question any prisoners that we brought in, and found they all had one thing in common, they possessed magical abilities, some more powerful than others, but all of them had powers. Prince Kalian obviously had a purpose for arresting these people, but I have yet to find out what it is."

"Prince Kalian has magical powers too," Aurie said. "He used them on me."

"Yes, I know, more than likely inherited from his Ancient bloodline. Our people do not believe in using our powers to do evil, and delving in the Dark Arts is dangerous. That is why he must be stopped."

At this point, Armitage picked up his pace, leaving Aurie and Seamus behind. Aurie could sense the condemnation in the wizard's deportment, and she did not run to catch up with him, she allowed him his privacy.

Chapter Nine

They walked for hours, periodically stopping to replenish their thirst. Aurie seemed to have more strength and stamina as the day wore on, and contributed it to the magical powers of the water. The cave vibrated with an energy that pulsed through her veins, she was aware of every rock, every stalagmite, every pond and frond of fern with heightened clarity.

Armitage led them off the path and stopped beside a glistening waterfall. The floor of the cave, covered in thick moss, made a comfortable place to rest. Seamus did not start a fire and they had a cold meal of jerky, cheese and barley bread. At the time, she had not wondered where the food had come from, and it was not until later that she thought about it. At this point, she was content in having a full stomach.

She lay down on the cool moss and tucked her backpack under her head, fell asleep straight away, listening to the song of the water, and did not open her eyes until Seamus shook her awake a few hours later. She drank deeply from the pool, and felt invigorated. Soon they were back on the trail.

They had not gone far when Armitage came to an abrupt stop next to a huge boulder. He raised his finger to his lips and pointed to a rocky overhang off to their right. Seamus nodded and then he took Aurie's arm and led her into the shadows. "Quick, get under and keep quiet," he whispered. "Don't move until I return, understand?"

Aurie nodded, and watched as Seamus rejoined Armitage. They walked down the path, and soon disappeared around a bend. She removed her pack and set it on the ground, and then she squeezed into the crevice and pressed her back tightly against the wall. It was not long before her old fear of the darkness overcame her. Time seemed to have stopped completely, she could feel her legs cramping. She felt something crawl over her hand, and she squeezed her eyes shut, clenching her teeth, talking herself out of panicking and bolting from the safety of the crevice.

She heard footsteps. She peeked out from under the overhang and was relieved to see it was Seamus. She grabbed her pack, and raced happily over to him. Seamus did not hesitate in his stride. Rushing forward, he grabbed her around her waist and flung her behind the huge boulder. A barrage of arrows arched through the air, barely missing his head. One of them ricocheted off the top of the rock and imbedded itself in the moss. Seamus reached inside his shirt and pulled out a knife. Aurie could not believe a man his size could move so quickly. Gesturing angrily for her to stay down, he crept forward on his stomach and peered around the rock. The arrows had come from behind a barrier of granite on the far side of the path. Their attackers had them pinned down.

Aurie lay flattened on the cave floor, terrified of raising her head. It was then the power manifested, flowing rapidly through her body, and vibrating down her arms. Taking a deep breath, she slowly rose and stepped from behind the boulder. She knew the soldiers would not harm her, as Prince Kalian wanted her alive.

Sparks erupted from her fingers, striking the rock barricade, there was a loud crack and an explosion, and a soldier was flung through the air, landing heavily on the path a few feet away from the boulder.

A second soldier appeared and raced in a zigzag route directly towards her. She summoned her magic but nothing happened. Shocked, she realized she did not know how to work the spell, and knew the soldier would reach her in seconds. Seamus leapt out from behind the rock, and flung his knife at the assailant, it buried deeply in his chest, and he fell with a grunt to the ground. Seamus cautiously approached the downed man, nudged his leg, and satisfied the man was no longer a threat, bent down and retrieved his knife. Wiping the blood on his pant leg, he replaced it inside his shirt.

Angrily, he turned and faced Aurie. "I told you to stay hidden until I called for you," he snapped, his face turning red. "If anything had happened to me, you would have been captured. From now on, you will obey my orders without hesitation, is that understood?"

Aurie stood rooted on the path, he had never been angry with her before, and the searing look in his eyes shook her visibly.

"Seamus, I... I'm sorry."

Not answering he turned sharply and headed down the trail. Aurie ran to catch up with him, regretting her impulsiveness.

They had not gone far when they saw lights bouncing off the rocks and the stalagmites. Seamus came to an abrupt halt in the middle of the path, and Aurie, who had been following him closely, bumped into him. Armitage was standing before a greyish-white tower of calcite, facing Prince Kalian. Aurie grabbed Seamus' shirt, grasping it tightly in her fist. The two men, oblivious to everything around them, were unaware of their presence.

"I thought I had disposed of you years ago," Prince Kalian said angrily.

"As you can see, Your Highness, I am alive and well."

"I had sent my best assassin after you, whatever happened to him?"

"He too is alive and well, and has become a loyal and trusted friend."

A venomous look crossed Prince Kalian's face. "I will not tolerate treason or disloyalty among my troops. He will pay for his treachery."

Seamus growled under his breath, and grabbed the hilt of his sword. Aurie grasped his arm, he looked down at her, and seeing the pleading in her eyes, he slowly released the sword handle. He lowered his hand protectively on her shoulder.

"Instead of worrying about one wayward soldier, perhaps you should worry about your present predicament," Armitage said coldly.

"You take too much for granted, Lord Armitage. My powers have increased greatly since last we met. You will find I am not that easily disposed of."

"Is gaining magical power so important you must eradicate innocent people?"

"They mean nothing to me, but they are useful in allowing me to reach my goal sooner. One day I will be more powerful than you can ever imagine."

"You are mad and no good can come from delving in the Dark Arts. Surely you are aware of the perils if you continue with your goal?"

"Spare me your warnings, Mage. Once I dispose of you and the rest of your pitiful tribe, nothing can stop me."

"It's been twelve years, Your Highness, and you still haven't succeeded in finding them. What makes you think you ever will?"

"I will find them, and when I do I will show no mercy, and that goes as well for the young slave girl you are trying to protect. How I missed discovering her when she was right under my nose all this time confounds me. With her powers, I will be that much closer to my goal."

Armitage roared in anger, raised his staff, and instantaneously a shield surrounded him. Then the powerful sage pounded the ground with the bottom of his staff, and the walls of the cave shook. In terror, Aurie flung herself behind Seamus. Prince Kalian's face turned dark with rage, and then he collapsed.

Armitage turned and faced Seamus and Aurie. "It's all I can do for now. His powers are strong. It will not take him long to recuperate, and his soldiers are not far behind. We must leave."

"Yes, we know, we ran into a couple of them a few minutes ago," Seamus grunted.

Once again, the three fugitives were on the run, the deeper they traversed into the cave, the narrower the track became. The soft glow from Armitage's staff provided enough light to guide their steps. They raced down the passageway and around a sharp corner, before them was a flight of stairs carved out of stone, leading upwards. They started to climb and it was not long before Aurie's legs were cramping and she was fighting for breath. She listened intently for sounds of pursuit

Armitage stopped, and Aurie noticed the stairs had split, heading in two different directions. "Why have we stopped?" Seamus asked, as he headed towards the left passage. "Are we not going to the exit?"

Armitage rubbed his chin. "That's exactly what Prince Kalian wants us to do. I am sure by now he has a whole squadron waiting for us. We're going to go the long way, over the Abyss."

Seamus grunted, but said nothing.

"I'll go first, and Seamus you take up the rear. Aurie, listen carefully, do not stray from the path, and do not stop unless I tell you to, which is very important. Come, we have a long way to go."

Armitage shifted his backpack higher on his shoulders, and turned right. They climbed steadily upwards, navigating deeper and deeper into the cave, Aurie concentrated on placing one foot in front of the other, it was getting hotter and more humid, and the back of her neck was wet with perspiration.

The trail ended abruptly, and Aurie stared in disbelief, they were standing on a narrow ledge that looked down into a deep chasm. A red glow radiated from the depths, and hot steam and a strong odor of Sulphur belched from its bowels, fire spewed from between the rocks and fissures. A wooden bridge with rope handrails led across the void and disappeared into the darkness on the far side.

Aurie followed Armitage down the embankment, walking sideways in the loose dirt and pebbles to stop from plunging headfirst down the steep grade. Armitage approached the bridge, signaling for Aurie to remain where she was. When he had taken half a dozen steps, he stopped, closed his eyes, and lifted his staff above his head. He motioned Aurie to follow.

Aurie found it hard to breathe, a terror buried deeply inside her made its way to the surface, she saw flames rising into the sky, heard piercing screams. She sensed Seamus standing next to her, and she opened her eyes. Armitage gestured once again, and knit his brow when she remained motionless. "Come Aurie," he said quietly. "I won't let you fall."

Taking a deep breath, she stepped onto the bridge, tightly grasping the handrails on either side. She placed her foot down on the first board, then she took a step, and then another. The plank cracked and she hastily withdrew her foot, watching in horror as a splinter of wood spiraled into the fiery inferno beneath her.

It was then she saw it. A huge monster, covered in gold scales, flew out of the flames and landed on a rocky perch above them. Its eyes were amber, and it had a long reptilian body with a spiked tail. Its legs ended in claws and its wingspan was enormous. Roaring loudly, flames spewed from its mouth and trails of smoke streamed from its nose.

Aurie froze, her legs refused to move.

"Aurie, remember what Armitage said about stopping," Seamus yelled from behind her. "You have to keep going."

"I... I can't move. What is that thing?"

"Nothing to fear. Just do not look down. Lift your head, what do you see in front of you?"

Aurie tore her eyes away from the creature. "Lord Armitage," she replied.

"Alright, then let him guide you, put your trust in him."

Aurie took a deep breath and shuddered. Slowly she took a step, then another. She grasped the handrails so tightly her knuckles turned white. She gritted her teeth and she put all her concentration in reaching the far side. Finally, she was standing on solid ground and had never felt so relieved in her life. She collapsed to the cave floor and laid her head on her knee, she was shaking violently and her teeth were chattering.

"What is that thing?" she stammered, staring in dread at the huge beast resting on the rocky ledge.

"A dragon," said Armitage casually as he lowered himself to the ground and opened his pack.

"A what?"

"A dragon. Surely you've heard of dragons?"

"But I thought they were make-believe."

"I'm a wizard, and you believe in me, don't you?"

Aurie nodded.

"Then what's so different in believing in dragons or Elves for that matter? Just because you've never seen one, doesn't mean they don't exist."

"Mrs. Black told me ...."

"That there was no such thing as elves, Faeries, or Pixies," Armitage said, interrupting Aurie. "If that is the case, why is magic forbidden in Westcott if these magical creatures do not exist? Where would the magic come from?"

"I guess from the Ancients?"

"Yet you had no knowledge of the Ancients before today, why hasn't anyone questioned where the magic comes from?"

"Even talking about magic could get you arrested, so no one ever does."

"Fear and ignorance, a deadly combination," Armitage responded, sighing deeply.

"Are there lots of dragons?" Aurie asked quietly, changing the topic.

"There used to be, but most of them were slain in the Magic War, a long, long time ago. There are a few left and only a small number of people know where their lairs are."

"And all this time there's been a dragon living underneath Windermere Castle, right here in Westcott?"

"Yes, his name is Owain, he's a metallic dragon and he's been Guardian of the Abyss for over five hundred years."

"What's he guarding?"

"Although he has never admitted it to me, I think he has a cache of valuable gems and artefacts that he's hidden somewhere close by, you see, dragons are very protective of their treasures."

"Is he your friend?"

"Yes. We have known each other for a very long time. Dragons can sometimes be greedy and predatory, but Owain is a very noble and virtuous dragon, and I have profound respect for him."

"Is that why you were chanting, to protect us from him?"

"I wasn't chanting, child, I was conversing with Owain, asking his permission to cross over the Abyss, after all, this is his realm, and we are trespassing. Sometimes he agrees and sometimes he doesn't."

"What if he didn't agree to let us cross?"

"Then we would have had to turn back, which would have made our escape a little more difficult. I have heard some fearful stories about him. It's a known fact that if he doesn't like you, he'll roast and eat you."

Aurie raised her head in alarm, and stared at Armitage. He was not smiling and she could not tell if he was joking or not.

"That's why Prince Kalian won't follow us," said Armitage as he picked up his pack. "Owain does not like Prince Kalian, and he told me he has not eaten a man in centuries, which by the way, is one of his favorite meals."

By now, Seamus had crossed the bridge and had joined them. He had overheard the last part of their conversation, and chuckled quietly. Aurie wondered if Armitage and Seamus were joking with her, but she did not know them well enough to make that assumption. Armitage walked over to the edge of the Abyss and faced the dragon, he nodded and Aurie wondered if they were talking to each other again. Armitage bowed deeply in reverence to the mighty beast, Seamus, who was standing next to Armitage, did the same.

Aurie stood up, but she did not have enough courage to go any closer. She looked at Owain's eyes, and her fear slowly dissolved, she felt as if she was drowning in a pool of liquid gold. Mimicking Armitage and Seamus, she lowered her head and bowed to the magnificent creature. Owain regally lowered his head in response to Aurie's gesture. He flapped his mighty wings, lifted his enormous body off the ledge, and flew back into his fiery lair.

"Owain asked after you," Armitage said, after he had joined her on the path.

"Me?" Aurie said in surprise.

"Yes, he seemed to be fascinated by you."

"Does he want to eat me?"

"No," Armitage chuckled. "He said your magical abilities are very strong, but first you must learn how to use them properly, once you have done so, you will be a powerful sorceress."

"Do you think he's right, Armitage?"

"Yes, Aurie, I do. I sensed it in you from the moment we met."

"I don't know if I want to be a sorceress, it scares me."

"Good, you have just passed your first test."

Chapter Ten

Aurie drank her water sparingly, as she did not know how long it would be before their journey would end. The heat was sweltering, as periodically flames blasted out of a deep fissure. There was a constant outpouring of steam from the sinkholes and the air in the cave was oppressive, it was a harsh and tumultuous surrounding void of all vegetation.

Aurie trudged stoically along the winding trail. Everything had happened so fast it was hard to believe she had just encountered a dragon and had crossed a fiery abyss. Why had she been so terrified of the flames? Whose screams had she heard? She shook her head in bewilderment, gleaning old memories. Did her fear stem from her past, the reason why she had suppressed her memories?

Armitage stopped and motioned for Seamus to join him.

"I'm going to scout ahead," he said. "There's a place to hide behind that scree. Wait there for me."

"I don't know if I like you going on your own, my Lord," Seamus exclaimed anxiously.

"You must stay and protect Aurie. Your sword will not stop anything I meet in the Fire Cave. I might be a while, so now is an appropriate time for the two of you to get some rest."

Seamus nodded in agreement. Armitage handed his backpack to Seamus, and disappeared into the haze. It was eerily quiet except for the hiss of escaping steam, Seamus left the path and walked over to a pile of loose rock scattered around the base of a steep incline, off to the right was an overhang unseen from the path. Seamus approached it and from her position, Aurie spotted a small entrance. Seamus looked cautiously around, and when he seemed satisfied the way was clear, he squeezed through the access, motioning for Aurie to follow.

They found themselves inside a small cavern, it would hold no more than two or three people, the roof was very low and Seamus had to keep his head lowered. He walked over to the far wall, and then sat down on the dirt floor. He placed his backpack behind his head using it as a pillow. Aurie stretched out on the ground, exhausted, and immediately fell asleep.

When she awoke, it took a few seconds for her eyes to adjust to the darkness. The glow radiating from outside the small cavern provided sufficient light for her to discern the shape of the walls and the ceiling. Seamus was snoring quietly, his back propped against the wall. She thought he looked terribly uncomfortable and realized that over the years as a soldier, he had probably slept in worse places than this. She quietly rose and wandered restlessly around the small recess, she had sensed something when she was sleeping, yet she could not see anything in the small chamber that might cause any threat or concern. Aurie did not notice the burrow until she was almost on top of it. Squatting, she peeked inside, wondering how far back it went. If she got down on her hands and knees, she would not have any trouble maneuvering down the narrow passageway. She wondered what kind of animal could carve a tunnel through solid rock.

She was undecided as to whether she should wake Seamus. Not sensing any danger, she began crawling. She had not gone far when she heard a growl. She froze, a second growl followed almost immediately, she realized she did not have any room to turn around. Terrified, she shuffled backwards as quickly as she could, and in her haste scraped her elbows on the rocky walls. With one last push, she flew out of the tunnel, landing with a thud on her back. Something heavy pounced on top of her chest, pinning her to the floor, she could smell its hot fetid breath, and she screamed and grabbed the beast around its neck pushing it away from her face. It had dark glowing eyes, huge fangs, and black fur, and it grabbed a mouthful of her hair and pulled hard. She let out a sharp yell.

Seamus jumped up, clasping his knife tightly. He raced over to where Aurie was struggling.

"Seamus, help me!" Aurie cried. "I'm being attacked."

"By a mean vicious puppy," snorted Seamus, holding his sides and laughing uproariously. "Watch out, or he'll lick you to death."

It was then Aurie realized that the bundle of fur tearing at her hair and smothering her face with drool was a young pup. She grabbed it by the nape of its neck and lifted it off her chest. Whimpering and whining, the young animal wiggled, trying to get free.

"Kind of a funny looking dog," she frowned.

Seamus stopped laughing and grabbed the pup from Aurie. "That's because it's not a dog, it's a wolf."

"Wolf!" Aurie exclaimed. "How did it get here in the Fire Cave?"

"I don't know, it's a young male, and it can't be very old."

Seamus placed the young animal on the ground and turned it in the direction of the den. When it refused to move, he stamped his foot hoping to startle it, but the wolf cub sat on its haunches, turned its head sideways, and whimpered.

"He's really cute," said Aurie.

"Cute and dangerous, don't forget it's a wild animal."

"I wonder where his mother is."

"I'm sure we'll find out soon enough."

Seamus returned to his original position near the entrance of the cave. Aurie stood up and dusted her leggings. "He's not going back to the den," she pointed out as she strode over to Seamus and sat down next to him.

"I know." Seamus said. "We'll have to listen for the mother. If we hear her returning, we will leave the cave, there is not much room in here, and if she thinks her pup is in danger, she could be dangerous. I don't want to hurt her."

However, the mother wolf did not make an appearance. By now, the cub had slowly inched its way over to where Aurie and Seamus were sitting. It licked its paws, yawned, and stretched out on the floor. "He thinks he's fooling us by pretending to be asleep," Aurie grinned.

Seamus grunted and closed his eyes. Aurie dug in her pocket and pulled out what was left of her dried meat. She threw a chunk to the cub wondering if he was old enough to eat it. It soon disappeared. The cub sat up, looked pleadingly at Aurie, and whined.

"Alright just one more piece. I have to save the rest."

She bit off a small piece, and extending her arm, she offered the meat to the cub. He lay flat, resting on his stomach, creeping closer and closer to the tempting morsel. Grabbing the meat, he spun around and raced over to the far side of the cave. This time he threw the meat into the air and pretended to catch it, then he jumped on it, and lastly rolled on it, making Aurie laugh at his playfulness. When he had tired of the game, he took the meat between his paws, chewing contentedly on the treat.

Time crept by slowly, the wolf pup fell into a restless sleep, Seamus was snoring loudly, and Aurie wished she had the ability to fall asleep as quickly. She knew she should be resting, but she was worried about

Armitage. The powerful wizard would be safe no matter where he was, but she would have felt a lot better if he had been with her and Seamus.

Without warning, the young cub jumped up and growled. Seamus opened his eyes, reached inside his shirt, and withdrew his knife, gesturing for Aurie to be still. A scraping noise came from outside the cave. There was something prowling around.

"Is it the mother?" Aurie whispered.

"I don't know," Seamus replied. "Something is making the pup nervous. If it was his mother, he wouldn't be growling."

"What should we do?"

"I'm going to have a look. Hide in the burrow, and don't come out unless I call for you."

Aurie immediately obeyed, she ran to the tunnel and slid in backwards. A wet nose poked her face. The cub had followed her.

"It's all right, Aurie," Seamus grunted, as his face appeared in the tunnel entrance. "You can come out now."

Aurie pushed the cub out of her way, and scrambled out. Armitage was standing by the exit drinking from his water skin.

"Did you see anything?" Seamus asked.

"Nothing alive," Armitage answered, shaking his head. "Prince Kalian won't follow us. He is no match against Owain. Right now, however, he is not our worry; there are other things in the Fire Cave just as dangerous."

The young cub walked over to Aurie and plunked himself down on top of her feet, leaning against her legs to get her attention.

"Well, well, well. What do we have here?" Armitage asked, as he reached down and picked up the young pup.

"I found him in a burrow at the back of the cave," Aurie replied.

"Seems to be abandoned," Seamus interrupted. "No sign of the mother anywhere."

Armitage sighed and shook his head. "On my way back, I came across a recent kill. Whatever was devouring it ran off when it heard me coming."

"Do you have any idea what killed it?" Seamus asked.

Armitage massaged the back of his neck, looking fleetingly at Aurie. "No, but I did get a look at the animal that was slain. I remember thinking at the time it was wolf, although I dismissed that thought because it is very rare to come across one in the Fire Cave. However, it seems as if I was right."

"Do you think it was the mother wolf?" Aurie asked.

"There's a good chance it was," Armitage answered as he placed the pup back on the cave floor.

"What's going to happen to him?"

Armitage shrugged. "We have to leave him and hope he can survive on his own."

"No, we can't. It's just a baby."

"And there's a good chance he might be a dire wolf," Seamus said sharply. "We don't dare take the chance. The most humane thing to do would be to dispose of him before we leave."

"No," Aurie said loudly looking beseechingly at Armitage.

"Let me have another look," Armitage said, as he stooped over and picked up the cub once again.

"I don't detect anything, he's not big enough to be dire, his eyes are blue, not yellow like a dire wolf, and he appears to be quite intelligent and gentle. The mother might have been chased into the Fire Cave, and she found this cavern to have her pup."

"Then can we take him with us?" Aurie asked.

"Aurie, we have to keep moving. Neither I nor Seamus have time to worry about his safety."

"I'll carry him! Please Armitage."

"We have a long way to go, and he's too heavy for you to carry."

"I can do it, I'm strong. Please Lord Armitage," Aurie pleaded.

"All right, Aurie," sighed Armitage. "But if he turns out to be more than you can handle, then you will have to leave him behind. Is that understood?"

Aurie nodded solemnly. She opened the back of her pack, and put the cub inside. Then she lifted the pack onto her back. Seamus grunted, picked up his own pack, and flung it over his shoulder. Aurie knew that he was not pleased with Armitage's decision, but he did not say anything to the wizard.

They travelled quickly, keeping a steady pace. Armitage spun around, grabbed Seamus by his arm and pointed. Seamus immediately drew his sword, taking a fighting stance, Armitage raised his staff in the air, and Seamus gestured for Aurie to stand behind them. The young pup started to squirm in the backpack, and Aurie scolded him sharply, he seemed to sense her urgency, and immediately settled down.

It was then Aurie saw them, their skin was yellow, orange, and red, with deep shades of brown, their hair was black, and they had big, pointed ears, and large sharp teeth jutting from their mouths. They were not much larger than a man was, but their fierce looks sent an icy chill down her back. She watched in terror as the hideous beasts bore down on them, screaming and howling. There was a loud crack and bolts of light flashed from Armitage's staff, the creatures in the front of the pack went flying, landing against the huge rocks, or falling into pools of boiling liquid. Seamus was swinging his blade wildly, causing as much destruction as Armitage. When the monsters in the flank saw what was happening, they turned and fled. Armitage lowered his staff. "Put away your weapon, my friend," he said to Seamus. "They won't be back. Goblins are not brave. As soon as one of their members is injured or killed, they run off."

Seamus wiped his blade on his pant leg, and replaced it in its scabbard.

"Are you sure that's what they were?"

Armitage nodded solemnly, a concerned look on his face. Aurie removed her pack, and took out the frightened pup, he tried to squirm out of her arms, and she stubbornly refused to put him down.

The three travelers did not linger. Aurie anxiously approached every corner with trepidation, wondering what they would encounter next. A stone rolled down a small embankment, and she jumped, her heart pounding in her chest. At first, the young pup was not hard to carry, but as the afternoon passed, he got heavier and heavier, her arms were aching, but she dared not complain.

All at once, the walls started to shake, dirt and rocks dislodged from the ceiling of the cave tumbled onto the path. Aurie held on tightly to the pup, she knew that if he got loose, he would run away in panic, and they would never find him again.

On the far side of the cave, a huge crack opened in the wall. Horror-stricken, Aurie watched as a black swarm poured out of the gaping hole, heading straight towards them. She screamed, and threw herself to the ground, covering the pup's body. Armitage raised his staff, and a bright glow wrapped itself around them, creating a protective shield. The swarm hit the barrier with dull thuds, bouncing harmlessly onto the path and into the surrounding rocks. The din from their high-pitched squeaks echoed throughout the cave, penetrating the magical shield.

Aurie raised her head and stared in disbelief. They were bats, but unlike any she had ever seen, they were ferocious looking with sharp dagger-like teeth and glowing red eyes. They swooped and darted leaving a trail of fire behind them. Black, writhing bodies covered the cave floor. Aurie did not know how long Armitage could keep the shield around them, and instinctively knew anyone using magic expended energy, and confronting Prince Kalian, the goblins and now the bats would take its toll on Armitage's strength.

As quickly as they had appeared, the bats turned and flew back into the fissure. Armitage waited until the aperture closed, then he released the shield.

"Is everyone okay?" he asked.

Aurie heard the exhaustion in his voice.

"Fire Bats," Armitage chuckled. "I must say Prince Kalian is getting more creative all the time."

Aurie could not understand why Armitage was joking at a time like this, and realized he was probably doing it for her benefit. She, on the other hand, could not wait to get out of the Fire Cave, and to see the open sky and smell fresh air once again.

"Do you think they were Prince Kalian's doing?" Seamus asked.

"Yes, and the goblins as well," Armitage replied. "I'm not sure how he's doing it, but he appears to be controlling them, only a wizard with powerful magic has that capability."

"If that's the case, why didn't he fight back when he confronted you earlier?"

"His powers are not as strong as mine, he's using something else to control the elemental beasts and the goblins, and I'm not sure what it is."

"I wonder if Prince Kalian will be waiting for us when we get to the exit," asked Seamus, once they had started walking again and had covered some ground.

Armitage shook his head. "No, it's too long of a trek around the mountain, and even a squadron of soldiers on horseback could not reach it before us."

Armitage approached a deep crevice in the rock, turned sharply to the right, and disappeared. Aurie followed directly behind him and found herself outside, standing on a narrow ridge, sheer walls of rock rose sharply above them. Below a dark green expanse of trees covered the landscape, a ribbon-shaped stream flowed through the dense foliage and in the far distance, she could see the misty outline of rolling foothills and high peaked mountains. The view was breathtaking.

"I know where we are," Aurie blurted. "This is Lindell Forest, isn't it? A few years ago, I picked mushrooms in the woods near Windermere Castle. I didn't like it very much, it was dark and scary."

"Lindell Forest is over a thousand years old," Armitage responded. "There are deep bottomless pits, dangerous bogs, and marshes. Man-eating beasts dwell in the caves and stagnant waters. It is not a place for the weak-hearted."

"Then why are we going there, everyone knows it is off-limits to travelers?"

"That's just more lies and propaganda instigated by Prince Kalian. Yes, for some it may be a dangerous and perilous place, but for others it can be a sanctuary."

"Come, we have to get off this ledge," said Seamus. "It's a steep climb down, and we do not have many hours of daylight left."

He reached over and took the wolf pup out of Aurie's arms. She was very grateful, but did not say anything, Seamus was a kind-hearted man, but she knew he had not agreed with taking the young pup with them, he felt it slowed them down, and could prove to be a nuisance during their trek.

The path leading to the gully below was steep and dangerous, at one-point Aurie began to slide in the crumbling dirt. She managed to grab a rock jutting out of the soil and stopped herself from falling headfirst down the embankment. The back of her legs and ankles were aching with the strain, and she knew that if Seamus had not taken the young pup, she would not have been able to make it down the steep slope.

At last, they reached the bottom. Armitage led them to a footpath and after walking for a short distance, they came across a bubbling brook. Seamus set the pup down, and it lunged into the water, splashing playfully. Aurie knelt on the ground and scooped up a handful of the delicious water, drinking greedily. She splashed water on her head, and sighed when it trickled over her hot face and down her neck.

"I know you're exhausted Aurie," Armitage told her. "But we can't stop long. Refill your water skin, and if you haven't fed them all to that young pup, have a piece of jerky."

"Yes, sir."

"Do you think we can make it to Primrose Cottage tonight?" Seamus asked.

"I don't plan on going there, at least not right away," Armitage replied. "The closest route is through Whitehawk Pass, and Prince Kalian will deduce that is exactly where we'll go. I'm sure he and his soldiers are riding there as we speak."

"Is there an alternative route?"

"Yes, Bloodroot Swamp."

"Bloodroot Swamp, surely you must be joking? Those tales about the Bog Hag might just be true. After everything we've come across in the Fire Cave, I wouldn't be surprised."

Armitage shrugged and smiled at Seamus. When the wizard did not provide any answers to Seamus' concerns, Aurie felt uneasiness in the pit of her stomach. The name of the swamp alone was enough to cause her apprehension. Things were not looking good.

Chapter Eleven

Armitage led them deeper and deeper into the forest. The energetic pup raced down the path ahead of them, turned, and scampered back, stopping just before he collided into Aurie.

Massive firs and cedars towered high above their heads, the coolness of the forest felt invigorating after the oppressive heat of the Fire Cave. After walking for some time, the trees disappeared and they found themselves in an open field, the ground was wet and spongy, and tall bulrushes and cattails grew in abundance. Aurie followed closely behind Armitage, maneuvering around succulent fronds and skirting deep pools of water with cow-lilies floating on the calm surfaces, while the resonating croak of a bullfrog beckoned from the reeds.

Aurie spied some swamp hedge-nettle, which she had at one time picked to provide poultices for Mrs. Black's aching joints and headaches. Off to her right she spotted a swamp lily, and she inhaled the sweetness of its scent.

As the sun slowly set, a soft glow emitted from Armitage's staff, providing light to navigate around the dense foliage and avoid tripping on the gnarled roots that covered the treacherous path. Armitage raised his hand, signaling Seamus and Aurie to stop. "Stay on the path and keep an eye on your young friend, Aurie."

She whistled softly and the wolf cub came running over, she picked him up, holding him tightly in her arms. He whined and struggled to get down, but she covered his muzzle with her hand, warning him to be quiet. Once again, he obeyed, and she was amazed at how quickly he responded to her commands.

Aurie stared into the darkness, sensing a presence, and wondered if the story of the Bog Hag was true.

A flash of light erupted out of the shadows, temporarily blinding her. Armitage lifted his staff and sparks ricocheted into the darkness. A dazzling blast followed almost immediately, and once again, Armitage diverted it. "You are no match for me Eleanor, show yourself."

There was an unnerving silence, and Aurie waited anxiously for the next assault.

"Do my eyes deceive me, or is that Lord Armitage, High Wizard of the Ancients?" a melodious voice said from the shadows.

"You are most perceptive, My Lady," Armitage chuckled.

There was a rustling sound from the bushes, and a graceful creature, grasping a spear, stepped onto the path. She was tall and slender, wearing a long flowing gown with a metallic cape, her hair was silver and flowed down her back, her face was heart-shaped, and she had slanted silver eyes and pointed ears.

Aurie stared in astonishment. She had never seen such an enchanting creature. She had imagined that a Bog Hag would be ugly and vile, reeking of the swamps and decay.

"What brings you to Bloodroot Swamp?" Eleanor asked, as she stared firstly at Armitage, and then openly at Aurie.

"I seek your presence, Eleanor Elderberry."

"How did you know I would be here?" Eleanor enquired, lowering her spear.

"Owain told me."

"That prehistoric lizard, is he still around?"

"Yes, hale and powerful as ever. He sends his greetings."

"I bet he does."

It was evident that Armitage and the willowy creature knew each other well as their light-hearted bantering held no malice.

"We have travelled a long way," Armitage said. "There is much I have to talk to you about."

"I do not wish to be disturbed, I enjoy my solitude."

"Is that why you started that rumor about the Bog Hag?"

Eleanor snorted, turned, and headed away from the path and into the bushes, Armitage gestured to Seamus and Aurie to follow him. After walking for a short distance, they left the marsh and entered the dense forest once again. A cold mist had risen wrapping itself sinuously around the trunks of the stately trees. Before long, they arrived at a waterfall, which cascaded into a deep pool. The light from Armitage's staff reflected off the spray like a million tiny fireflies. An enormous willow in full bloom grew next to the pool. Eleanor led them to the base of the tree where, concealed in its long sweeping branches, was a sprawling tree house. She quickly scaled the wooden ladder leaning against a broad platform that circled the tree house and disappeared into the shadows.

"Stay here and keep your eyes and ears open," Armitage whispered into Seamus' ear.

"You don't trust her My Lord?"

"With my life, but as much as I count Eleanor as a friend, I have learned to not let my guard down when I am in the presence of an Eldoran warrior and sorceress, especially Eleanor Elderberry. It would be wise to remember she is a high elf, and a creature of White Magic."

Seamus nodded and took a stance next to the ladder, placing his hand defensively over the hilt of his sword.

"Leave the pup here with Seamus," Armitage instructed Aurie. "Climb up. I'll be right behind you."

As Aurie entered the tree house, she sensed a slight presence of magic. She stared in amazement, there was a table and four chairs in the middle of the room, and a fire burned in a rock hearth on the far wall, casting an amber glow on the room and its furnishings. There was a closed doorway on the left, and ivy and flowers grew over the walls. Eleanor was setting a teapot and some mugs on the table. "I'll have a pot of primrose tea ready shortly, and here are some chokecherry scones. I don't have much else, I wasn't expecting company."

"That will do nicely Eleanor," Armitage replied as he and Aurie sat down at the table.

The kettle whistled, and Eleanor walked over to the hearth and removed it from the coals, returned to the table and sat down in a vacant chair. She poured the boiling water into the teapot and set the empty kettle on the floor.

"Eleanor," Armitage said. "This is Aurie. I want you to meet her."

Eleanor stared for the longest time at Aurie, and then she reached over and pulled her hair back from her face. She raised her eyebrows, looking questionably at Armitage.

Armitage shrugged, saying nothing.

"What is it you wish to discuss?"

"I assume your search for your sister has not been successful?"

"I will not stop searching for her and King Sebastian. I have sworn to my mother and father that I will find them, and find them I will."

For a few moments, there was silence, and then Eleanor leaned forward and poured tea into the empty cups. "You did not travel all this way to talk about my sister," she said, looking directly at Armitage, "or for that matter, to introduce me to a young girl with Elf blood."

"I'm not an Elf," Aurie said, interrupting rudely. "I'm just an ordinary girl."

Eleanor looked at Armitage who shrugged saying nothing.

"Do you mind if I ask you a few questions?" Eleanor asked, turning to face Aurie.

"I guess that's okay," Aurie replied quietly.

"You have excellent night vision, you heal quickly, you probably know how to read, is that not the case?"

Aurie lowered her head and stared at the table. "Yes, My Lady."

"Then with your appearance I would definitely say you are at least half Elf."

"But I don't want to be an Elf."

"One day you will feel differently. Now, I believe Lord Armitage wishes to discuss something with me. Have some tea and a scone."

Armitage then told Eleanor about his suspicions Prince Kalian was using Dark Magic to call up the creatures from the Underworld. When he mentioned their encounters with the goblins and the fire bats, Eleanor stood up and walked over to a side window, staring silently into the dark forest.

"I fear you may be right High Wizard, two days past, a bear attacked one of our knights, and she barely escaped with her life. The encounter was so swift, that had she not been one of our more experienced warriors, she would have perished. It was only after she had destroyed the creature did she realize it was twice the size of an ordinary bear, with vicious claws and teeth. With what you have just told me, it must have been a dire bear, although it has been over a century since one was seen on Earth."

"I feared there would be other sightings," Armitage said quietly.

"If Prince Kalian is using black magic, then he must have inherited his magical abilities from his Ancient mother. It takes a lot of power to control elemental creatures and beasts, how is it that he has become so strong?"

"I have been watching him for a long time, and at first I thought he was learning to use his innate powers, but more and more I came to realize he was more than just a supernatural wizard. He has been obtaining his skills from outside sources."

"How can such a thing be?" Eleanor asked, turning sharply.

"By power absorbed from those who have magical abilities, thus the reason for his never-ending quest to find the surviving Ancients. He grows stronger by the day, but there are not many villagers left in Westcott who can provide him with the magic he needs. Although I have managed to find this out, I still do not know where he takes the prisoners."

"I know where he takes them," Aurie murmured, looking first at Armitage and then Eleanor. Armitage turned in his seat and stared at Aurie in astonishment.

"I was with Tony, he's one of the boys from the street gang I lived with in Westcott before.... before," Aurie said, unable to finish her sentence. "He was exercising Prince Kalian's horse near the field bordering Lindell Forest. I had some time on my hands, so I went exploring. I came across a hollow tree trunk, and I went inside and there were stone steps that led to a large cave. There was a deep pool, with a stone pillar in the middle, with a glass case sitting on top, and inside was a beautiful crystal. When I touched the water, I was thrown across the room. There was magic down there, because I could feel it, and I had a really bad headache."

She told them about the tunnel leading to the antechamber, and finding the empty cages. She told them about the screams she had heard, and overhearing the soldiers' conversation.

Armitage listened intently until Aurie finished her story. He shook his head in disbelief. "Why did you not say anything about this earlier, Aurie?"

"I knew how dangerous it was overhearing those soldiers, and I couldn't take a chance that Prince Kalian would find out and do something to Tony, or the other boys in the band. They were my friends. Then with everything that has happened since we escaped from prison, I guess I forgot all about it until now. I'm sorry."

Armitage reached over and gently patted her hand. "Don't fret child. You did the right thing. There is nothing dishonorable in protecting your friends."

Armitage rubbed his chin, and stared for the longest time at the wall. "Aurie, you mentioned a brilliant gem inside a glass case, can you describe it to me?"

"Yes, My Lord. It was shaped like a... a... I do not know the word, but it had six points on it. And it was so bright it lit up the whole chamber."

"It's called a hexagon and I wish I were wrong, but I fear it may be the Fire Crystal."

"What's the Fire Crystal?"

Eleanor returned to the table and sat down. "It was forged at the beginning of time by the Dwarves." she said quietly "and is one of the most powerful artefacts in the Magic Kingdom, and can only be controlled by Dark Magic."

"That's why you had such a bad headache, Aurie," Armitage said. "Prince Kalian must have somehow managed to get his hands on it. That's how he's able to absorb powers from those who have magical abilities and how to control the beasts we encountered in the Fire Cave."

"What happens to those people?" Aurie asked in trepidation, remembering the empty cages in the buried dungeon.

"I am afraid they would not have survived. The power of the Fire Crystal is devastating. Prince Kalian has learned how to control it, and I fear he does not fully understand how dangerous it is. The price he will pay will be disastrous. Experimenting in the Dark Arts can only lead to one outcome. He not only puts himself but the entire natural world in peril. We must stop him before he succeeds with his plans."

"You mentioned you could feel the magic in the cave," Eleanor asked, as she turned and faced Aurie. "You have magical abilities?"

"Surely you must have sensed it in her the moment you touched her?" Armitage commented.

"Sooner than that, when she passed through my shield at the door, I knew she had abilities. Her powers are not strong, so she must have just come of age?"

Armitage nodded.

"Why have we never met? There are no Elves living in Lindell Forest, not since the Magic War."

Aurie squirmed in her chair. Sensing her discomfort, Armitage reached over and gently touched her arm. "Aurie and I met two days ago in Prince Kalian's prison."

Eleanor raised her eyebrows, but said nothing.

"I was a guest in Prince Kalian's prison. I was hoping to find out where he kept the prisoners, but unfortunately, I was not very successful. Aurie was in the cell next to mine. After talking to her, it did not take me long to realize why Prince Kalian had arrested her. Aurie has indeed just come of age, and I was amazed at how powerful her magic was."

"Which makes sense," Eleanor remarked. "Combined with her innate powers and her Elf blood, I am surprised Prince Kalian had not discovered her sooner."

Armitage nodded, took a sip of his tea and continued. "We managed to escape and flee through the Fire Cave. Rather than go to the exit, I decided to cross through the Abyss as I knew Lord Kalian would not follow us there."

"That explains Owain."

"I do not doubt Prince Kalian will be waiting for us at Whitehawk Pass with his troops. Our only chance to bypass him is to walk over Beargrass Mountain."

"You and your friends are welcome to stay the night," Eleanor offered as she stood up and walked towards the closed door. She soon returned carrying four mats and placed them on the floor next to the hearth. When she saw Aurie's enquiring look, she chuckled quietly. "One is for the wolf cub. All forest creatures are welcome in my home."

"Thank you, Eleanor, you are very kind," Armitage said.

"First thing in the morning, I will return to Fey Wild, the Eldorans must be warned immediately."

"The tribes living in Lindell Forest must also be warned. Now more than ever we must combine our strengths. I fear there are dark days ahead for all of us."

The next morning after Eleanor prepared a hasty breakfast of tea and scones, she rummaged through her larder for supplies, apologizing that she did not have more on hand.

"You have done more than enough, my friend," Armitage said. "If luck is with us, we will arrive at our destination before the sun sets."

Eleanor walked into the back room and returned carrying a long, black box. She placed it on the table and almost reverently lifted the lid. Inside was a long-sword made of gold and silver, with jewels embedded in the cross guard and intricate designs etched on the metal.

"It has been a long time since I have had need of this weapon," she said as she put the sword into the scabbard, and then strapped it to a leather belt she wore around her waist. "Not since the Magic War."

Armitage nodded sadly. Aurie remembered what he had said to Seamus last night about Eleanor being a fierce warrior and sorcerer.

Soon everyone was standing beneath the tree house. Eleanor grasped Armitage's elbow with her right hand.

"Please pass on my greetings to King Esmond," Armitage said. "And let your father know that when the time is right, he will hear from me."

Eleanor bowed her head in reverence to the High Wizard, and then nodded at Seamus and Aurie. Turning, she strolled towards the waterfall, waded into the deep pool, stepped under the cascading water, and disappeared.

"Come," Armitage said. "We have a long walk ahead of us, and we will not be safe until we reach Primrose Cottage."

Before she walked into the heavy undergrowth, Aurie looked one last time at the waterfall. She did not know how long it would be, but she knew she would meet Eleanor again.

Moss and ferns grew in abundance on the ground, tufts of hair lichen hung from the branches of the cedars and pines. The woods were quiet and the only sound was the shuffling of their feet. The path gradually got steeper and by late afternoon, they had left the forest and had climbed above the tree line, skirting the top of the mountain.

A dark speck soared lazily in the azure sky high above their heads, and Aurie marveled at the strength and power of the muscular bird. Sometimes when she was working in the garden back at the castle, she would see golden eagles circling high above the crests of the firs in Lindell Forest. The young cub growled bravely, but when he realized the bird was out of his reach, he turned and went exploring among the rocks. Aurie looked down into the valley far below and spotted a roadway snaking its way through the trees.

"There's Whitehawk Pass," Armitage said, pointing to the right. "It's the perfect place for an attack because the road is bordered by cliffs on both sides, there is no way we could have outrun Prince Kalian's mounted troops if we had taken that route, it would have been a death trap."

"It won't take him long to figure out we took a different route," Seamus said, coming up behind them.

They continued on their way, and Armitage allowed them to stop for a short break. Seamus had packed Eleanor's chokecherry scones, and Aurie hungrily ate the one she found in her pack.

"Lord Armitage," she asked. "Is Eleanor an Elf? Is that why she was so curious about me?"

Seamus snorted, and took a long drink from his flask. "Better not let her hear you call her that."

"Why?"

"Eleanor is an Eldoran, Aurie," Armitage answered. "Eldorans are high elves and they share a lot of similar features to the Elves, as well as a kinship with them. They are generally taller in stature and possess stronger magic. They have telepathic abilities as well as longevity, teleportation, and like the Elves, dwell almost exclusively in Fey Wild, which is located on a different plane than Earth."

"Then why is Eleanor living here?"

"Eleanor is a very powerful sorceress and has the ability of Dimensional Travel, which means she can move between the two worlds. She is also a warrior and a royal princess."

"As a matter of fact," Seamus said. "Queen Elyse is her sister, and when Prince Kalian tried to slay her and King Sebastian, he made a powerful enemy of the Eldorans."

"I thought she was nice," Aurie replied. "She's the most beautiful person I have ever met."

"Yes," Armitage said. "That's very true. But remember that Eleanor is not human, she is Eldoran, so referring to her as a human is incorrect."

"Yes sir."

"Now, I suggest we keep moving. We have a long way to go."

A few hours later, they reached the summit of Beargrass Mountain. Bearberry Wolf willow shrubs grew along the pathway and the sweet heavy perfume of silverberries tickled Aurie's nose, and she inhaled deeply. She always loved their scent. Although the sun shone warmly on her head, small patches of snow remained under the rocks, and she wondered if it stayed around for the entire year or eventually melted. A cool breeze caressed her cheeks, the strenuous climb made her warm, and she braided her hair, letting it hang down her back. She took off her jacket and wrapped it around her waist. The view was breathtaking. The mountain range extended for miles and in the distance, the blue hue of a lake, nestling in a deep valley, shimmered through the haze.

"That's Woodfern Lake," Seamus pointed out as he stopped next to her. "It's where we're headed. Primrose Cottage is located right next to it. You'll soon grow to love it there."

"Am I going to live there, with you and Armitage?"

"I imagine Lord Armitage decided that would be the case when he first met you, unless you want to live in a cave with your new wolf friend?"

Aurie grinned but said nothing. Happily, she lengthened her stride to catch up with Armitage. She lost her footing and quickly steadied herself, chastising herself for being so careless, as it would have been very easy to twist an ankle, which would have slowed down their progress.

Soon they were back among the trees. Trilliums and wild roses grew abundantly along the trail, a sign that a late spring had finally reached the valleys. The sound of rushing water could be heard in the distance. The trail ended abruptly, and she crept cautiously over to the edge of the embankment. Far below was a deep gorge, a turbulent stream cascaded through the ravine, crashing over huge boulders, fallen trees lay haphazardly among the rocks and deep eddies. Directly before her was a wooden bridge, like the one crossing the Abyss in the Fire Cave; she silently hoped this one would be more stable.

Armitage stepped out first, walking cautiously on the slippery boards. Aurie followed, holding tightly to the handrail. This time she remembered to not look down.

The wolf cub had followed her, but quickly skirted around her legs, loped past Armitage and was soon on the far side. He lay down in the cool grass, waiting patiently for them to join him. With apprehension, Aurie took a step, then another, wishing she was as agile and fearless as the cub. She sighed with relief when she realized she was halfway across, the bridge appeared to be well-built and she relaxed.

All at once the young wolf yelped a warning, and Seamus let out a loud bellow. Armitage, who was almost at the end of the bridge spun around sharply. A dark shadow blotted out the sun, and Aurie raised her head. A huge bird was plummeting out of the sky, heading straight towards her, it was dark golden brown and looked like an enormous eagle. When it was almost upon her, it flapped its enormous wings, and Aurie was buffeted by the updraft rushing through its feathers. Losing her hold on the ropes, she was flung violently onto the boards, before she had time to recover, she felt herself being lifted upwards into the air. She heard Armitage yell and she frantically grabbed the handrail, wrapping her legs and arms tightly around the rope.

The bridge was swinging wildly, and Armitage had a precarious hold on his staff and struggled to keep himself upright. Seamus had taken only a few steps when he lost his footing. Aurie watch in horror as he plunged over the side, however at the last second, he grabbed the handrail. She could see his arm muscles straining as he clung desperately to the rope, attempting to pull himself back onto the boards.

The bird screeched as it hovered above her. She could see its razor-sharp talons. Again, she sensed the familiar tingle along her arms, sparks flew from her fingertips, and she aimed directly at the bird's chest and struck the raptor with a burst of light. With a shrill cry, it turned in mid-flight and flew away. It circled high above, preparing to attack again. Armitage raced over to Aurie. Seamus had pulled himself back onto the bridge, and reached her seconds behind the wizard.

"Excellent job, Aurie," Armitage praised. "Stay where you are, and don't let go of the ropes no matter how rough it gets."

"This time we'll be ready for it," Seamus snarled, drawing his sword.

The bird continued to soar high above them, it flapped its powerful wings, ready to launch. Surprisingly, it veered sharply, and flew off in the direction of the cliffs, its shrill cry echoing throughout the canyon.

"What happened?" Aurie asked.

"I believe it was summoned, probably by Prince Kalian," Armitage said.

"You can bet he knows where we are now," Seamus growled angrily.

"What was it?" Aurie asked shakily.

"It was a Thunder Hawk," Armitage replied.

"I've heard tales about them, but didn't know they actually existed," Seamus said, still holding his sword.

"It's an elemental creature, the same as the Fire Bats, and they don't exist on Earth, at least they're not supposed to."

Armitage helped Aurie to stand. When they reached the far side, she was so relieved she threw her arms around the cub's neck and gave him a big hug. He in turn, licked her face and playfully nipped her cheek.

She would be very relieved when they reached their destination.

Chapter Twelve

Just before dusk, they arrived at a beautiful lake, surrounded by rolling hills. The rays from the setting sun shimmered off the water, shrouding the rocks and trees with a soft glow.

"This is Woodfern Lake," Armitage said. "And that is Primrose Cottage."

Aurie stared in astonishment. Before them was a large meadow smothered in wild flowers, columbines, red paintbrushes, daisies and lupine. She had not noticed the small, white cottage with the thatched roof until Armitage pointed it out to her. How could she have missed seeing it? It was located at the end of the meadow, sheltered on all sides by graceful willows and swaying elms, wild primrose bushes grew beneath the windows.

She followed Armitage wearily across the field, the young pup was exhausted and was having difficulty keeping up with them, he plopped himself down in the grass, whining to get her attention. Aurie turned and retraced her steps, but the look on Seamus' face stopped her.

"You might as well start training him now to let him know who the boss is," he muttered. "Or you'll never earn his respect."

The young pup yelped to get her attention, and as difficult as it was, Aurie turned and walked away, ignoring his whines. He would catch up with her once he realized he was not going to get his way.

Aurie could sense the magic surrounding them. Armitage released the shield, the cottage door swung open, and she followed him inside. A stone fireplace dominated the back wall. Beneath a window on the right was a long wooden bed, which could only belong to Seamus because of its length. On the left side of the room were a second window and a chestnut oak cabinet filled with blue dishes. A table and four chairs, sitting on a colorful braided rug, filled up the remaining space in the small, cozy room. There were two closed doors, one on either side of the fireplace.

Armitage placed his backpack on the floor next to the hearth, flicked his fingers and a fire started to burn briskly. Seamus picked up two wooden buckets and left the cottage, returning shortly with water in each of the pails. The young wolf followed Seamus into the cottage, and made a beeline directly to Aurie, jumping up on her legs, begging her to pick him up.

"No, no," she said wagging her finger at the excited pup. "You have to stay outside."

"Nonsense," said Armitage. "He's quite welcome to join us. He's far too young to be on his own. You never know what could be wandering around out there, especially after dark."

Aurie happily picked up the pup. "We have to give you a name," she speculated, staring into his eyes. "Hmm, let's see. What do you think of Torin?"

"An excellent choice," nodded Armitage. "It means chief and I have a feeling that your new friend will wear his name well."

"Torin," she repeated quietly. "Torin of the Wolves."

"Come with me Aurie," Armitage said as he walked over to the closed door on the right and swung it open. Aurie set Torin on the floor and followed the wizard into the room. She stopped, staring around in amazement. The curtains hanging on the window, and the duvet covering the bed had a matching pattern of green ferns and tiny pink roses. There was a small washstand under the window, and an armoire on the back wall. Armitage opened the closet door and she was delighted to see it was full of colorful dresses. She smiled as she spotted a shelf of leggings and loose flowing shirts.

"This will be your bedroom and these are your clothes," he said as he left the room. "Why don't you have a look around, and we'll call you once Seamus has prepared something to eat."

Aurie explored every nook and cranny, and then she flung herself backwards onto the bed, and landed in a cloud of softness and warmth. Torin tried to climb up after her but she pushed him down, lecturing him sternly that the bed was off limits. Wolves slept on the floor. She sighed contentedly, finding it hard to believe this was happening. She stood up, walked over to the washstand, and noticed there was water in the pitcher and a bar of soap sitting next to it, she filled the basin, and washed her face and hands.

"Foods on," Seamus called. Aurie left her room in a daze and sat down at the table. There were three bowls of steaming lentil soup, and fresh boysenberry biscuits in a basket. A bowl of soup was lying on the floor next to the hearth, and Torin raced over and lapped hungrily. He yelped and jumped back. "Torin, silly pup," Aurie laughed. "Wait until it cools down."

The young pup ignored her and circled the bowl, then he began eating again, and Aurie chuckled at his eagerness, he would soon learn.

A teapot sat in the middle of the table, and Seamus poured the hot brew into their cups. Aurie had no idea where the food came from, as she remembered Armitage saying they were absent from the cottage for a long time. How did he know she would be coming to Primrose Cottage, and why was the bedroom set up for a girl, with a closet full of girl's clothing, exactly her size? Although she had known Armitage for only a brief time, she was beginning to realize things did not always happen, as one would expect. She recalled the alcove in the cave, where Seamus had found the ingredients to make a stew, and was able to pack fresh cheese and bread in their packs. If this was one of the benefits of knowing magic, Aurie could hardly wait to start her training.

When their meal was finished, she cleared the table and poured hot water into a metal basin sitting on the counter. She washed the dishes and stacked them on the shelves, humming quietly to herself. Armitage was sitting in a rocking chair close to the fire, smoking his pipe and staring solemnly into the flames. Seamus had disappeared outside, and Aurie could hear him chopping wood.

"I know you have a lot of questions to ask," Armitage said, puffing on his pipe. "But we'll talk tomorrow after we've all had a good night's sleep."

Aurie strolled over to Armitage, put her arms around his neck, and kissed him on his cheek, then she whistled to Torin and he followed her into her bedroom. She found a throw rug lying across the foot of her bed, and placed it on the floor. The young pup paced in a circle three or four times, plunked himself down and was soon snoring quietly. She opened a drawer in the armoire and found a nightgown, opened her bedroom window, and then snuggled deeply into the soft quilt. She stared at the stars twinkling in the sky, an owl hooted close by and a wolf howled in the distance.

Torin growled softly in his sleep, and Aurie rolled over and was soon fast asleep.

Chapter Thirteen

The morning sun streaming through the window warmed Aurie's face and arms as she contentedly ate a biscuit and drank a second cup of mint tea.

"Is this where you and Seamus live?" Aurie asked Armitage.

"Yes, this is our home, I have lived here for a very long time, and of course Seamus joined me a few years ago."

Aurie nodded, and then she reached inside her blouse and pulled out the pendant, she held it up to the rays and smiled when prisms of light bounced off the ceiling and walls.

"Do you mind if I have a look at your medallion again?" asked Armitage as he reached across the table. Aurie took it off and handed it to him. Armitage examined it closely, spoke softly, and pressed the stone in the middle of the cross, there was a light click and it sprung open. He handed the medallion back to Aurie, inside was an image of a man and a woman. The man had a strong face, deep violet eyes, and light brown hair, the woman was beautiful with long blond hair, silver eyes, and pointed ears.

Seamus rose from his chair and looked over Aurie's shoulder. "It's King Sebastian and Queen Elyse," he said, shaking his head in disbelief.

"Yes, I know," Armitage massaged his chin, a gesture Aurie had come to recognize to mean he was deep in thought. "When Aurie first showed me her medallion in the prison, I had a feeling I had seen the crest before and just now it triggered my memory. It's a family crest and the wording around the outside is a message."

Aurie stared intently at the image, and then she placed the medallion carefully on the table. "Why is there a likeness of King Sebastian and Queen Elyse in my medallion?"

"The cross and the gemstone, which is a crystal, are the joint crests of the House of Hawthorn and the House of Elderberry, representing the bonding of the two houses when King Sebastian and Queen Elyse married."

"What does the message say?"

"It says "The secret within can only be opened by royal blood. I think it is time we find out exactly what the secret is, come with me outside for a moment."

When they got to the front yard, Armitage asked Aurie to hold the medallion above her head with the crystal pointed toward the sun.

"I would ask you to repeat aloud these three words: solada, solana, solange."

Aurie stumbled with the first word, and then she relaxed, and began again.

At first, nothing happened, and then without warning the stone in the center of the pendant began to glow, a beam of light shot outwards, projecting an image. Floating in the air were full body imageries of King Sebastian and Queen Elyse. King Sebastian spoke:

"I am King Sebastian and this is Queen Elyse and you are our daughter Aurialana Edelyse Hawthorn. By now, you will have discovered how Prince Kalian slew our people, and those of us who survived fled into the mountains. Many of our people died while we were hiding, some from their wounds and others from hunger or illness. You were born shortly after the massacre. Prince Kalian was relentless in his pursuit and for many years, we lived in underground caves or in ramshackle shelters. Fearing for your safety, your mother and I arranged to leave you with a kindly couple who lived on a farm in Lindell Forest. Prince

Kalian was not aware of your birth and should anything happen to us your existence would remain unknown.

We left your guardians this enchanted medallion. If we had not found a safe haven and retrieved you by your fifth birthday, your guardians were to give it to you, with instructions that you never take it off. Cloaked by a protection shield, only someone with strong magical powers can open it.

If you are listening to this message, then our plans have failed and Lord Armitage will be with you. You must obey him at all costs, as he is a powerful magician and can teach you what you need to know. In the meantime, be patient, my daughter, and soon we will be together."

At the end of the message, the images disappeared. Aurie stood rooted to the spot, tears streaming down her face. Seamus put his arm around her shoulder and led her back inside the cottage. He handed her a cup of tea.

"No thanks," she said.

"It will do you good."

She sighed, took a sip, and almost immediately felt better.

Armitage had followed them inside, and was standing quietly by the hearth. "I believe I know why we have not been successful in finding the Ancients," he exclaimed, turning to face Seamus.

"According to the message," he continued. "The survivors were looking for a safe haven, and that could only mean they are no longer living on Earth."

"I don't follow you," Seamus said.

"There's only one place where they can be. They must have crossed over to Fey Wild. Queen Elyse always referred to Fey Wild as her safe haven."

"If that's the case, why didn't Eleanor mention it to us?"

"It was probably decided by King Esmond and King Sebastian to say nothing to anyone lest word get back to Prince Kalian. It is hard to know who your friends are and who your enemies are in these dire times."

"That still doesn't explain how Aurie came to be living at the castle," Seamus said. "Something must have happened to the couple taking care of her."

"Aurie," Armitage asked. "Do you recall anything about how or when you came to the castle?"

Aurie sat down on the stone mantel and rested her chin in her hands. "My first memory was the foundling home, and then working in the kitchen, carrying wood, scrubbing, milking the cows, that sort of thing," she said shaking her head. "I would have to have been around five or six years old to do those chores. I have no recollection of my life before that time. It's almost like it didn't exist."

Armitage massaged his chin. "Of course. It's your medallion," he said animatedly. "It all makes sense now. The cloaking enchantment on the medallion made you forget things from your past. It was your parents' way of protecting you, should you fall into Prince Kalian's hands. Now that the spell has been broken, your memories should start coming back to you."

"You said that Eleanor Elderberry was a royal princess of the Eldorans, and that Queen Elyse was her sister."

"Yes Aurie," Armitage replied, "which makes Eleanor your aunt. It seems you are not half-Elf at all, but rather half-Eldoran, and half-Ancient. That could explain your powers, having inherited them from both your mother and your father."

"Then why did Eleanor say she had not found her sister when you asked her when we were at her tree house?"

"Your parents must not have stayed in Fey Wild with the rest of the Ancients. I can only assume they returned to earth to continue their search for you, and something happened to them, thus the reason Eleanor remains and has not returned to Fey Wild. She will not stop until she has found them."

"Do you think they are dead?"

"No, I don't, child. Eleanor would have told us if that was the case. The Eldorans look at death differently than humans."

"Well, well Aurie. It seems you are a royal princess. How does that make you feel?"

"No different, I guess. I'm still just Aurie."

"Good," the burly man said. "Because you still have to do your chores around the cottage, and take care of that spoiled wolf pup."

Aurie grinned up at her friend, and then patted Torin, who had joined her at the hearth and was trying to climb onto her lap.

Armitage stared into the flames. "Now that we know what Prince Kalian is planning," he said, turning to look at Seamus. "I must talk to the tribes as soon as possible."

Seamus grunted. "Do you think they will listen to you?"

"They have known me for a long time, and know my words are to be trusted."

"Some of the leaders can be pretty stubborn, and they don't all get along with each other."

"They must put their petty quarrels aside, and understand how important it will be for them to join forces. If I am correct about the Fire Crystal, Prince Kalian will continue his destructive path. We must act now before he gets any stronger."

Armitage looked down at Aurie. "Starting tomorrow, your training begins. Now that the medallion is open, your parents will know you are with me and are safe. They will come when they are able to do so. In the meantime, we must be patient. We have much work to do."

Aurie sat quietly for a few moments, and then she rose and walked into her bedroom. Torin followed her inside, and she quietly closed the door.

Part II
Armitage's Army

Chapter Fourteen

"Concentrate, concentrate. If you don't try harder, you'll never learn to master that spell."

"I'm tired. We've been working on this for over four hours," Aurie moaned, as she turned and faced Armitage.

The patient wizard shook his head in frustration. "We'll do it for another four until you get it right. And we both know you don't get tired when you use your magic."

"Well I'm bored. Can we try the weather spell again?"

"Not until you practice a while longer. It's vital. What good would it do you if you were forced to use your magic, and you couldn't hit the side of a barn because you can't control your powers?"

"I know, but I just can't seem to get this spell to work."

"You must sense the kinetic energy, which is all around us, and use it to power your energy blasts. Then it is merely a matter of choosing what your target is."

Aurie slumped to the ground. "I don't even know what that means how can I possibly learn something I don't understand?"

"It is not intelligence you lack, my child, but confidence in your abilities. Manipulating the elements, accelerated healing, and telekinesis are wonderful powers to have, but they won't do you any good if you're facing Prince Kalian and he's using Dark Magic. Now, stand up and let's try again."

Realizing he would not back down Aurie doggedly rose, no matter how hard she tried, she just couldn't seem to control the energy blasts. Whenever she tried a disciplined spell, she would lose control, it was as if her mind was all jumbled and words kept bouncing all over the place. Since Armitage had taken on the role as her guardian and mentor over three years ago, her abilities had improved under his guidance, but for some reason this part of her training had caused her nothing but grief.

The sun had fallen behind the crest of the tallest cedar before Armitage allowed her to stop for the day. Aurie plodded wearily into the cottage, it was her turn to prepare supper, but she was too tired to cook a large meal. She realized how fortunate she was her magic did not drain her energy, Armitage said he knew of only one other wizard in his lifetime having that ability, and thought she probably inherited it through her mixed bloodline.

She fried the last of yesterday's potatoes and fish, and quickly set the table. She had never been a good cook or housekeeper, preferring to be outdoors. It was fortunate Seamus and Armitage were not overly concerned if the furniture was dusty, or the floors needed sweeping. Her bedroom generally looked like a cyclone had hit it, and Armitage discreetly suggested she keep the door closed, especially if guests were expected. At the beginning of her training, Aurie had tried to use her magic to whip up a quick meal, but it had been disastrous. She had burned the food so badly it took a week to get the smell of burned onions out of the cottage. Using her powers to tidy her bedroom was even more catastrophic. Her armoire had flown across the room and her bed had turned upside down and landed on top of Torin, who had been sleeping on his mat. He had run howling out of the cottage, and would not come from under the garden shed for two days. At that point Armitage had intervened, and had warned her that unless she was taking lessons from him, and unless it was a matter of life or death, she was not to use her magic again for such trivial matters.

At one time, when supplies were getting low, Aurie had asked Armitage why he didn't just conjure up more food. His answer was always the same. The forest provided a natural bounty of fish, wild herbs, berries and nuts, which they could eat until Seamus brought back the needed supplies the next time he went to Westcott.

Armitage poured himself a second cup of primrose tea, and walked over to the hearth and sat in his rocking chair. He stared moodily into the flames and began rubbing his chin, a sign he was deeply worried.

After she had finished washing and drying the dishes, Aurie set up her slate. Every evening she worked on her reading and figures, she had a lot of catching up to do as she had not received any schooling while she lived at the castle. Although she had always known how to read, the rest of her education had been sadly neglected.

A scratching at the front door interrupted her thoughts, she flung it open and Torin entered the room, walked over to Armitage's chair, pushed his nose against the wizard's arm in greeting, and then lay down next to the hearth. He had grown into a powerful wolf. His coat was charcoal in color with silver fur under his chin and down his chest, and deep blue eyes that shone with intelligence. Strangers kept well back from his snarling fangs, and Seamus generally found chores to do outside when Torin appeared at Primrose Cottage.

Aurie sat down next to her friend and wrapped her arms around his neck. He licked her faced, lowered his head and was soon asleep.

"I wonder why he's shown up so late in the evening." Aurie said.

"Torin comes and goes as he pleases," Armitage answered. "He probably senses something is amiss, as I have for the past few days."

"Is that why you've been worried?"

Armitage smiled, but did not answer.

"Animals have a sixth sense, don't they? Is that how Torin knows when something is wrong?"

"A few people have empathic capabilities as well," Armitage replied, as he took a sip of his tea. "Especially those who possess magic. You should try to sharpen that skill, as it could be very useful."

"I don't think I have it," Aurie replied, sighing deeply. "I can never tell if a person is upset, or happy or for that matter, angry with me."

"That's because you never pay attention to what is happening around you, that's half the reason why you have problems mastering certain spells."

Aurie did not answer, as she knew Armitage was right. She reached over and patted Torin's head. "You don't think he'd hurt anyone, do you?"

"As long as they don't threaten you. You're the one who found and nurtured him and as far as he's concerned, you're a member of his pack."

Aurie stood up and walked over to the window, she stared outside at the darkness, deep in thought.

"You're worried about Prince Kalian, aren't you?" she asked, turning to face Armitage. "Do you think he knows where we are?"

"If he did, he would have shown up by now," Armitage grunted, as he rose from his chair. "It's getting late, Aurie, and tomorrow we have much to do."

Aurie yawned, relieved at getting out of doing her studies. She headed towards her bedroom, Torin opened his eyes, rose and followed. As she was closing her door, Armitage commented "You can do your lessons first thing in the morning before you start working on your magic. Good night Aurie."

Aurie leaned against the door and groaned quietly. She flung herself across her bed and stared at the ceiling. Muffled voices came from the other room, and she assumed Seamus had come inside and joined Armitage. Creeping quietly over to the door she opened it slightly, but could not see the two men from where she was standing although she could hear them talking.

"It's almost three years since Aurie first came here," Armitage said quietly. "Magic comes to her naturally, but she lacks self confidence in her abilities, which makes it difficult for her to learn the more intricate spells. Once she has mastered them, I feel she will be close to completing her first level of training."

Aurie felt a twinge of guilt, not only because she knew it was wrong to listen to their private conversation, but because she realized Armitage was referring to her inability to control her spells. She vowed she would work harder, first thing in the morning.

"Whitehawk Pass will open soon," Seamus said. "Most of the snow has melted, and the roads will be passable again. I must get to Westcott before Prince Kalian deploys his troops and sets up sentinels at the pass."

"He will never cease looking," Armitage murmured. "Although I have tried to keep Aurie's whereabouts a secret, I do not doubt he knows where we are. She poses a great threat to him, not only for her growing abilities but as the rightful heir to the throne. He must have deduced her powers would only grow over time, especially under my tutelage."

"There have been numerous reports of aberrant creatures being seen in Lindell Forest," Seamus commented. "At first their activities were restricted to the higher elevations, but they have become bolder, and now hunt in the valleys and along the river."

"Yes, I have sensed their presence."

"The magical folks are terrified, and do not wander far from their homes."

"Perhaps this will convince them as they have turned a deaf ear to my warnings. It has been a long time since the Magic War, and there are not many left who can remember the thousands who died and the desolation it caused. The clans do not have the means of protecting themselves as they have become complacent, and have not kept up their fighting skills."

Seamus grunted, and then Aurie heard a shuffling sound and a chair scraping across the floor. "It's getting late my friend. I believe I will retire as I plan to rise early. Good night, Seamus. Good night Aurie, sleep well."

Aurie quickly closed her door, but not before she heard Seamus' gravelly laugh. Armitage had been aware she was listening to their entire conversation. She jumped into bed, pulling her quilt up under her chin, finding it hard to believe so much time had passed and in a few weeks, she would turn fifteen.

As Armitage had predicted, after she had opened the message in her medallion, her memories had slowly returned. She would suddenly recall an event or a fleeting conversation, she remembered going to live with her guardians at a farm, and her parents visiting, sometimes months would go by before they returned. One day, a battalion of soldiers had attacked and she remembered the flames, the smoke and the screams, and now knew what had happened to her guardians. Their deaths must have affected her strongly, as she had blocked out the entire event over the years, and only now was she beginning to remember.

The most surprising revelation was when Eleanor Elderberry had finally admitted to Armitage that King Sebastian and Queen Elyse, as well as the last surviving Ancients, had indeed taken refuge in Fey Wild. Although it was unprecedented, Queen Elyse had sought asylum with the Eldorans. Surprisingly, her father King Esmond had consented, and they, along with the remaining Ancients, now resided in Fey Wild.

Also, as Armitage had thought, King Sebastian and Queen Elyse had returned to Earth to retrieve their daughter. Finding the charred remains of the guardians and the smoldering shell of the farm house, they were unable to find Aurie. All traces of her had vanished. They never gave up hope she had survived and they returned to Earth time and again, searching everywhere for her. When they failed to return after one of their quests, it was feared they had met foul play. Eleanor and two powerful warriors from Fey Wild had searched everywhere for them, but to no avail. Eleanor told Aurie she sensed her sister was still alive, and felt that one day they would be reunited.

When Aurie had spoken of her capture, ending up in a foundling home, and eventually becoming a slave at the castle, Eleanor's face had turned a deep shade of red, and she had grasped the hilt of her long-sword tightly, saying nothing. It was not until later Aurie came to understand why her aunt had reacted so violently to what Aurie had told her.

Discovering Eleanor was her aunt gave her a sense of belonging, knowing she was not alone in the world, and although she had never met her Eldoran grandparents, she hoped one day she would have the opportunity. She had been named after her grandmother, Queen Edelyse and Eleanor visited Primrose Cottage often, proudly passing on stories to Aurie about the Eldorans and the indescribable beauty of Fey Wild. Aurie had become very close to the powerful sorceress.

Torin rolled over in his sleep and snorted. Aurie smiled, comforted by his presence, she closed her eyes and was soon asleep.

Chapter Fifteen

The snow slowly melted and buds at last appeared on the crab apple and cherry trees, a few early wildflowers appeared in the meadow.

On her fifteenth birthday Armitage threw a surprise party for Aurie. Her closest friends Bluebell, who was a Faerie, and Phineas, a mischievous Pixie, arrived with their families early in the day. Many of the guests brought delicious food made from the herbs, roots and wildflowers growing in Lindell Forest, as well there was pheasant stuffed with wild chives and chestnuts, turnip roots and water parsnip stews flavored with pennycress and hyssops, strawberry and bunchberry scones and dandelion and violet salads. Seamus had made a huge kettle of mint tea, and he circulated among their guests, ensuring their mugs were kept full.

Aurie dressed in one of her gowns, it was a pale shade of lilac, and had a square neckline with flowers embroidered around the sleeves and hem. She had woven violets, matching the color of her eyes, through her hair, and her amulet hung around her neck. Seamus teased her about finally looking like a young lady and not a young lad, and Aurie giggled at his silliness. It was not often he or Armitage saw her in a gown, as she preferred the comfort and ease of wearing leggings and shirts.

Aurie was delighted when Eleanor appeared over the crest of the meadow, gliding gracefully towards the gathering. The guests stopped talking as they watched the arrival of the regal Eldoran. After Eleanor had greeted Aurie, the elusive sorceress joined Armitage and the leaders of the clans, who were sitting in a small group talking quietly. It was not often an Eldoran travelled to Earth, and most of the magical folks in Lindell Forest were not aware Eleanor spent a lot of time on this plane, residing in her tree house near Bloodroot Swamp. Her reputation as a powerful sorceress and warrior was well known to everyone and more than one guest was in awe, having never seen a High Elf.

The guests mingled while Phineas perched on a tree branch, playing his flute. Later, the three friends strolled over to the huge willow growing next to the stream. Aurie lay down on the grass, and Phineas leaned back against the gnarled trunk, Bluebell, who had changed back to her Faerie size, was perched on Aurie's knee. The energetic Pixie, much to Aurie's and Bluebell's annoyance, blew on a blade of grass, making shrill squeaky sounds.

"What do you think they're talking about?" Phineas asked, gesturing towards the small gathering of elders.

"What else?" Bluebell answered. "Doom and gloom."

"Oh yeah, Prince Kalian and his army of monsters and magical beasts," Phineas said, changing his voice to make it sound eerie.

Bluebell covered her mouth with her tiny hands and giggled, Aurie loved hearing her friend's laughter as it reminded her of tiny, tinkling bells.

"You shouldn't joke about that sort of thing," Aurie whispered, as a shiver ran down her back. "It's bad luck."

"Don't tell me you believe all those stories," Phineas asked jeeringly. "My dad says everyone is panicking over nothing, and that Prince Kalian doesn't have the power to do anything except call up a few elementals and magical beasts, nothing we magical folk can't handle."

"That's not true, I know for a fact Prince Kalian's getting more powerful all the time, and he's practicing

Dark Magic. Why would he be doing that unless he is planning something terrible?"

"Well, I don't think we should worry about it. Come on let's see if there are any scones left, I'm hungry." Phineas retorted, as he jumped up and ran in the direction of the cottage. Bluebell rolled her eyes and beating her silvery wings rose into the air and followed him.

Aurie was greatly disturbed by her friends' attitudes, and was beginning to understand why Armitage was so frustrated in his endeavors to forewarn the clans. What would it take for them to start listening to the High Wizard's warnings?

Soon the merrymaking was over, and the guests prepared to leave, many of them had a long journey ahead of them and did not want to be travelling after sunset. Aurie promised Bluebell and Phineas that she would see them again soon, and watched as the last of the guests disappeared into the forest. Eleanor remained and visited with her, and as a creature of the night, she had no fear travelling alone after the sun fell behind the mountains.

A few days later, Seamus arrived back at the cottage from one of his scouting trips. He announced Whitehawk Pass was open and he would be leaving within the hour. Although it was not the only route to get to Westcott, the pass was the quickest way to travel. Scaling Beargrass Mountain and cutting through Bloodroot Swamp was a safer route, but added on an extra day of travel. Seamus was a wily warrior and would have no difficulty evading the soldiers.

Armitage picked up his pace in Aurie's training. Overhearing Armitage's comment regarding her lack of self-confidence gave her the drive to work all the harder, but the control spell still eluded her. She sensed Armitage's frustration when she failed and she spent many nights in her bed, tossing and turning, hoping the answer would magically come to her.

Early one morning the wizard announced she was to accompany him into Lindell Forest, advising they would be gone for a while. When Aurie raced to her room to retrieve her backpack, he called her back and told her she was not to take any provisions. They headed across the meadow, and as Primrose Cottage disappeared from her view, she had a sinking feeling in the pit of her stomach.

They walked for hours, traversing deeper and deeper into the woods, Armitage walked ahead of her, not stopping as was his procedure to lecture or point out landmarks or herbs that he thought might interest her. Eventually they arrived at a large copse where water from an underground stream flowed into a dark pool. Armitage approached the pond and raised his staff, at first nothing happened, then suddenly the water began to roil and a plume rose upwards. In the center was a sinuous creature covered in green scales, with eyes the color of mud, its tongue flicking in and out of its mouth.

"To what am I owed this visit from the illustrious Lord Armitage?" the repulsive beast hissed.

"Greetings Finian," Armitage answered, stepping closer. "I come seeking information."

"I am flattered that you think I can be of assistance to one as powerful as yourself, oh mighty seer."

"Glib tongued as ever, I see."

Finian hissed, and then leaned towards Armitage. "What did you bring to bargain with?"

Armitage reached under his robe and extracted a package wrapped in a black cloth, laid it on the ground and unfolded it. Inside was a glistening gemstone and Finian's tongue flicked greedily when he saw the offered token.

"A mere bauble, what would I want with something as insignificant as this?"

"Forgive me," Armitage murmured. "I do not wish to insult you or take up your precious time, I hear Sorrell, King of the Marshes, has returned from his travels, and would be privy to the information I seek. Perhaps I should talk to him?"

Finian let out an intimidating hiss. "Do not trifle with me Sage. Do you think I am not aware of the game you play? No one knows more of what is happening in Lindell Forest than I."

"Then do we have a bargain?"

Finian hissed again, leaned over and snatched the gem from the ground. "What is it you wish to know?"

Aurie marveled at Armitage's ingenuity in coercing the sinister beast into accepting the jewel, but she hoped that the information he was seeking was worth the value of the gemstone.

"I sense disorder in the magic realm, Dangerous monsters and aberrant creatures from the Underworld have been seen on Earth." Armitage began.

"Yessss, that is true. But if anyone is aware of these occurrences, it would be you, Lord Armitage? What do you really wish to know?"

"Where is the portal located?"

"Portal? Of what portal do you speak?"

"The portal to the Underworld, you treacherous bog beast, the one Prince Kalian has opened. Need I remind you that we have made a bargain, and if you do not keep it, you will be in my debt forever?"

Finian turned a deep shade of grey, then a murky brown. "I do not need to be reminded of my obligation, oh mighty seer. The portal you seek is in the Fire Cave. The Abyss is the entrance to the Underworld. It has been opened by the Evil Lord."

Aurie saw the look on Armitage's face, and knew he was surprised at what Finian had just divulged about the portal. Apparently Owain, a mighty dragon that lived in the Abyss, had his own secrets, even from his best friends.

"What has happened to Owain the Guardian of the Abyss?" Armitage asked sharply. "And speak truthfully. I will know if you mislead me."

"It is said he fought bravely and stoutly, but he was greatly outnumbered by the Evil Lord and his summoned creatures. He barely managed to escape with his life."

"Where has he gone?"

"He dwells in a cave at the top of Beargrass Mountain. The Evil Lord sent out his creatures to find him, but Owain is wily. A dragon cannot be found unless it wishes to be found, especially one as powerful as Owain."

Aurie did not realize she had been holding her breath, and she sighed in relief on hearing the dragon was safe.

Armitage stepped back from the pool, signaling that his interview had come to an end.

"Who is this creature accompanying you? We have not been introduced." Finian asked, leaning down and stopping a few inches from Aurie's face, looking piercingly into her eyes. Aurie thought he smelled like a swamp on a sweltering day.

"Ah, I do apologize for my ill manners," Armitage responded. "This is Princess Aurialana, daughter of King Sebastian of the House of Hawthorne and Queen Elyse of the House of Elderberry."

"I did not know there was a child of their union? Does she possess magical abilities?"

"Some, but she is slow to learn and lazy. Her powers are weak and ..."

Finian coiled upward, a look of anger crossing his face. "I can sense her powers, you cagey Mage. What secrets are you harboring?"

Aurie listened intently to the interchange, wondering what the wizard was up to.

"I should have realized I could not fool you Finian. Indeed, with her Ancient and Eldoran bloodline, she is a great sorceress and her powers are remarkable. But I beg of you, please do not tell anyone of her existence. I do not wish the Evil Lord to find out that a powerful sorceress resides in Lindell Forest."

"You can be assured I will say nothing. Your secret is safe with me," Finian responded, as he slithered back into the dark pool and disappeared.

"Will he keep his promise?" Aurie questioned.

"Absolutely not, and I am counting on just that."

"But I heard you tell Seamus that Prince Kalian already knows about me."

"True, but Finian is not aware of that. However, not everyone in Lindell Forest knows of your existence, or about your terrifying powers," Armitage answered, smiling at the perplexed look on Aurie's face. "I'm hoping once they realize an Eldoran sorceress of the House of Elderberry is living in Lindell Forest and under my tutelage, I will gain their confidence and perhaps they will heed my warnings."

Aurie nodded, although she still could not see the logic behind Armitage's ruse. It would not take the leaders of the tribes long to realize that Aurie's powers were not in the least powerful, let alone intimidating. However, she did not question his actions as Armitage did nothing unless it had a purpose.

"Why didn't Owain tell you about the portal?" she asked. "And how did Prince Kalian find out about it?"

"Those are answers I do not have," Armitage replied. "Come. We still have much to do and it is getting late in the day."

With those words Armitage turned and headed back into the forest. Aurie picked up her pace, she knew better than to ask him where they are going, and wondered what he was up to. The next few days could prove to be quite interesting.

Chapter Sixteen

They walked for hours, passing heaths covered in bracken, cedars draped in moss and lichen, and stagnant water holes.

The shadows lengthened and the warmth created by the rays of the sun gradually dissipated, a mist had risen, drifting around the branches of the stalwart pines. Aurie shivered in her light clothing, and she thought of her warm jacket hanging in her armoire.

Eventually they arrived at a small clearing, surrounded by massive cedars and pine. Armitage approached a large boulder and lowered himself to the ground, sighing as he rested his back against the stone. Aurie started to sit, but he shook his head and pointed into the trees.

"We will make camp here for the night. Gather some kindling and branches for a fire."

Aurie peered anxiously into the shadows, her deep rooted fear of the darkness making her nervous. She turned and looked at Armitage, but he had his head down and was staring at the ground.

Aurie walked nervously into the dense bush, and stopped next to a cedar. Armitage had not said she couldn't use her magic, and she quickly conjured an orb, it gave enough light for her to scrutinize the surrounding area. Soon she returned to the clearing with her arms full of branches and twigs and threw them in a pile next to Armitage. She sat down, and waited for him to start the fire, he did not move, and she realized he expected her to attend to the chore. She remembered what Seamus had done to start a fire in their pit back home, he had piled the twigs into the shape of a tent, and then he had stuffed moss and kindling inside. Deciding that was too much bother, she used her magic, and soon had a fire burning brightly. She leaned over and warmed her hands over the flames, sighing contentedly.

"There's not enough light left to look for food," Armitage muttered, as he rolled over and wrapped his cloak around his thin frame. "We'll have to wait until the morning."

"But, but...."

"Make sure the fire doesn't go out. You never know what might be lurking in the shadows. Good night, Aurie."

"Goodnight My Lord," she whispered

"And Aurie, I don't want you using your magic again until I say you can."

At first Aurie was too stunned to answer. But when Armitage started snoring, she realized the wizard meant what he had said. The ground was cold, rocky and unyielding, and soon she was shivering, she stoked the embers, and threw some more branches into the flames. A twig snapped in the trees, and she sat up in alarm and stared into the blackness, expecting any moment to be attacked and devoured by a ferocious creature. The fire had gone out, and all the wood supply was gone.

As magic was off-limits, she decided it would be too dangerous to venture into the forest on her own, lying as close to Armitage as she could, she curled up into a tight ball and tried to get some sleep.

At last the sun rose, and the forest awoke. A scuffling noise from the bushes caught her attention and a rabbit shot out into the open, she stood up quickly and raised her arm, pointing it at the startled animal. Suddenly Armitage' hand was resting on her arm. "No. Find food without using your magic." he said.

"But you use your magic all the time when we are camping."

"That is true, but you are a novice, a student of magic, while I have been a High Wizard for over six hundred years. When you have learned to master your skills then you will have earned the right to use your magic for whatever pleases you, but for now, you will do as I say."

"Yes Master."

"You must learn to survive on the bounty nature provides for us. There may be a time in your life when you cannot or are unable to use your powers, and it could mean the difference between life and death."

Armitage rose and walked away from the clearing. "Come, I am hungry."

They stayed in Lindell Forest for over a week. The wizard showed her how to make snares to catch prey, how to catch fish from the flowing streams by building a trap, how to start a fire with a stone flint and how to make a comfortable bed out of dead leaves and moss. He pointed out the plants, berries and herbs that were edible and those that were poisonous. The nights became warmer and the snow lying under the rocks and in the deep crevices began to melt. Wild crocuses appeared along the banks of the streams, and Aurie spied tiny violets growing behind rocks and under ferns.

They were sitting around a campfire early one morning drinking cedar bark tea and roasting a partridge that Aurie had snared the evening before. She found the tea bitter and had never acquired a taste for it, but it helped to take away the early morning chill.

Armitage announced it was time to return to Primrose Cottage, as Seamus would have returned from Westcott, and he wanted to see if he had gleaned any news regarding Prince Kalian. After they had eaten, and cleaned up their campsite, they began their long trek home. By late afternoon, Aurie spotted smoke rising in the distance. They followed a path skirting a lake, and when they arrived at a large field, she realized they were home. She raced happily across the meadow, and when she arrived at Primrose Cottage, she flung open the door. Seamus was sitting at the table drinking a cup of tea, and seated next to him was a striking young woman with sparkling green eyes and long auburn hair. She had a dark bruise on her cheek.

Aurie stared in astonishment, approached the table and whispered "Jasmine?"

The young woman rose and smiled, Aurie was stunned when she did not recognize her.

"It's me, Aurie."

"I'm sorry, but have we met?"

Aurie remembered the last time Jasmine had seen her, she was disguised as a young boy, and had never seen her without her cap pulled down over her ears and covering most of her face.

"You knew me as Aurie Mundy, and I used to work for you at the bakery, almost three years ago."

"I do remember a young boy by the name of Aurie, but he left quite unexpectedly. I assumed he had moved away with his family."

"That was me. There was no family. I made all of it up."

"I'm not sure what to say. You must have had your reasons in posing as a lad and keeping your identity from me, although now that I have had a chance to look at you, I must admit your appearance has not changed all that much. I see you are still wearing leggings and shirts."

Aurie grinned at Jasmine's comment, and Seamus grunted as he took a drink. Her choice of clothing was always an issue with him, as he felt she should wear dresses more often, although at times he reluctantly admitted it was more practical for her to wear boy's clothing.

"I had to leave in a hurry," Aurie said. "Lots of things happened."

Jasmine nodded but did not pursue the matter.

At that point, Armitage entered the cabin, strolled over to the table, poured himself a cup of tea, then sat in his rocking chair next to the hearth.

"Seamus, I see we have a house guest. Why don't you introduce us?"

"This is Jasmine Bates, My Lord."

"My Lord," Jasmine replied. She curtsied low, immediately recognizing Armitage as a man of power and authority.

Aurie sat down at the table, gesturing Jasmine to do the same. She poured tea into a mug and took a drink, enjoying the flavor of the mint over the bark tea she had been drinking for the past week.

"How is it that Jasmine has come into your company?" Armitage asked Seamus.

"Why don't you tell your story," Seamus said, looking at Jasmine. "I always forget the most important parts."

Jasmine nodded, smiling at Seamus. "I was an indentured servant to a vile man by the name of Nathan Trent and I ran away and found work at the Wild Boar Inn. Jack Mudd, my dear friend passed away and I was left alone to manage Trent's bakery, and the work was unbearable. I still have two years left before my indenture is paid off, but Trent can be very abusive, and I feared for my safety. The owner of the Wild Boar Inn had no love for Trent, as his reputation was well known in most of the ale houses in Westcott. After a long discussion between Trent and the innkeeper, it was agreed I would be permitted to keep my job, on the condition I paid half of my earnings to Trent to help pay off my servitude. I don't care how long it takes, as long as I don't have to go back to the bakery, and live under Trent's roof."

"Nathan Trent was the reason I left in such a hurry," Aurie said, interrupting Jasmine. "I recognized his voice when I met him in the bakery, I had overheard him and Mrs. Black, who's the head cook at the castle and who had seen me using my powers, making plans to turn me over to Prince Kalian for a reward. I ran away, and that's why I ended up in the streets."

"That doesn't surprise me a bit, Aurie," Jasmine said, as she stared into the fireplace. "Greed has always been his master."

"Please continue Jasmine," Armitage said.

"One day he and a few of his sleazy companions came into the inn, I saw the way he was looking at me, so I tried to escape out the back door, but he grabbed me before I could get away, and started to get rough. When I fought back, he got so angry he punched me in the face. That's how I got this," Jasmine said, placing her hand on her cheek.

For a few seconds, there was silence in the room.

"I was terrified," Jasmine continued, "and I knew I wouldn't get any help from the patrons in the pub. None of them would have the courage to start anything with Trent and his drunken friends, most of whom were Prince Kalian's soldiers. Thankfully, Seamus came to my rescue. I had met him a few years back when he had a booth at the marketplace."

"You know how I feel about any man coward enough to hit a woman," Seamus said angrily. "I would have gladly stayed and finished off the whole mob of them, but giving Trent what he deserved was satisfaction enough. I didn't want to make any more of a scene, especially as I prefer keeping a low profile. I'm not sure if I was recognized or not but you can be sure I'll not be forgotten."

"You could have done nothing else," Armitage said. "I'm just glad you were there to help. Aurie, why don't you take Jasmine to your room? Both of you might want to freshen up before we eat, and you can get reacquainted."

Aurie led Jasmine into her bedroom, and did not notice the look of amusement on the young woman's face when she saw the state of disarray. The bed was unmade, and there were clothes draped over the chairs and piled in the middle of the room, she opened the door to her armoire and Jasmine's mouth dropped in amazement at the sight of the silken gowns, velvet jackets, kirtles and lace chemises stuffed untidily on the shelves. Aurie opened a side drawer and grabbed a pair of clean leggings and a shirt. She poured water into the basin sitting on her night table and used her magic to warm the water. It felt wonderful after bathing in icy mountain streams for the past week.

"If you like you can wash up here, there's lots of water in the pitcher," she said to Jasmine. "I'd give you some clean clothing, but I don't think any of my dresses will fit you."

"No, you're still very slender, and you're taller than I am."

Jasmine had matured in the past three years and was now a young woman, and if possible, even more beautiful. Aurie looked in her mirror and glanced quickly at her reflection, with her hair tied back in a braid and dressed in her usual attire, she looked exactly how she was dressed, like a tall, thin boy.

"I hate gowns and fancy dresses," Aurie said too quickly.

Jasmine nodded, but said nothing. She continued to stare at Aurie, and Aurie suddenly realized that her appearance must be quite shocking to Jasmine. This was the first time she had seen Aurie's entire face. Learning she was a girl and now noticing the shape of her ears and the color of her hair and eyes, would be enough to unsettle anyone.

"Besides, Armitage makes me dress in gowns when we have company," Aurie muttered. "He says I have to portray a proper image."

"Why would he say something like that?"

"Because of who I am, I guess," Aurie replied, as she sat down on the unmade bed and pulled on her boots. "King Sebastian and Queen Elyse are my parents."

"Are you saying you're a princess?"

"Yes, I suppose I am, although I never really think about it. As you can see, there's no castle or beautiful gowns or jewelry, I'm just as poor as I ever was."

Jasmine once again looked around the room and raised her eyebrows, smiling at Aurie's comment.

"Armitage is my teacher and mentor. He's been training me for the past three years," Aurie continued.

"Training you in what?"

"Magic, sorcery. I'm a sorceress, or I will be one day."

The stunned look on Jasmine's faces made Aurie uncomfortable. "That's why I disappeared. When it was discovered I could do magic, I was turned over to Prince Kalian and thrown into his dungeon, and Seamus and Armitage rescued me and brought me here."

There was a sharp rap on the door, and both girls jumped. "Come in." Aurie said.

The door opened and Seamus poked his head inside. "When you two are finished gabbing, you better come and have a bite to eat."

"I'll be right out," Jasmine said as Aurie jumped off the bed. "I just want to wash up."

Supper consisted of tea and biscuits, and black currants and gooseberries.

"We can thank Jasmine for the berries," Seamus informed them. "We didn't pass a bush or plant without her stopping to fill her apron pockets."

"I see you are a very resourceful young lady," Armitage said. "We thank you for your thoughtfulness."

Jasmine blushed prettily, relishing the compliment from the elderly man. Throughout the meal, she would glance over at Aurie, then lower her head and concentrate on her food.

After supper, Aurie and Jasmine cleared the table and washed the dishes. Aurie happily noticed the larder had been stocked with supplies, she filled her mug with tea, and then she went and sat on the doorstep, hoping to catch the last rays of the day. Jasmine remained in the kitchen, cleaning the counters, and tidying up.

Aurie was half listening to what Seamus was telling Armitage, when she overheard a familiar name. She jerked, spilling tea over her hand.

"And you said their leader goes by the name of Tony Drummond?" Armitage asked.

Seamus nodded. "From overhearing the soldiers talking, apparently, they live on the streets, and call themselves the Falcons."

Aurie stood up and walked into the room, approached the table, and sat down. Armitage and Seamus stopped talking and stared at her.

"You're as white as a ghost," Armitage said. "Is something wrong?"

"I know Tony Drummond, and I know where he lives."

Armitage looked directly at Aurie, a questioning look on his face.

"Tony's the boy who saved me from the soldiers when I ran away from the castle. He lives in an abandoned warehouse down by the wharf, there's a back entrance that leads into the side of the mountain, it's full of tunnels and passageways and you could wander for days in them if you don't know where you're going. I remember thinking that when he led me through them."

"Sounds as if these young insurgents have means of evading the soldiers if they had to," Armitage commented.

"Probably, and I know where Tony works. He's a groom at the horse stables at the castle, he's the only one who can handle Cesar, Prince Kalian's war horse."

Seamus laughed loudly, shaking his head in wonderment. "I'm beginning to like this young man more and more all the time, planting himself right under Prince Kalian's nose, and all the while organizing a group of rebels."

"It appears we may have help from an unexpected source in Westcott," Armitage pondered. "We must keep an eye on the Falcons."

"I would be very careful in putting your trust in Tony Drummond." Aurie interjected.

"Now why would you say something like that?" Seamus asked, looking questionably at her.

"He's the one who turned me in to Prince Kalian," She said bitterly. "And I ended up a prisoner in the dungeons."

Aurie turned and walked towards her bedroom closing the door quietly, but not before she noticed Armitage's troubled look.

Chapter Seventeen

Jasmine spent most of her time indoors and soon Primrose Cottage was spotless. The biggest change was in Aurie's room, as Jasmine had cleaned, folded and hung Aurie's gowns and shifts in the armoire. It turned out she was a wonderful cook and baked the most delicious buns and bread, her years of working in the bakery soon evident to everyone.

As there were no other bedrooms in the small cottage, the two girls shared the same room. Aurie gave Jasmine some of her dresses and shifts, at first Jasmine refused to take them, as she felt they were far too exquisite for her to own. Aurie assured her the moths would get better use out of them than she if she didn't use them, so Jasmine reluctantly accepted the generous gift. As it was, Jasmine proved to be a very competent seamstress, and soon she had altered the gowns to fit. Secretly Aurie felt Jasmine did them more justice than she ever would.

From the very start, Jasmine slept on a pallet on the floor, adamantly refusing to share Aurie's bed. When Aurie insisted, the young woman admitted she was quite comfortable. Although the two girls soon became friends, Jasmine never quite let her guard down when she was around Aurie. Aurie wondered if it might have something to do with her discovering Aurie was not only a sorceress but also a royal princess.

The first time Torin strolled into their bedroom Jasmine hastily removed her pallet and set it up next to the hearth. Aurie assured her that the friendly wolf would not harm her, but Jasmine stayed clear of the enormous animal.

Seamus understood her sentiments, and sagely agreed she had made a sensible decision.

When Armitage travelled throughout Lindell Forest visiting the villages and meeting with the clan leaders, Aurie always accompanied him. Word of her magical prowess was spreading quickly, just as Armitage had predicted. Aurie disliked being under scrutiny, and when she complained to Armitage, he reproached her impatience, reminding her of her royal status. There was a possibility she would one day rule the kingdom and as she was both Ancient and Eldoran, she would need the loyalty of not only the residents of Westcott but of the magical tribes as well.

Aurie learned to manipulate the elements, summoning up the clouds to create rain, conjuring up lightning that shattered the heavens. She discovered where to find wild herbs and plants and how to make potions and tinctures. Yet no matter how hard she tried, she could not master the more intricate spells, and she could sense Armitage was becoming more and more exasperated with her.

It was purely by accident that one of her most astonishing abilities was revealed. Armitage had placed a row of acorns on top of a fallen tree trunk, approximately fifty yards away, and instructed Aurie to hit them. At the last second, she lost her train of thought, sparks shot across the yard, hitting the side of a huge pine tree far off to the left of her target. Seamus, walking towards the woodpile with his arms full of wood, barely escaped injury when a large branch came dislodged and missed hitting him by a couple of inches. He roared in anger, dropping his load of wood.

"Seamus," Aurie said in shock. "That's not a nice thing to say."

The burly man stopped and turned abruptly. "What do you mean?"

"You just said I had the brains of a slug and I was more dangerous than having an ogre as a playmate."

"How did you know I said that?"

"I heard you say it."

"Aurie, I didn't say it, but I thought it."

For a few seconds there was absolute silence, Armitage approached Aurie and placed his hand on her forehead and closed his eyes. Aurie stood frozen, wondering what was happening. He lowered his hand and sighed. "How long have you been able to read other people's thoughts?"

"I didn't know that's what I was doing," Aurie shrugged. "Words just pop up in my head out of nowhere."

"That explains a lot, and puts a whole new perspective on your training," Armitage sighed.

"Does that mean I've reached my highest level in magic?"

"Not at all, it's the exact opposite. Telepathy is a powerful gift. Once you have developed your mental and intuitive abilities, then you shouldn't have any difficulty in concentrating and learning the more intricate spells."

"Wonderful," Seamus said. "Now I have to think wonderful things about her all the time or she'll turn me into a toad."

Aurie laughed at her friend. "Don't worry Seamus. I haven't learned how to do shape shifting yet, so you should be okay for a while."

Seamus grunted as he picked up the scattered wood.

"Aurie, this is a very powerful gift," Armitage said. "But it is wrong to penetrate into someone's private thoughts. Heed me, you must never abuse it."

"Yes Master."

"And you must never try to use it on someone who has strong magical abilities, they will sense immediately what you are doing, and could retaliate before you have time to protect yourself. I am talking about Prince Kalian, he would prove to be a very dangerous adversary if you attempted to use it on him."

Sometimes there were times Aurie wished she did not have magical powers. If she could have known what was in store for her in the future, she would never have felt that way.

Chapter Eighteen

A few days later, while Aurie was sitting in the doorway enjoying the warmth of the sun, a figure appeared in the distance.

"It's Eleanor," she shouted excitedly, as she stood, covering her eyes from the bright rays.

Armitage appeared in the doorway and calmly waited for the willowy Eldoran to cross the meadow. They greeted each other cordially and then Eleanor hugged Aurie.

"I see you have grown another inch since last I saw you, young niece. At this rate, you'll be taller than Seamus and he's practically the size of an ogre."

Seamus had just come around the corner of the cottage and heard Eleanor's words. "Should have known trouble was here, the sky suddenly turned dark, and the birds stopped singing."

Eleanor laughed at Seamus' ribbing. When the two of them had first met, Seamus had found her abrasive and overbearing, but over the past three years, he had come to know her well, and had discovered that under her hard steely demeanor beat a heart of gold. Her affection for Aurie was genuine and Seamus knew she would protect the young girl to the death.

Eleanor followed everyone inside the cottage. Jasmine, who was standing at the counter drying a plate, stared at the sorceress in disbelief. Armitage introduced the two women. Jasmine stuttered a reply, and curtsied to the enchanting creature. Eleanor removed her travelling cloak and a bundle she was carrying on her back, and placed them at the foot of Seamus' bed. Soon everyone was drinking elderberry tea and eating the scones that Jasmine had placed on the table.

"How fares your father?" Armitage enquired of Eleanor.

"He sends you his greetings, Sage. Progress is being made each day, although not fast enough to his liking."

"Splendid, splendid. And to what do we owe this visit?"

"I wish to take Aurie back with me to Fey Wild."

Armitage laid his cup down on the table, shaking his head in refusal.

"Hear me out," Eleanor said. "I know she's in the middle of her training, and I promise to continue her lessons personally."

"This is a very crucial time for Aurie. Surely you are aware of that Eleanor?"

"My father and mother wish to meet their granddaughter. She is a young woman now, and they regret not having known her while she was growing up. I will teach her weaponry, and how to use the long sword, an Eldoran's weapon of choice. She should learn our ways as well as the Ancients, as one day she will be given the choice to choose which path she wishes to follow."

"I agree Eleanor, but Aurie is very close to completing her first level of training."

"If she is to become proficient in weaponry, she must start her training as soon as possible, most Eldoran children start training when they are very young. It is as important a skill as learning magic."

Armitage nodded in agreement. "Let Aurie complete her first level of studies, and then she may go with you to Fey Wild."

At first Eleanor did not answer, and Aurie could see that she was not pleased with Armitage's suggestion.

"The reason I wish Aurie to remain with me for a while longer is because I have just discovered she has telepathic abilities. I feel once she has learned to control that skill she will progress at a faster pace."

"I will agree with your proposal, Sage, but my father and mother will not be pleased, they were looking forward to meeting and getting to know their granddaughter."

"Aurie, you're old enough now to make your own decisions," Armitage responded, turning in his seat and facing her. "How do you feel about this?"

Aurie shifted nervously in her chair. Being placed in the middle made her uncomfortable, she did not want to disappoint either of them.

"I think Armitage is right. I must learn to take control of my powers before I learn anything new. Eleanor, I do so want to go with you to Fey Wild, and I promise to practice extra hard so that the next time you visit, I will be ready to return with you."

Eleanor shook her head, and then poured herself a second cup of tea.

"I can see I'm no match for either of you. And by the way, these scones are delicious."

"Jasmine baked them," Aurie said, pointing at the flustered girl.

"I see she is a good housekeeper," Eleanor added, as she surveyed the tidy room. "I trust you have been watching and learning from her, my niece."

Aurie laughed at her aunt's comment, relieved she was not angry at her for deciding to stay with Armitage. For the remainder of the day, she showed Eleanor how far she had progressed in her training, and listened intently when her aunt gave her suggestions and pointers.

"Your studies are progressing well, and one day you will indeed be a great sorceress, but now I must return to

Fey Wild and let your grandparents know they will have to wait a while longer for your visit. But before I go, I have a gift for you."

She retrieved her bundle from Seamus' bed, placed it on the table and opened it. Inside was a dagger, approximately eight inches in length, diamonds and rubies were embedded in the grip, and the blade was silver with gold trimming, it was very like the dagger Eleanor wore and Aurie glanced at both.

"Yes, they are very alike, except this one belonged to your mother, and has not been used since she left Fey Wild to marry your father. I know that she would want you to have it, and when the time is right, I will teach you how to use it properly."

Seamus pointed at the dagger and Eleanor nodded. He picked it up and balanced it on the palm of his hand. "It's a trifle too delicate for my liking, but I suppose it would protect a lady in peril."

Eleanor snorted, and then took it from Seamus. She gestured for everyone to follow. Armitage was smiling and said nothing. Once they were outside, Eleanor handed the dagger to Aurie and pointed to the far side of the yard.

"See the wooden bucket hanging on that shed. Hit it with the dagger."

Aurie stared in astonishment at Eleanor. "But it's over a hundred yards away, and I don't know how?"

"Of course, you do."

Aurie faced Armitage, beseeching him to intervene. The wizard calmly watched, saying nothing.

"Aurie, what part of your magical training has Lord Armitage had you practice the most?" Eleanor asked.

"How to stay focused so that I can control my magic."

"Well, there's no difference in using a weapon. It takes complete concentration, and you have to believe you can do it."

Eleanor handed the weapon over. Aurie gripped the dagger, and was surprised it felt so comfortable in her hand.

"Now," Eleanor said, "clear your mind of all thought, focus on the bucket, and the rest will come to you naturally."

Aurie did as her aunt instructed, taking a deep breath, she threw the dagger. It flew in a straight line, hitting the bucket with a dull thud. Seamus raced across the yard, and returned, carrying the pail. The dagger was buried deep in the wood.

"Excellent," Eleanor commented. "Once you begin your weaponry training, I am sure you will have natural propensity in this area. Promise me you will practice with your dagger at least once a day."

"I promise," Aurie said.

"Now I must leave, as I have a few stops to make before I return to Fey Wild. When you are ready, I will return for you."

Aurie watched sadly as her aunt strode away from the cottage. The prospect of going to Fey Wild to learn weaponry and to meet her grandparents excited her. She promised herself she would practice diligently, and achieve her first level of magical training as soon as possible.

Chapter Nineteen

Stretching her aching muscles, Aurie poured a cup of tea for herself and Armitage, when suddenly a disgruntled Seamus flung open the front door and stormed into the room.

"It's Telford," he shouted. "He wants to talk to you right away, says it's important."

"Thank you, Seamus, invite our guest in," Armitage replied calmly.

Muttering under his breath, Seamus left the room. He soon returned, followed by a short stocky creature with a gruff looking face, bushy eyebrows and a long brown beard that almost touched the ground and carrying a large ax, which he laid against the wall next to the door. Aurie knew that Seamus did not have any liking for the cantankerous dwarf, and tolerated his company only because dwarves were master miners and smiths, and were known for their fabrication of armor and weapons. Dwarves had never been friendly with humans, and had always co-existed with the magical tribes in Lindell Forest, although they preferred to live in the caves and higher reaches of the mountains.

Jasmine entered the room and when she saw the extraordinary creature, she hastily retreated, firmly shutting the bedroom door. Aurie covered her mouth to stop from laughing, which would have been very disrespectful to their proud guest.

Telford approached the table, Armitage gestured for him to take a seat. Aurie rose and went to the hearth and returned with the teapot, she filled a mug, and handed it to Telford. Then she placed the last of the stew and the scones on the table. The dwarf nodded curtly, and ate the food, all the while noisily slurping his drink

"You have travelled a long way, my friend. I trust you did not encounter any difficulties in your travels?" Armitage enquired, after the dwarf had finished eating.

"One would be foolhardy if he did not keep a vigilant lookout in these unsettled times. Much as it is against my nature to do so, I took refuge in the shadows most of the way, my Lord."

"You are wise, my friend."

"Lindell Forest is being besieged by aberrant beasts, not only in the high mountains but also in the lower meadows."

"Yes, we have seen them ourselves. What brings you so far away from your home, my friend?"

"My Lord, you must accompany me to Dwarf Mountain as soon as possible, it's Egbert again, this time he's locked himself in the vault, and won't let us have any of the metal. All weapon production has stopped, and he refuses to come out."

Armitage rubbed his chin, closed his eyes, and muttered a few words under his breath. This was not the first time Telford had complained about Egbert, who was a bulbous nosed, mean-tempered dwarf. Egbert did not want to part with any of the dwarves' treasures of gold, silver or other precious metals as he did not take Armitage's warnings seriously. It had taken Armitage a long time to convince the dwarves Prince Kalian was becoming more powerful every day, and that he was amassing an army of soldiers as well as beasts from the Underworld. Armitage was not about to let the bad-tempered dwarf undo years of negotiations.

"I fear you are right Telford. It is time for me to have a long talk with Egbert, this nonsense must stop."

Aurie sensed the frustration in Armitage's response, realizing the unexpected trip to Dwarf Mountain would put him farther behind in his plans. She would not want to be in Egbert's boots once Armitage confronted him.

The dwarves lived in a well-fortified city high in the peaks of Dwarf Mountain. Beneath their stronghold were their mines, which could only be reached by a labyrinth of hidden tunnels and mining shafts.

Seamus, who had been leaning against the fireplace mantle, cleared his throat. "Master, I was to leave first thing in the morning to go to Westcott. Should I cancel the trip until your return?"

"No Seamus, it is important we continue with our plans. I think now is a perfect time for Aurie to visit Fey Wild. You can drop her off at Eleanor's on your way through Bloodroot Swamp."

"And Jasmine?" Seamus asked.

"She will be fine here. Nothing can penetrate my shield, and I will not be long at Dwarf Mountain."

Seamus nodded in agreement.

"And I think Torin should accompany us as well, at least as far as Dwarf Mountain, he has an uncanny ability to sense danger, and we can use his cunning and strength. Unfortunately, Aurie, he cannot cross over to Fey Wild, and you would have to bid your friend farewell for a time."

"How soon did you want to leave?" she asked Armitage.

"It's too late to make it all the way to Bloodroot Swamp today, and I'd prefer not to travel at night. We will leave at first light tomorrow."

Aurie nodded and headed towards her bedroom to pack her clothing and personal effects, and to let Jasmine know of their plans. After she had talked to her, Aurie could see the young woman was nervous about being left alone. She assured her that all would be well, Phineas and

Bluebell would drop by to keep her company. When she explained to Jasmine who her friends were, the color drained from Jasmine's face. For someone who had never met a magical being in her entire life, Jasmine was learning very quickly.

Aurie placed her dagger inside her backpack, ever since Eleanor had given it to her, she had practiced every day. She could not wait to show her aunt how much she had improved since receiving the gift. While she was gathering her things together, her thoughts wandered. She was excited about meeting her maternal relatives. She was fascinated by the stories Eleanor had told her about Fey Wild, which was located on a different dimension where Eldoran's and Elves lived in harmony.

She wondered what the future had in store for her.

Chapter Twenty

Aurie shifted her backpack higher. They were crossing an open valley, and she knew they were exposed to anyone or anything that might be on higher ground. Armitage led the group, and she followed closely, Torin remained at her side, while Telford walked a few paces back, muttering angrily under his breath, Seamus brought up the rear, his hand resting on the hilt of his sword.

They had been walking for hours, but dared not take a break until they made it to the cover of the dense trees. Three years before, when Aurie, Armitage and Seamus had trekked through Lindell Forest, the forest, meadows and marshes had been green and lush. Sadly, most of the grass was dry and brittle, and the withered leaves on the bushes fell silently to the ground when they brushed against them. Although it was early May, no rain had fallen in months, it was as if the land was held in a pocket of dry air and was slowly dying.

"We'll rest here for fifteen minutes," Armitage remarked once they reached cover. "Have something to eat and drink."

"Drink your water sparingly," Telford warned. "Most of the water holes and rills have dried up, and are not safe to drink, it gets worse the higher you climb."

Aurie chewed on a piece of dried meat, and took a swallow from her water skin, then poured a small amount in her hand and offered it to Torin.

The rest of the day was uneventful, and they steadily climbed upwards. Eventually they arrived at the crossroads where the left path headed towards Dwarf Mountain, while the right path traversed the summit of

183 • Child of the Ancients

Beargrass Mountain, eventually arriving at Bloodroot Swamp.

Armitage turned to Aurie. "This is where we part. Do not slacken in your studies or training, and learn all you can from Eleanor."

Aurie hugged him, fighting back tears. She did not know how long they would be separated, but for some reason she felt uneasy. Then she knelt and hugged Torin. "Take care of everyone, Torin," She whispered in his ear. The huge wolf licked her face, then went and stood next to the wizard.

"Take care Master," Seamus said, as Armitage, Telford, and Torin disappeared over the hill.

At first, they kept up their pace, stopping only once for a short break half way up the mountain. The trek down went faster, and just as the shadows were lengthening, they spotted Eleanor's tree house. Aurie raced ahead of Seamus, but he grabbed her arm and gestured to her to keep alert, she felt her face reddening, and chastised herself in forgetting her lessons about being more attentive when heading into unknown territory. Seamus had warned her often that it could be her undoing one day. They walked stealthily towards the huge willow growing next to the waterfall, Aurie sensed the magic and realized Eleanor had placed a protective shield around her home.

"Seamus, I don't know if we can get through the shield," she whispered. "And I'm not sure how to summon Eleanor to let her know we're here."

Seamus smiled at Aurie, and without hesitation, he strolled towards the base of the tree. Aurie stared at him in amazement.

"Come on, climb up. I don't know about you, but I'm exhausted and hungry."

Aurie quickly scaled the wooden ladder. When she arrived at the top, she pushed open the door, Eleanor was sitting at the table, sipping a cup of tea. Seamus entered and placed his backpack on the floor, nodding in greeting to the sorceress.

"I see you got Armitage's message," he said to Eleanor.

Eleanor rose, and Aurie ran to her and gave her a hug. Her aunt smiled as she rose and returned with two mugs and a plate of berries, cheese and scones. "Eat, you must be hungry."

"Bet you thought some of that magic you're always doing had rubbed off on me," Seamus chuckled, as he noticed the bemused look on Aurie's face.

"I released my shield when I sensed you had arrived," Eleanor said. "Seamus has no more magic in him than this pot of tea."

Seamus grunted, and Aurie laughed at them both. She poured herself a welcomed cup of the hot brew, and took one of Eleanor's blueberry scones, secretly wishing it was one of Jasmine's. Her aunt excelled as a sorceress and warrior, but was not known for her culinary talents, obviously not a gift inherited by the Elderberry family.

It seemed to Aurie as if she had just fallen asleep when the sun rose and filtered through the leaves outside the tree house window. They ate a quiet breakfast, then Seamus said his farewells and hastened on his way.

"Aurie, I think we should leave immediately," Eleanor suggested. "There's a Portal under the waterfall which will deliver us directly to Fey Wild. We will be teleported to a protected area not far from the palace so do not let the surroundings alarm you."

Aurie picked up her pack, and climbed down the ladder behind Eleanor. Her aunt strolled over to the pool, and waded towards the waterfall at the far side. Aurie followed, and suddenly Eleanor disappeared under the falls. Aurie took a deep breath and dove under the raging torrent, clasping her backpack tightly under her arm. When she emerged, she noticed they were in a small cave, the roar of the water was deafening.

Eleanor pointed to a white stone lying on top of a small wooden box, took Aurie's hand, then reached over and touched the rock. Aurie felt as if the world was spinning out of control and she found it hard to breathe, there was a pop, and Eleanor grabbed her arm before she fell to the ground.

They were standing on an island, and except for a small patch of dirt where they stood, consisted of jagged rocks and spiked plants. The dark water surrounding them roiled in eddies, and Aurie thought she spotted something swimming past.

"Normally I would teleport directly to the palace, but there are a few things I would like you to see first," Eleanor said. "Take my hand."

Again, Aurie was catapulted through space, and when she opened her eyes, discovered they were standing in a large meadow surrounded by lush moss-draped trees, scented orchids draped and twisted around the trunks, with translucent ferns covering the forest floor. An exotic vibrant colored bird squawked noisily, and landed on a branch of a silver tree, the sky was a soft gray and the water trickling in a nearby brook was a deep shade of amber.

"Everything is so beautiful," Aurie murmured. "The flowers are so fragrant."

"Yes," Eleanor said quietly. "Fey Wild has a natural beauty that cannot be compared to anywhere else, we live in continuous twilight, and as is evident, prefer dark forests. Soon you will come to love Fey Wild as much as I."

Aurie had never mentioned to her aunt her ongoing fear of the dark, as she had discovered years before from Eleanor that Eldorans were creatures of the night and preferred nightfall to day. "It's so different from what I ever imagined," she whispered.

"Come, we are expected at the Crystal Palace, Mother and Father will be waiting for us, and knowing the Queen, she has probably planned a gathering to announce your arrival. It's a short walk from here."

"Will there be many people there?"

"Just a few Ancients, the rest will be Eldoran."

Aurie laughed at Eleanor's remark, realizing her error. They walked for a short while, following paths bordered by flowers. A bright red animal that looked like a hedgehog sauntered onto the path, and Eleanor waited for it to cross, she told Aurie what it was called in Eldoran, and Aurie wondered how long it would take her to master their language.

Surprisingly Aurie's clothes and hair dried in only a few minutes, Eleanor noticed her feeling her hair and chuckled. "Everything is magical in Fey Wild."

Eventually the tranquil forest changed into rolling hills. Aurie followed Eleanor up a gradual incline, fascinated by the foliage and remarkable species of animals and birds. When they arrived at the top, she stared in astonishment, below was a cerulean lake, and on the far side a beautiful white palace rose out of the mist. It was surrounded by massive cedars, pines and oaks, and in the background, magnificent mountains rose skyward, while waterfalls cascaded into pools that flowed into the lake.

"Welcome to Crystal Palace." Eleanor stated.

They walked down the path and soon arrived at a small pier, a boat was tied to the dock, and Eleanor gestured for Aurie to climb in. The small vessel crossed the water without their assistance, heading directly towards the front entrance of the palace. After disembarking, they walked up a white paved roadway towards a huge open gate, there was no drawbridge, parapets or walkways, the main tower had large multi-colored windows and glass porticos. The absence of guards struck Aurie as odd.

"Our castles do not have any defense mechanisms like the castles in the mortal realm, Eleanor said. "There has never been a war in Fey Wild, so it is not necessary."

Eleanor led Aurie across the bailey towards the keep, when they arrived the door opened silently on its own, revealing a large foyer. Before them was a huge sweeping stairway. Majestic chandeliers hung from the ceiling three floors above, murals and tapestries covered the walls, depicting lavishly dressed Eldorans carrying long swords, hunting with spears, or riding unicorns. Aurie could have stayed for hours, but Eleanor did not slow her pace. A beautiful female appeared at the top of the staircase, and she glided silently past them, nodding her head in greeting, Eleanor smiled and returned the gesture. When she was out of sight, Eleanor said. "That was Eugenia Eveningstar, she is very kind-hearted and I am sure you will like her once you get to know her."

At the top of the stairs, Eleanor turned right. Walking down a long-carpeted corridor, Aurie heard music and the sound of laughter in the distance.

"It seems they have started without us," Eleanor said.

They walked down one hallway then another, and eventually they arrived at a large ballroom, Aurie stopped in amazement. Elegantly dressed Eldorans danced gracefully to the sounds of flutes and harps yet there was no orchestra present.

A regal couple wearing crowns, were seated on raised thrones in the middle of the room. Eleanor strode towards them, and Aurie nervously followed, intimidated by the presence of such grandeur.

"Ah, my wayward daughter has returned," the King said. Eleanor climbed the four steps leading up to the thrones, knelt, then rose and kissed both the King and the Queen. She favored her father, with the same slender build, silver hair and silver eyes, her mother was tall and slender, as all Eldoran were, her hair was blonde, with silver highlights, and her eyes were emerald green.

"Mother, Father, this is Aurialana, your granddaughter."

The music stopped and there was silence in the room, Aurie stared at the floor, she held her cap tightly in her hands, conscious of her stained travelling clothes.

"Come before me Aurialana," the Queen said quietly.

Aurie climbed the steps and stopped a few feet short of the throne, the Queen reached over and drew Aurie towards her and lifted Aurie's chin. "You're the image of your mother, and you have your father's violet eyes."

King Esmond nodded solemnly at the Queen's remarks, Eleanor was leaning casually against the king's throne, smiling at Aurie's discomfort. Aurie was uneasy, wishing the floor would open and swallow her.

"Come, let me show you to your room. Eleanor, you may stay and visit with your father, I'm sure you will have much to talk about."

The Queen rose and swept down the steps. Aurie followed her across the ballroom floor towards the doorway, the dancers bowing and curtsying as they passed. A small group standing in the far corner approached the Queen, they did not resemble the Eldoran's in their appearance or coloring, and Aurie wondered who they might be.

"Aurialana," the Queen said regally. "I would like you to meet the Ancients, they have been living with us since your mother and father brought them here. Once you get settled, I am sure you will get to know each of them in turn."

One of the men stepped forward. "It is an honor to see you again Princess Aurialana, we never gave up hope that you were alive, and one day soon you will be reacquainted with your parents."

Aurie nodded solemnly at the small group.

"Come," commanded the Queen. "You shall get an opportunity to talk later."

She followed the Queen out of the room and into the hallway, when they got to the end of the corridor, the Queen turned right and they arrived at a flight of stairs.

"Ah, Eugenia, there you are," Queen Edelyse said as a young female appeared. "Please prepare a bath for Princess Aurialana and put out some clean clothing for her."

Aurie noticed it was the same Eldoran who had passed her and Eleanor earlier, she smiled at Aurie, curtsied, and then headed down the hallway.

"Eugenia will take care of your needs."

"But, but...Your Majesty, I don't need a maid."

"Eugenia is not a maid, there are no servants in Fey Wild, it was Eugenia's choice to serve the royal family, as she did not wish to pursue the path of a warrior, and please call me Grandmother."

"Yes Grandmother, and you can call me Aurie if you like."

The queen stared at Aurie, smiled indulgently and said, "This way please Aurialana."

Aurie followed the queen down the lengthy corridor. They stopped in front of a large metal door, and the Queen raised her hand and it opened silently. Aurie stared in astonishment. There was a huge canopied bed covered with a silk throw, and an armoire and a matching desk and chair. She walked towards a large floor length door, opened it and stepped outside onto a secluded balcony, the view was breathtaking.

"Come along Aurialana," the Queen ordered. "You are expected in the bath."

Aurie quickly stepped inside. The sound of running water could be heard and the Queen led Aurie over to a closed door on the far side of the room, she opened it to reveal Eugenia standing over a marble bath, pouring amber liquid into the water, bubbles filled the tub, and a scent of roses and gardenia wafted through the room.

"I'll have your bath poured in a few moments, Your Highness." Eugenia said.

The Queen nodded and turned and looked at Aurie, who suddenly realized Eugenia had been talking to her.

"Um, thank you," she responded, wondering if her grandmother would be upset if she told Eugenia to call her Aurie instead of Your Highness, however, considering her previous attempt she decided not to pursue the matter. Although Eugenia was not a slave or a servant, it was evident her grandmother would not have approved of any familiarity between Eugenia and a member of the royal family.

"This will be your room Aurialana," Queen Edelyse said. "I want you to feel comfortable and at home while you are here. If you need anything, just ask Eugenia and she will tend to your needs."

"Thank you, Grandmother."

"You certainly are quiet. Your mother was of the same temperament, while Eleanor is more forceful. Mind you, your mother was a powerful sorceress in her own right. It wasn't until she had met and married your father that she allowed her abilities to lapse. I wonder which path you will follow."

Her eyes followed her grandmother's back as she turned and left the room. The Queen's question surprised her, and Aurie realized she was not expecting an answer. It was the first time she understood she had other choices than becoming an Eldoran warrior, yet she intuitively knew should she decide to follow a different path, her grandmother would not be pleased with her decision.

Some questions were best left unanswered.

Chapter Twenty-One

The first few days passed quickly. Aurie attended a continuous stream of parties and gatherings. The Eldorans loved to dance, and when the Queen discovered Aurie had never learned, she introduced her to Erling Silverweed, who was a few years older than she. Besides being a good dancer, Erling was a very competent swordsman.

Soon Aurie and Erling were spending long hours together, much to her annoyance, Aurie discovered she was continually comparing him to Tony Drummond, who was as different as night and day. The slender, fair Eldoran laughed and joked incessantly. Tony, on the other hand, was muscular, dark, and more serious in his temperament. Ever since Seamus had brought him up in his conversation with Armitage, she thought of Tony often. She had not seen him in over three years and doubted if he would remember her should they meet again.

After he had shown her the finer points of dancing, Erling began teaching Aurie the basics of spear throwing and the long sword, which, as Eleanor had mentioned, was the preferred weapon of the Eldorans. The long sword was much lighter than the two-handed sword Seamus had been training her with. She discovered she had an aptitude for it, but did not pick up the basics of the spear as quickly. When time permitted, Eleanor gave Aurie lessons with her dagger, and was pleased to see how quickly the young girl learned to use the weapon. As an afterthought, Eleanor decided to train Aurie in the art of archery, although this weapon was not used by the Eldorans during battle. Aurie secretly preferred the bow and arrow to the long sword and the spear, but she kept her thoughts to herself.

The spear however was an entire different matter. After Aurie spent a few days in frustration and discouragement, she threw it angrily on the ground. Facing her aunt, she said "This is hopeless, I'm just not cut out to be a warrior."

"Nonsense," Eleanor responded. "You just have a smaller physique than most Eldorans your age and lack the strength in your shoulders and arms to throw the spear any great distance. Once you have matured, you will become more proficient."

When she was not taking lessons from Erling, Aurie was being tutored by Eleanor in magic. Her aunt began to teach her how to teleport, and was pleasantly surprised to learn that this ability came naturally to Aurie.

"Once you have completely mastered this skill, I'll teach you how to teleport others as well," Eleanor promised. "It's more difficult and can be dangerous if not done correctly."

Eleanor was a strict disciplinarian, and Aurie missed Armitage's patience and calm demeanor. Her aunt gave praise when she thought Aurie deserved it, or when she had mastered one of the intricate spells. Aurie had the utmost respect for the sorceress and concentrated on her lessons. In time, she began to understand how tolerant Armitage had been while she was under his tutorage and she vowed when she returned she would double her efforts to please him.

Soon a month had passed, then another and another. Late one evening, Aurie was resting in the rose garden with Eleanor and her grandmother, lying on the grass, captivated by the subtle hues in the sky and the songs of the birds.

"Eleanor, when are we going to return to Primrose Cottage? Armitage and Seamus would have returned by now, and they must be wondering where I am."

At first no one answered, Aurie sat up, and turned and looked at Eleanor and the Queen. Eleanor glanced at her mother, who hastily lowered her head and stared at the grass.

"Don't you like it here?" Eleanor asked.

"Yes, of course I do, it's beautiful, but I have to get back to Primrose Cottage. All my clothes are there, and I miss Torin."

"You have a closet full of clothes here, and anything else you desire."

"I know, but we've been gone a long time," Aurie replied, staring at her elegant gown, wishing for the hundredth time for the comfort of her leggings and shirts.

"Aurie, in Fey Wild there is no time, there is no change of seasons, and no one ages. As long you as you remain here with us, you will enjoy longevity."

Aurie did not answer her aunt, and she felt a chill of foreboding. Why hadn't her grandmother answered her question? What if Eleanor refused to take her back?

Later when she was alone in her bedroom, she went and sat on the balcony, staring longingly at the distant mountains, wondering what Armitage, Seamus and Jasmine were doing. She hoped that Torin was well, and that he was not missing her. She tried not to let anyone know how much she missed her friends on Earth, they were so kind to her, and she knew how much her grandparents enjoyed her company.

Aurie concentrated intensely on her lessons, Eleanor was relentless in her training, pushing her harder than ever.

One day as Aurie was walking down the upstairs corridor, she heard voices coming from a side room. Her name was mentioned, so she stopped outside the doorway, which was slightly ajar. She peeked around the corner, and spotted Eleanor and the Queen on the far side of the room, standing next to a large window, their backs were turned and they did not notice her standing in the doorway. She remembered the last time she had eavesdropped behind a door, and hoped she would not be discovered, she doubted the Queen would be as tolerant as Armitage.

"Mother, we can't do this anymore," Eleanor said sharply. "It's not fair to Aurie."

"Honestly Eleanor, you're being overly dramatic, the girl is perfectly fine."

"No Mother, she is not. She doesn't smile or laugh anymore. She's homesick, and she misses Primrose Cottage, her friends, and for some reason, that massive black wolf."

"She has plenty of friends and family who love her, right here in Fey Wild."

"But we aren't Armitage."

"We're her family, not he, and soon she will come to realize that."

"Mother, they have a bond that neither you nor I could ever break. You must remember she is also half Ancient."

"She must continue with her studies. Lord Armitage is far too busy right now to spend any time with her, and she must not fall behind in her combat training."

"Lord Armitage has never faltered in his duties as Aurie's mentor, and Seamus may be a human, but he is very competent and a great warrior in his own right."

"What of Erling?"

"Erling has taught her all he can."

"I was hoping that something would come of their friendship, that they would come to care deeply for each other."

Aurie's face turned a deep red, and she fought back her anger.

"I believe they are good friends, but that is all," Eleanor said. "As for teaching her magic, I have gone as far as I can. She knows as much as I do. The only one who has the ability to advance her powers is Armitage."

Eleanor placed her hand on her mother's shoulder. "I know how much you miss Elyse, and no matter how much you try, Aurie will never take her place."

The Queen's face turned rigid, and then slowly she relaxed. "Have I been that obvious?"

"Mother, Aurie's destiny lies elsewhere. Armitage has told me that she will become a powerful sorceress, more powerful than any of us."

"You are right," the Queen said sadly. "I have been very selfish, thinking of my own needs before hers. As soon as you can, take her back to Armitage."

"Thank you, Mother, I know you are making the right decision."

"Losing her is like losing your sister all over again."

"We're not losing her Mother, but we can't stop her from becoming what she was meant to be."

Aurie hastily retreated down the hallway, she slid behind a huge urn located at the end of the corridor. Waiting until she heard their footsteps, she stepped out and almost collided with them.

"Ah, there you are Aurialana. Come, join us outside," the Queen suggested. "There is something we must discuss."

Aurie followed them outside to the rose garden and although she was sad to be leaving, the thought of returning home lifted her spirits. She might even forgive her grandmother for trying to pair her up with Erling.

Chapter Twenty-Two

Aurie had been practicing with Seamus for well over two hours, when he suggested they stop for a break. She propped her sword against the trunk of the willow, and took a long drink of water from the stream. It was only a few weeks since she had returned to Earth, and although she missed her family in Fey Wild, she was happy to be back. Torin had materialized out of the shadows the first day she had returned, and then he disappeared just as mysteriously. She wondered if he had found a pack, and secretly wished that was the case. There were times she worried about him, not only because of his size but of his fierce appearance. She had heard rumors from some of the magical folks that a dire wolf had been seen in their valley, and Aurie was afraid that Torin might be mistaken for it and slain.

Sensing a disturbance, she quickly stood up, grabbing her sword as she passed by the willow. Seamus noticed her movement, and immediately followed, his sword drawn as well. Aurie pointed silently towards the far end of the field, where a group of dark figures could be seen outlined in the trees. As they slowly approached, she recognized King Glendon, leader of the Centaurs, and at least a dozen members of his herd.

Seamus whistled softly in surprise, she nodded solemnly in agreement, King Glendon never ventured far from the meadows high in the mountains passes. She was curious as to why he had wandered into their valley. The door of the cottage opened and Armitage stepped out, he waited as the Centaurs galloped across the open field, stopping a few feet short of the protection shield. Raising his staff, he released the safeguard, King Glendon nodded his massive head, and then slowly approached the wizard.

"Greetings Lord Armitage," he said in his loud booming voice. "I trust you fare well?"

"I do Your Highness."

"Greetings, Princess Aurialana, daughter of King Sebastian of the Ancients, and Queen Elyse, daughter of King Esmond and Queen Edelyse of the Eldoran's."

"Greetings King Glendon," Aurie responded solemnly, bowing her head in deference to the ruler of the Centaurs.

"And greetings to your servant."

Aurie sensed Seamus bristling next to her, and she quickly answered on his behalf. "Seamus Stark, who is a great warrior among his people, greets you King Glendon."

"Please allow me to offer you and your herd water and food," Armitage interjected, smiling at Aurie's quick response in correcting King Glendon's error as to Seamus' status.

Aurie knew that politeness was imperative to the Centaurs' culture, and business was never discussed until formal greetings were made and water and rations were offered. It was a great insult if these formalities were not met.

"I thank you My Lord, but I must pass on your generous offer, we do not wish to tarry. Two days past, four of my warriors came across a small group of humans and their horses taking shelter in a cave at the base of Beargrass Mountain, they fled into the trees, although a few stood their ground and prepared to fight."

A look of concern spread over Armitage's face. "I pray a battle did not ensue?"

"No, we did not raise our arms. Their leader was riding an experienced war horse, I decided to talk to him instead as he seemed to be quite intelligent."

"I can only assume the reason the humans retaliated was because they had never encountered Centaurs before."

"That is what the war horse said. He introduced himself as Cesar, and told us his human had been attacked by the Evil Lord, and driven from the man village. They fled to Lindell Forest and after a long pursuit managed to lose them, finding cover in one of the caves."

Aurie listened uneasily to the conversation between the wizard and the Centaur, she had to stop herself from interrupting and asking questions. She realized it would have been extremely rude, and Armitage would not have been pleased with her, as he had spent a long time earning King Glendon's loyalty and respect.

"Cesar informed me his human was brave and honorable," King Glendon said. "I then allowed the human to speak to me, and forgave him when he did not greet me in the manner that was expected."

Armitage nodded seriously, saying nothing as the proud ruler continued with his story.

"I finally convinced him that it would be foolish to remain where they were. Food and fresh water are scarce on Beargrass Mountain, and their small group would be no match should they encounter any of the Evil Lord's beasts."

"How did he respond?"

"At first, he was distrustful, but then I told him I knew a powerful wizard and a sorceress with healing powers. A few members of his tribe are wounded, and being a wise leader, he saw the merit in my words, he allowed us to lead him here"

"Where are they now?"

"I left them in a glen about two miles north, on the west side of Woodfern Lake."

"Thank you King Glendon. Your kindness will not be forgotten. Please set up camp next to the stream, as you must be tired from your long journey."

"Once again, I must decline your kind offer, as I wish to return to our home as quickly as possible. These are not safe times and I fear for the safety of my herd. Until we meet again Lord Armitage."

King Glendon turned sharply, and he and the Centaurs galloped across the meadow, and soon disappeared into the dark forest.

"Seamus and I will go and retrieve them," Armitage said to Aurie. "Better warn Jasmine that there will be wounded arriving."

Aurie nodded, then went inside and informed Jasmine of their impending visitors. The capable young woman immediately filled the kettle with water, placing it over the flames to boil. Aurie set out a stack of towels and sheets to be used for binding, then returned outside, and sat on the doorstep, she did not have long to wait.

Cesar was the first horse to appear, his rider was holding an injured boy in his arms. She counted a dozen men, and only half of them were mounted. It wasn't until Caesar was almost at the cottage before Aurie recognized the man who was riding Cesar. It was Tony. She slowly rose, and waited until he dismounted.

She nodded curtly, and led him inside the cottage and had him place the boy on Seamus' bed. Tony did not greet her and she wondered if he even recognized her. He was well over six feet, his face was unshaven, and there were dark shadows under his eyes, his black curly hair long and unkempt.

Aurie sat on the edge of the bed next to the injured boy, the cloth wrapped tightly around his chest was red from the flow of blood.

"He took an arrow," Tony said quietly. "I did all I could, but I am no healer."

At that point, Armitage and Seamus entered the cottage, half-carrying a young man who was using a branch as a crutch. Armitage guided him over to the table and had him sit in one of the chairs.

"These two are the most seriously injured," he said to Aurie. "Jasmine and I will tend to this one while you take care of the young lad."

"And I will see to the others," Seamus said, as he filled a bucket with water and took some of the torn sheets, quickly leaving the cottage.

Aurie slowly removed the dressing from the injured boy, the wound was deep. She pressed her ear against his chest and listened to his heartbeat, it was very weak. She summoned her magic but instinctively knew she could do nothing. She looked up at Tony and shook her head, seeing the anguish in his eyes.

"The best we can do is keep him comfortable. I've placed an incantation on him, and he's not feeling any pain. I'm sorry, but he will soon enter a different plain. There is nothing I can do."

She walked over to the man sitting at the table, not knowing what his reaction would be if he saw her using her powers. She quietly said. "Your wound is deep, so I'm going to use magic to heal it."

He nodded and said nothing. Aurie placed her hand over the wound, and the man gasped as the gash closed and the bleeding stopped, he shook his head in amazement, and thanked her for helping him.

"Come, we'll see how Seamus is doing," Armitage said.

Aurie and Tony followed him outside. Seamus was winding a strip of cloth around the head of one of the injured men, and he pointed towards two others lying on the ground. Aurie immediately tended to their injuries, and was relieved to see they were not seriously wounded.

The rest of the group were sitting or lying quietly on the ground, their faces gaunt and their clothing hanging loosely, evidence they had not eaten in a long time. The cottage door opened and Jasmine came outside carrying a huge basket, filled with barley bread and cheese which she passed around, Seamus walked to the stream and filled the emptied bucket with cold water.

When everyone had been attended to Aurie headed towards the creek and scooped water into her hands and drank deeply, closing her eyes, distressed that she could do nothing for the young boy. She heard a movement in the grass, and spotted Cesar by the willow. She walked over to the war horse and spotted Prince Kalian's magnificent saddle on his back, and wondered how Tony had managed to get possession of it.

"Hello old friend," she said, stroking his neck.

Cesar pushed his muzzle against her shirt and snorted.

"How have you been Aurie?"

She spun around, Tony was standing a few feet away. At first, she did not answer, and then she shrugged. "I'm doing fine Tony. I was wondering if you knew who I was."

"You're a lot taller, but I would have recognized your golden hair and violet eyes anywhere."

Aurie was at a loss for words, she turned her back.

"Aurie, I'm sorry about everything. We heard that you had escaped, but I know it still doesn't make things right."

"Forget about it Tony. It was a long time ago."

"I can't forget about it. I wish there had been another alternative, but I had no choice. If Prince Kalian found out I had let you go, he would have arrested me. I was responsible for the safety of others, not just Sam and Fred, but for the Falcons as well. I hope you can understand and forgive me."

203 • Child of the Ancients

Aurie had been carrying around so much anger and hurt inside for the past three years, she did not know if she would ever be able to trust Tony again and for some reason that thought only made it more painful.

"I'll be back in a few minutes to sit with Bobby," Tony said, when he realized that Aurie was not going to answer. "I want to unsaddle Cesar and give him a good rub down."

Patting Cesar one last time, Aurie turned and headed back towards the cottage, she sensed Tony watching her as she crossed the field, but she could not bring herself to turn around.

Chapter Twenty-Three

Aurie sat quietly at the table, sipping a cup of hot chamomile tea as she massaged the back of her neck, willing her eyes to remain open. The kitchen was hot and stuffy, and Armitage had opened the front door and the two windows on either side of the room, allowing a cool breeze to flow through. The young boy had died not more than ten minutes before, and Aurie felt drained. On Armitage's instructions, Tony had carried him outside and placed him in the garden shed, they would bury him in the morning.

"You did everything you could," Armitage said quietly.

"I have the power of accelerated healing. I should have been able to do more."

"No amount of magic could have saved him, not even someone with your abilities."

Tony had returned and had overheard Armitage's comments. "His name was Bobby Fuller. I've known him since he was six years old."

"Was he one of the street kids?" she asked quietly.

"Not at first. His father was arrested and slain by Prince Kalian as he possessed magic. Bobby and his mother lived in a hovel down by the wharf, and money and food were in short supply. His mother became ill, but did not survive. Bobby did not possess any magical abilities, so he was of no use to Prince Kalian. I found him wandering the back alleys, hiding from the soldiers and living on pickings from the garbage heaps."

The door swung open and Seamus clomped into the room, he sat in the vacant chair at the table. Pouring a cup of tea, he reached over and took one of the strawberry scones Jasmine had set out earlier. "Everyone has been provided with water and food. The temporary shelters will make do for the night. Tomorrow we'll set up a more permanent camp."

"I think the best place would be at the far end of the meadow, adjacent to Woodfern Lake," Armitage suggested. "There's plenty of fresh water, and anyone approaching the valley can be seen for miles."

"I want to thank all of you for everything you've done," Tony said. "But we have overstayed our welcome."

"Your small band will not survive in Lindell Forest, and this is the safest place to be right now," Armitage said. "Prince Kalian does not know of our whereabouts. Seamus is a highly trained soldier, and Aurie is well trained in weaponry as well. I think this would be a good opportunity to train your small band so that when the time comes, they will be able to defend themselves."

"I have been training them," Tony replied stiffly. "Some of them are pretty good fighters."

"Then they should learn quickly, but fighting magical beasts is different from fighting an armed trooper. They must know how to do both."

"We are indebted to your friends. I don't know what would have happened if the Centaurs hadn't found us and brought us here."

"Although they tend to not trust humans, most of the magical clans in Lindell Forest are friendly and helpful," Armitage commented. "They would never abandon anyone who needed help, magical or non-magical."

"Then, on behalf of the Falcons, I accept your generous offer, My Lord."

"Your band is known as the Falcons?"

"Yes, although this is only half of them. I pray those who have remained in Westcott are not discovered by the troopers."

Armitage nodded, then turned and faced Aurie. "I noticed you talking to that fair, quiet man, and wonder if he might be a friend?"

Aurie glanced fleetingly at Tony.

"His name is Sam Murdoch," Tony interjected. "Aurie met him when she lived with us at the warehouse."

"I see that Fred is still lurking around in the shadows," she said curtly.

"He's just as churlish as ever, but he's good in a fight and I need every man I can get."

"And you trust him?" She grunted in response.

"Not entirely, he's been spending as much time with the troopers as he has with the Falcons. His loyalties are divided right now, but I believe I can sway him my way. We've gone through a lot together."

"If he stays away from me," Aurie said curtly, "Then he has nothing to worry about."

Tony ran his fingers through his hair. He stood up and walked over to the fireplace, he leaned against the mantel, deep in thought. "I worked as a groom at the castle caring for Prince Kalian's horse," he said, looking at Armitage. "A few years ago, I discovered a door leading to the dungeons under the stables. I discovered many of the prisoners were being tortured, but there was nothing I could do because there were too many guards. I never found out what happened to them after they were taken from the cells."

Aurie's thoughts returned to the time she was interrogated by Prince Kalian in the dungeons, and she shivered remembering the terror she had felt.

"I think we can answer that question for you," Armitage said, interrupting Tony. He quickly told him about Aurie's discovery of the subterranean cave, the Fire Crystal, and the conversation she had overheard between the two soldiers. Tony stared at her in disbelief.

"You mean you knew at the time, and you never said anything," he asked sharply. "Why would you keep something like that a secret?"

"If Prince Kalian ever found out I had discovered the cave and had overheard those two soldiers talking, none of us would have been safe. I was afraid for you and Sam, and even Fred, although he doesn't deserve it."

"I think Aurie's decision was a wise one at the time," Armitage commented, sensing the tension between the two-young people. "Tony, please continue with your tale."

Tony shrugged. "Our street gang had grown, and we called ourselves the Falcons. At first, our main goal was survival. The soldiers became more aggressive, and anyone found wandering the streets was arrested, whether they had committed a crime or not. The young boys and men were forced to join Prince Kalian's army, if they refused to cooperate they ended up in the quarry. The young girls and women were taken to the castle to do kitchen or scullery work, or for the few unfortunate, keeping the troopers entertained.

"The Falcons began fighting back. Prince Kalian posted a warrant for our arrest, dead or alive. He didn't give any of us the luxury of choosing between his army and the quarry. He was sending out a message to the villagers, that dissidents would not be tolerated.

"He did not know that I was the leader of the Falcons, so I continued working in the stables, which allowed me to often overhear the troopers making plans.

"I began to notice a drastic change in Prince Kalian's appearance, his face became thinner, almost gaunt, and his eyes glowed red. The horses in the stable were terrified of him, and even Cesar was nervous, especially when Prince Kalian rode him."

"The dark magic is transforming him," Armitage mused.

"About a week ago, Bobby came to the stables in a panic," Tony continued, as he nodded at Armitage's comment. "A battalion of soldiers had attacked the warehouse, and he had managed to get away unseen. Two of the young grooms working in the stables with me, James and Randy, are also members of the Falcons. You might remember them Aurie," Tony said, pausing in his tale, and turning to look at her.

Aurie nodded.

"They immediately left the barn to warn the Falcons. In the event something like this ever happened, we were to meet at a rendezvous point in Lindell Forest. No sooner had they gone than I heard hooves in the courtyard. I had just finished saddling Cesar to take him for his run, and I jumped on his back, grabbed Bobby and threw him in the saddle behind me. Cesar charged straight into the soldiers, catching them by surprise, we were outside the castle gates, and barreling towards Lindell Forest before they realized what had happened."

At this point, Tony sat down at the table, poured a second cup of tea, and then leaned back in his chair.

"We arrived at the rendezvous point, but there were only a dozen Falcons waiting for us. James and Randy were not among them, and I hoped they had managed to get to safety.

"We galloped the horses for hours, with the soldiers only a few paces behind, until the sun was starting to set, and I knew we had to find cover. We were at the base of Beargrass Mountain, so I decided to try and find refuge higher up. I discovered an animal trail, and we started climbing. Suddenly Sean fell forward in his saddle, he had taken an arrow in his thigh. I did not know Bobby had been hit as well.

"The soldiers were shooting our horses out from under us. All would have been lost except a powerful lightning storm appeared out of nowhere, washing away all signs of our trail. It was then I noticed the cave, and I steered the horses towards it. We did not see the soldiers again, so they must have given up their search. We stayed in the shelter for almost a week, foraging for water and food, but we found nothing."

"You were lucky you did not encounter any of the beasts from the Underworld," Armitage commented.

"Yes, the Centaur king warned me about them," Tony said.

He rose and paced nervously around the room. Stopping at the hearth, he leaned heavily on the mantle. "There is one thing I have been wondering about," he said, looking directly at Armitage. "If Prince Kalian is practicing Dark Magic, and has control of the beasts, and is so powerful, why has he not attacked?"

"I have thought about that myself. Prince Kalian is aware I have been gathering the tribes together, and that the Eldorans and Centaurs are our allies. He is also aware that a young sorceress lives in Lindell Forest, but he does not know the extent of her powers."

With these words, the wizard rose and entered his bedroom, closing the door quietly, and leaving everyone with their own thoughts.

"You need to find out which one of your men is the traitor," Aurie said, as she faced Tony. "Someone told the soldiers about the warehouse, and I have a good idea who it is, but you have to discover that on your own. Now, if you'll excuse me, I think I'll call it a night."

Chapter Twenty-Four

Early the next morning they buried Bobby under the willow tree. Sensing the depression among the Falcons, Tony put everyone immediately to work setting up a base camp. Shelters made of wood and cedar boughs and tents made of animal hides were erected in the woods bordering the open meadow, which was soon turned into a training field.

Aurie arose each morning at sunrise, and after a quick breakfast, joined Seamus and Tony at the camp. The training she had learned while in Fey Wild soon became evident.

Armitage insisted she keep up her magical studies along with her combat training. Every night she staggered into her bedroom and collapsed on her bed, almost too exhausted to undress.

One morning Armitage stopped her on her way out the door. "Aurie, I want to commend you on your arduous work. With so many people in the vicinity, I hope you have been taking the opportunity to practice self-discipline regarding your telepathy."

Aurie's face turned a deep shade of red, she guiltily looked away, then slowly returned to the table and sat down. Armitage raised his eyebrows, waiting for her reply.

"I know you told me not to, but I read Fred's mind once, but nothing happened. It's kind of empty in there."

Armitage choked, and then turned his head, his shoulders shaking in suppressed laughter. When he had composed himself, he turned and faced Aurie.

"Is that the only time?" he said sternly.

"No sir, I tried reading Tony's mind too. But it didn't work, something was blocking his thoughts."

Armitage scowled, a look of disapproval shrouding his face. "Aurie, what did I tell you?" he said, shaking his head.

"I promise I won't do it again."

"I'll take your word on it, but you must try harder. I can't stress enough how important it is you not abuse this gift. A person's innermost thoughts are personal and private, and no one has the right to intrude on them. The only time you should use this gift is under the most crucial of circumstances, and even then, utmost care must be taken. Now you best get going. Seamus will be wondering where you are."

The rest of the morning went quickly. At noon, Jasmine came to the practice field carrying a large flask of water, and a basket filled with rye bread, cheese, onions and berries. Aurie sat next to her on the grass, while Seamus and the young men wandered over to the shade under the huge elms. She watched in disgust as Fred grabbed a handful of bread and a large onion, stuffing them greedily into his mouth. She refused to spend any time in training him, and understanding her hatred for the man, Seamus had not insisted.

One of the lads made a comment, and Tony laughed out loud. The men looked over to where the two girls were sitting, Aurie knew they were watching Jasmine, as her beauty drew attention wherever she went.

"He's so handsome, isn't he?" Jasmine sighed ignoring the looks of admiration directed her way.

Aurie stiffened, wondering why Jasmine's comment irritated her. "Sure," she said quietly, "if you like them tall, dark and moody."

"Tall, dark and moo ...., Oh, you think I mean Tony. No, no. I'm talking about Sam."

Aurie stared at Jasmine, a surprised look on her face. It was the first indication she had that Jasmine liked Sam, although she could understand the attraction, as Sam was a kind and gentle man.

"Promise you won't say anything to anyone. If Sam knew I liked him, I'd be so embarrassed."

"Why should you be embarrassed? Besides, I can understand why you like him, any girl would be happy getting someone like him."

"But he's definitely not your type."

"What do you mean by that?"

"I would say your type is, let me see, tall, dark and moody," Jasmine said, laughing lightly.

"That's ridiculous. Tony thinks I'm a little kid, he always has."

"He'd have to be blind if he didn't notice how beautiful you are; besides, I notice him watching you all the time, especially when you're training the men. The two of you are a perfect match, although neither of you have figured it out yet."

"I don't have time to think about such nonsense. My training keeps me busy, and my path is very different from Tony's."

"Why, because you're a princess, and a sorceress, or whatever else you may be. You can choose any path you want to Aurie, and someone like Tony doesn't come along very often. Perhaps it's time you forgave him and came to realize how special he really is."

With those words, Jasmine rose, gathered up the empty water jug and food basket, and headed across the meadow towards the cottage.

For the rest of the day, Aurie found it difficult to concentrate, as Jasmine's words kept interrupting her thoughts. She had come to respect Tony for his prowess and fighting abilities, but she was not sure if she would ever forgive him.

Training was over for the day, and Aurie was gathering her equipment, when suddenly Eleanor appeared at the edge of the forest. Aurie ran across the field and greeted her.

Armitage was waiting for them in the doorway, and he extended his arm in greeting. "I trust all is well, Eleanor?"

"I fear not My Lord," the sorceress answered. "I teleported here as quickly as I could. I do not bring glad tidings."

"Come inside." Armitage said, ushering the sorceress into the cottage. Jasmine immediately poured a cup of tea and placed a hot scone on the table.

When Eleanor had refreshed herself, she stood up and starting pacing around the room, she walked over to the fireplace and looked down at Armitage, who was sitting in his rocking chair.

"Strange phenomena are occurring in Fey Wild, the land is changing, and some places have been thrown into permanent winter. As there is no time in Fey Wild, these changes will remain that way evermore."

"I think we can all agree that Prince Kalian is behind this," Armitage commented, rubbing his chin. "He is definitely getting stronger."

"We suspect that he has created a rift between Fey Wild and the Mortal World. Although he and his aberrant beasts are unable to pass into our realm, he is able to send dark energy through which is causing irreparable damage."

"What message do you bring from your father?"

"We must protect our homeland. Our magic is strong, but we will need all of our warriors to cover the rifts and deflect the energy blasts."

"We can wait no longer. I will go to the Centaurs and the Dwarves and let them know what is happening in Fey Wild. They can assist in passing my message on to the other tribes."

"I will warn the tribes living east of Beargrass Mountain," Eleanor said solemnly. "Before I do, I will go directly to the Dryad camp. With their teleporting abilities, their assistance will be invaluable."

With these parting words, Eleanor rose and left the cottage. Aurie followed her outside, Eleanor seeing the look on her face said. "I am sorry I could not visit longer. You will be safe here with Armitage."

That evening, while Jasmine was preparing supper, Aurie, Seamus, Armitage and Tony gathered around the kitchen table, it was a habit they had fallen into every night to discuss the training progress of the Falcons. Armitage brought Seamus and Tony up to date and informed them he would be leaving first thing in the morning to meet with the Centaurs and the Dwarves, and Eleanor was on her way back to the portal to return to Fey Wild and planned on stopping at some of the villages to report the status of events.

"This is impossible," Tony cried. "We have just begun our training; how can we possibly meet Prince Kalian in battle?"

"The Eldorans are in trouble, and unless we take immediate action, Prince Kalian will not stop until he has destroyed Fey Wild. They will not leave their homeland, be assured they will fight to their deaths."

Tony rubbed his hands wearily down his face. "What can we possibly do? We are so few, and none of us have ever seen battle. It would be suicide to confront Prince Kalian's soldiers."

"That is not what I had in mind for your small group of rebels. There are other means of fighting an

215 • Child of the Ancients

enemy. The Eldorans are great warriors and powerful sorcerers. They will be able to defend Fey Wild, but unfortunately, it greatly reduces the strength of our army here on Earth. While I am gone, you must continue with your training, doubling your efforts."

While everyone sat quietly, deep in their own thoughts, Armitage rose and walked over to the fireplace, he stared into the flames, his back facing the table.

"Tell me how strong your magical abilities are?" he asked, turning and looking directly at Tony.

Tony's face flushed a deep red. "I... I don't know what you mean?" he stuttered.

"Young man, I am a high wizard of the Ancients, and can detect if someone has magical powers."

Tony twisted his head and looked directly at Aurie, seeing the look on her face, he shrugged his shoulders. "I guess I've known since I was around eleven or twelve," he replied, facing the wizard. "But my powers are very minimal. I can control the weather and I have a bond with animals, certainly nothing like what Aurie can do. How long have you known?"

"I suspected something when you told us about the unexpected storm that appeared while you were being pursued by the soldiers, also, something Aurie told me a while back. She has telepathic abilities and she told me she had tried to read your thoughts, but for some reason was not able to do so. Only someone with magical abilities can block a telepathic intrusion."

Tony looked sharply at Aurie, and she shamefacedly turned away, realizing he had every right to be angry at her.

"Hmm, something we'll talk about later," he murmured.

"I don't imagine it has been easy trying to hide your powers from Prince Kalian," Armitage pointed out.

"He must have known I had some abilities because I was the only one who could control Cesar. I obviously wasn't a threat to him, and I suppose that was the reason I was never arrested." He stood and walked towards the door. "I think I'll make it an early night. I need to bring the lads up to speed."

Later, while lying in bed, Aurie thought about Tony possessing magic and how he had kept it a secret from everyone. How could he have turned her over to Prince Kalian when he had powers of his own? Was that the reason he showed remorse and regret, or was it because he had the Falcons to protect? It was still difficult for her to forgive him, but she had begun to realize he could not jeopardize the lives of so many for one street kid. If she had been in his place, she would have made the same decision.

Sighing, she rolled over and closed her eyes, silently wishing Eleanor a safe journey.

Chapter Twenty-Five

Aurie was up each morning before the sun peeked over the tree tops. Jasmine always had a hearty breakfast ready, and after everyone had eaten, they went directly to the training field. Before leaving, Armitage made her promise to work on her spells and incantations.

Aurie felt her powers growing, she had learned to control her magic, and Armitage had shown her how to block other people's thoughts. After the noon meal, she spent time with Tony helping him hone his abilities. He proved to be a capable student as he never forgot anything he was taught.

Four days had passed before Armitage returned to the cottage. King Glendon and the Dwarves were sending their warriors out to all the tribes to prepare them for battle. The following evening, Eleanor returned to Primrose Cottage. Armitage sent Aurie out to get Seamus, who was in the back, chopping wood and Tony, who was at the base camp. He asked Sam to join them, as he was beginning to rely more and more on the level-headed man.

Jasmine was working at the hearth when the cottage door opened, her face flushed from the heat. She had tied her hair up into a bun, and when she saw Sam, she raced into the bedroom, quietly closing the door. No sooner had everyone taken a seat than the door opened, and Jasmine re-appeared. Aurie noticed her hair was loose and cascaded down her back, and she had changed into her new flowered apron. Sam's face was flushed, and he looked everywhere except at Jasmine, who placed mugs and a steaming pot of rose hip tea on the table.

Eleanor soon brought everyone up to date on her travels. She had talked to the tribes located on the far side of Lindell Forest, and with the help of the Dryads, had convinced them of the urgency. Aurie noticed the lines of weariness etched on her aunt's face as Eleanor took a drink and massaged the back of her neck. "Our warriors are keeping matters under control, but it is a stressful and continuous battle, I cannot remain on Earth I must return to Fey Wild and stand at my father's side."

Noticing the concerned look on Aurie's face, Eleanor reached over and squeezed her shoulder. "Everyone is well and you must not worry."

"We will leave at first light tomorrow," Armitage said. "Eleanor will return to Fey Wild, and we will go to Westcott."

"Westcott?" Seamus said in surprise.

"Yes," Armitage said. "We must get the Fire Crystal back and return it to Owain. Once that has been done, Prince Kalian will no longer have control of the Underworld. His powers will be greatly diminished and then we will make our move."

"How do you plan on getting to the subterranean pool?" Tony exclaimed. "I'm sure he has soldiers guarding the area day and night."

"Seamus and Sam can have the Falcons create a diversion in Westcott, which should keep the troops busy for a while. In the meantime, Aurie can take us to the location of the tree trunk, with our combined powers, we shouldn't have any difficulty disposing of any of the soldiers who might be guarding the Fire Crystal. We will meet Seamus and the Falcons at a rendezvous point in Lindell Forest. It won't take Prince Kalian long to learn we have taken the Fire Crystal and he and his troops will not be far behind. We will lead them to Whitehawk Pass, where

King Glendon, the Dwarves and the rest of the tribes will be waiting for them on the ridge overlooking the canyon."

Aurie rose, a frown creasing her face. She walked over to the door and opened it, looking at the darkness.

"Is something wrong?" Tony asked.

"I thought I heard movement outside the door, but there's no-one here."

"You've just got a case of pre-battle jitters."

"I guess so," Aurie shrugged, as she returned to the table. Only half-listening to what Armitage was saying, she continued to stare uneasily at the closed door. Maybe Tony was right, and she was just nervous about tomorrow.

After the meeting broke up Aurie went to her room, but couldn't relax, she paced back and forth. Jasmine was lying on her pallet, and she finally rolled over and said in exasperation. "Aurie, you must get some sleep tomorrow will be a long day."

"I'm sorry Jasmine. I guess I'm just nervous."

"I can understand that although I feel you're much too young to be going into battle."

"I have an advantage, so do not worry about me."

"Aurie, you may be a formidable sorceress, and you may have been trained by the most powerful wizard alive, but I'm still going to worry about you."

"I know you are uncomfortable staying here on your own. Will you be alright?"

"It is the safest place for me to be, I have become used to Phineas and Bluebell popping up at the strangest hours. They are quite entertaining, and good company."

Aurie smiled at her friend's comment. "Good night Jasmine."

It was many hours later before Aurie finally fell into a restless sleep.

Chapter Twenty-Six

Long before the sun rose the next morning, everyone was on the road. Aurie had hidden her dagger in her boot, and had buckled her sword around her waist, although she chose to leave her spear behind. She found it more of a nuisance, especially while riding horseback.

Many of the Falcons rode double as there were not enough mounts for everyone. Aurie rode with Tony, as Armitage felt that Cesar's training as a war horse and his speed would prove to be invaluable if they should encounter any difficulties.

Eleanor walked with them for a while and just as quietly as she had appeared, she vanished into the trees. Aurie wished she could have gone to Fey Wild with her, but understood that her duties lay elsewhere.

Armitage refused a mount, and he had no difficulty keeping pace with the riders. The young rebels watched him in amazement as he tirelessly led them through the forest and down the steep mountain trails.

By late afternoon, they arrived at a fork in the trail. Sensing they were close to their destination, the small entourage rode silently through the tall cedars and pines. Climbing steadily upwards, they soon arrived at the crest of a steep hill, far below was Whitehawk Pass.

As had been planned, Aurie dismounted, and Seamus and Tony guided their horses down the wide path, leaving a cloud of dust in the air. Everyone quietly waited for their return and they did not have long to wait.

"The road is clear," Seamus whispered to Armitage. "I'm surprised there aren't any guards posted."

"Keep alert," Armitage warned, as he helped Aurie climb onto Cesar's back. "Take Sam and half of the men and wait here. Make sure anyone who goes with the first advance is riding. When we get to the far end of the pass, wait for my signal and then join us. If we get into trouble, get away as quickly as you can, we'll meet back at Primrose Cottage."

Seamus nodded. He spurred his horse around, and then pointed to Sam and four of the Falcons. "Take my horse," he whispered, as he dismounted and approached one of the young men who would be accompanying Armitage. Sam did the same.

"I'll stay too," a raspy voice said.

Aurie turned in the saddle and stiffened. Fred was steering his horse out of the line.

Armitage frowned, and staring directly at Fred said. "If that is your wish, but trade mounts with one of the lead men in the advance party. Your horse is more seasoned and he's faster."

Fred glared at the wizard, and Aurie thought he was going to protest, but the man was not foolhardy enough to question Armitage's authority. He quickly turned away, but not before looking at her. His demeanor and posture disturbed her, but she dismissed it as being part of her intense dislike of the man.

Armitage, who was standing next to Cesar, placed his hand on her leg, and gave it a reassuring squeeze. Was he sensing her anxiety?

Tony removed his sword from his scabbard and Aurie leaned forward and wrapped her arms around his waist. He steered Cesar down the winding trail, the grade was steep but the horse had no difficulty maneuvering his way down the slope. The rest of the selected horsemen followed, while Armitage walked a few paces behind the last horse. The penetrating cry of a hawk circling high above them pierced the stillness. Aurie tightened her hold, and Tony covered her hands and squeezed them reassuringly.

The three men chosen to be in the lead rode past Cesar, who was fighting his bit as he did not like to have other horses in front. The last three men rode behind Cesar, and they spread out on the road. Armitage walked next to Cesar, comforting Aurie by his presence.

The clopping of the horses' hooves echoed off the towering cliffs.

Heavy undergrowth and bushes crowded large boulders on both sides of the pass. They had ridden half way down the trail when an arrow whistled through the air, striking one of the lead Falcons. He cried out as he fell from his horse, crashing to the ground. In horror, Aurie watched as mounted soldiers swarmed from behind the rocks. Without hesitating, Armitage swung his staff in a wide arch, and an energy blast hit half a dozen of the attackers. One of the soldiers spurred his horse straight towards Cesar, Aurie propelled a blast of energy, hitting him squarely on his chest.

"Great shot Aurie," Tony exclaimed.

A second soldier galloped past the downed trooper making a beeline towards Cesar. Leaning over, he grabbed the warhorse's reins. Cesar reared and his powerful hoofs struck the trooper's horse who bucked in terror, throwing the soldier from his saddle. The startled trooper landed beneath Cesar's thrashing hooves.

During the altercation, two foot soldiers had circled unnoticed behind Cesar, they separated, one approaching on the left flank and the other on the right. The soldier closest to Cesar reached over and grabbed Tony's leg, trying to pull him from the saddle. Tony twisted Cesar's reins around the saddle horn, leaving his left hand free. Relying on the warhorse's savvy in battle, he grasped the sword with both of his hands, then lunged, concentrating solely on disarming his attacker. Aurie realized she was hindering Tony. She released her arms from around his waist, and grabbed the sides of the saddle. She dared not use her powers in fear of striking him.

His companion, unseen by Aurie, reached up and grabbed her arm. She screamed, and tried to retrieve her sword from its scabbard, but she dared not release her precarious hold on the saddle. Realizing its uselessness, she summoned her energy, and sent a blast straight at the soldier. He was dead before he landed on the ground.

"Tony," Armitage yelled above the din. "Get out of here."

Tony nodded, dodging thrusts from the soldier's sword. Grabbing the reins with his right hand, he twisted Cesar's head, and steered the warhorse into the heavy foliage. Aurie felt herself falling, she released her grip on the saddle and wrapped her arms tightly around Tony' waist. Cesar crashed into the undergrowth leveling bushes and shrubs. Aurie lowered her head, leaned into Tony's back, protecting her face from the branches.

She heard the soldiers cursing when they realized they were getting away. Cesar stopped abruptly, almost unseating them. He stood on the edge of a steep slope, but he hesitated for only a second, and then lunged over, sliding down the scree, dislodging pebbles that rolled down the ridge. The soldiers, following in hot pursuit, stopped sharply when they arrived at the crest of the hill. Their mounts balked, ramming into each other and circling each other in terror. Their leader yelled angrily pointing in their direction, ordering them to follow. The troopers spurred their horses down the slope. All at once, the lead horse fell, and Aurie watched in dismay as it fell down the embankment. The soldier was thrown from his saddle, and the terrified horse rolled on top of him.

Cesar never faltered, although carrying two people was taking its toll on him. He was breathing heavily, and his withers and neck were drenched in sweat. When they arrived at the bottom, Tony steered him towards an animal trail. A stream flowed next to the path, and when Cesar tried to stop, Tony pulled his reins up tightly, refusing to let the exhausted horse near the water. It was brown and murky and had a foul odor. He urged Cesar to keep up his strenuous pace. The trail ended, they were in a clearing, surrounded on three sides by a steep wall of rock.

"Quick," he said to Aurie. "Jump down, climb up and hide behind that boulder."

"What are you going to do?"

"I'm going to lead them away from here, and whatever you do, don't show yourself."

"No, we have to stay together."

"Aurie, it's not me they want it's you. Now wait here until I return. I may be gone for a while."

Aurie squeezed Tony's waist and whispered in his ear. "Be careful."

Grabbing her backpack, she jumped off Cesar's back and headed to the boulder, quickly taking cover. Her heart was pounding as she watched Cesar gallop back down the trail and disappear around the bend. She heard a loud crashing and realized Tony had steered him into the heavy bush. He was making so much noise, it wouldn't take the soldiers long to locate them.

She lowered herself to the ground, and leaned back against the rock. She began to shake violently. How had matters turned so terribly wrong? She had slain two men with her magic, and she replayed the events over and over in her mind. She closed her eyes, and prepared to wait for Tony's return.

Chapter Twenty-Seven

A hand reached over and covered her mouth, Aurie struggled to get free.

"It's me, Tony," a voice whispered in her ear.

Aurie opened her eyes, the shadows had lengthened, and the sun had fallen behind the crest of the trees. She was so relieved she flung her arms around his neck. Tony chuckled, and realizing what she had done, she quickly lowered her arms, thankful he could not see her flushed face.

"What happened to the soldiers?" she whispered.

"I managed to give them the slip. Right now, they are barreling through the trees chasing a rider less horse."

"Will Cesar be alright?"

"They won't harm him. He's much too valuable, and if they did, Prince Kalian would have their hides."

Aurie stood up and shook her cramped legs.

"We can't go back down the path, there are troopers everywhere." Tony said.

"What do we do?"

"We go up."

"It's pitch black, we can't see a thing."

"Well, use your magic and make one of those little round things, except make sure it's not too bright."

Smiling at Tony's description, Aurie created an orb. Long black shadows cast off the boulders and the underbrush. She was relieved to see Tony had not forgotten his backpack.

"You go first," he instructed.

She strapped her pack onto her back and started climbing, grabbing sharp rocks, roots and branches to help keep her balance. The incline was steep and treacherous, Tony was breathing heavily. When they arrived at the top, Aurie made the orb disappear, if anyone below should happen to look up, they would see its light. The moon appeared from behind a cloud, they were standing on a plateau. It highlighted the shrubs and bushes in soft silver hues, in the distance the silhouettes of the trees and the looming mountains provided a charcoal backdrop.

"That's the way we must go," Aurie whispered, pointing straight ahead. "It leads to the swinging bridge which crosses the gorge and back to Primrose Cottage. Come on, let's go."

"Aurie, we can't go to Primrose Cottage. It's too dangerous."

"We have to, that's the rendezvous point, and everyone will be there."

"If anyone goes back, probably Armitage, it will only be to get Jasmine, but he won't dally. I'm sure Fred has brought Prince Kalian up to date on everything, and Armitage is aware of that fact. He'll take them all somewhere safe."

"So, you finally realize Fred's the traitor?"

At first Tony did not answer. "I always knew he was ambitious, and obviously money means more to him than loyalty. I should have listened to you at the very first, instead of letting my pride get in the way. I won't make that mistake ever again."

"You're not the only one who made a mistake. I don't doubt for a moment it was Fred listening at the door when we were going over our plans. It's exactly something he would do. I shouldn't have doubted my feelings."

"I guess we both have learned a lesson."

"But at a terrible price. Be forewarned, Tony, the next time I lay eyes on Fred, I will make him pay for his treachery."

Tony shrugged at her remark. "Next time I won't stop you. By the way, didn't you say your aunt lives somewhere near Beargrass Mountain?"

"Yes, at Bloodroot Swamp, in a tree house. I'm sure that would be where Armitage will take the survivors."

"What's the fastest route there?"

"It's almost due east of here, but there are too many gorges and rivers to cross, and unless you know where you are going, we could wander around Lindell Forest forever. We're going to have to walk northeast towards Beargrass Mountain, cut across the top, and then we can follow the trail south to Bloodroot Swamp."

They walked for hours, using the moonlight to guide their way. Tony fell behind her many times, and Aurie reasoned his lack of sleep was catching up on him. They had to find some shelter as they both needed rest.

Eventually the flat terrain ended, and they arrived at the tree line. Considering it safe, Aurie produced another orb. They came across a well-used animal trail and followed it into the dense forest. Tony tripped over a root, and Aurie turned to face him, his face was haggard and he was breathing heavily, if he walked another step, he would collapse.

Aurie spotted a large fallen tree half buried in the ferns, it was gigantic, and they could easily crawl inside the trunk and take cover.

"Come on Tony, let's stop for a while. You need to rest."

"I'm fine. We have to keep going."

"Tony, you can hardly stand up. Come on, they won't be looking for us in the dark. We'll rest for a couple of hours, and then we'll leave."

He nodded in agreement. Arriving at the huge trunk, Aurie glanced inside, and was pleased to see it was dry and warm, and gestured for Tony to crawl in first. The orb provided enough light for her to check out their surroundings. It was then she noticed the blood on Tony's shirt.

"Tony, you're injured," she exclaimed.

"It's just a scratch. I'm okay."

"That's a lot of blood for just a scratch. Let me look at it. Take off your shirt."

Tony unbuttoned his shirt and cringed when Aurie lifted his arm to help him remove it. She hissed through her teeth. There was a deep gash on his shoulder. "Why didn't you tell me earlier?"

"There wasn't any time and I thought it would stop bleeding. Guess it's deeper than I thought."

"Lie back and be quiet," she ordered. She summoned her magic, muttering under her breath as to how stupid men could be at times, and placed her hand over the wound. She sensed his weakness, and realized he had lost a lot of blood. He visibly relaxed, and the strain left his face. "Not many people have their own magical healer at their disposal," he joked.

"Just get some sleep," Aurie replied, as she took his water pouch out of his backpack and gave it to him. "Careful, just a small sip. It might be a while before we get fresh water again."

He soon fell into a fitful sleep. Aurie took off her backpack and dug out her jacket, the nights were cold in the mountains. In a few hours, they would be moving again, and Prince Kalian's soldiers would not be far behind.

She released the orb, and was instantly in darkness. Sleep did not come easily, as she kept reliving the battle, wondering if Armitage and the Falcons had escaped. The soldiers were no match against Armitage's powers. It was the Falcons she was worried about, as they had been greatly outnumbered and Prince Kalian's troops were seasoned soldiers. Instinctively, she knew Armitage would contact her when he was able, and would let them know where they were. There was something nagging her, yet she couldn't quite pinpoint what it was. She closed her eyes, and just as she started to drift off, she realized what it was. She sat up quickly, smacking her head on the knotted wood of the trunk.

"Tony," she whispered urgently, groping for his arm in the dark. "We have to leave."

Tony groaned. "Has it been two hours already?"

"No, but something's been bothering me, and I just thought of what is it. You must have left a blood trail."

"Damn," he said under his breath. "Give us some light."

Aurie conjured up the orb while Tony grabbed his backpack, and pushed her out the entrance. It was only a few hours to daybreak, and it wouldn't be long before the soldiers resumed their search. Once they found the blood trail, it would not take them long to catch up on horseback.

For the first hour, they alternated between running and walking. Lack of sleep was taking its toll on Aurie, and her muscles screamed in protest. Her back ached from carrying her pack. She worried about Tony, as he was still weak from losing so much blood. They drank their water sparingly, and chewed on salt pork while they kept up their hectic pace. She discovered some cranberry bushes along the trail, and although the berries were shriveled and tasted acrid, they provided some sustenance.

The terrain was starting to get rockier and steeper, and Aurie knew they were not far from the base of Beargrass Mountain. Hopefully they would be able to find a cave and take shelter for a short rest. They would have a better chance seeing the soldiers if they were higher up.

Aurie stopped abruptly, and Tony almost collided into her.

"What's the matter?" he asked nervously.

Aurie raised her hand for him to be quiet.

Aurie, it's me, Armitage, are you and Tony alright?

Yes, the soldiers are still following us, but we hope to find shelter soon. Where are you?

I went to Primrose Cottage and picked up Jasmine. Torin joined us on the trail and is here with us. Seamus is taking Sam and the others to Eleanor's. I'm sorry Aurie but none of the Falcons in the advance party survived. And Fred has very conveniently disappeared, along with our only horse.

I guess I'm not surprised. I'll let Tony know.

Aurie, we mustn't use telepathy again and you can't use your powers. If Prince Kalian is in the vicinity, he'll be able to locate you by sensing your location. Be careful.

Okay, we'll meet you at Eleanor's late tomorrow afternoon.

Aurie told Tony about Armitage's message. The most difficult part was when she told him about the Falcons.

"What about Fred?" he asked sharply.

"Gone. I imagine he's in Westcott by now, and he's told everything to Prince Kalian, including the location of Primrose Cottage."

"He'll go straight there you know?"

"He won't find anything if he does. While Armitage was talking to me, I saw a vision of the cottage. He's destroyed everything, there's nothing left."

"Come on, we have a long way to go," Tony said wearily.

"We can stop for a rest if you like. You're white as ghost."

"I'm fine. Let's keep moving. We can rest later."

Aurie realized Tony's sharpness was not directed at her, but was his way of hiding his feelings. The Falcons were close friends of his, many of whom he had known most of his life. He had coerced them into joining the rebels, and she sensed he was putting the blame on himself for their deaths. Obviously her empathic abilities were stronger than she had thought.

They decided to take one of the many animal trails that branched off the main path, the sharp rocks and roots would slow the soldiers' progress. She dared not use her magic to erase their tracks, as she did not want to leave any traces of magic. Once they got closer to the summit, they should be able to find shelter. They picked up their pace, each wrapped in their own thought, listening intently for any sounds of pursuit. It was strangely quiet.

The bush was so dense, it was difficult to make out the trail. Aurie stopped and looked nervously around, something was following them. A black shadow leapt from the foliage, she spun around hurling an energy blast, striking the creature on its side. It howled in fury, landing on the ground on all fours. It was the size of two large men, had enormous fangs, and coal red eyes.

Tony pulled his sword. "Be careful, it's going to charge again."

The second bolt hit the creature in the middle of its chest, it landed in the dirt, stunned. Slowly it rose, growled menacingly, and then disappeared into the trees.

"By the gods, that's the biggest panther I've ever seen," Tony stammered.

"It's a Fey Panther, it's a supernatural creature touched by magic," Aurie said. "Armitage told me about them, but I never thought we'd get a chance to meet one."

"We're not making appropriate time, and we both need some rest, we have to find cover, and soon."

"I imagine Prince Kalian, if he's anywhere in the vicinity, knows exactly where we are, he'll sense I've used magic."

"Come on, there have to be caves in the area."

The sound of horses charging through the underbrush startled them both, the soldiers had caught up with them.

"This way, hurry," Tony whispered.

They tore through the woods, crouching low as they skirted tree trunks and climbed over huge rocks. Tony grabbed her arm and pointed. "Look over there."

Huge boulders, smothered in moss, littered the forest floor, tendrils of lichen dripped from the branches of the trees, and ferns grew as high as Aurie's waist.

"I don't think we should go in there," Aurie whispered. "There's something in there that's not safe."

"We have no choice," Tony replied. "The soldiers are almost on top of us."

The gigantic trees created an ethereal atmosphere. It was then Aurie noticed that the moss was glowing.

"There has to be some place we can take shelter," Tony whispered. "Look, there's an overhang over there, and it looks like it goes back a way into the rock. Come on."

Tony took a step, and started to fall, and reacting on instinct, Aurie grabbed his arm.

The last thing she remembered was Tony yelling "no, stay back" and then everything went black.

Chapter Twenty-Eight

Aurie groaned and opened her eyes. Tony was leaning over her, an anxious look on his face.

"What happened?" she said.

"We're in a cave. We fell, I tried to warn you but it all happened so fast."

"How long was I unconscious?"

"Long enough to scare the hell out of me."

"Sorry."

"I could hear the soldiers moving around but it's been quiet for a while now, hopefully they've given up on finding us and have left."

"I doubt it, they'll keep looking you know. They can't go back empty-handed."

"Let's move into the shadows, if they should find the opening and look down, they'll see us."

Aurie nodded, tried to sit up and gasped as excruciating pain shot up her leg.

"What's wrong?" Tony asked.

"I think my ankle's broken. Let me heal it before I try moving."

Tony nodded. Aurie summoned her magic, but nothing happened. She tried a second time, and again nothing happened.

"My magic, it's gone," she said uneasily.

"What do you mean?"

"What do you think I mean. It's gone. Is that so hard to understand?"

Tony pulled back in surprise at her sharp words, but he said nothing.

"I'm sorry," Aurie said. "I shouldn't have yelled at you. I guess I got scared."

"It's okay, I would have reacted the same way."

"There's strong magic here, maybe it has something to do with the glowing moss."

"What glowing moss?" Tony asked as he looked around. "The rocks and walls are covered with moss, but it's not glowing."

"Funny that you can't see it. Maybe your powers aren't strong enough."

"You just said you have no powers at all, so why can you see it and I can't?"

"I don't know, and this place is strange, I can't quite place it, but I don't think we should stay here any longer than we have to."

"Well we have nowhere else to go now, and since you've lost your abilities and can't heal your ankle, and the soldiers are prowling around outside, we might as well get some rest while we can. We'll wait until morning, and then we'll figure out a way of climbing out of here. Maybe when we are away from this glowing moss your powers will come back and you can heal yourself."

He reached over and removed her backpack. "This might hurt a bit."

Picking her up, he walked into the shadows, then set her down next to a large boulder and opened her pack. He dug around until he found her water pouch, then handed it to her. "That's the last of the water and we're out of provisions. I'm going to look at your foot, hold still."

Aurie leaned back on her elbows, her head back, and she winced when Tony slowly removed her boot. Something heavy was placed on her stomach, and she looked down and spotted her dagger. She had forgotten she had hidden it in her boot.

"It might be a good idea to keep that close at hand." Tony suggested. "We have no idea what's living in this cave."

She placed the dagger on top of her pack within easy reach.

"There's not much I can do with your ankle, at least until we get out of this cave and I can see better," Tony said.

"Help me unbuckle my sword," Aurie replied. "I'll be more comfortable with it off."

Tony removed both their swords and placed them on the ground. "Elevate your foot on my jacket," he said. "That might help a bit. Try and get some rest, you're in for a long night." Then he lay down beside her, and shoved his pack under his head. Having not slept in two days, it did not take him long to fall into an exhausted sleep.

Aurie kept waking up every time she moved, her foot was throbbing, and she was frustrated she was not able to use her powers to heal it. She worried about the morning, and wondered how they were going to climb out of the cave. For a moment, she was annoyed at Tony, he always coped with stress so much better than she. But having someone like that around at a time like this did have its benefits.

Time passed slowly, and she gave up trying to sleep. There was a shuffling noise in the far corner of the cave and she lifted her head straining to see into the shadows. The moon had disappeared behind the clouds, and the glow from the moss was so subtle it was difficult to see more than a few feet.

The sound of a pebble being dislodged startled her, she slowly reached over and grabbed her dagger. At that moment, something touched her arm. Aurie screamed and swung her dagger, but it was wrenched roughly from her hand.

Aurie froze, she could see nothing. "Who are you, what do you want?"

There was no answer.

Suddenly the moss turned a bright fluorescent green, lighting up the cavern. Tony was standing a few feet away, his arms pinned behind his back by a man holding a knife at his throat.

Tony's captor was of medium-build, with long golden hair that reached half way down his back, pointed ears, high cheekbones and sapphire eyes. His face was severe and angular, painted with a fern design that ran from his forehead down to his chin. He was dressed in a dark green tunic, and leather pads covered his shoulders and knees. A longbow and a quiver filled with arrows hung over his shoulder.

Squatting on the floor next to Aurie was a second man, who was clutching her dagger tightly. His hair coloring and eyes were the same as his companion, but his face was bared of markings, and his clothing was made of finer silk. It was then Aurie realized it was a woman. The features of the two creatures were so similar, it was hard to tell them apart.

The female spoke but Aurie shrugged her shoulders, as the language was unknown to her.

"Come with us," the young female ordered. This time Aurie understood.

"I can't walk," she replied. "I broke my ankle."

The woman leaned over and placed her hand on Aurie's foot and almost immediately the pain stopped. These people were obviously magical, and had healing powers.

"Thank you," Aurie said. She stood, putting her weight on her foot, and collapsed. The woman grabbed her around her waist.

"Aurie," Tony said, reaching over to catch her. The man tightened his restraint on Tony's arms, and raised the knife closer to his throat.

"Tony keep still," she warned. "I'm okay."

Aurie faced the woman, sensing she was in no danger. "I don't seem to have any energy."

"Your magical powers are being absorbed by the moss," the woman said. "Lean on my shoulder, and your strength will return as soon as we leave this cave." She faced the man and spoke to him in their own language, he was obviously not in agreement with what she said. After a few tense moments, he lowered his knife, and released Tony's arm. Tony reached down to pick up his and Aurie's swords, but the young man immediately took them from him. Shrugging, Tony grabbed Aurie's boot, and the woman released her hold on Aurie. She waited until the boot was replaced, then she turned and headed towards a tunnel Aurie had not noticed earlier. As she had advised, the moment they left the cave, Aurie's strength began to return, although she sensed her powers had not returned.

They walked for over an hour, down numerous tunnels and labyrinths, passing spacious caverns and dimly lit chambers until they arrived at the edge of a huge drop off.

Water poured down the walls of the cave, and flowed into a dark lagoon, which was surrounded by lush ferns and foliage. A short distance from the pond was a village surrounded by towering stone pillars that rose hundreds of feet above the cave floor, disappearing into a ceiling obscured in darkness. The huts were made of stone, the roofs being held together by grass and mud. In the middle of the settlement, surrounded by the shelters, was a longhouse built of rock and granite. The cave was lit by magical orbs giving the appearance of daylight. Villagers sat before their dwellings, working, playing musical instruments or keeping a sharp eye on their young.

"Wow," said Tony in awe. "This is amazing."

"It's an entire underground city," Aurie said. "I wonder if the water is safe to drink."

The young woman, who had been following closely behind, overheard their conversation. She nodded and gestured towards the pool. She and her companion waited patiently while Aurie and Tony took a deep drink.

"Who are these people?" Tony whispered. "And what is this place?"

"I'm not sure," Aurie answered. "It's obvious they're not human, I think they might be Elves. They look a lot like the Eldorans except for their smaller physique, but I don't think their magic is as powerful. Also, they carry longbows and arrows, not swords or spears."

"Then how come you can't use your powers?"

"They must have placed a spell on the moss, which causes it to absorb them. I remember something Armitage told me about Elves. Even if I had my powers, I wouldn't be able to use them, as I believe they have a natural resistance to outside magic."

"Do you think they're friendly?"

"I believe so, although I have never met an Elf. When I was staying in Fey Wild, Eleanor talked about them, although legend has it that they all left Lindell Forest, and were no longer living on Earth. I wonder where these Elves came from."

When they had finished drinking, the female gestured for them to follow her down a path skirting the lagoon. When they arrived at the village, she led them towards the longhouse.

"Stay here," the male ordered, uttering his first words. He opened a large oak door and disappeared inside. He was gone for what seemed to Aurie a very long time. The female stood rigidly, and did not speak to them. The inhabitants of the village continued with their tasks, taking no notice of them.

The door opened and the male appeared, he nodded and the female gestured for Aurie and Tony to enter. Aurie waited until her eyes adjusted to the dark interior. A wooden table ran the length of the hall, and Elves were sitting on the benches, eating quietly. The walls were covered in brilliant tapestries, and swords and shields hung on display. At the far end of the room, an elderly male wearing a crown embedded with jewels and precious gems, reclined on a large golden throne.

Aurie and Tony followed the young man, and stopped a few feet from the throne. Listening to their conversation Aurie suddenly realized the language being spoken was very like that of the Eldorans, and although her knowledge of Eldoran was limited, she had managed to learn enough when she was in Fey Wild to understand most of what was said.

"The human warriors have set up a camp not more than a mile from the clearing. The male is human, but we do not know the female's tribe. Her magic is strong enough to penetrate our shields. She was injured when she and her companion fell into the moss cave. I took their swords, and the female tried to use this weapon, but Oria disarmed her."

The male handed the swords and the dagger over to the older man, who examined them carefully. He returned the swords to the young man, but kept the dagger, turning it over and touching the engravings.

"I sense this dagger was fabricated by Dwarf magic. I do not believe our guests are dangerous. We will make them comfortable and offer them some sustenance. Once they have rested, we will have the opportunity to question them."

"Yes, Your Highness."

"By what names are you called?" the young man enquired, as he led Aurie and Tony towards the door of the longhouse.

"She is called Aurie, and I am Tony," Tony answered.

"I am Oran. This is my twin sister, Oria, and our father is King Osmar of the Elves."

"It is an honor to meet you," Aurie replied. "May good health and happiness fill your days."

Suddenly the room became quiet, and Aurie realized she had answered them in the manner a High Elf greeted strangers. She chastised herself for being so careless.

"Come," Oria said, as she looked at Aurie reflectively. "We will find you a place to stay, and then after you have rested and changed into clean clothing, we will talk."

Aurie and Tony were led to a small hut located not far from the longhouse. "Your clothes need repair, and your shirt is covered in blood," Oria said, looking directly at Tony. "After they have been cleaned, they will be returned to you. Here are some clothes you may wear in the meantime."

"Thank you."

"Once you are presentable, King Osmar will grant you an audience," Oran advised, as he and Oria left the hut.

"I'd just as soon keep my own clothes," Tony muttered.

"It would be an insult if we appeared before their king dressed as we are. Manners are extremely important to the Elves, so it would be best if we followed their advice," Aurie said.

Shrugging Tony turned his back and began to undress. Aurie did the same.

"Did you understand what Oran and King Osmar were talking about?" Tony asked.

"Yes, their language is very like the Eldorans. They know you are human, and that I have magic, but they are not sure what my lineage is, I don't imagine they've ever seen someone like me before."

241 • Child of the Ancients

"Don't let them know you're a royal princess. We need to find out what they plan to do with us first, before we provide them with too much information."

Aurie remembered something else Eleanor had told her about Elves, they were fierce protectors of their own. "They could be violent if they think we are a threat."

"Well right now we are in their hands, and I don't want to make any enemies here. Hopefully they will permit us to leave without any problem."

"They know about the soldiers chasing us, and that they're from the man village, as most magical folks call it."

"I wonder how they know about Westcott and the soldiers."

"I'm sure they are aware of everything that is going on in Lindell Forest. We are not far from Whitehawk Pass and they must keep a close watch on travelers using that route, as well as the activities of the troopers. I would imagine they are highly trained warriors, as apparently they have managed to keep their presence a secret, not only from Prince Kalian, but from the rest of the inhabitants in Lindell Forest as well."

"That's what worries me. They're not going to be happy having two strangers fall into their midst."

"We better not delay any longer. Are you ready?"

At first Tony didn't answer, and then suddenly he sputtered. "I am NOT going out there looking like this."

Aurie spun around and covered her mouth, stopping from laughing out loud. Tony's leggings barely covered his knees, and his tunic was so tight, he couldn't get it buttoned up. When he looked up and saw Aurie, he stopped complaining and smiled in appreciation. She was dressed in a gown made of the finest green silk, with burgundy leaves embroidered throughout the material. It fit her perfectly, as she was close in height and had the same slim build as Oria.

"Wow, you almost look like a girl. I don't think I've ever seen you in a dress before."

Aurie punched him playfully on his arm as they left the hut and headed towards the longhouse. When they arrived at the door, Oria stepped out, almost colliding with them. She looked fleetingly at Tony and her eyes shone in merriment.

"I am sorry but we do not have any clothing your size. You are taller and bigger than anyone in our village," she apologized.

"Thank you for your hospitality and kindness," Aurie said, answering for Tony. "The material is exquisite. I have never seen the like."

"Our females spin and weave all of our fabrics. It is an art that has been passed down through the ages. Come, you must be hungry. We will eat, and then King Osmar wishes to have an audience."

Aurie and Tony were offered a seat half way down the table. A beautiful Elf dressed in a russet-colored gown walked towards them. She had long golden-brown hair, the most exquisite blue eyes Aurie had ever seen, and was wearing an emerald and diamond necklace. She laid a plate of food and a tankard of water before each of them. Tony thanked her, and watched her as she glided gracefully across the room. Aurie knocked Tony's goblet with her elbow, and the water landed in his lap. He jumped up in surprise, and glared at Aurie, but she ignored him, and concentrated on eating her meal. He muttered under his breath, then reached over and set his goblet upright. After they had eaten, Oran approached them. "Come, the King awaits your presence."

Aurie and Tony followed the solemn Elf to the throne. "I trust you enjoyed your meal?" King Osmar asked, smiling as he looked at Tony's attire and wet trousers.

"The food was excellent Your Majesty, and we thank you for your hospitality," Aurie answered, bowing low.

Oran turned and faced Aurie. "We are aware that your companion and defender is human, but King Osmar wishes to know the name of your tribe. We are not aware of any other Elves who reside in Lindell Forest."

Aurie started to correct Oran's misconception of Tony's status, but Tony shook his head warning her to say nothing.

"I am not Elf, I am half Eldoran, and half Ancient. For many years, I lived in the man village as a slave."

A united gasp resounded throughout the room and Aurie saw anger and disbelief in the faces. She remembered a similar reaction from Eleanor when she had learned about Aurie's servitude. For an Elf or an Eldoran to be held captive as a slave, especially by a human, was inconceivable.

King Osmar stared into Aurie's eyes for the longest time. "How it is the Eldorans did not free you and demand retaliation?" he asked sharply. "They do not bring their offspring to Earth, only their most seasoned warrior's travel through the dimensions."

"They did not know I existed, Your Majesty," Aurie answered. "I was rescued by a warrior from the man village and a powerful wizard, and I now reside in Lindell Forest. It is a long story."

"There is nothing we like better than a good tale."

Aurie glanced at Tony and shrugged.

"Yes, Your Majesty," She responded, thinking of how much he reminded her of Armitage.

"Come sit on these cushions and make yourselves comfortable."

Aurie sighed, and then she settled back and began her story. It would be a long night.

Chapter Twenty-Nine

Aurie opened her eyes and stretched. Tony's pallet was empty.

King Osmar had kept her them up late into the night. In telling their story, Aurie had left huge gaps, not mentioning her amulet or finding out who her parents were. She made no mention of Eleanor or visiting Fey Wild. When she told them she lived with Armitage Ravenswood and he was her teacher and mentor, everyone in the longhouse began talking at once. It seemed that Armitage was well known everywhere, even with Elves who kept their whereabouts a secret.

"That old goat," King Osmar chuckled, "Is he still around. I haven't seen him in over five hundred years."

When Aurie mentioned Prince Kalian, she was surprised at the reaction. The Elves were aware of his presence, but did not seem to be overly concerned. When she tried to explain how imperative it was they remain alert, King Osmar nodded his head and smiled. Aurie knew she had not got through to him or anyone else in the longhouse. At that moment, she sympathized with Armitage and could fully understand his frustration.

Their lack of sleep soon caught up with them, but it had been late before they were permitted to return to their hut. They collapsed on their pallets and had fallen asleep almost instantly. When she awakened, she spotted her clothes lying on the table, they had been mended and cleaned. Her dagger had been returned as well but there was no sign of her long sword. Tony's sword was leaning against the wall behind the door.

She dressed quickly. The villagers were attending to their chores, and a few of them nodded as she passed them on her way to the longhouse. She opened the heavy door and stepped inside.

Tony was standing next to Oran and Oria a short distance from the entrance. His face was flushed, and Aurie sensed the tension as she approached the small group.

"I'm sorry, but I don't understand why King Osmar will not allow us to leave," Tony said through clenched teeth. "Lord Armitage and our friends will be expecting us sometime today. If we do not show up, they will be worried about our safety."

"We cannot allow you or Aurie to leave," Oran replied. "None of the tribes in Lindell Forest are aware that our village exists, and it must remain a secret."

Aurie stepped between Tony and Oran. She reached over and squeezed Tony's arm, shaking her head. Tony's face turned a deeper shade of red, and then he angrily looked away.

"We greatly respect King Osmar's decision," she said. "However, it is imperative that we be allowed to talk to him and explain our situation."

"He has made his decision," Oran responded curtly. "We will not discuss this matter again."

Aurie looked beseechingly at Oria, hoping the easier-tempered Elf would intervene on their behalf.

"Wait Oman, let us grant their request," Oria said. "Perhaps hearing what our father has to say will make them understand why his decision must be obeyed?"

Oman shrugged, then turned and walked towards the throne. King Osmar listened to the young man, and then he shook his head. His face was flushed and Aurie surmised he was not accustomed to having his orders questioned, Oman gestured for them to approach.

"Oman tells me you wish to leave."

"Yes, Your Majesty," Aurie replied.

"It is impossible."

"We give our solemn oath that we will not reveal your whereabouts to anyone. Your secret will remain with us."

"I do not take your promise lightly, as an Eldoran's word is her bond, but I cannot allow you to leave. Our village has been secluded for over five hundred years, ever since the Magic Wars. We have lived peacefully since that time and announcing our existence would destroy our way of life. I am sorry, but my decision is final."

"You must understand that it is only a matter of time before Prince Kalian finds you," Aurie responded, hoping she had not overstepped her boundaries. "And when he does, he will not be lenient. He plans on eliminating anyone who possesses magical abilities. He believes that is the only way he will have absolute control. Surely you must understand?"

"We can defend ourselves. We have strong magic and our warriors are well-trained." Aurie sensed the rising anger in King Osmar's voice.

"But your numbers are small, Prince Kalian is a powerful wizard, and practices Dark Magic. He has the beasts from the Underworld at his beck and call, and has his own army, who are well-trained in fighting and weaponry. You wouldn't have a chance against that kind of power."

"Then we will have to take our chances," Oran said angrily.

"Silence Oran," King Osmar commanded. "I will speak no more on this subject. Take them back to their dwelling."

Oran left them outside the door of their hut. After they went inside, Aurie sat down at the table while Tony paced angrily.

"We must get away from here," Aurie said. "Armitage has no idea where we are as I can't send him a message. And there's something else I thought of last night."

Detecting the seriousness in her voice, Tony stopped pacing.

"We know Prince Kalian was alerted of our plans and that he had his soldiers waiting for us at Whitehawk Pass. We were greatly outnumbered, yet you and I managed to escape, as did Armitage and the rest of the Falcons hiding in the trees above the canyon. Fred was with them, so I am quite sure he managed to alert Prince Kalian as to their whereabouts. Prince Kalian knew we wouldn't be able to return to Primrose Cottage, and we would be forced to go elsewhere."

"What are you saying?"

"Think about it. We were being pursued by hand-picked seasoned soldiers on horseback, and you and I were walking. Yet they never caught up to us. Their instructions were to push us, but to not capture us."

"By the gods," Tony moaned in dismay. "We were leading them straight to Eleanor's tree house."

"And the portal to Fey Wild. Prince Kalian may not be able to send the beasts to Fey Wild through the rift, but with his growing powers, he might have found a way to travel there on his own."

"It won't take the soldiers long to find out where we are. As soon as Prince Kalian arrives, he will immediately detect the presence of magic. We must try to convince the Elves to flee before he gets here."

"You know they won't listen to us Tony, they'll stand and fight before they'll leave."

"Then we must leave, as soon as possible."

There was a sharp rap on the door and Aurie quickly ran and opened it.

Oria and Oran were standing in the doorway, and Aurie noticed the strained look on Oria's face. "Our King has decided to grant Tony his wish," she said. "We will release him but his memory will be wiped clean."

"You just mentioned me," Tony said. "What about Aurie?"

"She will remain with us. Should we release her, her powers will return, and our memory manipulation would not work on her. Her magic is too strong."

"No way," Tony said angrily. "I will not go without her."

"Then you both must remain with us, and this matter will not be discussed again, King Osmar is being more than fair."

Before Tony could respond, Aurie walked over and stood before the proud warrior. "Please thank your father for his most generous gift. How much time does Tony have before he is released?" she asked.

"He has one more day," Oria said as she and Oran walked away.

"This is ridiculous," Tony sputtered as Aurie closed the door. "Isn't there anything we can do?"

"Think of a plan before tomorrow morning." Aurie whispered. "And it better be a good one."

Chapter Thirty

The following morning, after having a quick meal, Aurie and Tony wandered around the village, chatting amicably with the inhabitants, gradually making their way down to the lagoon. They stopped and watched some youngsters splashing in the water, then they followed the stream leading to the base of the waterfall.

"What do you think?" Tony asked, looking up the embankment. "The water is cold, and not polluted like all the other streams in Lindell Forest. The source of the waterfall must originate somewhere deep under the mountain."

"I still think we should try going back to the moss cave, although I'm not sure if I can remember the way," Aurie frowned.

"Two reasons that's not a clever idea," Tony responded. "One, we wouldn't get more than ten feet from the village before we're stopped, Oran is a skilled warrior, and I'm sure he has guards posted everywhere. Two, assuming we did make it back to the cave, and we managed to climb out, the soldiers would be there to greet us. We can't take the chance your powers are back. It's just too dangerous."

Aurie shrugged, saying nothing.

"I think our only chance is to climb to the top of the waterfall and see if it's possible to follow the stream, there has to be a tributary somewhere that will lead us outside. I doubt if the Elves have only one entrance to their village, there has to be a backup route somewhere."

"Come on," Aurie said quietly, pulling Tony away from the falls. "We better get back, or they'll start looking for us, we don't want anyone to get suspicious."

Aurie and Tony had talked for hours the evening before, trying to come up with a plan of escape, and just when they had run out of ideas, Tony had thought about the waterfall. It was all they had, and they knew if their plan failed, they would not see each other again. The remainder of the day went quickly. After eating their evening meal, they returned to their hut and bundled their provisions in their packs.

"Aurie," Tony said. "I want you to know that if this doesn't work, and we get caught, they'll separate us right away, and I won't be able to tell Armitage anything about this place or where you are, not with my memory erased. You have to keep trying to get away, promise me you'll do that?"

"I promise Tony, but I don't plan on being anywhere near this place when Prince Kalian makes his move."

"Good, because I think my life would be very dull if I didn't have soldiers chasing me all the time and fey panthers, or whatever you call them, trying to make a meal out of me."

Before Aurie could respond, Tony leaned over and kissed her softly on her lips. "You've become very special to me, Princess Aurialana."

"And you to me," she whispered.

"We'll discuss this later, but right now, we need to get out of here."

"I wish we could do something to help the Elves, I talked to Oria today and I stressed to her how imperative it is they leave."

"What would their chances be if Prince Kalian does find them?"

"None, especially against Dark Magic and he won't come alone, I'm sure he will have some of his beasts with him, they would be slaughtered."

"All we can do is hope Oria believes what you told her, and she can convince King Osmar to do whatever it takes to get everyone to safety."

Tony found a torch and a flint, and stuffed them inside his shirt, then he and Aurie put on their backpacks. He retrieved his sword and buckled it on. "King Oswald never returned your long sword, we'll have to make do with mine."

Then he opened the door and peered outside, except for the sound of the waterfall in the distance, the village was quiet. Most of the orbs had been extinguished, and the few that remained provided sufficient light for them to see. They stayed in the shadows, walking around the perimeter of the village and hiding behind the enormous columns. When they arrived at the lagoon, they picked up their pace, it took them a few minutes to get to the base of the waterfall. Tony gestured for Aurie to go before him, the embankment was steep, and she struggled to keep her footing. Grabbing a large rock for support, she dislodged a pebble and it clattered down the slope, she froze, her heart pounding wildly.

Nothing stirred, breathing a little easier, she continued climbing, taking special caution to not step on any loose rocks. Arriving at the top, they were relieved to see the fern-shrouded entrance was wide enough for them to pass through. There was a rocky path following the stream, which allowed them to walk single-file without having to wade through the icy stream. It was not long before the darkness completely enveloped them. Aurie grabbed the back of Tony's shirt, fearing they would become separated. When he finally lit the torch, she visibly relaxed.

They followed the never-ending path deeper and deeper into the bowels of the cave, yet no branches or tunnels diverted away from the stream. Aurie sensed they were going downhill, and suspected Tony's suspicion that it was an underground river was correct. Yet there was something unusual about the flow of the stream, she suddenly realized what it was, the water was flowing upstream. She marveled at their ingenuity.

Unfortunately, there were times when the path narrowed and disappeared, and they were forced to climb over boulders or wade through the raging torrent. For one terrifying moment, Tony lost his footing on the slippery rocks but managed to keep a tight grip on the torch. It sputtered but did not go out and Aurie breathed a sigh of relief. Without her magic, she would not be able to conjure an orb and the thought of wandering around in a cave in total darkness was alarming. They turned a corner, and Tony stopped dead in his tracks, she was only a few paces behind and almost knocked him over.

The stream had ended and the water gushed into a large pool. The florescent moss was growing everywhere, on the ground and over the walls of a huge cavern carved out over the millennia by the continuous movement of the water. At that moment, the torch went out.

"Tony, can you see anything at all?" she asked nervously.

"Just barely, the same as when we first fell into the cave, how about you?"

"The moss is glowing again, and it's affecting me the same way."

Tony removed his backpack. "Here, sit down and try to save your strength. I'm going to see how deep the pool is, maybe there's a way of getting out that way."

Before Aurie could protest, he dived and disappeared. She shook her head in frustration, angry once again at his impulsiveness. Just when she began to worry he surfaced, and swam over to the edge of the basin.

Noticing the worried look on her face, he reached up and squeezed her knee in reassurance.

"It opens up into another cavern and there's a light source coming from somewhere, probably the moss," he wheezed. "It's a long swim, do you think you can make it?"

Aurie nodded.

"We'll have to leave our packs and my sword, their weight will drag us down."

"What about our water and food?"

"It can't be helped, we have to keep moving, when the Elves find out we're missing, it won't take them long to figure out the route we took. They'll be on us in no time at all. Oran is a skilled warrior, and I don't know if I'm good enough to fight an Elf who has magical powers."

"Maybe we should hide everything instead of just leaving them out in the open, it might give us more time if they don't find our belongings."

Tony nodded, climbed out of the water, and gathered everything in his arms. He walked over to the boulders and immediately found a deep crevice, he stuffed the packs and the weapon inside and returned to where Aurie was sitting.

"I wonder if anyone will ever find them, they could remain buried forever," Aurie said sadly.

"Can't be helped," Tony said, "Come, the longer we wait, the weaker you'll become."

Realizing Tony was right, Aurie lowered herself into the chilly water.

"The deeper we go, the darker it gets," Tony said as he joined her in the water. "Take my hand and hang on tightly."

Aurie nodded, took a deep breath, and then dove.

The pull of the current was strong, and soon her legs felt heavy, and she struggled to keep up with Tony, terrified she would lose her grip. Her lungs were burning, and just when she thought she could go no farther, he gave her arm a tug and pulled her upwards. They climbed out of the frigid water, and collapsed on a rock, breathing hard, shivering uncontrollably. Surprisingly, the cave floor was warm to the touch.

"How can that be, when the water is like ice?" Aurie chattered,

Tony shrugged and stood up. "Elf magic I suppose, are you rested enough to do some exploring?"

Aurie smiled, Tony always accepted events the way they happened, never fretting as to what lay ahead, eagerly willing to face any obstructions he might encounter. At times, she wished she was more like him in that respect.

"I'm feeling a lot stronger," she answered. "I don't see any moss anywhere, I wonder if my powers are back."

She tried to conjure up an orb, but nothing happened. "It's too soon I guess."

"There's no moss," Tony pondered, "and we can see, that means there has to be a light source fairly close."

"This cave is immense," Aurie said.

"Let's just follow the wall and hopefully we'll find an exit out of here, I'm getting really tired of caves."

Aurie stood up, reluctant to leave the warmth of the stone. They passed several passages leading to other caverns, but they continued walking in as a straight a line as possible. The underground lake was miles behind them, they had not passed any other streams since they began their trek.

It had not taken their clothing long to dry, as the walls of the cave, and the huge boulders and rocks radiated heat.

Hours later, Tony stopped, looking up at the cavernous expanse of the cave. "What's wrong?" Aurie asked nervously.

"It's getting darker, so it must be close to night fall, we need to find a place to rest."

"Look, there's a small fissure over there, about half way up that pile of rubble."

They climbed up to the crevice, and using all her concentration, Aurie conjured up an orb, it appeared in her hand, and she smiled happily. Her powers were slowly returning.

She guided the light into the crack and leaned over to look inside, a rustling sound startled her, and she jumped back in fright. Something flew past her head, and she screamed.

Tony laughed, and then patted her shoulder lightly. "It's only a little bat. Don't worry, it won't hurt you."

Aurie crawled into the crevice, choosing to ignore his comment. The rocks were warm and would keep them comfortable during the night. Tony followed her inside, it would be crowded but they would be safe if anything passed below while they were sleeping.

Aurie laid her head down on her arm, conscious of Tony's closeness. She shuffled over, trying to get comfortable.

"Keep still," he muttered. "There's not enough room in here to breathe, let alone move." He reached over and pulled her close, and in a few minutes, he was snoring.

Aurie was exhausted and finally drifted off to sleep, but not before she whispered. "Not all bats are cute and cuddly Tony. One day I'll tell you about the Fire Bats."

Chapter Thirty-One

They awoke hours later, stiff and hungry. They followed a stone path that twisted around huge boulders, leading them farther and farther into the immense cave. Aurie examined the plants that grew among the rocks, but she had never seen them before and did not know if they were edible.

Tony pointed upwards, above them was a huge opening. The sun, partially obscured by a dark cloud, was shining obliquely into the cave.

"I think we've found our way out," Tony said. "You ready for another climb?"

Nodding, Aurie stepped in front of Tony and grabbed the edge of a huge boulder. She pulled herself up, and then looked down at him with a grin on her face. "Try and keep up, okay?"

There were numerous footholds and the rock walls were uneven and not difficult to climb. When they got to the top they stopped to catch their breath, surveying the landscape. Dense trees and withered foliage and bushes grew everywhere, and Aurie was again reminded of the changing landscape in Lindell Forest.

"Tony, I think I know where we are, the shape of those mountains seems familiar. Look, there's a trail over there, heading north east, it leads to the gorge and the swinging bridge. We have to climb over the pass on Beargrass Mountain, which leads us to Eleanor's, we should make it to the gorge just before dusk."

"Armitage will be worried, we've already lost so much time, are your powers strong enough to teleport us?"

"I think so, but I don't think it's a smart idea if I used my magic, teleporting takes a lot of energy and would be detectable by Prince Kalian even if he were a distance from here."

"We'd have time to warn Armitage and the others and then we'd all be gone before Prince Kalian figures out our location."

"True, but there's another problem. I know how to teleport myself, but I've never tried it on anyone else, I didn't get that far in my training."

"So how different can it be if you teleported both of us, what could go wrong?"

"You could be disintegrated, exploding into a million pieces, or you could be split...."

Tony gulped, and his face went pale. "Never mind, we'll walk."

They quickly slid down the embankment and headed towards the path. Along the way, Aurie searched for edible plants, and was pleased when she found some dried cranberries, she also spotted a patch of wild chives growing under a rock.

"Dried berries and wild onion," Tony muttered. "Never thought I'd see the day when I thought they would be a feast."

"We'll get something to eat when we get to Eleanor's. For now, we need to keep our strength up," Aurie replied, handing the berries to Tony.

Stopping for only two short breaks, they eventually arrived at the river. The water was brown and murky, and was just as turbulent as Aurie remembered it to be when she had passed this way three years earlier. Dark clouds had been building up for the past hour, and a strong wind had picked up, causing the huge trees to sway and bend. A bolt of lightning lit up the sky, and rain began to fall in cold, icy sheets. Aurie shivered. The downpour did not last long, but it was enough to soak their clothing. Not wanting to waste valuable time, they had not taken refuge from the thunderstorm, but continued walking.

A few hours later they passed the swinging bridge, the ropes had been cut. Aurie was not overly concerned. The soldiers must have arrived after Armitage and the Falcons had passed this way.

A fine mist had rolled in after the rain and now clung to the ground and wrapped around the branches of the trees. The forest was eerily quiet, and Aurie reached over and pulled Tony's sleeve, getting his attention. He was already aware something was amiss, and raised his finger to his lips, warning her to be quiet. He pointed to a huge boulder a few feet ahead of then. Aurie nodded, and just as she moved towards it, a dark shadow exploded from the underbrush and landed heavily on Tony, throwing him to the ground. It was the fey panther, it must have been stalking them for miles.

The cat's claws raked Tony's shoulder, his arms strained as he twisted the beast's head, trying to keep away from its lethal fangs. Rolling over and over on the pathway, he flung the panther to the side. Breathing heavily, he stood up and stepped back, preparing for a second assault. Aurie reached down and removed her dagger from her boot. Tony noticed her movement, and moved closer to where she was standing. The bank, weakened by the heavy rain, crumbled and Aurie watched in horror as he fell backwards. At that moment the huge cat pounced, twisting sharply, she threw her dagger, and it imbedded in the panther's chest, but it did not stop the huge cat. Summoning her powers, she blasted it with a powerful bolt and the animal fell heavily to the ground just a few inches from where she was standing.

She spun around, and raced over to the ledge, looked down, all she could see were huge rocks and the turbulent river as it wound its way through the gorge. She called loudly, but there was no way Tony could have heard her over the roar of the water. She stopped shouting, realizing that if the fall had not killed him the raging torrent would have pulled him under. She turned and numbly walked back to the panther, she cautiously poked it with her boot, but it lay motionless. Reaching down, she pulled the dagger from its chest, wiping the blood on her leggings. Swaying in agony, she fell to her knees as the tears fell unheeded down her face, it had happened so quickly, she found it hard to believe Tony was gone.

She moaned, suddenly realizing it would not take Prince Kalian long to discover her whereabouts. She must get to Eleanor's as quickly as possible, and the fastest means of getting there would be to teleport. Summoning her powers, she pictured Eleanor's treehouse, the ground shifted beneath her, and she felt as if she were being pulled into a tornado. Her head spun dizzily, and she landed heavily in the dirt. She stood, looking slowly around. The devastation before her was overwhelming, the treehouse, no more than ten feet away, had been torched and the charred branches of the willow twisted grotesquely. The air was filled with heavy smoke, and she covered her nose with her hand, trying not to inhale the acrid fumes.

Walking past the charred remains, she hugged her arms tightly to her chest, using all of her willpower to keep walking. She headed towards the pool, the water barely reached her knees, dead foliage and scum floated on the surface. Wading through the contaminated water, she ducked under the waterfall, which was now a mere trickle. The portal had been destroyed, the white stone and the wooden box had been shattered, closing off the only means of getting to Fey Wild.

She turned and retraced her steps. Climbing wearily out of the pool, she walked over to a huge boulder located in the middle of the yard and leaned against it. She stared despondently at the vast destruction, unsure of what to do next. Where was everyone? Had they arrived here before or after the devastation? If Armitage had managed to escape, why hadn't he contacted her to warn her away? Her thoughts flew in all directions.

She sensed a change in the surrounding energy, and she stiffened. The smoke parted, and a man dressed in a long black robe, and holding a staff walked steadily towards her. His features had changed drastically since the last time she had seen him, his body was emaciated, he was bald and his eyes burned in hatred.

"You led me on a long chase young sorceress," he said impassively, "but this time I won't under-estimate you as I did before."

A blast of energy hit her and she fell forwards, landing heavily on the ground. She lay motionless, and pain such as she had never experienced coursed through her body.

"Where's Drummond?" Prince Kalian asked sharply.

"Do you think I would tell you that?" Aurie answered bitterly, lifting her head.

"You really must learn to control your thoughts a little better, so young Drummond is dead, well, that's just one less matter for me to worry about, as I have no time for traitors."

"He's no traitor, he was brave and decent," Aurie said, staring at the charred ground.

"Oh, how touching, you had feelings for him. Surely you can do better than he?"

Aurie refused to rise to his taunt. "What have you done to Lord Armitage and Princess Eleanor?"

Prince Kalian squatted, so that his face was almost level with hers.

"Worried about your friends. How noble."

"Something you would never understand," Aurie whispered, all the revulsion she felt for the man reflected on her face.

Prince Kalian rose; he leaned on his staff, looking at the devastation surrounding them. "It appears Lord Armitage knew he would be walking into a trap, so he's hiding somewhere with his pathetic band of survivors, his disappearance does not concern me at this moment."

"It should because he's more powerful than you'll ever be, and when he finds you he will destroy you."

"That remains to be seen," Prince Kalian said. "As for Princess Eleanor, now she was a worthy opponent, and put up a valiant struggle."

Aurie felt an icy pang of fear. "But she escaped, didn't she? I saw the portal and it's been fractured."

"That is true, and considering the extent of her injuries, I'm surprised she had the fortitude to make it to the portal at all."

"Fey Wild will be closed to you forever," Aurie said, clenching her jaw.

"For the time being, but for now it's merely an annoying deterrent."

Prince Kalian spun around and walked towards her, a bemused look on his face. "Your concern for that magical creature puzzles me, now why would you care about her wellbeing?"

"Her reputation is known far and wide, she's a great warrior and a powerful sorceress."

"Of course," Prince Kalian said slowly. "She's your aunt. You really haven't quite mastered your telepathic abilities, have you?"

Aurie shuddered, remembering everything Armitage had told her about controlling her fears and allowing Prince Kalian to get into her mind.

"Interesting, that makes you half Eldoran and half Ancient, which explains your powers. You must have inherited them from both bloodlines," he continued. "And to think you were living all these years at Windermere Castle, right under my nose."

"Ironic, isn't it?" Aurie sneered. "All those lives you took trying to gain your powers and you could have reached your goal so much faster if you had only known about me. You only have yourself to blame, your greed and corruptness has left you blind to everything around you."

Prince Kalian's face turned dark with rage, he raised his staff and Aurie rolled behind the boulder, anticipating his next move, the rock exploded, and fragments ricocheted in all directions. She felt a searing pain in her thigh.

Prince Kalian approached her, and she felt both anger and intense fear, before she could retaliate, he hurled a second blast directly at her. The pain was so intense, she screamed, her body shaking convulsively, she rolled onto her back, lying motionless on the ground. She opened her eyes and stared at Prince Kalian, standing directly over her, a bored look on his face.

"You are no match for me, young sorceress."

"Does ruling Westcott mean so much to you that you must kill all who stand in your way?" Aurie panted. "If that's the case, you can have the throne; I want no part of it."

Prince Kalian laughed manically, sending shivers down her back.

"Do you think that's my goal, to rule an impoverished village with a handful of starving peasants and a castle falling into ruin?"

"You've never shown otherwise."

"My path lays elsewhere young sorceress, and Lord Armitage is quite aware of my ambitions, I'm surprised he never told you."

"You're talking in riddles."

"He never told you about the Prophesy, did he?"

Aurie shook her head in confusion, "What Prophesy, what you are talking about?"

"I must say I am intrigued, now why would he keep that information from you?"

"You're talking nonsense, and if he thought I should know about some Prophesy, he would have told me."

"Even when it directly involves you?"

Aurie stared in stunned silence at Prince Kalian. 'You'd say anything to turn me against Lord Armitage, but it won't work."

"You're but a pawn in his plans, unfortunately, you won't be alive long enough to find out what I'm saying is true. But know one thing, he has used you, when you die all of Lord Armitage's hopes and dreams will be for naught."

Aurie stared defiantly into his eyes, her thoughts turned to Tony, and the future they might have had.

But the final blow did not come, as suddenly the silence was disrupted by a roar that echoed through the forest shaking the ground with its intensity. Howling in anger and rage, Prince Kalian disappeared, but not before she heard his parting words in her mind. "Fate is with you once again, young sorceress, but we will meet again."

An enormous creature swooped out of the sky, its massive wings beating rapidly. Aurie tried to defend herself, but an impenetrable shield protected it from her blast of magic. The last thing she remembered was being plucked from the ground by razor sharp talons, and then everything went dark.

Chapter Thirty-Two

She was in a cave, with stalagmites hanging from the roof, and steam hissing out of fissures. A shuffling noise came from the far side of the cavern, she stood up quickly, fighting dizziness and nausea, a burning pain throbbed down her leg, and she remembered the rock shattering and a splinter hitting her thigh. Leaning weakly against a boulder, she summoned her powers, ready to defend herself.

A gigantic creature emerged from behind a huge block of granite. Aurie shook her head in disbelief, it was Owain. She froze, although every fiber in her body screamed for her to flee, instinctively she knew she must not show any fear.

Owain lumbered to a stop a few feet away, she bowed her head. "Greetings Lord Owain."

Smoke and flames erupted from the dragon's mouth and nose, slashing his tail from side to side; he lowered his massive head and stared into her eyes.

"Greetings young sorceress. I will not harm you," he said in a deep sonorous voice.

"Thank you, My Lord."

"You are in my lair and safe from the Evil Lord. He cannot follow you here."

Aurie lowered herself to the ground as she suddenly felt light-headed. "Forgive me My Lord, I am very weak."

"You have been injured and your wound is deep. It will take time to heal."

Aurie placed her hand on her thigh, the pain slowly subsided and the deep gash disappeared. She could feel the strength returning to her body.

"You possess the power of Accelerated Healing?" Owain asked.

"Yes, My Lord."

"That is good. You will need sustenance to regain your strength. Come, I have water and food."

Aurie followed Owain through the cave; there was a lingering odor of sulfur. Soon they arrived at a second chamber and she cringed when they passed a pile of bones. The dragon had prepared his nest out of dried reeds and moss, and a stream of water trickled down the wall into a dark pool. Aurie remembered Eleanor telling Armitage that Owain lived in a cave on Beargrass Mountain, and she wondered if they were on the summit, as she could not see any tree tops outside the enormous entrance.

"The water is not pure, but it is safe," Owain said. "I will return shortly with nourishment." Owain spread his majestic wings and soared into the darkness.

Aurie knelt next to the pool, and scooped brown and murky water into her cupped hands, it had a metallic smell, it might be safe for a dragon, but not for anyone else. She used her powers to make the water drinkable, but drank sparingly. She wandered over to Owain's nest. Her clothes were still damp from yesterday's downpour, and although the cave was warm, she shivered. Prince Kalian's words kept running through her mind. What Prophesy was he talking about? Armitage would never have withheld information of that magnitude from her if it was true, and she wondered if Prince Kalian's hatred for them was so intense he felt the need to make disparaging remarks, even at the time of her death.

She did not have long to wait for Owain's return. He swooped into the cave, and landed just short of where she was resting. In his mouth was a deer, which he placed on the floor.

"Eat Princess Aurialana."

Aurie stared at the offering placed before her, then looked quickly away.

"This food is not to your liking?" Owain asked.

She did not want to offend the generous dragon, and wondered how she could tell him she seldom ate the meat of the creatures living in Lindell Forest as they were her friends. Except for what Seamus brought back from Westcott, her food consisted of berries, herbs, plants and nuts from the forest, and occasionally pheasant, rabbit or fish. She shrugged her shoulders, hoping she was not breaking some dragon protocol. Owain lumbered over to the far corner of the cavern and poked his head into a large hole chiseled in the rock, he shuffled around for a few seconds, and then he turned and walked back to Aurie. In his mouth was a wilted plant, which he deposited at her feet.

Aurie picked it up and looked at it closely. "Watercress," she said, looking up at Owain."Yes, sometimes I get blisters on my mouth, and the watercress helps."

Aurie laughed, imagining a two-ton dragon munching on watercress to soothe a burned mouth, if a dragon could smile, then Owain came close to doing just that.

"Eat," he commanded.

She did as she was bid, the watercress might not have been her choice for a meal, but she liked its peppery flavor, and it could be eaten raw, it was filling, and it had been a long time since she had any food. After finishing the watercress, she thanked Owain.

"I must contact Lord Armitage," she said. "He has not heard from me in a long while and will be worried."

The dragon lowered his massive body to the ground. He stared directly into Aurie's eyes. "Lord

Armitage has told me you have telepathic powers. I am most impressed with your abilities, young sorceress."

"Thank you, my Lord."

"As for Lord Armitage, he did not go to Eleanor Elderberry's, he and a small band of humans are at Dwarf Mountain. They are alive and well."

"I must get to him right away."

"That can be arranged, young sorceress, but first you must rest, and I will take you to him in the morning. Yet I sense there is something else bothering you."

"It was just something Prince Kalian said, just before you arrived. He told me about a Prophesy. Why have I never been told about it?"

Owain sighed deeply.

"It's not true, is it?" Aurie asked, as she tried to keep her voice from trembling.

"Yes, young sorceress, there is indeed a prediction that was foretold a long time ago, but it is not my place to tell you about it, you are Lord Armitage's apprentice, he is your master, so you must ask him yourself."

With those words, Owain lowered his head and closed his eyes. It took Aurie a long time to fall asleep as her thoughts turned to Tony, and she wiped the tears from her face. In one day, her entire life had crumbled, losing Tony was devastating, but Armitage's betrayal was almost more than she could bear.

Chapter Thirty-Three

Aurie woke just as the sun rose over the tree tops, Owain was waiting by the entrance, and when she approached him, he nodded his head in greeting.

"Climb onto my back, young sorceress, and I will take you to Lord Armitage."

For a moment Aurie was not sure how she could manage this feat, but Owain lowered his massive body to the ground, and Aurie climbed up his leg and onto his back, and wrapped her legs tightly around his scaly neck.

Owain flapped his wings, and then flung his body off the ledge. She suppressed a scream as the gigantic beast fell rapidly, and at the last second, soared upward, away from the sharp-edged crags protruding from the face of the mountain. The cedars and pines passed in a dark blur as Owain flew over their crests, heading towards a distant mountain range, the air was bracing, and she had never felt so alive.

She began to recognize some of the landmarks, shortly they arrived at the swinging bridge and she quickly looked away from the spot where Tony had fallen. They arrived at the junction in the trail, and Owain veered to the left, heading towards the summit of Dwarf Mountain. He descended, landing in a meadow surrounded by sharp cliffs and stunted pines. Aurie climbed off his back, and looked up at the dragon. "Thank you, My Lord," she said. "I envy you the freedom of the skies."

"You are welcome, young sorceress," Owain replied, as he raised his head, "I believe you are expected."

Aurie spun around, Armitage was standing on the edge of the field with Torin by his side. The wolf yelped and raced across the clearing, almost knocking her over in his excitement. Armitage approached and bowed to Owain.

"We meet again, good friend. I thank you for delivering Princess Aurialana safely back to us."

"Her safety is vital, Lord Armitage. The Evil Lord must be kept under constant surveillance, I fear he grows stronger and he will not relent in his pursuit of the young sorceress."

Then he spread his mighty wings, lifted his body off the ground and soon disappeared into the horizon.

Aurie buried her face in Torin's neck, and the huge wolf squirmed and licked her face. She sensed Armitage watching them, and she stared at the ground, finding it difficult to look into his eyes, she did not want him to know how angry she was.

Armitage reached down and touched her shoulder. "Have we been apart so long you are not sure of how to greet me?"

"No, My Lord," she whispered.

"I know much has happened, Aurie, and we will talk about it soon. But first, there are others anxiously waiting for your arrival. Come."

She followed him into the trees onto a path that climbed steadily upward, eventually arriving at a boxed canyon surrounded by sheer cliffs. Aurie spotted Dwarves patrolling on top of huge boulders, they recognized Armitage, nodded and allowed them to pass. When they were almost at the summit, they came to a barricaded fortress, as they walked through a wooden gate, Aurie was surprised to see a thriving village consisting of square dwellings made of solid granite. A community well dominated the center of a large square, a female Dwarf was drawing water and when she noticed Armitage she waved as she picked up her bucket, then strode towards one of the huts. Armitage continued walking, turning down alleys and narrow streets. The fortress was much larger than Aurie had first thought. Young Dwarfs laughed and played in the dirt, and with a start, she realized there were no males anywhere.

"They work in the mines during the day," Armitage said.

Aurie stopped in her tracks. "I thought you told me it was rude to intrude into people's thoughts."

"I did not have to read your thoughts Aurie, I knew what you were thinking, and yes, it is still rude to read other people's thoughts."

"Someone should have told Prince Kalian that," she said bitterly.

Armitage raised his eyebrow, but said nothing. "Ah, here we are," he said jovially. He approached a tavern, opened a door and stepped inside. There were tables and chairs filling every spare inch of space in the room, a staircase, on the far side led up to the second floor. An elderly patron, sitting in the corner, was drinking from a mug, and a rotund Dwarf was standing behind a long counter wiping a glass.

"Krystal, would you please bring some food and tea up to the room." Armitage said as he walked towards the stairs.

"Yes, My Lord," Krystal answered. She frowned when she noticed Torin standing next to Aurie.

"I'm afraid Krystal has no love for Torin," Armitage commented as they climbed the stairs. "He scares away her customers."

Armitage led Aurie down a corridor, they stopped at the last door on the left, and he gestured for her to enter before him. She stepped over the threshold, and then froze.

Tony was standing in the middle of the room, his right leg was bandaged, and he leaned heavily on a cane.

"Well, aren't you going to greet me, or are you going to make me hobble all the way over there?"

She flew across the room, and flung her arms around his neck. "Whoa, be careful," Tony chuckled.

"How, how ..." Aurie stuttered, as she buried her head in his shoulder. "I thought you were dead, I saw you fall off the cliff."

"I was lucky, well I think I was, a boulder stopped my fall, and I fell into a crevice. By the time I came to, it was night. I called but you were long gone."

"I teleported to Eleanor's. Tony, everything is gone. Eleanor was injured, and she closed the portal to Fey Wild and ... "

"Why don't you take care of Tony's injuries first," Armitage said, interrupting.

Aurie spun around and stared solemnly at Armitage, and the wizard studied her face, "There's a protection shield around the city," he said quietly. "Your magic won't be detected by Prince Kalian."

She led Tony over to his cot and had him lie down. Using her powers, she mended his leg, two broken ribs, and the deep claw marks on his shoulder. He smiled at her and she remembered him joking about her being his personal healer.

"What happened to the panther, or should I even ask?" he asked teasingly, looking down at the blood on her clothing.

"He won't be bothering us again," Aurie answered tersely.

There was a light rap on the door, and Armitage opened it and took a tray from Krystal. He placed it on the table and beckoned for Aurie to eat. The food was delicious, and Aurie smiled, remembering the meal Owain had provided just a few hours before, the stew and hot buns were better than the watercress and questionable water.

When she was finished, Armitage strode across the room and opened the door, Jasmine rushed in and raced over to the table. The two girls hugged, laughing and crying at the same time. It was then Aurie noticed there were others in the room, Seamus, Sam and Kevan, one of the Falcons Aurie had trained, stood in a row in the doorway, watching the two girls greet each other. Seamus strode across the room and grabbed Aurie, giving her a bear hug and almost crushing her ribs, Sam grinned and Kevan nodded a quiet greeting.

Were these the only survivors? Aurie thought to herself.

"There's tea, buns and cheese here for everyone." Armitage said.

Jasmine filled several mugs, and passed them around.

"Tony has brought us up to date from the time you fled the battle," Armitage said, as he sat in a chair. "What happened after the panther attack?"

Torin padded over to the far side of the room, and lay down next to the door.

"I called and called for you Tony," Aurie said as she turned and faced him. "When you didn't answer, I thought you had drowned in the river, so I teleported to Eleanor's place hoping to find everyone."

"We never made it that far." Armitage said.

"Yes, Owain told me you had not gone to Eleanor's."

"After I picked up Jasmine, we met Seamus and the others at the swinging bridge, but something didn't sit right, as I couldn't understand why the bridge had not been destroyed, which I would have thought the soldiers would have done to stop us from crossing. I decided to send Torin ahead to scout around."

When the wolf heard his name, his ears perked up, but he did not open his eyes.

"He soon returned," Armitage continued, "He was very agitated, and kept walking in circles, someone or something had used the trail before us and I didn't want to take a chance of walking straight into a trap. Rather than go to Eleanor's, I decided it would be safer to go to Dwarf Mountain. I knew you and Tony would be trying to get to Eleanor's tree house, and she would have known our whereabouts. If she got into trouble, she's quite capable of taking care of herself. Unfortunately, we did not reach our destination without a fight, we were attacked by trolls, and lost three men. They had to be the reason Torin was so upset, he must have picked up their scent."

"The bridge ropes were cut," Aurie said. "There's no way of crossing the gorge, I sensed magic when I passed it."

"Which makes sense, not only would our means of escape be cut off should we have had to backtrack, but I would not have been able to magically repair the damage, what you sensed was Dark Magic," Armitage said. "Prince Kalian wasn't taking any chances."

"He was waiting at Eleanor's," Aurie said quietly.

"I'm sorry you had to confront him on your own, Aurie, but I was not able to tell you about our change of plans, as it was just too risky, Owain had been following your progress and was aware Prince Kalian was at Eleanor's."

Aurie fought back tears as she described the devastation, and how the portal had been destroyed, and the apprehension she felt about her aunt's injuries. She did not go into detail as to what had transpired between her and Prince Kalian, instead she talked about her rescue, and the exhilaration of flying over the mountain tops on the back of a dragon. There was a lull in the conversation, yet she sensed Armitage was aware she was holding something back. When the time was right, she would ask him about the Prophesy, but now was not the time.

"It seems as if you're meeting the Elves was meant to happen, although you may not think so right now," Armitage said, changing the topic. "King Osmar is an old friend who I have not seen in many years. After the Magic War, he and his entire tribe mysteriously disappeared, and we all assumed they had travelled to a more distant realm. I was not aware of their presence in Lindell Forest. It is fortunate you managed to escape, because the Elves are quite adamant about keeping their existence a secret."

"He kept my long sword, but I did get my dagger back."

"Does not surprise me, King Osmar always had a particular desire for weapons made by the Dwarves. I'll have him return it to you."

"When I think about it now, I wonder if we would have been better off staying with the Elves," Aurie said quietly.

Again, Armitage said nothing. Turning slowly, he faced Tony and said. "Why don't you tell Aurie what happened after you two were parted?"

Tony nodded. "Realizing I could not climb back up the embankment because of my injuries, I walked, or to be more accurate, staggered along the river bank for a short while, but my progress was slow. I spotted a large tree trunk that had been washed ashore, so I grabbed hold of one of its branches and managed to push the trunk into the water. I thought I would make better progress in the water. I don't know how far or how long I floated, but it had to be a great distance, and the rain started again, adding to my misery. I was very weak, and had no idea how long I would be able to cling to the trunk. Just when I thought all was lost, I noticed two short, muscular men walking along the river bank, and I yelled to get their attention. They helped me ashore and built a carrier made of two long poles and cedar branches, and dragged me to this fortress. Imagine my surprise when I found Armitage and the others were taking refuge here and my rescuers were Dwarves.

"We were very worried about you Aurie, as I had no idea what had happened after we were separated. Lord Armitage was greatly relieved when Owain contacted him and told him you were with him at his lair."

"Right now, Tony needs to rest, and the rest of us can spend the day catching up. The two young ladies can bed in this room."

Aurie followed Tony out to the corridor, quietly closing the door.

"Prince Kalian thinks you're dead, Tony," Aurie whispered, as she looked up at him.

"I don't care what Prince Kalian thinks, and I don't want to talk about him right now."

"What do you want to talk about?"

"Who said I wanted to talk."

Then he gathered her in his arms, and they held each other tightly. Words were not needed.

Part III

The Fire Crystal

Chapter Thirty-Four

Aurie stood on the edge of the ridge, staring moodily at the churning water. She wrapped her cloak tightly around her shoulders as the relentless rain pounded the already saturated ground. The weather was cold for this time of year, and the wild flowers and herbs grew sparsely.

Time had crawled by, her eighteenth birthday had come and gone, and she wondered if she would ever find peace and happiness again. Unable to cross over to Fey Wild, there was no way she could find out how Eleanor had fared after her encounter with Prince Kalian. A large part of her discontent was Torin. Her thoughts turned back to the time they had stayed at Dwarf Mountain, almost three years ago. Krystal, the barkeep, had never hidden her dislike of the huge wolf and Armitage had thought it prudent to keep him hidden. Torin had been miserable in the cramped room and paced constantly. Unable to bear his distress, Aurie had slipped away one night. The wolf had followed her down the steep mountain trail. When they arrived at the meadow, she had knelt on the ground, burying her face in his neck, and then she had ordered him to leave. Torin had whined, and pushed his nose into her hand, then he had silently turned and disappeared into the darkness of the trees. He had never returned, and she hoped her friend had found a pack and was happy with his own kind. Periodically a wolf call would waken her during the night, and she sensed it was Torin, letting her know he was safe.

They had stayed with the Dwarves for almost three months, their presence was tolerated, but it was obvious their generous hosts were not comfortable hiding humans in their midst. Knowing Prince Kalian was searching for the runaways, they feared for their homes and the lives of their families. Although they were never asked to leave, Aurie sensed the dread hanging over Dwarf Mountain like a dark cloud.

One evening, Armitage announced it was time to depart from their haven. He knew it would only be a matter of time before Prince Kalian found them, and the evil sorcerer would not hesitate to seek retribution on the generous Dwarves. They packed their meager supplies, and left early the following morning.

At first, they lived in caves or abandoned mines but the food supply was sparse, and the continuous snow and bitterly cold winds made their lives miserable. Armitage finally led them down the mountain and back to the lower reaches of Lindell Forest. Although the weather was not as harsh as the upper ranges, the berries, nuts and herbs were almost non-existent.

They discovered a secluded clearing deep in the forest and built a small hut, it was very cramped but the fugitives were protected from the harsh weather, and no-one complained.

Armitage had sought out the magical tribes to see how they had fared after the skirmish at Whitehawk Pass. When they had realized the small advance party had walked into a trap, they had quietly dispersed and returned to their homes. No amount of persuasion on Armitage's part could convince them to regroup. Although he was distressed, he never stopped trying. Too often Aurie wondered why he insisted she continue with her studies when they did not have the support from the magical folk in Lindell Forest.

Aurie's thoughts returned to the present, she kicked a stone into the shrubs. The heavy rain had subsided, and a fine mist continued to fall. Shivering, she turned and headed back to the cottage. Picking up her pace, she followed the stream down the gorge that flowed into the meadow. She could have drawn on her magic to keep warm or for protection from the rain, but she restrained from using it whenever she was away from the protective shield surrounding the cottage. Attentiveness was a trait she had learned over the years. It was highly unlikely Prince Kalian would pick up such small traces of magic this far from Westcott, but it was not a risk she wanted to take. Should Prince Kalian find her, he would not hesitate to dispose of her friends as well.

It was almost two weeks since Armitage, Seamus, and Tony had gone to Westcott. Armitage had felt it would be too dangerous for her to accompany them, as he did not want to take a chance someone would recognize her. Shortly after leaving Dwarf Mountain, Armitage had resumed their earlier practice of keeping a close surveillance on Prince Kalian and his army. The first time Seamus and Tony had gone to Westcott, Kevan had accompanied them as he had decided he would not return. They were sorry to see the quiet, young man leave but understood his desire to return to his family.

Aurie had never discussed the Prophesy with Armitage, although she thought about it continuously. Often during her training, Aurie had been on the verge of bringing it up, yet something held her back, perhaps she was afraid her relationship with Armitage would deteriorate to a level from which she would never be able to return.

The cottage was a welcome sight and Aurie opened the door and quickly closed it against the chill. The heat radiating from the hearth in the cottage was welcoming. Sam was sitting at the table and Jasmine was laughing, her face flushed. The couple's relationship had grown and they were seldom apart.

Aurie removed her wet cloak and hung it on the wooden peg on the door, pouring herself a cup of mint tea she sat down on the rough bench pulled up to the table.

"Not the best weather to be out walking," Jasmine said. 'It's miserable out there."

"I know," Aurie replied, reaching for a scone. "I just had to get away for a while. This place feels like a prison cell."

The three friends were sitting quietly at the table, relishing the heat from the hearth, when the door swung open, and a gust of frigid air blew into the small room. Armitage, Tony and Seamus were standing in the doorway, water dripping from the cowls of their cloaks. Seamus and Tony placed the large bundles they were carrying on the counter.

"Here are the supplies Jasmine," Seamus said. "Couldn't find everything you wanted, but it'll have to do. Things are pretty tough in Westcott."

"Thanks Seamus," Jasmine replied as she stood up and began opening the parcels. "We'll make do."

The three weary men poured themselves a hot drink, and Armitage went and stood next to the hearth, staring into the flames.

"How was your journey?" Aurie asked, as Tony sat down next to her.

"Wet and cold," Tony replied. "And I discovered the Falcons have disbanded, I ran into James and Randy, and they were not very happy to see me pop up again. Being branded a fugitive made them nervous. The people are living in constant terror and are barely surviving."

"I'm sorry, Tony," Aurie said, as she reached over and placed her hand over his.

"Matters have deteriorated even more since our last visit," Seamus commented. "Windermere Castle is in ruins, the barracks are empty, and all of the attached buildings have been abandoned. I imagine the soldiers have been garrisoned elsewhere. We searched for them but so far no luck."

"I wonder what happened to Mrs. Black," Aurie wondered, more from curiosity than concern.

"From what I can gather," Seamus said. "She's living with her brother."

"Nathan Trent?" Aurie asked, turning to look at Jasmine. The young woman's face turned pale.

Seamus nodded. "Nathan spends most of his time in the pub, guess there ain't no love lost between them."

"They deserve each other. We're well rid of them," Tony murmured.

"There's no law and order anywhere," Armitage said as he walked over to the table and poured a second cup of tea. "A person would be foolhardy to wander the streets alone. We went to the subterranean cave. It has been destroyed, and the Fire Crystal is gone."

"What happened to it?" Aurie asked.

"Since Prince Kalian now controls the Fire Cave, I imagine that's where the Crystal is."

"Without the Crystal, we cannot hope to defeat him."

"I know things look bleak right now, but we cannot allow our fears to take over."

"My Lord, he has possession of the Fire Crystal, which gives him control of the Underground, and power over the creatures. He no longer considers us a threat."

"We must not let our guard down, he will never stop looking for us."

"You mean, he will never stop looking for me," Aurie replied, raising her voice.

There was silence in the room, and Aurie bit her lip. The look on Armitage's face settled her indecisiveness, she knew the time had come to speak.

Shirley Bigelow DeKelver • 282

"It's because of the Prophesy, isn't it?" she asked, looking directly at the wizard.

Armitage sighed, and then placed his mug on the table. "How long have you known?"

"For over three years. Prince Kalian told me. He said there was a Prophesy, and it involved me, and you knew about it. He didn't get a chance to tell me much more before Owain appeared."

"Aurie, I'm sorry you had to find out that way."

"I asked Owain about it, but he said I had to ask you. I tried to bring the matter up several times, but I couldn't do it. I suppose I've been waiting for you to tell me, but you never did."

"I certainly did not want you to find out this way. The Prophesy was foretold almost five hundred years ago, during the time of the Magic War. Earth had been thrown into darkness and despair, seeing no end in sight to the slaughter and destruction and the suffering of those caught in the middle, an uneasy truce was called. The most powerful wizards on Earth and Fey Wild, both good and evil, gathered together to find a solution.

"The negotiations went on for many years, it was a trying task to get everyone to agree on a suitable compromise. Eventually, it was unanimously agreed that if the War continued Earth would never recover from the destruction. It was unlikely any of the inhabitants, both magical and non-magical, would have survived. A truce was reached, although many of the wizards were not pleased with the outcome.

"The wizard heading the negotiations was the most powerful mage on Earth, and he made a prediction. There would be five hundred years of peace, and at the end of that time, a powerful sorcerer would open the gates to the Underworld. The world would be thrown into chaos, and once again evil would clash with good. During this time, a young sorceress would be born. She would become very powerful, and would be the only one having the ability to challenge the evil sorcerer. They would meet in battle, and only one would survive, the outcome would determine whether good or evil would reign on Earth for another five hundred years.

"The Prophesy was written on a scroll buried deep in the Abyss, and when Prince Kalian gained control of the Fire Crystal, he must have found the scroll. That is why he is so adamant in destroying you, as you are the one person who has the capability to stop him from succeeding."

"How can you be sure that I'm the one the Prophesy talks about?" Aurie asked vehemently.

"The Prophesy foretold the young woman would be of mixed, royal blood, possessing powerful magical abilities."

Aurie stared in stunned silence at Armitage, the only sound in the room the crackling of flames in the hearth.

"You should have told her about it sooner," Tony said angrily.

Armitage sat down next to Aurie. "At first, I did not say anything as I needed to be absolutely sure you were the sorceress mentioned in the Prophesy, and most assuredly, at that time, you were far too young and immature to be told something of that magnitude. Worrying needlessly would not have done you any good. I wanted to wait until your training was complete."

"Perhaps the meaning of the Prophesy has been misinterpreted," Aurie suggested. "Five hundred years is a long time."

"Owain was one of the wizards at the gathering," Armitage said, shaking his head, "and has been Keeper of the Prophesy since that time."

Aurie stared despondently at the table, unable to look directly at Armitage. He reached over and placed his hand over hers. "I was the seer who foretold the Prophesy."

Aurie quickly pulled her hand back, the room began to spin and she found it difficult to breathe. Jumping up, she walked over to the door and retrieved her cloak. Tony rose to join her but she shook her head, and opening the door she stepped outside. Right now, she needed to be alone.

She spent hours walking through the forest and climbing the steep mountain trails, unanswered questions running repeatedly through her mind. Did Armitage keep silent over the years because he wanted to ensure her training was complete, as he needed her absolute concentration in learning her skills? Was he genuinely worried about her well-being and wanted to wait until she was mature enough to handle it? The wizard had always treated her with respect, and finding out about the Prophesy in this manner was shattering.

If she wanted to find any answers, she realized she had to do it on her own.

Chapter Thirty-Five

A few days later, after the evening meal, Armitage asked everyone to remain seated. Rubbing his chin, he rose and walked over to the hearth, staring at the flames. "As everyone is aware," he said, turning to face them, "I am making no headway with the tribes, many of them feel Prince Kalian is seeking retribution because of the altercation at Whitehawk Pass and they do not want to antagonize him any further."

"We all know that's not the case," Seamus said, shifting uneasily. "Surely, they must realize how devastating matters are, both in Lindell Forest and in Westcott. We're barely surviving as it is."

"It is true, the continuous rain and cold winds have destroyed the vegetation, the waters are polluted and the sun has not shone for a long, long time. Prince Kalian will have his Kingdom of Darkness to rule over; something must be done, and soon."

"With the tribes not backing us, we don't have enough manpower to retaliate in any event," Tony said bitterly. "Without the aid of the Eldorans, it would be suicide to attack, and we have no means of getting to Fey Wild now that the portal is closed."

"I was not talking about a battle, Tony, we must try to retrieve the Fire Crystal from the Abyss. It's our only hope to stop the damage Prince Kalian is inflicting on Earth and in Fey Wild."

"The front and back entrances to the Fire Cave are guarded night and day," Tony remarked. "How can our small group get past that many soldiers?"

"We can't. That's why only you, I and Aurie will be going to Westcott in the morning. Seamus, Sam and Jasmine will remain here."

Everyone started talking at once. Seamus jumped up and angrily pounded his fist on the table. "I will not stay behind. You will need my fighting skills."

Armitage waved his hands, and waited until everyone had calmed down. "No-one can equal your fighting prowess, Seamus, but I need only those with magical abilities. That is why Tony and Aurie will accompany me."

Seamus rose and angrily left the cottage, slamming the door in his frustration.

Aurie rose, and headed towards the door.

"Wait Aurie, do not worry," Armitage said. "He has a short fuse, and once he has calmed down and realizes why I have made my decision, he will be his jovial, pleasant self once again."

Aurie spun and faced Armitage, her mouth open in surprise. When she noticed the twinkle in Armitage's eyes, she giggled. Jovial and pleasant did not describe her old friend.

Aurie and Jasmine cleared the table, leaving the dishes in the basin for Jasmine to wash in the morning. Later in their curtained-off corner, Jasmine stopped brushing her hair. "Aurie, what do you think your chances are of getting the Fire Crystal?"

"I don't know," Aurie said, as she pulled her blanket over her shoulders. "Armitage must feel we have a chance or he wouldn't have suggested it. We won't have any problems getting by the soldiers, and ..."

"I wasn't thinking about the soldiers. I was thinking about Prince Kalian, he'll know immediately you're in Westcott, especially if you use your powers."

Aurie did not answer her friend. She rolled over and faced the wall, her thoughts in turmoil. Jasmine blew out the candle.

The next morning, a subdued group watched as Armitage, Tony and Aurie left the cottage. When they passed the edge of the shield, Armitage reached for their hands.

"Are you ready to teleport?' he asked. "And remember, Aurie do not use your powers unless I tell you it is safe to do so."

"But won't Prince Kalian be alerted when he senses you and Aurie using magic?" Tony asked. "Why are you including her in this?"

"I do not have the power to manipulate the Fire Crystal on my own, and although I can use a magical defense so he won't be able to detect me, it is very advanced magic, and beyond Aurie's capabilities to create one for herself. I can place a shield around Aurie, and I'm hoping we will have enough time to get the Crystal and leave before he is even aware of our presence. Tony, be assured I would do nothing to jeopardize Aurie's safety."

They arrived at their prearranged destination in the ravine below the Fire Cave. More than a dozen troopers were guarding the back exit, most of them were asleep, while a few tended the campfire.

"Tony, why don't you create a diversion?" Armitage whispered. "I'll signal you when it's safe to join us at the entrance."

The sky turned grey, and the wind picked up, swaying the branches, dirt, rocks and debris lifted from the ground, spinning wildly. Aurie noticed the smile on Tony's face and the gleam in his eyes, and realized he was enjoying himself. She had witnessed the same fervor in Seamus and Eleanor when they were engaged in fighting, and surmised that some men and women enjoyed the excitement of danger and living on the edge, while others preferred caution to risk.

One of the soldiers noticed the unexplained storm, and pointed it out to his comrades. They ran to the edge of the cliff, leaving their posts to watch the phenomenon.

Armitage and Aurie teleported directly to the cave exit, the troopers had their backs turned, and were unaware of them until it was too late. Before they could draw their weapons, Armitage had sent an energy blast into their midst and they lay sprawled on the ground, those who were asleep having no idea what hit them.

"I don't envy any of them when they wake up," he said. "They're going to have terrible headaches."

Walking over to the edge of the cliff, Armitage gestured to Tony, it did not take him long to scale the steep grade.

"Be alert for guards," Armitage commented as they entered the Fire Cave. Surprisingly, it was deserted. Aurie wondered why Prince Kalian had not set up more sentinels. With his rapidly growing powers and the Fire Crystal under his control, was he getting complacent?

Once again Armitage teleported them, and they landed behind a large boulder. Aurie doubted if she would ever get used to the sensation of teleportation, yet at times it had its advantages.

She peered around the boulder, and as before, was humbled by the overwhelming fury of the Abyss. She spied the Fire Crystal floating in a glass case suspended in the middle of the burning inferno. She shook Tony's arm to get his attention and pointed it out. They left the shelter of the rock, and Armitage walked towards the Abyss, Aurie followed, keeping a safe distance from the edge.

"I can only shield you for a brief time," Armitage said to Aurie. "We must do this quickly."

Simultaneously, she and Armitage used summoning spells to manipulate the Fire Crystal from its magical prison, powerful energy bursts deflected off the glass case, bouncing erratically off the rocks.

Armitage raised his hand and gestured for Aurie to stop. "You must concentrate as you have never done before, use all of your powers, and do not hold back."

Aurie nodded, and swallowed nervously. She summoned her magic, sensing her energy combining with Armitage's as it struck the glass case, it began to spin rapidly, and beams shot outwards in all directions. Armitage grabbed her arm and pulled her back to the safety of the boulder, rocks exploded, the fire in the abyss roared as it intensified, and the walls of the cave shook.

"Why can't we summon it?" Aurie asked breathlessly.

"The Dark Magic is too strong." Armitage muttered.

"Then why don't we create a combined counterspell."

"No, you know how I feel about Dark Magic, it is too dangerous."

"Then all is lost, Prince Kalian has indeed won."

"For now," he said wearily. "There will be other opportunities, just not this time."

"Where's Tony?" she asked, suddenly realizing he was missing. Armitage shrugged, and wearily laid his head back against the boulder.

"Aurie, I'm over here," a voice echoed from behind them. "Come here, I've found something."

Aurie sensed the pull of magic before she got to the small alcove where Tony was waiting. She followed him inside, on the far wall were two large glass enclosures, one containing a man and the other a woman.

Aurie's face turned white, and then she dropped to her knees in shock.

"Aurie," Tony said in alarm, running over to grab her arm.

"It's my parents," she whispered. "Tony, it's my mother and father."

"Are they dead?"

"No," Armitage said, as he entered the alcove. "They are in a deep trance."

"Is there nothing we can do for them?" Aurie asked.

"It's not too intricate of a spell, I believe that once the glass enclosures are opened, they will awaken. Aurie, would you mind. My strength has not returned."

Aurie cast a spell, and suddenly the glass pillars shattered, everyone covered their faces to protect their eyes from the flying shards. The prisoners landed on the ground.

'Well, I suppose that's one way of freeing them," Armitage said, wiping fragments of glass from his robe, "I was thinking of unlocking the clasp but this works just as well."

Tony chuckled, and Aurie punched his arm lightly.

King Sebastian opened his eyes and slowly sat up, seeing the Queen, he reached over and gently touched her face. Queen Elyse awoke, and smiled, King Sebastian put his arms around her waist and helped her to stand. It was then they noticed they were not alone.

"Is it you, my old friend?" King Sebastian said faintly as he faced Armitage.

"It is, and I am pleased to see you are both alive."

Aurie approached her parents, brushing the glass from her hair and clothing.

"It cannot be," Queen Elyse said. "Aurialana?"

"We thought you were dead," Aurie whispered.

"We were captured by Prince Kalian," her father said. "And held prisoners in an underground cave for a very long time. My powers were no match against the Fire Crystal. When it was moved, he brought us here and encased us in these glass prisons."

"Why would Prince Kalian let them live all these years?" Aurie asked Armitage. "He spent so much time trying to capture them, it doesn't make sense."

"I have ceased trying to understand Prince Kalian's actions in anything he does, it might have been revenge, or perhaps he thought he could use them as bait to capture you."

Queen Elyse raised her hand and gently touched Aurie's face. "Has so much time gone by, that you are now a young woman?"

"I am sorry to interrupt, but we must leave immediately" Armitage said. "We will have an opportunity to talk and get reacquainted once we are away from this place. Aurie has used her powers, and it is imperative we leave before Prince Kalian arrives. I'll explain everything later.

"We will take the long way through the Fire Cave and enter through Windermere Castle, I'm quite sure the back exit will be blocked off by now, and Prince Kalian will soon find out you have been freed."

They crossed the swinging bridge although its condition had not improved greatly from the last time Aurie had crossed it. At first, they walked slowly, as her parents had not regained their strength and their powers were slow in returning. Aurie took her mother's arm and quickly introduced Tony to her father, who gratefully accepted his assistance.

"We need to move faster," Armitage murmured. "Aurie, I still have not regained my full strength, please teleport your mother and Tony to the interrogation room next to the dungeons, and I'll take your father."

Aurie noticed the alarmed look on Tony's white face. "It's alright Tony, I've learned to safely teleport others now."

In a few seconds, they appeared in the room, they walked down the dark corridor passing the dungeons. The cells were empty, and the doors hung on their hinges, while spider webs covered the walls and the ceiling, and rats scrounged in the moldy straw strewn across the floor. They soon arrived at the steps leading to the tack room, the wooden door was closed but Armitage opened it easily. Tony walked over to the far wall and lifted an old blanket, underneath was Prince Kalian's saddle, the leather was cracked, and the silver was badly tarnished. A whinny was heard from the stables, and everyone froze. Drawing his sword, Tony walked quietly towards the door, Aurie followed, her dagger in her hand. A fleeting smile crossed her mother's face when she recognized the weapon.

Tony placed his ear against the door, then he pushed it gently with his foot, it opened with a creak. Satisfied there was no-one waiting for them, he gestured the others to follow.

The devastation was overwhelming. Rafters had fallen from the overhead lofts, landing on the stalls and shattering them beyond repair. Some of the stalls were still intact, and to everyone's dismay, held a few horses. There was no water or feed and the enclosures had not been mucked out in a long while. The smell was overwhelming, and bile rose in Aurie's throat as she realized the animals had been abandoned to fend on their own.

Tony headed towards Cesar's stall, one side of his stall had been destroyed. It was evident the distraught horse had tried to escape. When he recognized Tony and Aurie, he tossed his head and snorted. Tony reached over and patted his neck, and Aurie fought back angry tears. Could she hate Prince Kalian any more than she did now?

"Why were these horses abandoned?" Tony said furiously. "We can't leave them here, they need food and care."

"We will take them with us," King Sebastian pronounced. "No animal should be treated this way."

Aurie helped Tony gather feedbags hanging on pegs in the tack room, most of the equipment was gone, but a few old saddles and harnesses remained, and they decided to take them as well. It was soon apparent why the horses had been abandoned. Most of them were in no shape to be ridden long distances by the troopers, and without Tony's assistance, Prince Kalian would not have been able to handle Cesar. He no longer required a steed, as he could teleport wherever he chose.

They left by the back entrance.

"I'll check the compound to see if anyone is around. I'll be right back," Tony said.

"I'm going with you," Aurie said, and before he could protest, she was walking down the path bordering the barn.

"Where is everyone?" Aurie whispered, when they arrived at the courtyard.

The peasants' huts were abandoned, and the gardens were overrun with weeds. Much as she hated being back at Windermere Castle, seeing it in this condition was disheartening. There were no people in sight, and the emptiness was distressing.

"I'll go get the others," Tony said, as he turned. He stopped and looked directly into Aurie's eyes. "Don't leave this spot," he said adamantly.

Aurie nodded, shortly Tony returned with the others. The shocked look on her parent's face when they saw the disrepair of their home was upsetting, they were quickly discovering the extent of Prince Kalian's destruction.

The small group headed towards the front gate of the castle, each person holding the reins of a rescued horse, expecting at any moment to be discovered, but they made it safely down the drawbridge. Soon they were in the field behind the castle, Lindell Forest rising darkly in the background.

They were just a few feet away from the stream when a shout stopped them in their tracks. Tony and Aurie turned sharply, their weapons drawn. A squadron of soldiers was galloping across the field, heading straight towards them. Queen Elyse and King Sebastian had their hands full calming the terrified horses. Armitage turned and faced the troopers, a determined look on his face. The soldier leading the unit spurred his horse forward and Aurie was stunned when she recognized Fred; the anger and hatred she had been carrying inside for years quickly rose to the surface, and she angrily cast a spell. There was a loud crack and Fred fell heavily to the ground. The remaining soldiers sharply reined in their horses, and in terror they turned their mounts and raced back to the castle.

The despair in Armitage's eyes made Aurie step back. "You must undo your spell," he said sharply.

"I will not."

"You are using Dark Magic, and I have warned you before how dangerous that is. Do not trifle with dark powers."

"I will not change my mind. What is done is done."

Aurie had felt both terror and elation when she had cast the spell and understood Armitage's warning as to how easy it would be for the magic to control her. She walked slowly over to Fred. He was lying on his back, a look of shock etched across his face seconds before he had been turned into stone. Aurie did not regret her decision, and the satisfaction of getting her revenge on Fred was exhilarating.

She turned and quietly walked back to the others.

Chapter Thirty-Six

It had taken the small group almost three days to walk to the hut because of the horses weakened state. Armitage nervously wondered why there were no soldiers at Whitehawk Pass. Obviously, Prince Kalian did not feel they posed a threat since they had failed to take possession of the Fire Crystal.

Seamus and Sam immediately took over the care of the horses. Cesar was no different in temperament, and his care was left solely up to Tony. Jasmine saw to King Sebastian and Queen Elyse's welfare.

Two weeks passed and Armitage had remained quiet, refusing to talk to Aurie. Her parents had said nothing to her but she sensed their disapproval as well.

The horses were slowly gaining weight, although the grass was brittle and dry. Tony had hauled Prince Kalian's saddle back with him, and spent hours cleaning it, not satisfied until the leather was once again soft and supple and the silver gleaming as before.

With Jasmine's nurturing, it did not take King Sebastian and Queen Elyse long to regain their strength. An extra room was added to the hut, which provided privacy for the royal couple. Two extra pairs of hands were appreciated. Everyone pitched in weeding the garden and hauling water from the stream, exercising the horses, and foraging for herbs, berries, and pinecones. Jasmine still reigned in the kitchen, as none surpassed her cooking talents.

Aurie continued practicing her magic and accomplishing intricate spells that amazed her parents. Seamus and King Sebastian were both skilled swordsmen, and it wasn't long before Tony was as proficient. As the spear and long sword were not weapons of choice for either Seamus or King Sebastian it seemed Aurie's training with these weapons would have been neglected if not for Queen Elyse, who proved to be as skilled as Eleanor.

Aurie told her mother about the time she had gone to Fey Wild, when Eleanor had spent hours trying to improve her skill with the spear, and finally throwing her hands up in dismay. Queen Elyse laughed, and told her stories of when she and Eleanor were young, and how they often got into trouble with the Queen, who was strict and demanding, continuously reminding them they were royal princesses and not wild sprites.

Aurie wondered if her mother ever resented her decision to marry her father, and being banished from the Mortal World, thus losing all her powers and her longevity. However, when she saw her parents together, their love for each other was evident, and she knew they were content.

Armitage increased his efforts to gather the tribes together. Upon discovering King Sebastian and Queen Elyse were alive, many of them returned to the gatherings.

Aurie spent as much time as possible with her parents, catching up on the years they had been separated. When she told them of her renewed memories, when she was captured by the soldiers and how her guardians had perished in the fire, they comforted her and let her talk about the experience often. Having someone listen to the trauma she had suffered, Aurie's fears began to dissipate, although her deeply rooted terror of fire would remain with her for years to come.

Aurie told them about the foundling home, and how she became Mrs. Black's slave. They became angry and distressed when she told them about her life at the castle, and the abuse inflicted by evil woman.

It had been difficult for Aurie to tell them of Eleanor's confrontation with Prince Kalian, and how she feared her aunt had been seriously injured. When she mentioned the destruction of the portal to Fey Wild, they looked at each other but said nothing.

One day, Queen Elyse told Aurie she wished to talk to her in private. Feeling the need to leave the confines of the crowded hut, Aurie took her mother to the summit of the waterfall, where they sat on a huge boulder, enjoying the panoramic view of the valley.

At first, her mother talked about trivial matters, then she brought up the topic of Tony. She asked Aurie if she had feelings for him. Aurie assured her they were only friends and wisely her mother said nothing. How could Aurie tell her about their stolen kisses, how her heart raced when she was alone with Tony, and how she thought of him continuously?

"I'm glad you feel that way, Aurie," she said quietly. "You're only eighteen, and you have so much to experience before you pursue a relationship with anyone."

Perhaps her mother was right. The anguish she went through when she thought Tony had died after the panther attack was something she did not ever want to go through again. With her future being so uncertain, perhaps keeping a safe distance was for the best.

There was a lull in the conversation, and Aurie leaned back on the rock. The mist had lifted, and it was pleasant not having to cope with the relentless rain.

"Aurie, I brought you here for a reason. There's another portal to Fey Wild, hidden deep in the glens of Lindell Forest, known only to the Eldorans, and which can only be opened by a member of the royal family."

Aurie sat upright and stared at her mother. "Why haven't you told me about this before?"

'Your father and I thought it best to keep its existence a secret. The less people aware of it the less chance Prince Kalian has of finding it. You talk continuously of Eleanor, and I too am worried for my sister. Your father and I have discussed this matter with Armitage, and we have all agreed it is time you and I go to Fey Wild."

"When do you wish to leave?"

"Early tomorrow morning. Do not pack any clothing or provisions, as we cannot remain long."

Early next morning, they saddled two of the horses and rode away from the cottage well before anyone had arisen. At first, Aurie had been so anxious to get to the portal, she had suggested she teleport them there, but her mother reminded her that to do so would be foolish and dangerous.

Late that evening they arrived at a lake obscured by the shadows of the gigantic trees. A doe and her speckled fawn were drinking at the water's edge, they calmly lifted their heads, showing no fear. After they hobbled their horses next to a large oak growing close to the water's edge Queen Elyse approached a large boulder jutting out into the water. On top was a white stone like the portal at Eleanor's tree house.

"Aurie, open the gateway to Fey Wild, and when we arrive, it will be safe for you to teleport us to the Crystal Palace," Queen Elyse said. "Prince Kalian cannot use his magic against you once we have left this realm."

Aurie took her mother's hand, and then she placed her hand on the rock. Once again, she was reminded of how much she hated this manner of travel. Landing heavily on the ground, she opened her eyes, and her lips parted in dismay. The devastation was catastrophic. Huge fractures in the amber sky created an atmosphere of bleakness and despair. They had landed in the middle of a large meadow surrounded by mighty trees. The flowers and foliage were wilted and brown, and the wooden sentinels that had stood for time eternal, had been demolished and left to rot in the dying mosses and lichen.

"By the gods," she murmured. "What has happened?"

"Only powerful magic can cause such destruction," Queen Elyse whispered. "Black magic. Be alert, Aurie."

The sight awaiting them at the Crystal Palace was heart-rending. The tower on the north wall lay in ruins, and the drawbridge was raised. The white wall surrounding the castle was covered in black soot.

Aurie saw a small boat lying on its side in the bulrushes, she upended it, and she and her mother climbed in. Using her magic, Aurie guided the boat towards the dock. They disembarked, and stoically approached the gate. Aurie immediately sensed the magical shield.

"Mother, there's a shield cloaking the castle. I'm not sure if I can disable it."

"Use your telepathy. See if you can contact Eleanor, and let her know we are here."

Aurie concentrated on contacting her aunt. A voice broke into her thoughts, and she grabbed her mother's arm.

"It's Grandmother. She will release the shield and we are to enter by the side gate."

Two armed warriors met them at the entrance and accompanied them to the courtyard, where Queen Edelyse stood waiting for them. The three women rushed across the yard, and held each other tightly.

"My daughter, my granddaughter, how I have longed for this day," the Queen said quietly. "Come, you must be exhausted from your travels."

"Mother, we are fine," Queen Elyse replied. "Please, we have come to see Eleanor."

Queen Edelyse did not reply, but instead turned and walked towards the keep which was in no better shape than the rest of the castle. Aurie and her mother followed the stately queen.

Soon they were on the second floor, and they headed towards the living quarters of the royal family. Queen Edelyse stopped at a door. "I must warn you that Eleanor has changed greatly since either of you last saw her. She was gravely wounded by the Evil Lord, and we have done all we can to keep her alive. I fear we are losing our battle."

"But that was three years ago," Aurie said. "Why has she not improved?"

"Granddaughter, three years on Earth is but a short span of time on Fey Wild. She knew you would eventually come and has been waiting for you."

"Perhaps I can do something," Aurie said.

Her grandmother slowly opened the large wooden door, the room was in semi-darkness, and there were two attendants standing next to Eleanor's bed. The scent of jasmine and a foreign herb wafted throughout the room. Eleanor was covered by a quilt made of silver spider webs, and her face was drawn and pale. Aurie reached over and placed her hand on her aunt's chest. She summoned her healing powers.

Eleanor slowly opened her eyes, covering Aurie's hand with her own. Noticing her sister standing next to Queen Edelyse, she smiled weakly.

"I knew you would return," she whispered. "Now I can leave in peace."

"No," Aurie implored. "You must get better. Tell me what I have to do."

"Aurie, there is nothing that can be done. You cannot undo Dark Magic."

Aurie stood rigid, fighting back the tears. "I wish to try."

"No Aurie, you cannot." Queen Elyse gasped, grabbing Aurie by her arm. "The only way to counter a Dark Magic spell is to use Dark Magic, and that you must not do."

"Your mother is right," Eleanor whispered. "Black Magic is dangerous and should never be used, no matter what the circumstance might be."

"I cannot stand here and watch you die," Aurie whispered.

"You must stay strong," Eleanor said quietly. Then she closed her eyes, took a shallow breath, and slipped into a deep coma.

Aurie sat on Eleanor's bed, her eyes never leaving her aunt's face while her mother and grandmother remained standing at the foot of the bed chanting softly. In the early hours of the morning, Eleanor stirred.

"Aurie, your powers are truly strong, and you must remain true to your path in life."

"Is it because of what the Prophesy says?"

"The Prophesy is merely a foretelling but the outcome is up to you." Eleanor coughed raggedly, and Aurie squeezed her hand. "May good health and happiness fill your days," she whispered to them all, and then she was gone.

Queen Elyse reached down and placed her hand on Aurie's shoulder. Aurie stiffened, shrugged her off, and then ran from the room. She raced down the corridor, and headed towards the staircase, and across the courtyard. When the guards saw the look on her face, they stepped aside and allowed her to pass. She did not stop running until she arrived at the foot of the waterfall. Eleanor had been more than her aunt, more than her teacher and mentor, she had been a mother to her over the years. Aurie sensed the power surging through her body, and at that moment she felt she could have destroyed Prince Kalian with one blow.

She did not return to the castle for hours. A young woman stepped from behind a curtain when Aurie entered her chambers, and she recognized Eugenia Eveningstar. Aurie shook her head, indicating she wanted to be alone. Eugenia understood Aurie's wishes and quietly closed the door as she left the room.

For days, Aurie wandered the corridors and the gardens, refusing to talk to anyone. She took her meals in her room, sitting for hours on the balcony, staring at the charred remains of the garden below. She overheard her mother and grandparents talking in hushed tones, and she sensed the strain in her mother's voice. It wasn't until later she discovered her grandfather had gone to Earth. He had contacted Armitage and asked that he retrieve the horses as he did not know how long it would be before Aurie and her mother were ready to return.

In Fey Wild, a solemn ceremony was held celebrating Eleanor's life where stories were told of her brave deeds. The Eldorans believed that when one of their own died, they moved on to a higher level to begin a new life. Aurie attended the ceremony, quietly standing next to her mother and grandparents. When she left early, she heard them talking quietly and knew they were concerned about her.

One afternoon, almost a week after Eleanor's death, Aurie was requested to appear before her grandfather. She would have preferred to stay in her room, but one did not refuse a summons from the High King. She allowed Eugenia to dress her in one of the beautiful gowns hanging in her wardrobe, unaware and not caring which one was chosen. She entered the large antechamber, and when she walked across the floor, all talking ceased as she approached the throne and curtsied.

"Aurie, come before me," King Esmond ordered in his deep voice.

Aurie walked up the steps and stopped a few feet from the throne and stared at the floor. She knew it was extremely impolite, but she was unable to look directly into the king's eyes.

"I do not feel Eleanor would have wanted you to hide in your room. She has not left us, and one day we will see her again. You must face your destiny if any of us are to get through the dark days that lie ahead. Do you understand what I am saying, granddaughter?"

Aurie raised her head and looked at the king. She was not surprised he knew about the Prophesy, as her mother would have discussed it with him and her grandmother.

"You come from a lengthy line of warriors and sorcerers, from both your Eldoran and your Ancient bloodlines. Your birth was foretold in a Prophesy over five hundred years ago. Be assured your family and friends will always love you and the Eldorans will be standing by your side when the time comes."

Her grandfather had always frightened her a little, but at that moment Aurie saw the love and pride displayed on his face, and she was ashamed of her behavior.

"You are right Grandfather. It is time I returned to the Mortal World. I will confront the Evil Lord, and I will avenge Eleanor's death."

With these words, she turned and left the room, her mother following closely behind.

Chapter Thirty-Seven

Aurie kept herself busy with her training, although her heart was not in it. Queen Elyse passed King Esmond's message on to Armitage, assuring him the Eldorans would join them when the time came. The remaining Ancients residing in Fey Wild waited as well, as they were prepared to fight the Evil Lord along with the Eldorans.

Early one morning, a few days after her return, she was greeted at the front door by Torin, it had been a long time since she had seen him and she knew he had somehow sensed her distress. At first her parents were reluctant to approach the massive animal, but when they saw how gentle he was, particularly with Aurie, they soon relaxed.

Aurie sensed the change in her old friend, he did not have the same tolerance for humans and humanoids as he did when he was younger. Armitage had warned her that one day he would not return and would remain forever with his pack, she dreaded that time, but knew it was the only solution for the wolf's happiness.

Receiving King Esmond's commitment improved Armitage's mood immensely, and he immediately informed the magical tribes the Eldorans would join in the ensuing battle.

Seamus and Tony kept a constant surveillance on Westcott and on the movements of the troops. There was a dark, ominous cloud hovering over the Fire Cave, evidence the Abyss was now permanently open, permitting the beasts to cross the threshold to Earth whenever they were summoned by Prince Kalian.

One evening, after a particularly grueling day of training, a commotion from the corrals had everyone racing from the cabin in alarm, Seamus and Tony drew their swords and tore across the field. The rest of the group waited by the cottage. Two massive shapes appeared in the darkening sky, flying directly towards the meadow. Aurie immediately recognized Owain, and was surprised to see a smaller dragon flying in his wake.

Sam protectively placed himself in front of Jasmine, who gaped in astonishment, then turned and fled into the cabin. At the horse corral, Seamus and Tony had their hands full trying to calm the terrified horses. When Tony realized the dragons were headed directly towards the cabin, he drew his sword and tore across the open field.

"Wait," Seamus yelled as he followed Tony. "They're friends."

Aurie spotted Tony racing across the meadow, his weapon raised. Although she knew he was coming to protect her, she smothered a laugh, watching him race across the field, his sword raised above his head, coming to rescue her from two gigantic dragons.

"It's alright," she said walking out to meet him. "It's Owain, the dragon who saved me from Prince Kalian. Come, I'll introduce you to him."

"No thanks," Tony panted. "I think I'll stay here, you go say hi to your friend."

Aurie smiled and squeezed Tony's arm. She went and stood next to Armitage and her parents and waited while the two dragons gracefully landed. After Armitage had greeted his friend, Aurie approached Owain and bowed in deference, Owain lowered his enormous head and stared into her eyes. "I bring you news from Eleanor Elderberry, she says she is well and happy, and to tell you she will always be with you."

Aurie nodded numbly, unable to respond, as talking about her aunt was still very painful.

King Sebastian and Queen Elyse had always been aware a dragon resided deep in the bowels of Fire Mountain and Armitage introduced them. While they were conversing, Aurie examined the smaller dragon, she was beautiful, and was covered in gold scales, with eyes the color of dark ocher. When the conversation had ended, Owain spread his wings, turned and lifted his massive body off the ground, the female followed, and they quickly disappeared into the darkening sky.

When they returned to the cabin, Jasmine began preparing the evening meal, her face still pale, Aurie did not doubt the young woman had been terrified by the massive creatures. After Jasmine's delicious stew and scones had quickly disappeared, Aurie waited patiently while Armitage poured a second cup of tea and walked over to the hearth, warming his hands in the flames.

"I imagine everyone is wondering about our recent visit from Owain," Armitage said. "He wishes to join us in battle against Prince Kalian, along with his friends."

"Friends?" Aurie asked.

"Yes, you might recall I had told you years ago about the small numbers of dragons left on Earth, besides Owain, there are four others, you just met Owena, his mate. Of the three remaining dragons, two of them are metallic dragons and will follow Owain without hesitation. They have no love for mankind, but they don't have any love for Prince Kalian either. One dragon is worth five hundred men in a battle, and our odds have greatly increased."

"You said there were five dragons in total," Tony asked. "I sense some uncertainty about the last one?"

"His name is Thaine, and he is a Chromatic Dragon, which means he is a creature of the shadows. It is not through loyalty that he joins forces with the other dragons, but without the Fire Crystal, every dragon residing on Earth, chromatic or metallic, is in peril."

"Do you think Thaine can be trusted?"

"Not for a minute. However, Owain is a formidable dragon and will be able to keep Thaine in line."

"Evil sorcerers, malevolent dragons, creatures from the Underworld, it gets better all the time," Tony muttered, as he stood up and walked towards the door. "Can't wait to see what tomorrow brings."

Chapter Thirty-Eight

Aurie swatted a mosquito away from her face, and then squished another that landed on her arm. The clouds hung low in the sky, threatening to open at any moment, it was humid and muggy, and she half-wished it would rain. The parched trees and bushes could have used a good soaking, but whenever it did rain, it was usually a cold, bitter downpour that made travelling and being outdoors unpleasant.

"How much longer before we get to Faerie Glen?" she asked.

"You just asked me that an hour ago," Armitage grunted. "You must learn to be more patient."

"I know, it's just that I haven't seen Bluebell in ages, we have so much to talk about."

"You will not have a lot of time to visit with your friend, as we must return to the cottage before nightfall. I'm expecting an important message from King Glendon."

When Armitage had mentioned he would be going to Faerie Glen to talk with the Faerie Queen, Aurie had begged to accompany him, she had not seen Bluebell in a long time, and missed her friend. At first Armitage was reluctant but when he noticed how disappointed she was, he finally relented, warning her again about using her powers away from the protection of the cottage.

It was soft underfoot where the dead pine needles and leaves littered the forest floor, there were no flowers growing in the meadows and along the sluggish streams, and a few shriveled berries, missed by the birds, clung stubbornly to the branches of the bushes. A small animal was heard in the underbrush, scurrying for safety.

Eventually the dense trees tapered off, and they arrived at the edge of expansive grassland. Aurie and Armitage waited silently in the shadows. On the far side was a hidden glen where the Faeries lived among the toadstools and ferns. Sensing nothing amiss, they walked down a trail that twisted through the brittle thistles and wild sage. The dark ominous rain clouds had drifted towards the mountains, once again depriving the dying foliage of moisture.

Without warning, Aurie sensed a disturbance, she looked at Armitage, and knew he had felt it as well, as he had stopped abruptly on the path. The blast came so quickly, neither of them had a chance to protect themselves, Aurie was lifted off her feet and flung through the air, landing heavily on the ground. Armitage raised his staff to form a protective shield, but was not quick enough to deflect a second burst, and he landed with a thud in a patch of stinging nettles.

Aurie shook her head in disbelief, the Thunder Hawk was flying directly towards them with Prince Kalian perched on its back. The bird was almost on top of her when she reacted, and she teleported to the first place that came to mind. There had not been enough time for her to relay her thoughts to Armitage and she hoped he had been conscious when she disappeared, so that he would know where she was.

She landed on the trail that followed the river forging its way to Beargrass Mountain, not far from where Tony was attacked by the panther. A large crack sounded directly behind her and the Thunder Hawk flew through the breach.

The huge raptor landed awkwardly, with its wide wing span it smashed heavily into the branches of the tall cedars and pines, screeching as it lost its footing. The bird stumbled on the edge of the ravine. Prince Kalian swore angrily, and lifted the Thunder Hawk slowly into the air, setting it down a few feet away from the drop.

"Well played, young sorceress," he growled, as he jumped off the back of the agitated bird. "This time I will finish what I started."

"Of course, you must fulfill the Prophesy."

"Lord Armitage finally told you, did he?"

"Yes, we discussed it, and he explained he was waiting until I was old enough before he told me anything, nothing more."

As soon as Aurie spoke these words, she realized the truth in them, any resentment she had been holding against Armitage dissipated. The wizard had been aware of her deeply rooted anger yet he never brought up the matter, realizing in time she would comprehend the truth.

Aurie sidled over to the edge of the ravine. Impatience reflected across Prince Kalian's face, she realized she had only a second to make her decision. This time she knew he would not hesitate in his decision, he meant to rid himself of her once and for all.

Looking directly into his eyes, she took a deep breath, and jumped. The astonished look on Prince Kalian's face was the last thing she remembered before she landed with a heavy splash in the water.

Struggling against the rapid current, she was immediately pulled under, gagging and sputtering, she submerged yards downstream. She concentrated on avoiding the dangerous rocks and floating tree trunks. She heard a piercing scream over the roar of the rapids. Taking a deep breath, she dove and swam towards a cluster of reeds growing next to the riverbank, the water was murky and she had difficulty seeing. Lifting her head, she located the huge bird, it was flying directly towards her, a few feet above the stream, its talons skimming across the water. How was it possible that Prince Kalian knew where she was? In shock, she realized he had to be reading her thoughts, and it would not be long before he spotted her.

Grabbing a long reed, she uprooted it, broke it in half, put it in her mouth, and lowered her head into the water, leaving only an inch of the reed exposed. She inhaled and her lungs filled with air. Relaxing, she concentrated on controlling her fear, and emptied her thoughts.

Aurie did not know how long she stayed submerged, the cold slowly crept into her body, and she knew she could not stay any longer in the bone-chilling water. Lifting her head, she looked cautiously around. She could not sense the presence of either Prince Kalian or the Thunder Hawk.

Swimming over to the edge of the stream, she pulled herself up the embankment. Her legs and arms were numb, she had swallowed some of the murky water while struggling to keep afloat. The taste in her mouth was foul.

Pale ribbons of moonlight fell through the branches of the tall trees as she rose and staggered towards a huge cedar. She gathered dried leaves and pine needles into a small pile, and then lay down, burrowing underneath until she was completely covered. The last thing she remembered was the croaking of frogs and the light splash of an animal entering the stream.

She opened her eye, and brushed her hand across her face, she was covered with leaves and pine needles. She sat up, shivering in her wet clothes.

She rose, fighting a wave of dizziness, the bile water heaved into her mouth and she retched violently. She sat down and leaned against the trunk of the cedar, shaking uncontrollably. Remaining here was dangerous, and she had to get as far away from the river as possible.

Aurie had no idea how far she had travelled downstream, she had to be somewhere between the swinging bridge and the trail that led to Beargrass Mountain. If she had known the way to Owain's lair, that would have been the best solution, but she could wander for weeks in the mountain passes trying to find it. That's when she thought of the Elves, their village was not far from here, and it would be the safest place for her to go. She did not know how they would greet her, but an Elf never turned away anyone who needed help, especially one of their own.

She followed the river downstream, still weak from her ordeal, climbing over large boulders and wading across numerous brooks flowing into the river, making it difficult to make valuable time. At this speed, she should arrive at the Elves' home sometime late in the afternoon. She found a few wild onions and devoured them and scrounged for nuts and berries, which helped slack her hunger, yet she dared not drink any of the contaminated water.

She prayed Armitage was uninjured and had made it to Faerie Glen and eventually back to the cottage. There was nothing he or the others could do to help her until she contacted them.

She travelled for hours, but she did not recognize any of the landmarks, she knew she should have arrived at the path by now.

A shuffling noise came from a thicket directly in front of her, but it was too loud to have been made by a small animal, she looked around in panic for somewhere to hide. She was standing beneath a massive cedar and grabbing one of the branches, she pulled herself up, and kept on climbing until she was almost at the top. She pressed against the trunk, hiding behind a heavy bough and waited.

It wasn't long before the intruder appeared, it stopped beside the cedar, and raised its head and sniffed. Aurie held her breath, keeping as still as possible. It was a massive bear, with lethal claws and teeth, and she did not doubt that it was one of the creatures summoned by Prince Kalian from the Underworld. It swayed its massive head from side to side, stood on its hind legs and growled, raking its claws along the bark, growling vociferously.

The bear lowered itself onto its four paws, and walked around the trunk. It had picked up her scent, and Aurie prayed it would not look up and see her, it looked powerful enough to knock down the cedar. All at once it turned, and barged into the brush, following her back trail. She remained motionless. She would sleep for a couple of hours, then she would continue her trek. Creating a nest out of the boughs, she leaned back against the trunk and fell into a restless sleep.

At the first sign of light, Aurie climbed down the tree, then continued on her way. A few hours later she realized she was utterly lost, and had no idea where she was. The dense trees blocked out the weak sun but she knew she was heading east, as the tree trunks were covered with moss, and she remembered Armitage telling her moss always grew on the north side of a tree. By mid-morning she heard the trickle of an underground brook, and she followed it for the rest of the day, sensing she was walking deeper and deeper into the shrouded woods.

Hours later, she was so disoriented, not knowing if she was travelling east or west, when she stepped out from behind a large bush and stopped in amazement. She was facing a wide expanse of water.

She walked over to the edge, knelt, and scooped up a handful of water, gagged and spit it out. The water was salty. Excitedly, she realized the only body of salt water near Lindell Forest was the Marek Ocean, if she followed the shoreline, she would eventually arrive at Dolphin Cove. There were still a few hours of daylight left, so she decided to continue walking. She arrived at an impenetrable wall of rock, and as she tried to detour around it, she realized there was no way of getting around the barricade, short of swimming.

Not relishing the idea of getting wet again, Aurie waded into the icy water. Something caught the corner of her eye, and she spotted the hull of a boat buried in a patch of sand not fifty feet away. She headed towards the shore, unable to believe her luck. The boat was old, and there were oars lying inside, she hauled it into the water, and pulled herself over the side. There was a small leak, but not enough to stop her from using it. She rowed away from the dangerous rocks, heading towards the open water.

Aurie's arms and legs began to ache from the unaccustomed strain in rowing, yet she dared not rest, she must find a safe landing spot before it got dark.

Before long the wind picked up and the waves got higher, the little boat pitched and tossed.

Aurie was sitting in water up to her knees, her clothes were soaked, and she was chilled to the bone. The skies darkened, and then opened and icy rain poured down. Miserably, she hunched over, frustrated she was not able to use her powers to get to safety. It seemed no matter where she was Prince Kalian had a perilous hold over her.

As if it was a small piece of driftwood, the boat was lifted into the air by a huge wave, it started to list, and Aurie was thrown overboard, landing with a splash in the frigid water. She tried to swim, but a second wave followed, pulling her under. She struggled and thrashed her arms wildly. Powerful arms grabbed her by her waist, lifted her out of the water and deposited her on a flat rock surrounded by the crashing waves.

She raised her head to see who her rescuer was, but she was alone. Had she imagined that someone had pulled her out?

The waves smashed into the reefs and she wondered how she would be able to make it back to shore. Deciding it would be safer if she remained on the rock, she raised her knees and wrapped her arms around them, hoping to preserve some of her body warmth. The storm would not last forever.

A head rose out of the water, and then just as quickly disappeared. A second head appeared, then a third, and another, and soon they formed a ring around the rock. Whatever they were, they had slanted eyes and pointed ears, and their faces sparkled with multi-colored hues. One of them dove into the tumultuous surf and Aurie noticed a glistening tail as it struck the water. She realized they were Merfolk, and she remembered Armitage telling her about them, warning her they were a gentle, fun-loving race, with the ability to prophesize catastrophes but should you be captured by them, became extremely possessive.

As quickly as it had started, the rain stopped, and the ocean calmed. One of the Mermen swam up to the edge of the rock. "You will come with us," he said.

"I cannot, I must continue with my journey."

Ignoring her response, he pointed the trident at her and immediately she was encased in a bubble. "This will allow you to breathe under water."

Then he lifted the bubble off the rock, and dove underwater, it happened so quickly Aurie did not have time to prepare herself. The Merman was a powerful swimmer, and it did not take him long to reach the ocean bed. There were other Mermen and a few Mermaids that made up the group. The Mermaids had long flowing hair of vibrant hues of blue, green and yellow, they swam among the corals and floating kelp, playfully dodging large schools of fish. The ocean floor was beautiful and peaceful, and Aurie relaxed, she did not feel threatened.

As they traveled, she noticed lights in the distance, and the closer they got the more distinct they became. It was a magnificent underwater city. The Merman swam into a cave and followed a dark tunnel until they arrived at a large hollow cave, lit by magical orbs. At the far end was an enormous opened shell, and seated inside was a Merman wearing a crown. He had a long white beard, and was holding a golden trident.

The Merman swam towards the shell, and placed the bubble on the ground.

"Greetings," a deep voice said.

"Greetings Your Majesty," Aurie replied.

"I am King Maynard, and this is Oceana, home of the Merfolk."

"I am Princess Aurialana, daughter of King Sebastian Hawthorn of the Ancients, and Queen Elyse, daughter of King Esmond and Queen Edelyse Elderberry of the Eldorans."

King Maynard looked at her in surprise. "I have heard of you Princess Aurialana. It is said you are a great sorceress. If that is the case, why have you not used your powers to free yourself?"

Aurie hesitated in answering, and then quickly made her decision. "I am being pursued by the Evil Lord, and I cannot use my magic, as it would be dangerous to let him know where I am."

"His Dark Magic cannot penetrate our shields."

"I dare not take the chance. The Evil Lord's powers are strong, and he has the Fire Crystal, which gives him control over the beasts from the Underworld. Surely you are aware of this?"

"We are, as we have come across fearsome creatures that do not belong in our oceans."

"Then you must understand why I cannot remain here in Oceana. I must go to the human village as quickly as possible. I have friends there who will help me."

"These are challenging times, and although it is not in our nature to do so, we shall release you and take you back to the surface."

"That is good. Even now the magical tribes residing in Lindell Forest are preparing themselves for battle."

"We have heard these accounts, and I am pleased you are able to confirm their truth. We shall act as sentinels of the oceans and will help in any way we can to stop the Evil Lord. You have my pledge, Princess Aurialana."

"Your assistance would be invaluable Your Highness, and will not be forgotten," Aurie replied earnestly.

She regretted not being able to stay longer with these gentle creatures of the deep, and she silently promised, if possible, to return.

Chapter Thirty-Nine

The Merfolk accompanied Aurie to Dolphin Cove and vanished as silently as when they first appeared. She waded ashore, just as the sun began to set.

The dock was abandoned, and a few unmanned ships were anchored in the bay, evidencing the absence of trade in Westcott.

The Wild Boar Inn was where Seamus and Tony stayed when they came to Westcott. They would be coming to Westcott in the next few days, and as the innkeeper was reliable and was no friend of the soldiers, Aurie decided she would leave a message with him. It would be easier for her to wait than to walk back to the cottage and chance missing them on the road. Her absence would be a great concern for everyone, yet if anything had happened to her Armitage would have sensed it.

Aurie headed towards the abandoned villas bordering Lindell Forest, most of the houses had been destroyed or burnt to the ground. She walked solemnly through the empty streets, listening to the wind echo through the collapsed walls. Just as she was ready to turn around, she noticed a house set back in the trees, buried by vines and overgrown tree branches. The roof had collapsed, yet the ground floor was still partially intact. She found refuge in one of the rooms, and though it did not offer any amenities, she was at least protected from the rain and the relentless wind.

During the long night, while she lay awake, Aurie sensed the restless spirits of the slain Ancients. Sadly, she realized Armitage, her father and the few survivors living on Fey Wild were the last of the pure-blood Ancients. Ever since she discovered she was half-Ancient, Aurie had accepted her ancestry with pride, perhaps her mixed heredity was a sign of what the future held.

Early the next morning, she covered her hair and ears, and as she was dressed in her leggings and tunic, decided it would be safe for her to wander around Westcott without being recognized. She headed to the marketplace first, there were a few booths opened, but the produce and goods being sold were far below standard. Having no coins on her person, she wandered past the stalls, eyeing the bread and buns. One of the merchants gave her a cup of drinking water, and she thanked him, realizing it was more valuable than bread, and she appreciated his charity. She could survive without food for a while, and if she found water, she should be able to wait for Seamus and Tony for at least three more days.

She left the marketplace and walked to the Wild Boar Inn. The booths were empty and the sole occupant was the barkeep, who was standing behind a counter wiping a tankard. Aurie introduced herself as Aurie Mundy, and he said his name was Mac. She asked him if he had seen Seamus or Tony Drummond in the past few days as she was an old acquaintance of Tony's and understood he often stayed at the Wild Boar Inn, so she thought she might take a chance he might be in Westcott. Mac shook his head, and promised to pass along her message if the two men showed up. Tony would immediately know it was her as he would recognize the name she gave to Mac.

The Wild Boar Inn was the gathering spot most evenings for the soldiers, and was also where Jasmine had worked before she was rescued by Seamus. Aurie decided it would be prudent to drop by early in the morning, and not take the chance of running into either Nathan Trent, Rufus. Although it had been many years since either of them had laid eyes on her, she did not want to take the change of being recognized.

On the third morning, she noticed there were more soldiers than usual patrolling the streets. She hid in an alleyway, watching their movement. They were edgy, and questioned anyone they came across. It did not take the villagers long to disappear. Something was astir, and Aurie decided to find out what it was. As the soldiers were originally bivouacked at the castle she decided that would be the most logical place to look.

She kept to the dark alleys, cutting through tenements and warehouses. The streets were abandoned, so she decided to head towards the main thoroughfare and make faster time. Turning a corner, she almost barged into an old man pulling a rickety wooden cart. He raised his head, nodded curtly, and hurried away, muttering to himself.

Finally, she arrived at the castle, the gate and the portcullis were open, and she could see into the courtyard. She crept up the drawbridge, but did not enter the compound, instead, she turned down the path skirting the outer wall. Half way down the pathway she looked towards the field and stopped. Fred was still lying in the middle of the field frozen forever in his stone prison, partially buried under dried grass and thistles. A pigeon landed on his head, and Aurie smiled when a white stream trickled down his face. Obviously, it was a frequent perch for the bird. Her feelings for the man had not changed, and she did not regret what she had done.

Arriving at the back gate, she lifted the hatch, and was relieved when it opened easily. Keeping low, she raced across the field, and soon arrived at the back door of the stables. The barn was in the same dilapidated state it had been when they had rescued the starving horses. She wondered where the troops kept the remaining mounts. The hidden passageway in the tack room and the fissure in the stone wall were both wide open.

Soon she was inside the Fire Cave, she had not travelled far down the pathway when she heard voices coming towards her. Noticing a massive round boulder at the top of the scree, she ran and scrunched down behind it. A squadron of soldiers, marching in single file, appeared. Aurie immediately recognized Rufus, who was in the front, evidently, he had received a promotion, which did not surprise her in the least.

He stopped directly beneath her hiding place. He turned facing the soldiers and raised his hand to get their attention. "At ease men. We'll wait here for the rest of the platoon. There's been some trouble reported at the wharf, so they've gone into the village to check it out."

A few of the soldiers sat down in the moss bordering the path, the rest remained standing. A young trooper left the ranks and headed towards the boulder.

"Hey, Rob, where are you going?" one of his comrades asked. Someone whistled lewdly, causing the others to laugh.

"I'm going to take a leak, okay?" answered the badgered soldier. "Not that it's any of your damn business."

The soldier appeared around the corner of the boulder, seconds before Aurie had stepped backwards, taking cover in a dark recess. She waited until the young man had returned to the ranks, then she knelt, pressing her back against the stone wall.

"Hey Sarge, how long do we have to wait?" one of the soldiers asked.

"As long as it takes for the captain to return," Rufus snarled.

"Seems as if all we ever do is wait," someone else muttered. "When are we going to see some action?"

"Sooner than you think," Rufus replied, shrugging his shoulders.

"What you mean, Sarge?" a pimply faced soldier standing at the end of the line asked.

"I overheard the captain talking this morning, and it looks like Prince Kalian is ready to make his move, we'll be mustered by the end of the week."

All the troopers began talking at once. Rufus scowled angrily. "You ain't supposed to know so keep your voices down. These orders are confidential, understand?"

"Where are they deploying us?" A grizzled haired trooper asked, spitting a wad of tobacco on the ground.

"Far as I know, Whitehawk Pass."

"You mean we ain't gonna see no fighting?"

"Our job is to make sure no one gets through the pass, coming or going. Prince Kalian is sending the creatures to Greenlea Meadows, where he plans to fight the battle. I don't think they're smart enough to know whose side we're on, so we're better off being where we are."

Aurie half rose and leaned closer to hear better, and dislodged a rock. Frowning, Rufus turned and stared in her direction. Raising his hand for silence, he walked towards the boulder.

Aurie stepped backwards and lost her balance, she reached to grab something to stop from falling, but there was nothing there. She found herself standing at the top of a flight of stair, and without hesitating, she raced down the steps, as the sound of pursuit echoed behind her in the darkness. Reaching she bottom she felt a slight pressure along her arms and legs, and hesitating for only a second, she stepped forward, recognizing she had passed through a shield. Rufus would find nothing but a stone wall.

She was standing in a hollowed-out chamber, lit by torches that flared when she passed through the shield. The walls were coated with mold and dust, creating a frosted patina of white, evidence the space had not been disturbed in a long while. Ancient artifacts and leather-bound tomes were piled in the corners.

She walked across the floor, knelt, and blew the dust off the top of a wooden trunk. Lifting the lid, she was surprised to discover its only contents was a scroll sealed by wax. Lowering the lid of the trunk, she sat down, and unrolled the parchment. It was written that a plague had struck the Town of Westcott, and King Thomas and the young heir, Prince Donahue, had not survived. For some unforeseen reason, the plague had wiped out all the Ancients, except the High Wizard Armitage Ravenswood, who had been away from Westcott on a diplomatic visit. Prince Kalian as the only surviving member of the royal family, became the ruler of Westcott. Nothing more was said, and at the bottom, it was signed "Percival Hastings, Royal Scribe."

Aurie shook her head in disbelief, she stood, lifted the lid and in disgust, threw the scroll back inside, slamming the lid down violently. The force knocked the trunk over, there was a sharp splintering noise and the bottom fell open, revealing a hidden compartment. A second scroll fell out, rolled a few inches, and stopped next to her foot. She bent and picked it up, broke the seal, unrolled it and began reading.

"I, Percival Hastings, Royal Scribe to King Thomas, of the House of Whitmore, hereby confess I was coerced in producing a false statement setting out the events leading to the death of King Thomas and Prince Donahue. I produce this second declaration detailing the actual events that occurred, and I do solemnly attest the following is a true and legitimate accounting of what transpired. Be it known that Prince Donahue did not perish as stated in the false attestation, and at the time of writing this declaration, was alive and residing in the Village of Westcott.

King Thomas had become privy to a plot that Prince Kalian was planning to massacre the Ancients and was incarcerated by his brother, along with Prince Donahue, in the royal chambers. The small son of King Thomas' valet, who was the same age as the small prince, was very ill and not expected to survive. As the young prince's life was in peril, King Thomas persuaded the grieving father to switch the two boys. The valet dressed the young prince in servant's clothing, and fled from the castle. Sadly, his son died a few hours later. Knowing Prince Kalian would want to verify the young prince's identity King Thomas spread word among the servants the young boy had died from a terrible disease, with symptoms similar to the Black Death. None of the servants dared enter the bed chambers for fear of contacting the contagious disease, and it was reported to Prince Kalian that it was indeed the young prince who had succumbed to the illness. I can attest that this did happen as I was aware from the onset of the two boys being switched. King Thomas urged me to flee from the castle, as he knew my life, as well as his, was in danger, not only because of my position as Royal Scribe but as his close friend.

I placed the first scroll in a trunk as ordered by Prince Kalian, but this scroll I have hidden in a false compartment, and hopefully one day it will be found and the truth revealed. I have placed a cameo and a ring bearing the royal insignia in the trunk as well. The images in the cameo are of the late Queen Wilona and Prince Donahue, painted when he was four years old, shortly before his disappearance. The ring can only be worn by the rightful heir to the throne, as I have placed an enchantment on it. I pray someday the truth will be revealed, and Prince Kalian will be punished for his greed and evilness.

I will remain with my King to the end and his fate will be mine.

Percival Hastings, Royal Scribe

Aurie lowered the scroll, visibly shaken by the message. Stepping back from the trunk, she stepped on something sharp that was lying on the ground next to the trunk. It was the ring, which must have fallen out with the scroll. It was made of gold, and there was a huge gemstone in the middle, with words engraved around the outer rim.

She spotted a second object lying on the ground. It was the brooch mentioned in the scribe's attestation. Picking it up, she clicked it open and saw two portraits, one of a woman wearing a crown, and the other of a young boy, and for some reason his likeness was vaguely familiar. Her mouth dropped in astonishment, there was no mistaking the curly, black hair and the vivid blue eyes. It was Tony! Tony was Prince Donahue.

Aurie stuffed both scrolls inside her tunic, and placed the seal and the cameo in her pocket.

As much as she wanted to explore the rest of the cave, she realized she must find Seamus and Tony and return to the cottage as quickly as possible to tell Armitage all she had heard.

Time was running out.

Chapter Forty

Aurie sat in the darkened corner, her back against the wall. The pub was quiet this early in the morning, and except for the barkeep, she was the only person in the room. If Seamus and Tony did not show up today, she would have no choice but to return to the cottage without them. Two hours passed, and just as she was about to leave, the front door flung open and Seamus and Tony entered.

"Mac, how about pouring two pints for a couple of weary travelers?" Seamus shouted. Mac raised his hand in greeting, and placed the mugs on the counter, he looked over at Aurie, but she shook her head. She remained seated, intent on watching her friends, not realizing until that moment how much she had missed them.

Seamus chugged his drink and handed the empty mug to the barkeep, who quickly refilled it. Tony's face was drawn and he looked tired, as if he had not slept for a long time.

"Can't a person sit in peace around here?" Aurie yelled.

Tony stiffened and placed his hand on the hilt of his sword. Looking in her direction, he shook his head in disbelief, then he ran across the room, lifted her from the chair, overturning it in his haste. Seamus roared, lumbered across the room, and wrapped his massive arms around the two of them. Tony grunted, and Aurie laughed, even though she felt as if her ribs were being crushed.

Over Seamus' shoulder, Aurie noticed the surprised look on Mac's face. She shrugged and removed her cap, letting her hair cascade down her back. He grinned, and continued wiping the counter, unconcerned about her deception.

"We can't talk here," Aurie whispered, "Come with me, I have a place where I've been staying."

She led them through the vacant streets, the three friends walking silently past the shuttered tenements. As they approached the burned villas, Aurie asked Seamus about Armitage. She was relieved when the big man told her the wizard had returned to the cottage, shaken and bruised, although he was angry he had agreed to let her accompany him to Faerie Glen. Once again, he had underestimated Prince Kalian's vehemence and in letting down his guard, had allowed the cruel sorcerer to surprise and attack them.

"We can't be more vigilant than we already are," Aurie replied.

"Maybe so," Seamus grunted, "but I think Armitage plans on keeping you a prisoner at the cottage from now on."

Aurie shrugged, not answering the big man.

"Here's the house I've been staying in," she said as they neared the partially burned villa. The two men followed her inside.

She then told them how she had given Prince Kalian the slip by hiding in the reeds and briefly mentioned her contact with the Merfolk, and how they had pledged their support by patrolling the oceans and the seas. Lastly, she told them of the conversation she had overheard between Rufus and the squadron of soldiers.

"I've been expecting this for some time," Seamus muttered, "but not quite this soon."

"We must return to the cottage as quickly as possible," Aurie continued. "I'm going to teleport back."

"Aurie, you can't," Tony said.

"I sent a telepathic message to Armitage a few minutes ago and he knows I'm safe and with you two. I have told him what I overhead and he's in agreement with my plan."

"Which is?"

"I have to go to the Elves, and make sure they are safe, and find out if they will support Armitage. I won't stay long in one place, as I'm gambling right now Prince Kalian has his hands full getting his army together. Are you ready?"

Everyone at the cottage was happy to see them, but as they were all aware of the danger Aurie was in, none of them delayed her departure.

She went to her sleeping quarters, and hid the scrolls, the ring and the cameo under her pallet, placing a shield around them so Jasmine would not find them. She had not brought up her discovery of the scrolls to Tony because if he had wanted anyone to know his identify he would have told them about it a long time ago.

Hastily she changed into a clean tunic and leggings, returned to the kitchen, and took Tony's hand and led him outside, quietly closing the door.

"When this is all over," Tony said quietly, "I'm never going to let you out of my sight again."

Aurie wrapped her arms around his neck and whispered in his ear. "I love you."

"I know, and I love you too."

"I told my mother we were just friends, but I think she realizes by now I wasn't being exactly truthful."

"You think she doesn't approve?"

"My parents like you Tony, they just feel I'm too young to get serious about anyone right now, and I think my grandparents were hoping I'd eventually find someone in Fey Wild."

"I suppose you're talking about that Erlie Something weed or whatever?"

Laurie chuckled. "You mean Erling Silverweed. My grandmother had hoped something would come of our friendship, but I think she now knows that will never happen."

"He is an Eldoran, and has powers, I can't compete with that."

"You have nothing to worry about, Erling and I are good friends but it stops there. Besides, someone told me once that I preferred my men tall, dark and moody."

"Hey, I'm not moody."

"Well okay, tall, dark and handsome."

"That's better. However, now is not the time to talk about this, but you must promise me you'll be careful."

"I will, I'm always careful."

Tony rolled his eyes, gave her a quick kiss, and stepped back.

Aurie teleported to the ledge overlooking the lagoon in the Elves' underground city and stared in amazement. The entire city was gone, all the dwellings, any sign of habitation whatsoever, had disappeared. There were no signs of a battle, and Aurie hoped they had all escaped. If the Elves were in the vicinity, it would not take them long to detect her presence.

She sat down, facing the waterfall, remembering when she had first met the Elves, how Tony and she had escaped, and wondered if King Osmar would be angry they had disobeyed his orders.

She sensed them before she saw them. A dozen warriors surrounded her, and she solemnly waited for their welcome.

"I see our magic no longer has any effect on you," Princess Oria laughed softly as she stepped forward and approached Aurie. Prince Oran bowed his head in greeting, and as was his nature, quietly accepted her presence.

"I was greatly concerned when I first arrived," Aurie responded, as she turned and looked at the deserted city.

"It is because of you that we are safe," Oria said. "I thought about your warning of the Evil Lord, and raised the matter with my father and the High Council. The troopers had not returned to the man village, but waited in their camps not far from the place where you and your companion fell into the cave. Our warriors hid in the shadows and overheard their plans. They were waiting for the Evil Lord, laughing of the devastation he planned to invoke on our village. It was then we realized everything you had told us was true. We could not remain where we were. We moved our entire city to a location deeper in the bowels of the earth."

"I am relieved King Osmar took action when he did," Aurie said.

"This location was indeed discovered by the Evil Lord, but he found nothing. We had lifted the incantation reversing the flow of the stream, allowing the lagoon to dry up and moved to our new location before he arrived. Our warriors are constantly vigilant and have been watching the Evil Lord's movements closely. The Elves will not be found by Prince Kalian."

"Sadly, the destruction does not stop here in Lindell Forest," Aurie said. "He has opened a rift between Earth and Fey Wild, and there has been devastating destruction. I am here as I seek an audience with King Osmar."

Oria nodded, walked over to her brother and spoke to him. As quickly as they had appeared, he and the warriors disappeared.

"I have sent Oran ahead so he might inform our father of your request. In the meantime, I sense you have something to say."

"Your empathy does not betray you," Aurie said. "It is good we can talk before I seek your father's advice. When Tony and I were last here, I purposely did not reveal my identity. My father is King Sebastian of the Ancients, and my mother is Queen Elyse, of the House of Elderberry. I am their daughter, Princess Aurialana."

Oria stared in shock, then lowered her head in respect. "You are a royal princess of the Eldorans?"

"Well, only half-Eldoran. I did not divulge who I was at the time because I was not sure of the reaction I would get. Tony and I thought it best to keep my identity a secret."

"We have heard of you and your abilities, Prince Aurialana. Come my father awaits your arrival."

Oria took Aurie's hand and teleported them to the New City. Oran was waiting for them at the longhouse and went inside. Aurie and Oria remained by the entrance and Oran soon returned, gesturing for Aurie to follow.

When she arrived at the throne, she lowered her head, waiting for King Osmar to acknowledge her presence.

"Greetings, my old guest, it is an honor to see you again," the King smiled.

Aurie raised her head, her face burning. Before she could respond, Oria stepped forward and announced to the entire assembly Aurie's identity.

As was the reaction when she had confessed to Oria, the room became quiet.

"If we had known you were an Eldoran princess," King Osmar said, a frown crossing his face, "We would have welcomed you in a much different manner."

"Please understand it was my choice to not disclose who I was. No dishonor has been placed on me or my family."

"We thank you, Your Highness."

"May good health and happiness fill your days," Aurie replied quietly.

King Osmar bowed his head, as did everyone in the longhouse.

"Your Highness," Aurie said. "I must break protocol and ask your tolerance in foregoing the proper greetings. The Evil Lord is at this moment gathering the beasts from the Underworld and will be deploying his soldiers by the end of the week. Messengers are being sent to all the tribes and inhabitants of Lindell Forest. The battle is to be fought at Greenlea Meadows and Lord Armitage hopes to arrive before Prince Kalian's army. He feels the element of surprise will be in our favor."

King Osmar nodded gravely, politely waiting for Aurie to continue her petition.

"On behalf of Lord Armitage, I seek the assistance of the Elves in ridding Earth of the Evil Lord."

King Osmar stood, facing his warriors. Every head was lowered in approval. "My warriors will be ready, the proud king announced.

"I am pleased, Your Highness. Be assured that King Esmond of the Eldorans has pledged his support, and will join us when the time is right. However, there is another matter I wish to discuss, before I leave. May I speak?"

"You may."

"When the battle is over, things will be harsh in Lindell Forest. Your underground haven is one of the last remaining places that has been left untouched by the Evil Lord. I would implore that your produce and fresh water be made available to all who survive. I not only ask this for the magical folk, but also for the humans living in the man village, who are starving and living in constant terror.

"If we succeed, the cleansing rains and the return of the sun will make the fields bountiful once again, and the foliage, trees and flowers will flourish, but it will take time for Earth to heal."

Aurie waited patiently for King Osmar's answer, although she fully realized should Prince Kalian triumph, there would be no place on Earth that would be safe for any of the survivors, the Elves included.

"I will grant you your wish," he replied, looking directly at Aurie. "However, I do ask something in return. When the time is right, I ask that the Elves be allowed to return to Fey Wild, to live once again in harmony with our kin, the Eldorans. Our presence on Earth will no longer be a secret, and it is time we returned to Fey Wild. We have been too long on the Mortal Plain."

"I will bring your petition before King Esmond. The final decision, of course, will be his, but I do not think he will refuse your request."

"I understand, and I thank you, Princess Aurialana."

Aurie prepared to return to the hut. Perhaps one day she and Oria would become close friends, but for now Aurie was thankful to have the skills of the Elves on their side.

Also, she must remember to tell them Tony was more than her companion and defender, he was a warrior and prince in his own right. She knew they would find it difficult to accept that an Eldoran princess would choose someone who was half-human and half-Ancient to love and spend her life with. Wisely, she decided to keep that information to herself.

Chapter Forty-One

Lookouts from the magical tribes were sent to Whitehawk Pass with instructions to report back immediately should they spot any activity. Armitage teleported Aurie and Queen Elyse to the hidden portal, Elyse was returning to Fey Wild to bring King Esmond up to date on matters and to ensure the Eldoran warriors were prepared and ready to teleport to Earth as soon as they were summoned. King Esmond would bring Queen Elyse back to Earth within the day.

Armitage's distrust of Prince Kalian had only heightened after their attack at Whitehawk Pass, and since her return from the Elves, Aurie was not permitted to leave the shielded meadow. As she was the only one with the power to open the portal, and as he had no choice, Armitage agreed to let her accompany them to the gateway but as soon as her mother was safely in Fey Wild, he teleported Aurie back to the cottage.

The strain of being continuously on alert was taking its toll on everyone, tempers were short, and the overcrowded cottage only made matters worse. To keep herself busy, Aurie spent hours practicing her magic and weaponry. She handled the spear well, but she would never be proficient with the long sword as her mother and Eleanor had been. Although she pushed herself to the point of total exhaustion, deep inside, she sensed her confrontation with Prince Kalian would have nothing to do with weapons but would come down to a battle of magic.

Most days, after their evening meal, Aurie and Tony would walk down to the horse corral so they might have some time alone. Armitage insisted, however, they stay in sight of the cottage, and remain in the confines of the shield. The matter of Tony's identity dwelled on Aurie's mind and she thought about it continuously, he never brought up the topic of his childhood, even when Aurie had provided him with the opportunity to do so many times.

It was drawing close to the end of the week, and Aurie decided to reveal her discovery. She removed the scrolls, the ring and the cameo from under her pallet, put them in a leather pouch and placed it inside her shirt. Although the wind was cold, the rain had finally stopped, and when they arrived at the corral, they sat on the damp ground with a wool blanket wrapped around their shoulders. Taking out the pouch, she emptied the contents, handed Tony the first scroll, saying nothing. He unrolled it and began reading, his jaw tightened, and then he angrily threw it aside. "Where did you get this?" he asked sharply.

"Before I tell you, read this one," Aurie said, handing him the second scroll. "When I went to the castle to check out the soldiers, I had to take cover in a hurry, and that's when I discovered the room where these were hidden, it was purely accidental."

Tony quietly read the second scroll, and then he laid it in his lap. "I've always been aware of my identity. Since I had no way of proving it, I felt it more prudent to say nothing. These scrolls are the proof I need. I was never told the entire truth about my father's death, and now that I know, I want nothing more than to see Prince Kalian defeated."

"There's more, Tony."

She handed him the cameo and the ring, he sprung open the latch on the locket, and stared at the images. Silently he placed it in his pocket. He rolled the ring around in his hand.

"Aren't you going to put it on? It belongs to you," Aurie said.

"We have enough on our agenda without complicating things any further. As long as Prince Kalian rules Prince Donahue does not exist."

"Do you want me to tell the others?"

Tony shook his head, and then he placed the two scrolls and the ring inside the leather pouch, and handed it back to her. "No, this must remain our secret. Please put these in safekeeping for now, and when the time comes, I will ask for them."

"Tony, are you sure?"

"I am."

Aurie nodded, she would respect his wishes.

"After you were taken from the castle when you were five, what happened?" she asked, leaning back on her elbows.

"I lived with my father's valet, Richard Golden, in a small hut down by the wharf, and he managed to pick up work when he could at the quarries. No one questioned his disappearance from Windermere Castle, as a rumor was spread that his son had contacted the deadly illness that had taken Prince Donahue, and he had left to care for him. Richard kept in contact with a few of my father's more faithful servants, and I remember the day he told me my father was dead. I was so young at the time, I didn't fully understand everything he had said, and all I knew was that I would never see my father again. When I was ten years old, Richard left for the quarries as he did each morning, but he never returned. The neighborhood where we lived was a breeding ground for cutthroats, thieves and murderers, and I was old enough to realize he probably met an untimely death. The few coins he earned each day at the quarry would have been a temptation to those who had nothing.

"After that, I lived on the streets, and I soon learned to survive as so many other kids did. Although I was young, I understood how dangerous it would be to expose my identity, as Richard had warned me often to not reveal who I was. Prince Kalian must never find out I had survived. That was when I took the name Tony Drummond."

"I'm so sorry Tony, your life was not easy, was it?"

Tony smiled, and he pulled her up and put his arm around her shoulders. "No different than yours."

"So how did you come to work in the stables?"

"It was a few years later, I was probably around fourteen at the time, when a platoon of soldiers rode through the streets. I hid behind a wagon. Prince Kalian was in the front and he was riding Cesar, who was wearing my father's saddle, and having a tough time controlling him. I was aware of Cesar's unpredictability, as he had been my father's horse, and I knew there were few men who could ride him. Cesar had always been gentle with me, and I had no fear of him. Prince Kalian was hitting Cesar with a crop, and I had to stop myself from barging out of my hiding place and interfering.

"After they rode away, I had an idea, I would get a job at the stables and keep a closer watch on Prince Kalian, as well as be with Cesar. I suppose I had the grand idea that one day I would confront Prince Kalian and tell him who I was, but that was just a young boy's fantasy, and would have been foolhardy. I realize now, Prince Kalian had no designs whatsoever in claiming the throne. If he decided to retaliate my deception, it would not be because I was Prince Donahue and the sole heir to the throne, it would have been because I had been right under his nose for all those years and had deceived him. When we have rid the world of Prince Kalian, then and only then will I step forward. Do you understand why I have to do this?"

"Yes, Your Highness," Aurie said chuckling softly. Tony scowled, then said. "It's Tony, just Tony," then he leaned over and kissed her.

Chapter Forty-Two

Two days later a message was received that a battalion of soldiers had just left Westcott. Immediately, Armitage sent out messengers to all the tribes to converge at the rendezvous spot overlooking Greenlea Meadows.

Aurie, Seamus, Sam, and King Sebastian rode the four rescued horses. Aurie chose a black mare by the name of Jetta, although she was small, she was fast and had a lot of spirit. Tony was riding Cesar. Jasmine and Queen Elyse would arrive the following day in a covered wagon pulled by two oxen. They would be bringing the medical supplies, fresh water and provisions. When Seamus had gone to Westcott a few months earlier, Armitage had instructed him to buy the two animals and the wagon, and Aurie had wondered at that time why he would want them. She should have known he never did anything without a reason.

When Armitage joined the riders at the corral, he informed them he would not be accompanying them as he had an important errand elsewhere. Aurie was not happy to hear this, but she did not question his decision.

The five riders pushed their mounts, stopping for short breaks to rest the horses, and late in the afternoon they arrived at the ridge overlooking Greenlea Meadows. Aurie was stiff and sore as she was not used to riding. Setting up a cold camp they unsaddled the horses and fed oats and fresh water to the weary animals. A light rain began to fall and everyone took what little shelter there was under the canopied leaves of the cedars, shivering in their wet cloaks.

King Sebastian suggested they retire early, as it had been a long ride, and they would need their strength for the upcoming day. Aurie tossed and turned, her mind racing wildly. It would take the soldiers most of tomorrow to arrive at Whitehawk Pass, and she wondered if Prince Kalian and his entourage of beasts would arrive at Greenlea Meadows around the same time. There was no conceivable way he would have discovered his plans had been overheard, yet for some reason, she felt anxious.

Unable to sleep, she rose and crept quietly away from the camp. She stood on the edge of the ridge, surveying the landscape, the rain had stopped, and a fog was snaking its way across the open plains. The mountains in the background rose sharply against the darkening sky, and the serpentine path of the river wound through the dense trees and bush. Whitehawk Pass was southeast, but it was too dark to make out the outline of the high cliffs. Aurie instinctively knew the battle would never get that far. It would be fought here, and it would be swift and deadly. Prince Kalian was aware his soldiers could not match the fighting prowess of the beasts, and he was using them as a backup in the chance anyone managed to flee from the battle.

A branch cracked, she spun sharply, reaching for her sword. Tony walked over, put his arm around her waist and drew her close. "You really should get some sleep."

"There's no sense keeping everyone awake," she replied, relaxing in his embrace. "Tony, what do you think our chances are?"

"Aren't you asking the wrong person? Armitage is the one with precognition abilities."

Aurie smiled, and lowered her head to his shoulder. "What if I fail the Prophesy?"

Tony released her and walked over to the ledge, angrily he kicked a rock and watched as it rolled down the embankment.

"I sometimes wish you had never found out about that insufferable Prophesy. You have the most powerful wizard on Earth, your father, the Eldorans and the Elves, all of the magical tribes, and five ferocious dragons and me backing you up, now what more do you need?"

Aurie walked over to Tony and took his hand. She was so thankful for him, as he always seemed to know when she needed his strength and support. Quietly they returned to the camp, each deep in their own thoughts. They lay down together, wrapping their cloaks around each other for warmth. Before she fell asleep, she quietly said, "I've decided that once all of this is over, I will release the curse on Fred, but he has to pay for his treachery. Since I turned him into stone, I thought banishing him to the quarries would be a suitable punishment."

"That's a wise decision," Tony muttered drowsily. "Lord Armitage and your parents will be relieved to hear that."

"And I don't intend to stop at Fred, Nathan Trent will pay for what he did to Jasmine, and Rufus better hope he never sees me again."

Tony yawned. "Be quiet and go to sleep. Tomorrow will be a long day."

The weather had not improved any by the next morning. The rain continued to fall. Campfires were still forbidden, and the miserable conditions did not help the morale. The different tribes began arriving, the Dwarves, Dryads, Faeries, and Pixies, and although campsites were set up, there was little mingling. The thunder of hooves announced the arrival of the Centaurs, and their stern countenance and fierceness created a respectful silence.

Wherever she strolled, Aurie could feel their eyes following her, and she was uncomfortable. She angrily wished for the hundredth time Armitage was there. She wandered into the woods and found a patch of grass next to an old tree and lowered herself to the ground. She wrapped her cloak tightly around her body to keep out the damp chill. She leaned against the tree's trunk, deep in thought. Sensing someone was watching, she lifted her head and was surprised to see her father.

"Aurie, don't you think you should be mingling with the tribes?"

She shrugged, a frown crossing her face.

"Armitage is not here to do it, and that duty falls on you," he said quietly.

"Why is it my duty?"

"Has Armitage been training you all these years for naught?"

"Armitage is their leader, not I. It's his army."

"That is true, and rest assured he will be here to lead them when the time comes, but in the meantime, you must do what is expected of you."

"I wouldn't know what to say."

"The words will come, and if you wish, I will accompany you."

Aurie did not stand, lowering her head, she stared at the wet ground. "I didn't ask for any of this."

"That is true, and it is a large burden to be placed on one so young. Your birth was foretold by a powerful sage over five hundred years ago, and as predicted, your abilities are remarkable. It is a gift you must embrace, not resent. You are a formidable sorceress, and a skilled warrior."

"Everyone gives me more credit than I deserve."

"That's because you don't see yourself as others do."

"Sometimes I wish I could just run away from everything, disappear forever."

"Would that resolve your uncertainties, your self-doubts?"

"Perhaps not, but I would be happier."

"Happiness must be earned Aurialana, by all of us. You can only do your best, and that is all that will be expected of you."

"Then why do I feel so terrified, why do I feel I will fail?"

King Sebastian sighed deeply, and then he knelt before his daughter and placed his hand on her shoulder. "When you face Prince Kalian, you must not let your fear overshadow your purpose, you must discover his weakness. If you cannot find the strength to do this, then all will be lost."

Aurie stared into her father's eyes, she was ashamed of her outburst. Her parents were two of the bravest people she had ever known.

"I'm sorry, I can't seem to throw this feeling of anxiety."

"It's your dread of Prince Kalian that cloaks your confidence, he is a man, not some powerful god, and although his abilities are strong, he is not infallible. You must believe that."

Aurie rose, and her father held her close. "At first, when your mother and I were reunited with you, we felt anger and despair that you were placed in a situation beyond your control. We had missed so much of your childhood, and questioned Lord Armitage as to the wisdom of pursuing your training, preparing you for the ultimate confrontation with Prince Kalian. Yet as time passed, and the more powerful the Evil Lord became and the more damage and destruction he caused, the more we came to realize Lord Armitage was on the right path. The only thing Prince Kalian fears is the Prophesy. You are the one person on Earth who can stop him from victory."

Aurie closed her eyes, then pulled away from her father's embrace. She knew her father was right, and she also knew what needed to be done.

Soon they were walking from campsite to campsite, talking to the warriors, joking with them, calming their fears. The tribes were pleased to see King Sebastian. He was known to most of the elders and leaders, and he spent time talking to each of them.

Later in the day the Elves arrived and their superior military bearing did wonders for the overall morale. When Oria spotted Aurie with the horses, she waved and walked across the field to join her. They greeted each other happily. Oria advised King Osmar had not escorted them as he felt he was too old to fight. He had handed control over to Oria and Oran. Their fittest and most experienced warriors were present, and other than the Eldorans, no greater fighters existed.

A dark creature rushed out of the trees and ran directly towards Aurie. Oria immediately pulled an arrow from her quiver, turned, and faced the charging animal.

"Oria, stop," Aurie yelled. "It's alright, he won't hurt me."

Oria slowly lowered her bow.

"His name is Torin," Aurie said. "We've been friends since he was a young pup."

Oria eyed the huge wolf and shook her head in amazement. "I believe I'll join my brother." Then she turned and headed towards the Elves' camp.

Aurie smiled at Oria's uneasiness, then scratched Torin behind his ears. She was not happy he was here as she feared for his safety. Although he was a powerful and a cunning hunter, he did not have the power to fight any of the dire creatures, or Prince Kalian's beasts. If he thought she was in danger, he would not hesitate to protect her.

Just before nightfall Jasmine and her mother arrived with the supply wagon. They looked exhausted, their cloaks splattered with mud. Aurie, with Torin following closely at her side, walked over to greet them. Their trip had to have been grueling, as the narrow roads and trails were rocky and deeply rutted, and the constant rain had made the trek arduous.

A soft tinkling came from inside the wagon, Bluebell flew over to Aurie, and landed in her cupped hands. "Your Highness. I trust you are well," Bluebell said, her silver eyes shining brightly.

"How many times must I tell you," Aurie said sharply. "You do not have to call me Your Highness, I am just plain Aurie."

Bluebell flew upwards, reached over and touched the tip of Aurie's nose with her tiny finger. "Why are you not happy I am here?" she asked solemnly.

"I am happy to see you, but this is no place for you Bluebell, it's too dangerous."

"Everyone is in danger. I have offered my assistance to your mother and Jasmine. There will be many wounded, and I have healing powers."

"I'm sorry Bluebell," Aurie sighed. "I'm just on edge. Your assistance is invaluable."

"Did you think the Faeries would not fight? We are brave and quick, and our magic is strong."

"You are right, my friend. Please be careful."

"You might as well know, Phineas is here as well," Bluebell said, as she flew over to the wagon. Aurie was surprised when the little Faerie landed on Jasmine's shoulder. It seemed a friendship had developed between her little friend and Jasmine.

Aurie returned to her camp, reflecting deeply. The thought of Pixies and Faeries fighting against Prince Kalian's terrifying creatures unnerved her. She was tired of worrying about everyone and everything that might happen tomorrow, and knew the reason she was so short-tempered was because of Armitage's absence.

Tony was sharpening his sword, and when he saw the look on her face, he wisely lowered his head, concentrating on his task.

The camp was awakened early the following morning by the sound of a horn echoing throughout the glade, creating pandemonium everywhere.

Aurie joined Tony at the horses, Sam, Seamus and her father had finished saddling their mounts. They stood off to the side, watching the warriors as they rode, walked or flew past, heading towards the roadway that would lead them down to the plains and to their assigned locations. Many of them nodded, saluted or raised their weapons in greeting. There was no joviality or cheering as each of them was aware what they would be facing, and their chances of coming through the battle alive were slim. They were fighting for their families, their lives, and their freedom to live peaceably.

When the clearing was empty, King Sebastian mounted his horse, and the rest of the small group followed his actions. As they passed the wagon, Aurie caught a movement in the corner of her eye. Jasmine and her mother were standing side by side, watching silently. Her mother nodded, her head held proudly, while Jasmine wiped her eyes with the corner of her apron. Bluebell was perched on Jasmine's shoulder, trying to comfort her. Jasmine blew a kiss to Sam and he pretended to catch it, holding it against his heart.

They rode over to the edge of the cliff and saw in the far distance a black mass slowly approaching. King Glendon and his centaurs stood in the front lines, behind the centaurs were the dwarves, Pixies and Dryads and off to the right were the Elves, standing in military formation. It was then Aurie noticed the Eldorans on the far left and picked out King Esmond standing in the foreground, dressed in gold armor, his long sword hanging from his waist, clasping a spear. He lifted his head and stared at Aurie, nodded and then turned back to face the approaching horde.

Tony noticed the exchange between Aurie and the imposing warrior, and knew him to be someone of regal bearing. He raised his eyebrows enquiringly.

"My grandfather," she mouthed quietly.

"Of course," he said pragmatically. "Who else would it be?"

Aurie reached over and squeezed Tony's leg. Oh Tony, she thought quietly to herself, don't ever change.

Her father led the small group of horsemen down the steep grade, gesturing for Aurie to follow. Torin loped behind Jetta, but he made her nervous, so Aurie ordered him to keep well back. Cesar was the next horse in line, but he had no fear of the huge wolf.

Something had been nagging at the back of her mind, yet she couldn't quite place what it was. She jerked Jetta's reins, Cesar slid on the slick path and collided into Jetta's buttock, and he reared and spun nervously on the narrow path. Cursing under his breath, Tony tightened his hold on the reins. King Sebastian stopped when he heard the commotion, and Seamus and Sam backed their horses up, waiting for Cesar to settle down.

"I'm sorry," Aurie apologized. "It's just that something has been bothering me all morning, and now I know what it is. Armitage hasn't shown up."

"And I don't see Prince Kalian anywhere either," Tony said.

"You don't think Armitage has gone and done something stupid, do you?" Aurie asked, not looking at anyone.

"If you mean has he gone to confront Prince Kalian, the answer is no," Seamus replied from the back of the line.

Aurie turned in her saddle.

"He said we were to trust him, and trust him we will."

"I imagine Prince Kalian is at the Abyss," King Sebastian said, "He has the Fire Crystal to control the beasts, so there is no reason for him to be here."

Aurie knew her father was right. Squaring her shoulders, she urged Jetta forward. The path wound its way down the steep slope, gradually leveling into an easy grade, they did not have far to travel before they arrived at the edge of Greenlea Meadows. When Torin noticed the beasts in the distance, he growled deeply in his chest, and bared his fangs. A screaming melee of Orcs was in the lead. Aurie had never seen these creatures before now and understood why they were the most savage of the marauders. They were dressed in leather armor, and carried war axes the size of a boulder. They were muscular, had grotesque faces, and huge dagger-like teeth. Fighting them in hand to hand combat would be impossible. The only warriors capable of stopping them were the Elves and the Eldorans as they possessed the strongest magic.

Following the Orcs were creatures even more hideous to behold. They were monstrous in size, dressed in fur loincloths and carrying spears, clubs and chains. She knew they were Ogres. What child living in the magical world did not know of these cruel, dull-witted creatures, which often fought alongside the Orcs? She spotted dire wolves and bears, and fey panthers, dismayed at their numbers. The Goblins, as was their cowardly nature, brought up the rear. She knew the beasts would be unstoppable, with no thought of surrender or retreat. With the Fire Crystal in his possession, Prince Kalian had complete control over them.

The Elves and the Eldorans stood patiently, their bows and long swords drawn. The Dwarves, although small in stature, looked formidable. Their choice of weapons was clubs and picks. Flying among them were Pixies and Faeries, and just as she turned away, Aurie spotted Phineas in the foreground. He looked so small, her heart pounded, and she prayed for his safety. He caught her eye, waved, and Aurie returned his greeting with a salute. An icy feeling of dread passed through her body, but she quickly pushed it aside. She must put all her concentration on the ensuing battle.

King Glendon stood proudly, surveying the scene before him. When the surging mass of beasts was almost upon them, he gave the signal, and the magical army surged forward. Aurie looked over at Tony, and before he lowered his face shield, he whispered "I love you," then he spurred Cesar into a gallop, joining the herd of Centaurs surging across the field. The hooves of the horses churned up the wet soil, turning it into mud. With a howl, Torin tore after Cesar; Aurie yelled at him to come back, but the wolf paid her no heed.

She drew her sword half-way out of its scabbard, and at the last second replaced it, realizing her greatest strength was in her magic, not her weapons. She had the ability to use her powers and not become tired, so now was the time to take advantage of her gift.

The first blow was struck by King Glendon. A dire bear had surged ahead of the charging Orcs and Ogres, but soon met the Centaurs massive hoofs. The Elves released a barrage of arrows, finding their targets in the stampeding beasts. Aurie spurred Jetta forward, and soon found herself in the center of the melee. An Orc raced towards her, arm raised, clasping an axe. Summoning her powers, she aimed a bolt directly at its chest, the creature disintegrated, and two of its companions who were following close behind stopped in their tracks. Having more intelligence than the Ogres, it did not take them long to realize they were facing a powerful adversary, and they hastily retreated and reassembled a safe distance from Aurie's blasts.

The beasts forged steadily forward, killing and maiming. It soon was apparent to Aurie the tribes did not have a chance against the relentless bludgeoning. Spurred on by the magic of the Fire Crystal, Prince Kalian would not stop until all of them had been annihilated.

Aurie steered Jetta towards a small party of Dwarves who were stalwartly fighting a horde of Goblins. Remembering the Goblin's tactics of fighting and their cowardliness when overwhelmed, she summoned her powers, and hurled a massive bolt into their midst. Watching their numbers fall, and realizing they were outmatched, they quickly retreated. The leader of the Dwarves raised his axe in gratitude, and Aurie recognized Telford. Surprisingly, Egbert, who was standing next to Telford, nodded his head in thanks.

At one point, she spotted her father fighting an Ogre. He directed a blast at the intimidating creature, and it howled in anger, a second burst soon disarmed it, and it fell heavily to the ground.

She spotted Tony at a distance facing an Orc warrior. The blood-crazed creature swung his battle-axe missing Cesar by inches. Tony pulled sharply on the reins, and the terrified horse spun around, leaving Tony vulnerable. Aurie spurred Jetta towards them, creating a path of carnage, but soon realized she was too far away. Suddenly a flurry of wings flew directly at the Orc, flying around its head and in front of its face, distracting it enough to allow Tony to move to a better position. Jetta never faltered in her stride and when Aurie was close to the Orc, she shook her head in disbelief, as she recognized the attackers, they were Faeries and Pixies. In horror, she watched as the Orc swung his axe hitting one of the Pixies. In anger she charged, releasing a powerful bolt, which immediately felled the Orc. She stared at Tony, but he quickly turned away, but not before she saw the look of dismay in his eyes. Lowering her gaze, she spotted Phineas lying in the mud, his body twisted and still. She shook her head in disbelief, then a searing agony filled her body. Two of Phineas' friends flew down, gently picked him up and disappeared.

She sensed Tony's nearness and she lifted her head and looked directly at him. He raised his face guard and said, "I love you." Then he turned and rode Cesar back into the fracas.

Aurie lost all sense of time, she disarmed or destroyed anything that crossed her path, seeking revenge, helping those who were most in need. She concentrated on keeping her seat, as Jetta was finding it difficult to maneuver through the slick mud. The beasts were keeping well away, and soon she and the stalwart horse were standing alone in the middle of the field. A screech was heard over the din of the battle, Jetta reared, and Aurie struggled to stay seated. Looking upwards, she saw the Thunder Hawk, it must have been circling overhead, and waiting for Prince Kalian's order. Now she understood why the beasts had stayed so far back. Prince Kalian had been following her progress, and was aware of her position throughout the entire battle.

Grabbing the saddle horn tightly, she wrapped the reins around her left hand securing it in place. She knew this was dangerous because if she got thrown, she could get hung on the saddle, and get trampled, yet she needed her right hand free to use her magic on the huge raptor. She relied on Jetta's common sense and bravery.

The massive wings of the raptor created a wind rush as it descended, lifting mud and debris off the ground. She dared not cover her eyes, as it would give the bird an advantage. Freeing her mind of the sounds of the battle, she focused her concentration. She knew she would only have one chance. Without warning, a massive beast leapt from the skirmish, and pounced on Jetta, raking its claws down her hindquarters. Jetta screamed in agony, as the brute strength of the predator pulled her to the ground. Aurie unbound her hand and jumped out of the saddle seconds before Jetta was overcome by the vicious leopard. She hit the ground hard, smacking her head on a rock. Standing up quickly, she was overcome with nausea, her vision blurred. She wiped her hands across her face and forehead, it was covered in blood.

Ignoring her injury, she concentrated on the Thunder Hawk. She would not have time to summon her full powers to stop the bird, but she did not plan on going down easily, she would not give Prince Kalian the satisfaction.

The ground shook, and a bolt of lightning slashed across the overcast sky. Aurie glanced upwards, and spotted a huge creature flying over the tree line. It was Owain.

When he was directly above the Thunder Hawk, a fire erupted from his mouth and the raptor was engulfed in flames. It screamed as it spiraled towards the ground, landing in a smoldering heap a few feet from where Aurie was standing. She raised her head to thank Owain, and only then did she notice Armitage sitting on his back. He certainly knew how to make a grand entrance. Before the beasts had a chance to retaliate, the four remaining dragons appeared overhead, it seemed Owain had control over Thaine after all, and the chromatic dragon was fighting as fiercely as his companions. The ferocious Orcs and Ogres fought for their lives. The destruction caused by the dragons was horrific, and the beasts fell back.

For a short while, it seemed as if the battle had turned, but Aurie knew Prince Kalian could summon up as many beasts as he wanted. They would continue to come until all of them, including the dragons, were slain. It was then Aurie knew what she must do. She relayed her thoughts to Armitage, and he nodded solemnly. Her last words to him were, "Tell Tony I love him."

Then she disappeared.

Chapter Forty-Three

Prince Kalian was standing on the far side of the swinging bridge tightly clutching the Fire Crystal, which dangled from a gold chain hanging around his neck.

"I have been waiting for you, young sorceress," he said in a raspy voice as Aurie appeared on the far side of the bridge. She was shocked when she saw his appearance, the dark magic had consumed him completely. He was emaciated, his body withered, his eyes glowing feverishly, more a creature of the Underworld than the beasts he controlled.

"Surely you must be aware that the battle has turned, that your beasts have no chance of surviving," Aurie countered.

"For now, the dragons are keeping them at bay. I will continue to summon the beasts until every dragon and every miserable member of Armitage's army has perished."

"It seems to be an unsatisfactory victory, does it not?" Aurie murmured. "Will you be content to rule your earthly kingdom alone? How I pity you."

Prince Kalian's face remained impassive. Her words did not seem to penetrate and she sensed his madness. He would be more dangerous now than he had ever been.

Prince Kalian raised the Fire Crystal, and a bolt surged across the expanse of the bridge. Aurie had anticipated his reaction, and flung herself to the ground, rolling and then landing on her feet. A second bolt, and then a third followed and each time she managed to evade them.

A low rumble and sharp crack sounded behind her. She turned to see a huge boulder catapulting through the air, she leapt over the rock, seconds before it landed with a crash in the middle of the path where she had been standing. Prince Kalian laughed gleefully. Aurie realized this was merely a game to him, and when he grew bored, he would put an end to it.

Calling up the flames from the Abyss, she directed them towards the maddened sorcerer. Immediately, he created a wall of ice, and the fire evaporated.

"Is that all you have?" he taunted. "I can wait until you have expended all your energy sorceress, or I can be merciful and end it now."

"Then you will be waiting a long time."

"You have magical endurance," he said, laughing manically. "With our combined abilities, we could have had total control, not only of Earth by Fey Wild as well. You could have stopped a lot of bloodshed."

"I would never use my powers in such a manner," she answered disgustedly.

"Yet you have used Dark Magic, it surrounds you, young sorceress. Can you not feel its power coursing through your blood?"

An icy chill ran down Aurie's back. She closed her mind to Prince Kalian's words, struggling against the pull of the Dark Magic. Prince Kalian raised the Fire Crystal above his head, and brilliant beams radiated outwards lifting her from the ground. Aurie felt as if her lungs were being crushed. Agony ripped through her body. She crashed to the ground, the pain was excruciating, and she bit down on her lip, tasting blood.

Was this how it would end? How easy it would be to succumb, to close her eyes and wait for the final blow. It was then she remembered her father's words. "You must find out what Prince Kalian's weaknesses are."

What was his greatest fear other than the Prophesy?

Suddenly the answer came to her. It was not her powers that he feared, it was her mixed bloodline. The magic and abilities of both the Ancients and the Eldorans flowed through her veins, making her impregnable. That was why he must destroy her, with her destruction, he would have sole supremacy.

Aurie slowly rose, ignoring her pain, and concentrated completely. She summoned the Fire Crystal. It grew in intensity, its rays almost blinding her, then they turned a fiery red. With a cry, Prince Kalian staggered, as the chain holding the gemstone snapped. Aurie lifted the Fire Crystal into the air, guided it across the bridge, and grabbed it in her left hand. The power surged through her body. It was exhilarating. Her senses were attuned to the slightest sound, and the objects surrounding her took on a startling clarity.

The madness glowered from Prince Kalian's eyes. He stepped onto the bridge, racing towards Aurie. Lifting the crystal, she summoned all her powers, and the hem of Prince Kalian's robe burst into flames. The blaze spread quickly, consuming him, he shrieked in agony but continued his approach.

Aurie reached inside her boot. She grasped the handle of her dagger, then slowly and calmly, she threw the weapon. Prince Kalian stopped, staring in disbelief at the knife protruding from his chest. By now the flames had spread over the handrails and were devouring the wooden planks. The bridge collapsed, and with a howl of anguish Prince Kalian fell into the burning inferno of the Abyss.

"That's for Eleanor, you bastard," Aurie whispered.

She stood rooted on the path, unable to move. Holding the Crystal tightly, she stared into its depths, feeling her body absorb the magic. She understood the control it held over Prince Kalian. It would be so easy to surrender to its powers.

Shaking her head, and frightened by the overwhelming desire she felt, she lowered the Fire Crystal. If peace was to ever return to Earth and Fey Wild, it must be returned to the rightful guardian of the Abyss.

She teleported back to the battle. The beasts, realizing their ties to Prince Kalian had been severed, were running blindly in all directions, seeking to escape from the fiery blasts of the dragons, the arrows and spears of the Eldorans and Elves and the thundering hooves of the Centaurs.

The skies grew dark, the earth trembled and the ground split open. As if an invisible hand had reached out of the darkness, the beasts, the Orcs, the Goblins, and the Ogres, were pulled into the depths of the fiery pit. They disappeared, and as quickly as it had opened, the rift closed.

A victorious roar erupted from the tribes, many of them were jumping in glee, or hugging their companions. The Eldorans and Elves stood regally watching the bedlam, as if such behavior was beneath them. Her father, Seamus, Sam, and Tony were standing in a small group on the far side of the field, weary but jubilant. For a moment her heart contracted, as she noticed the blood on Tony's tunic and down Cesar's side. He raised his head, removed his helmet and smiled, sensing her anxiety. She felt his love, and knew he would wait for her to join him.

Bodies were scattered across the field, there would be sadness along with the joy. Battles were never fought or won without terrible losses.

The dragons circled overhead, and one by one they landed in the middle of the field. The tribes kept a respectful distance from them. Although they had been fighting on the same side, they still held a deeply imbedded fear of them.

Aurie solemnly approached Owain. She opened her hand and said. "I believe this belongs to you."

Owain lowered his head, and Aurie placed the Fire Crystal around his massive head. Armitage, who was still seated on the dragon's back, jumped lithely to the ground.

"Well done, sorceress," Owain said.

Then he and the dragons flapped their massive wings and soared as one into the air.

"Guard it well, My Lord," Aurie whispered, as they flew towards the forest and disappeared over the crest of the trees. "Guard it well."

The End

About Shirley Bigelow DeKelver

Growing up, if I didn't have my nose in a book, I would be drawing and painting, and it wasn't until later I discovered I had a passion for photography as well. I worked as a paralegal in law firms in Calgary law firms for well over 40 years. In 2004, I received a diploma for Writing for Children and Teenagers from the Institute of Children's Literature, and in 2006, a second diploma, Writing Children's Books: The Craft and the Market. I am Past President of the Shuswap Writers' Group, and currently a member of the Writer's Nook writers group. I am also on the Executive for the Shuswap Association of Writers, and the Planning Committee for the Word on the Lake Writers Festival held in Salmon Arm annually. I also coordinate and emcee Cafe Lit, a special coffee house launching the Festival. As well, I am a member of the Writers Union of Canada.

Social Media Links

Facebook: https://www.facebook.com/Shirley Bigelow DeKelver/

Federation of BC Writers: http://www.bcwriters.ca/profile/shirley-dekelver/

Website: http://www.shirleydekelver.com

LinkedIn: https://ca.linkedin.com/in/shirley-bigelow-dekelver3a534450

Twitter: https://twitter.com/ShirleyDeKelver

Writers Union of Canada:
https://www.writersunion.ca/member/shirley-dekelver

If you enjoyed this story, check out these other Solstice Publishing books by Shirley Bigelow DeKelver:

Lilacs and Bifocals

A clandestine meeting with an elderly woman named Annie, and her young granddaughter Hanna, will start a chain of events that will change fifteen year old Caroline Lindstrom's life forever—paranormal encounters, eerie illuminations, unexplained time shifts, traveling back in time to 1902 through a mysterious portal. Warned by Annie of a devastating disaster that occurred in the past but which can only be changed by someone from the future, Caroline must find the answer before the gateway closes forever.

Caroline's relationship with her angry, controlling grandfather contributes to the ongoing source of her frustration and discontent and although the year is 1955, she feels as if she is living in the Dark Ages. When her life spirals out of control, she returns to the past, realizing she must stop the catastrophe that will befall Annie's family. Will she find the courage to confront the past and change the future, or will she fail in her mission?

https://bookgoodies.com/a/B00ZIXGAW6

Made in the USA
Columbia, SC
27 October 2017